CW00921094

CHRISTMAS ACTUALLY

LISA DARCY

BLOODHOUND
BOOKS

First published in 2024 by Bloodhound Books.

www.bloodhoundbooks.com

Print ISBN: 978-1-917214-63-6

For Chris. Thank you for your infinite love, humour and kindness.

CHAPTER 1

I never thought I'd be the sort of person to submit to a mid-life crisis. I'm not sure I ever believed in such an event. Mid-life crisis? Surely a phrase made up to name ongoing boredom, malaise, and restlessness?

As for my dreams? Well, I certainly never thought I'd give up on them.

When I was twenty, in my final year of photography studies, I hoped by the time I turned forty, I'd have:

1. A gorgeous, happy husband and two sweet-natured children (sex didn't matter) to whom I'd be like a big sister.
2. A successful photography business that allowed me creative freedom and financial independence as well as time to lunch, shop and travel.
3. The confidence and desire to pursue my dreams.

Whenever I fantasised about my future, I saw myself living the perfect life.

Well, I'm about to celebrate that milestone and I'm not

exactly where I'd hoped I'd be. I've got the family part happening, but as far as the illustrious photography career—

Maybe my poor mood was because Christmas was looming and I hadn't put up the tree, decorated the house, or hung fairy lights. My festive spirit was seriously lacking.

I glanced at my vibrating mobile. My sister Robyn.

What I didn't have on my future bingo card was my younger (by two years) sister becoming an Instagram sensation, a high-profile, social-media influencing, Instagramming smash hit. Who could have predicted that?

'Katie?' Robyn's high-pitched voice bordered on hysterical. 'I'm about to have a baby. I'm... labour... need photos. Documentation. If I don't follow up immediately...'

She was referring to her latest Insta post a few days ago which had garnered over 400,000 likes. Captioned *Sun-Kissed and Salty*, I'd photographed Robyn on the beach in a fetching indigo bikini, pale-azure chiffon wrap and oversized straw hat (with lollipop-pink ribbon) and she'd posted it together with the following: *#32weeks #livingmybestpregnancy #bodypositive #selfcare #greenjuice #cleansedontdiet #juicecleanse #grateful #blessed*

Instagram Perfect: staged, styled, angled, face-tuned (together with a smattering of cute freckles) and airbrushed. Bouncy hair. Blemish-free skin. Flawless.

Never let reality get in the way of your dream life. *#makebelieve*

At what point did my photos cease being documentations of real life and become *#distortions #exaggerations #sendups #cartoons*?

After reassuring both of us Robyn was not in labour and promising to take more *Insta perfect photos* of her as soon as humanly possible, I hung up.

Once upon a time photography was my passion. My

grandmother lit the spark when I was six. She had a fabulous collection of black-and-white photos, and I was struck by their significance, each print linked to a fascinating adventure, be it camel racing in Egypt or marching for peace in Sydney during the Vietnam War.

'History, Katie,' she'd say, examining a beloved photo through a magnifying glass. 'The exact moment this image was captured will never come to pass again.'

On my seventh birthday, she gave me her cherished Hasselblad. It fascinated me – learning the intricacies of the fixed-focus lens, discovering the dual positions for sun and cloud, and using the disposable flash for indoors. I still treasure it. After school, I turned my passion into a career goal, attending Sydney College of the Arts. In my final year, I won a photography scholarship overseas.

Back then, I had ambition. It seemed reasonable to want it all. After six months abroad and only a year at a leading Australian newspaper, I went out on my own and managed a hectic freelance schedule. I was one of those people who could cope with unpredictable weather and produce amazing photographs. My portfolio of natural-disaster photos was particularly impressive – bushfires in southern Victoria, drought in central New South Wales, cyclones and widespread flooding in Queensland. You name it, I was there, capturing images which revealed emotions that couldn't be put into words.

After Lexi, my now thirteen-year-old, was born, walking the tightrope between career and family became increasingly difficult. I retained my favourite clients and still did my best work outdoors, although I drastically cut back my hours. But I soon realised unless you keep accepting jobs and upping your profile, people forget you. Someone with newer, fresher ideas and a sharper eye comes into focus – and whammo, they're the 'next big thing' and you're a distant memory. So, when Lexi turned two, I went back to full-time work to rebuild my portfolio. The tightrope tightened further.

Fast forward two years. Seven months pregnant with Angus, I drove to northern New South Wales to photograph rampaging grasshoppers threatening to take over the small agricultural town of Moree. Those photos won several awards and led to a spate of commissions from *Australian Geographic.*

Not that I could fulfil them.

I assumed I'd keep working at the same frenetic pace after Angus was born, but who was I kidding? 'Having it all' proved impossible, what with a daughter starting school, a baby, breastfeeding, housework, life.

My photography career came to a standstill. I wasn't offered top assignments because I couldn't dash off at a moment's notice to flood-ravaged plains and infernos threatening the bush. After a while, I settled for a two-day-a-week job at a portrait studio where I was stuck indoors. I didn't last long.

Angus is eight now. I have no career and my personal and professional confidence is at an all-time low. So much for the perfect life.

While on the phone with Robyn, my mobile beeped with a new voicemail: '*Hi, Katie, it's Fern. Can you help me out of a fix? Our assistant photographer is a no-show for a couple of weeks, right as our Christmas campaign is launching. I immediately thought Katie. You'd be perfect. Give me a call.*'

A rush of adrenaline flushed my cheeks.

Thinking about getting back behind the camera professionally was thrilling... and terrifying. My skills haven't advanced since the late noughties and these days it was mostly digital – downloading SD cards and retouching on computer screens.

I listened to Fern's message again. *...you'dbeperfectgivemeacall.* She always ran her words together. I hesitated, worried I couldn't live up to Fern's expectations, and regarded the mountain of groceries that my cat, Cleo, was currently pawing on the kitchen bench.

I gently set her down on the floor. 'Thoughts?'

Fern and I met doing photography at college. After our first year, she switched to a Bachelor of Commerce at Sydney University, deciding she was more suited to corporate life. We remained great friends though, even flatting together for six months.

These days, Fern is a guru in the magazine world. She'd started as the editor of global corporation, Image Ink's *Home Interiors*, before being promoted to Australian Group Editor in charge of six lifestyle magazines. A couple of years ago, she advanced to Australasia's Editorial Head for all of Image Ink's more than twenty titles, digital and print, ranging from health and beauty through to sports, parenting and gossip rags.

I'd hardly seen her in the previous ten years and then, I'd seen her twice in as many days, the most recent being at Angus's swimming lesson today. We talked and she told me she had four kids, all under ten, one still in nappies. Phone to one ear, she was madly cheering on three of her children as they practised their strokes. And she looked immaculate. *Immaculate.* Matching toe, nail and lip colours. Hair styled, she dazzled in a merry pink sundress.

Meanwhile, I was wearing ancient jeans and a faded blue T-shirt, sitting on *the* most uncomfortable plastic chair, slumped in a heap, with barely enough enthusiasm to nod as Angus swam past me. Seeing her made me want to crawl into a hole and die.

I punched in her number.

'Kate, thankgoodnessyoucalled. I'm in a spot. Short story, our photographic assistant had an accident this afternoon. I need a fill-in for two, three weeks max in the lead-up to Christmas. Minimal travel, flexible hours, great pay. You'd be doing me and

Santa's elves a huge favour and it'd be great if you could start tomorrow.'

'Tomorrow?' Fear and excitement pulsated. *I couldn't possibly start a new job tomorrow. I'm too busy...* but was I really?

Clearly distracted, Fern took my question as a statement.

'Great, Katie, you're a doll. Tomorrow, here at Image Ink, say eight o'clock. I'll give you the lowdown then.' The line went dead before I could protest.

CHAPTER 2

With Lexi at netball practice and Angus playing outside with Rupert, our black labradoodle, I shoved the groceries into the fridge and pantry, then sifted through the day's junk mail, delighted when I spied a parcel from my mother-in-law. An early birthday present. Moments later, my delight evaporated. It was a book, imaginatively titled *Don'ts for Wives* by Blanche Ebbutt, first published in 1913.

Excuse me?

Was this Carol's subtle way of commenting on the state of my marriage? I flicked through the pages, sighing loudly as I read old-fashioned advice such as not considering it beneath you to put out your husband's slippers before he arrives home from work. Out where? In the garbage?

And another about not thinking you can each go your own way, but rather, pull together as a team. I stopped and considered her words. Pulling together and walking the same path was what Matthew and I didn't do often enough these days.

I was sitting at the kitchen bench surrounded by several ancient photography portfolios, when my mother appeared.

'Katie, I knocked, but—'

'Look at these, Mum.' I thrust an enormous folder of black-and-white prints of Central Park under her nose. 'Remember when I won a scholarship to New York?'

Mum looked through the folder and read the lecturer's comments aloud. '*Technical aspects outstanding; lighting and composition intuitively conquered... Looking forward to attending Kate's future exhibitions... Natural talent in abundance... A star in the making.*'

'How did I go from dreaming that one day my photos would be hanging in New York and Parisian galleries, to this?' I gestured at my messy kitchen. The pristine white cupboards, white marble benchtop, and white appliances looked a sickly grey. Even the parquet flooring looked dirty and tired.

'Birthday blues? You look sad enough to bring tears to a glass eye.'

My mother, Pip: always ready with a quick and colourful observation or three. I shrugged. 'Remember Fern McLeod?'

Mum looked blank. 'No.'

'Yes, you do. I was at college with her. Anyway, she's asked if I'd like to do some Christmas photography for one of the magazines she publishes, filling in for a couple of weeks. I said yes.'

Mum smiled. 'Great.'

'Yeah, but I'm worried about all the new technology.'

She made sympathetic clucking noises. 'You worry too much. You've been offered an opportunity to do something you love. Enjoy the moment. But—'

'But what?'

'Nothing, but you'll be busy. Christmas is around the corner.'

'Yes, well everyone will have to pitch in, I guess. Carol sent this for my birthday!' I picked up the offending tome. *Don'ts for Wives*. 'Is this meant to be a joke?'

'Carol's just trying to help. She's from the country.'

'She lives in Adelaide!'

'Speaking of birthdays, it's only a few days away. Are you and Matthew doing something exciting? Painting the town and the front porch?'

I laughed. 'Doubt it. He's so caught up with pressures at work, downsizing, end of year retrenchments, he may not even remember. Not many people do, being a month out from Christmas.'

In the old days, Matt would never have forgotten. We always made a special effort for each other's birthdays. One year, he surprised me by taking me to see the musical *Mamma Mia*, knowing how much I loved ABBA. We stayed at the Hyatt for a romantic evening and followed it up the next day with a full five-hour shopping spree. It was fantastic. For his birthday, I bought tickets to see *We Will Rock You*. Queen was more his speed.

In recent years, romantic gestures like those had fallen by the wayside, along with other intimate stuff.

'It's important you and Matthew spend time together, Katie. And I don't mean the time you spend sorting out the kids' schedules for the week. You need couple time to keep a marriage happy.' Her eyes strayed towards *Don'ts for Wives*. 'Strangely compelling title, don't you think?'

'Mum!' I didn't need to have this conversation right now. Besides, what did my mother know about happy marriages? My father had walked out on us years ago, and she hadn't had a serious relationship since.

'I saw your dad today,' she said, uncannily reading my thoughts.

'Really?' I looked up.

'I sort of ran into him.'

'Ran into him? How? Where? Doesn't he still live in Canada?'

Angus walked in, making a beeline for the pantry to fill up on whatever snacks he could find.

Mum reached out to hug him. 'How's my little guy?'

'Good, Nanna. What's to eat?'

After making multiple cheese and Vegemite crackers, I turned to Mum. 'You were saying?'

'I was at the art gallery, and we literally bumped into each other looking at the same painting.'

I pulled a bottle of soda water out of the fridge. 'Hang on.' I poured two glasses and took a large gulp before passing Mum hers. I gestured to the small kitchen nook overlooking the back garden, shuffled papers, books and an iPad aside, and we both sat. 'I don't know why you'd ever want to speak to him again.'

'Katie!' Mum shielded her eyes from the sun. 'Obviously, I was surprised to see him, but it wasn't as awkward as you might expect.'

'Awkward? How awkward should I expect it to be for you to bump into the man who walked out on us almost twenty-five years ago?'

After Dad moved out, he happened to discover an *intellectual and spiritual connection* with another woman. Mum found out when, in an attempt to reconcile, she flew to Melbourne to surprise him. As it turned out, Mum was the one surprised. Walking into Dad's suite at the Windsor Hotel, she found him and his intellectual and spiritual connection in bed together. It was three o'clock on a Thursday afternoon.

Dad later tried to explain to Robyn and me he'd fallen under the spell of a *truly inspirational woman.* It didn't escape our notice that this truly inspirational woman was ten years his junior and had spectacular breasts and lovely legs. Soon after divorcing Mum, Dad married Miss Inspirational. Since then, my contact with him had been practically non-existent. It helped that his new wife was Canadian, so they moved to Vancouver. These days, I rarely thought about Dad and actively avoided thinking about his second wife.

'That was a long time ago. It was lovely to see him today. Of course, he wanted to know all about you and Robyn and the children.'

'Of course. That's why he's kept in touch so diligently.'

'He did try, and I understand – and appreciate – why you and Robyn turned your back on him in support of me, but he is your father, after all.'

'Don't remind me.'

Mum looked out the window and smiled. 'You know, I'd played the scenario in my head so many times – what our first meeting would be like after all those years. In the early days, I hoped it would be at his funeral.'

'That's more like it.'

'But as soon as I saw him today, I realised I'm glad Bob's alive. I have no anger for him anymore. I was happy to see him.'

Happy to see him? I couldn't quite comprehend what Mum was saying. Or why she was talking so fondly about the adulterer who'd deserted her.

CHAPTER 3

'Great news,' I said to Matthew when he phoned after Mum left. 'Remember Fern, my friend at Image Ink? I saw her at Angus's swimming class today and she's hired me to do some photography on one of her titles in the lead up to Christmas. Starting tomorrow.' Breath steady. Voice upbeat. Positive. 'How about dinner out tonight to celebrate?'

Pause.

'Tonight's tricky, hon, with the Americans in town. I was hoping you might—'

'Matthew!'

'Just informal Aussie home-cooking, easy wining and dining. Don't go to any trouble... but they need to eat. I promise we'll celebrate your new job another night.'

A simple dinner party for six. Sure, no trouble.

I bundled Angus into the car and drove to the local shops to pick up a few extras, like a main course, then rushed home and set about creating the perfect dinner for guests from overseas, who were expecting a home-cooked Australian meal. I marinated a whole snapper in white wine with ginger and garlic, baked a pavlova with a Cointreau sauce and created a blender full of sublime mango cocktails. Perfect.

I set the dining table and even managed a passable festive theme: green-and-white crockery, sage candles, and a centrepiece of red holly sprigs and miniature pine cones. With these organisational skills, maybe I'd manage my return to working life after all.

I was in control and on schedule. In fact, so ahead of schedule, I picked up my phone to play Wordle. And then Lexi bowled into the kitchen.

I stood, open-mouthed. 'Your hair...' Honey-blonde since birth, Lexi's hair was now blue-black.

She brushed past, ignoring my horror, and opened the fridge door. 'There's nothing to eat,' she moaned, despite me having spent several hundred dollars at the supermarket that afternoon. She slammed the door and began rummaging in the pantry.

'Lexi...' I bit my tongue and busied myself at the kitchen sink, studying the label on the dishwashing powder. Hmm. Lemon fresh. Fabulous.

She ripped open a packet of double-coated Tim Tams. The top two buttons of her white school shirt were undone, and I swear I could see her rapidly developing breasts swelling before my eyes. Though Lexi has lovely cotton bras, today, for some reason, she was bra-less. And then there was her barely-there skirt, which rode up around her backside.

'Want to talk about it?'

She rolled her eyes. 'Mum! Blonde hair is so yesterday. Have you seen Billie? Her hair's awesome.'

'I don't care about the other girls in your class...'

She dismissed me with a laugh. 'Billie Eilish's a singer!'

'Lexi—'

'It's *my* hair. Anyway, it's done now.'

'Don't speak to me like that,' I said, voice loud and sharp. 'And why aren't you wearing your retainer? We didn't spend six thousand dollars on braces to have you—'

She held up half a biscuit. 'Eating!'

'Ahem.' Matthew and the Americans had arrived.

Immediately, I framed them, taking a mental snapshot: two fresh-faced women, one brunette, one flaxen, both wearing twinsets and elegant jewellery as if they'd stepped out of *Ladies' Home Journal*, circa 1965; and two overweight middle-aged men wearing baggy stone-washed denim jeans, white sandshoes and matching Utah baseball caps. I was also wearing jeans, but at least they weren't stone-washed.

I switched to hostess mode. 'Lovely to meet you.'

Lexi disappeared upstairs without another word, but within seconds, angry music (I guessed Billie) was blaring from her bedroom.

While Matthew settled everyone into the lounge room and calmly asked Lexi to turn her music down, I busied myself in the kitchen, pouring chilled mango cocktails. I sipped one to test it.

I'd really outdone myself. They were magnificent.

I walked in with the drinks, and everyone took one. Smiling, one of the men asked what was in them.

'Summer mangoes.' I grinned. 'And champagne.'

They put their glasses down in unison as if I'd said the drinks contained rat poison.

Matthew ushered me into the kitchen. 'What's wrong with you?' he demanded through gritted teeth. 'They're Mormons. They don't drink alcohol.'

I gulped some mango mix. 'Pardon?'

'I said, They. Are. Mormons. No. Alcohol.'

'Matthew, you said you were bringing home colleagues from America for an Australian home-cooked meal. Easy wining and dining, you said. So, naturally I thought we'd be *wining and dining*.'

The shock of Matthew telling me our guests didn't drink alcohol, at all – never ever – sent me into a spin. My wine-marinated fish, my Cointreau-soaked pav. Tia Maria Tim Tams!

He squeezed my shoulder and pulled a face. 'My bad. I'll fix it.'

When he walked back into the living room, I heard him apologise about the liquor misstep, and ask our guests what they'd like to drink instead. The women opted for *club soda,* and the men – *diet Pepsi, please.*

Pulling several lamb cutlets from the fridge, I threw them on a plate, then gave the appetisers the once-over. I crossed my fingers our guests wouldn't be offended by Kangaroo Island brie and kalamata olives.

I stared around the kitchen, desperate to find something to do – anything to delay the inevitable. But given I'd prepared the salads, and the garlic and rosemary potatoes were baking in the oven, I could procrastinate no longer.

I hadn't taken my seat with the group when Angus and Rupert came barrelling into the lounge room, followed by Lexi shouting, 'Freak! I'm going to kill you.'

I assume she meant her brother, not the labradoodle.

After dragging them out, all the while smiling at our guests, I threatened them (again, not Rupert) with ongoing pain and torture for the rest of their lives if they didn't behave.

'Only the two children?' Ruth, the brunette, asked after I'd re-joined them.

'Yes, thankfully. More and I'd kill myself.'

'We have six,' Ruth chirped, before smiling at one of the cap-wearers seated to her left.

'Six!' I spluttered.

'We have seven,' Sandi chimed in.

They both looked too neat to have given birth to any children.

'And you don't drink alcohol? You don't ever feel the urge to scoff liquor-filled chocolates?'

The evening remained a tragedy. While the men busied themselves at the barbecue cooking lamb cutlets and plain beef sausages (thin), I attempted to find some common ground with the women. But all my standard conversation starters were stoppers at this particular dinner party. I asked if they skied. They lived in Utah after all. No. 'Been to the Sundance Film Festival?' Nada. New York? Los Angeles? San Francisco? Nope. Maybe scrapbooking and needlepoint were more their thing. Although with so many children between them, maybe all their energy went into keeping house, as Blanche, no doubt, would have recommended.

I had to keep pinching myself to stay awake and animated, especially after Matthew gave me the sly thumbs up and took the men into the games room to play pool. I almost wished Lexi would have one of her meltdowns so I could be excused, but she remained curiously silent.

I contemplated bringing out the *Family Conversation Starters* cards, a Mother's Day gift from Matthew – an implication that familial relations needed improvement? I don't think the cards had quite the effect on the family he'd been hoping for; whenever the cards surfaced, bickering ensued, resulting in food fights and at least one of us stomping off to bed. We'd had some terrific fights over those cards. As recently as two weeks ago, I'd pulled them out during a lacklustre Sunday evening roast.

'*I would love my family to...?*' I asked Lexi.

'Fuck off,' she'd replied. Even Lexi seemed surprised when that answer popped out of her mouth. We promptly confiscated her phone.

But I persevered.

With half an eye on *The Great British Bake Off*, Matthew pulled out the next card and groaned before reading it aloud. '*The family member with the most annoying habit is...*'

Lexi jumped in quickly with, 'I absolutely know the answer to this one. Please! It's Angus because he's—'

'Don't say it,' I warned. Too late.

Lexi shouted over my words. 'A fuckwit.'

That night, she also lost her non-essential computer privileges for the week.

Okay, so maybe it was best not to drag those cards out tonight.

Over peppermint tea, I talked about how I used to be a mildly successful photographer. 'But about the only thing I've taken photographs of lately is my pregnant sister's belly, which is getting increasingly enormous every day.'

'I refuse to take snaps of the actual birth,' I soldiered on after Sandi showed a flicker of interest. 'Too much blood, and as for the greasy mucus and the placenta – well, you both know how gruesome *that* is.' I took a breath, then babbled, 'But she's a crazy influencer. May insist on me filming the whole thing.'

Somebody shoot me.

It was well past midnight by the time I'd finished clearing up after the disastrous dinner. Before heading to bed, I made the school lunches, put on a load of washing, fed the pets and put out the garbage.

Cleo sat with me as I wrote an extensive to-do list for Matthew for the following day. He'd offered to get the children off to school. I kissed her nose. 'Yeah, we'll see how it goes.'

Upstairs, I peered in at Lexi. She looked almost angelic, curled up asleep. Normally, she hid her cuddly toys in the cupboard but tonight she'd surrounded herself with them. It was too dark to see her hair colour, so I walked out of her room pretending she was still a honey-blonde. I loved her, but sometimes...

I was greeted in the master bedroom by a snoring husband. Several lights were on. Clothes were strewn across the floor, and he'd left the drawers open. I climbed in next to him and flicked on my computer to watch the news with the sound down low.

A young man with a huge smile and tidy hair had been arrested for his mother's murder. I wondered what her crime had been. Perhaps making him do his homework when he was a child or forcing him to eat carrots? I'd given up trying to make Angus and Lexi eat vegetables. I knew I'd never win any Mother of the Year awards but hopefully my behaviour wasn't so appalling that years down the track my children would conspire to kill me.

After I finally switched off the light, I lay awake worrying I'd forgotten an after-school activity, money for an excursion, cat food or something. Then I agonised over what to wear for my first day. I was scared that after years away from real photography work, I'd have lost the spark, the gift I once had for knowing the exact second to click the shutter to capture the perfect poignant moment.

CHAPTER 4

I arrived at Image Ink at ten minutes to eight – no mean feat considering the chaos that had greeted me when I walked into the kitchen after showering and dressing in record time that morning. Still, Matthew put on a brave face.

'Dazzle them with your brilliance,' he'd said before kissing me goodbye.

After spending twenty minutes finding a parking space, I turned off the car engine and swivelled the rear-vision mirror so I could see my face. I rubbed off a layer of blush overzealously applied in darkness, checked my lipstick and gave myself a final once-over – black sling-back shoes, long black skirt, black shirt and black jacket. *#funeraldirector*

I pushed open the front door, anxious, but also excited, determined to observe workplace culture, do my best to fit in, be always professional, enthusiastic, punctual, work hard and work fast. Sure. No pressure.

Several corridors sprang from the bright purple main foyer, and I had no idea where to go.

I didn't know which magazine I'd be working on, but it didn't bother me. I could find interest in most things: people, flowers, animals. I wasn't too keen on photographing food or cars, but aside from those, I was open to snapping anything. Given I'd spent the last months taking photos of Robyn's expanding girth, I was ready for a new challenge.

I followed several people rushing down a hall. At the end of the walkway, a huge studio was being transformed into a Yuletide Turkish bathhouse. People dashed around with clipboards, others spoke into microphone headsets and several builders made a lot of noise with hammers and saws creating impressive faux marble baths and fountains.

'Katie,' Fern boomed. She looked amazing, wearing a sixties-inspired navy satin shift, elegant peep-toe heels and minimal make-up. I self-consciously touched my thin mumsy hair and regretted wearing Lexi's 'too pink to be true' lip gloss. 'You're here.'

'Yes, am I supposed to be?'

'Not likely. This is jock central, part of a holiday advertorial campaign for *Action Sports*.' She waved her hand. 'Deodorant,' she said by way of explanation. 'Sorry, I don't have much time to brief you. It's absolute bedlam. Come with me.' Together, we walked out of the studio, back up the hallway and into the foyer. 'You'll be working upstairs assisting Graeme Grafton on *Delicious Bites*. His focus is on the monthly print edition, and I want most of your attention centred on the daily digital title. He'll show you the ropes.'

My heart pounded. 'Food?' I knew Graeme by reputation. A former Bachelor of the Year, Graeme was not quite pretty boy, not quite handsome. A master photographer, he was a sometime charmer and an absolute nutter to boot.

She nodded. 'Didn't I tell you yesterday?'

'No.' My ringing mobile momentarily halted further conversation. Matthew. 'What's up?' I asked.

'He's lost his homework,' Matthew shouted over Angus's incoherent ranting.

'In his backpack,' I replied. Pause. 'And don't forget he has soccer after school.'

'Can't you handle that?' he asked.

'Yes. I'm just reminding you so you can remind Gus to take his boots.' I tried hard to stay calm.

'Okay. Look,' – Matthew sounded uptight, verging on angry – 'I'm already late for work and Angus is going ballistic over his shoelaces. Who knows where Lexi is? We'll have to work out something better for the morning routine.'

Where had my lovely supportive husband of an hour ago disappeared to? Breakfast reality with the kids had set in, that's what. I wouldn't be able to keep up this charade for two days let alone two or three weeks.

'Adjustment issues?' Fern asked as she led me upstairs, past the *Delicious Bites* hub and into the white-on-white studio, where, presumably, I'd be spending most of my time. I was entering the frightening world of food photography, temperamental chefs, ambitious food stylists and precious photographers.

I recognised Graeme straight away: tall and slim, not weak-knee-inducing gorgeous, but interesting, nonetheless. Fern and I watched for a few moments as he focused his lens on a plate of what looked like spaghetti marinara – I've been around long enough to know it's near to impossible to photograph that dish well (most seafood looks colourless and that's before you notice the anaemic squid comes across as being covered in acne) – while a woman hovered slightly outside the frame, muttering. She darted forward every now and then with tweezers to rearrange a tiger prawn or iceberg lettuce leaf.

Seizing an opportunity while a crisp red napkin was being positioned for the fifth time, Fern introduced us. 'Graeme

Grafton, Creative Director. Kate Cavendish, Photographer extraordinaire.'

I was a little flustered. I'd never met a Bachelor before. He shook my hand.

'Graeme,' Fern continued, 'you know Kate's sister, Robyn?'

He smirked. 'Once sought-after influencer? Now scrambling to remain relevant?'

Rude. His mop of sandy-blond hair threatened to hijack his dark-rimmed glasses. Blue eyes.

He glared at Fern. 'We're on a deadline.'

She waved her hand. 'Every day's a deadline.' Fern turned to me. 'Graeme's just returned from Canberra. He judged a national photography competition last night.'

'Crap! Total rubbish. I disqualified all the contestants. None of their photos were even worthy of a retirement home fête. I would have preferred being locked in a public toilet cubicle for six hours. Without my phone.'

Bah humbug!

Unfazed, Fern indulged Graeme with a wide smile, then said to me, 'I'll leave you to it,' before disappearing out the door.

Graeme shot me a piercing stare. 'So? You up for it?'

'I don't—'

'Relax, Katie-Kate. Do as I say. Humour me on the rare occasion I get precious, and you and I will get along fine.' He flashed a megawatt smile and laughed.

What had I let myself in for?

'I'm not as volatile as people say, I just can't abide imbeciles. Hey, Mara?' He glanced at a woman dressed in a black skivvy shirt, black jeans and black ballet flats, who had just walked into the room.

Mara Milton, the *Delicious Bites* editor and head chef, was an Aussie icon, revered for her innovative take on traditional cooking. Our very own Nigella Lawson. Her restaurant, *Milton*, had been awarded three Michelin stars. She'd also been invited to appear on the new season of *MasterChef: The Professionals,* beginning next February.

Mara tossed him a benevolent smile and strode over to introduce herself.

'Lovely to meet you,' I stammered. 'I was so sorry when Milton closed. It was one of my favourites.'

She smiled. 'Thank you. I'll open another restaurant some day, but for now—'

'Enough with the love fest, ladies.' Graeme's glare was piercing.

Further conversation terminated, he dismissed me with an extensive list of fruit and vegetables and other ingredients he needed *immediately* for the afternoon shoot. I hurried out of the studio, past a huge open-plan office and, once I'd asked the receptionist for directions, set off to a nearby grocer.

After loading up with assorted green vegetables – peas, beans, broccoli, zucchini and lettuce; berries, cherries – I headed to a hardware shop for lacquer spray, then on to the two-dollar shop, where I bought celebratory baubles, garlands, and other trimmings. I was well qualified for this, given all the costumes I'd created for school and dance concerts over the years, not to mention my extensive knowledge of even the rarest vegetables in the world.

Graeme thanked me by having me make him a cup of coffee. 'Strong, black, two cubes of sugar. No instant sludge, either.'

I soon found out that as Graeme's assistant, my first job every morning would be to make his plunger coffee according to his written instructions, which he handed to me on a piece of white palm-sized cardboard with his initials embossed in silver in the top right-hand corner.

My elegant black shoes were going to be my downfall, among other things. I could feel the blisters growing on my toes.

I'd thought they'd get me through the day, the week, the month maybe. They were practical... enough. Though in fairness, I'd only worn them once before... to a restaurant, where the furthest I'd walked was the ten metres from the Uber to the chair where I'd sat on my backside for four hours.

I was washing green broad beans when my mobile rang. The alarm at home was going off. Six sensors were beeping, and the security company had phoned the police. I called Matthew, but he was in a meeting and couldn't be disturbed. Of course. I tried Mum. No answer on the landline, and she didn't have a mobile. Very convenient. I thought about calling Robyn but quickly came to my senses.

So much for good first impressions.

Thirty minutes later, I arrived home to find a security guard and two police officers hanging out on the front verandah.

'No apparent sign of a break-in,' one of the officers told me calmly as he took my keys and unlocked the front door.

As the four of us walked inside, I positioned myself at the rear of the group in case the burglars were still there.

No burglars. Merely animals rampaging hysterically through the house. Why couldn't Matthew have put Rupert in the backyard and Cleo in her catio before turning on the alarm?

I made my apologies to the police and to the gum-chewing security guy who said, 'No problem, fills in my day.'

After they departed, I took the opportunity to change shoes. My crippled feet thanked me as I rushed back to the car.

It was close to one thirty by the time I arrived back at *Delicious Bites*. So far, I'd achieved little more than foot comfort and superfluous set decoration. I was no closer to picking up a camera than I'd been yesterday or the day before.

CHAPTER 5

'Mum, why am I always the last to be picked up?' Angus asked later when he and his muddy-footed friends clambered into my car after soccer practice.

'Sorry, Gus,' I said, distracted by the coach, Arnaud, stretching his muscular legs barely three metres away from me. He saw me looking and I waved.

I returned my attention to my son. 'How was your day?'

No answer. Too busy making fart noises with friends in the rear of their personal taxi. How did I go from owning a cute Volkswagen Beetle to driving a people mover with a *Kids on Board* sticker plastered to the back window?

I turned the radio up and sang along to 'Jingle Bell Rock', smiling to myself, even though December wasn't yet upon us. Had Lexi been in the car, she'd be dry-retching about now. But then, if Lexi was in the car, I'd never get away with listening to this station or singing.

Parking in the driveway after dropping Angus's friends home, I suddenly felt exhausted. It had been a long day. I craved soaking in a hot bath, then curling up with a good book, though that was as likely as snow falling in the Sahara.

In the kitchen, I heard Taylor Swift blaring about unrequited love.

'Lexi, could you turn it down a few decibels, please?' I called, before noticing a handsome boy stuffing his face with chocolate biscuits. Lexi's new friend – boyfriend perhaps? What had happened to Luke from last week? A never-ending parade of adolescent boys seemed to pass through my kitchen, depleting our food supplies.

'Wassup?' he said.

Wassup! Great, just what Lexi needed – an *illiterate* new boyfriend.

'Hello.' I carefully enunciated my vowels. 'I am Kate, Lexi's mother.'

'Hunter,' he obliged.

'Hunter?' I repeated, before staring at his T-shirt which said, *Eat out more often*. Clearly not an advertisement for a restaurant chain, given the ink graphics of two bodies, a man and woman on top of each other, head to crotch.

Six months ago, Lexi barely acknowledged boys. Five months ago, Lexi turned thirteen. Now here she was, hanging out with a walking advertisement for oral sex. The blue-black dye job suddenly seemed less important than it had yesterday.

In my short experience as the mother of a teenage girl, I've learned the following:

1. They're so much more sophisticated than I was at that age.
2. iPhones are for texting best friends, Instagramming best friends or playing TikTok videos. Definitely not for answering their mother's calls and texts.
3. They go from shunning boys to having boyfriends with names like Spike and Hunter.

4. They go from asking lots of questions and expecting you to know all the answers, to accusing you of knowing nothing.
5. They hate their mothers and torture them by mutilating their own hair.
6. They may or may not know the finer points of fellatio.

At thirteen, I wore braces, and had no breasts to speak of. I didn't even own a bra. 'What do you want a bra for?' my mother had said. 'To hold up your imagination?'

My male friends amounted to two younger cousins whom I studiously avoided at family functions. Of course, there were boys on the school bus, but they never took any notice of me, instead focusing entirely on my big-breasted classmates. On the rare occasion a person of the opposite sex paid me the slightest attention, I'd crumple in an embarrassed, boobless heap. And I certainly didn't know what the hell fellatio was.

Lexi would have shunned me had she known me. Rather like she does now, I guess.

❄

'Hey, class mother, how's the new job?' my friend Diane asked when she phoned.

Diane (athletic, Zumba enthusiast, trivia queen) and I had met when Angus and her son, Tom, started preschool together. In the beginning, we only talked about kids, school and reality television. These days, few topics were taboo.

The downside of our friendship? Diane's a fitness fanatic – an eight-glasses-of-water-a-day girl who lives by the creed of no-carbs-after-midday. And she drags me out of bed at dawn twice a week to go walking with her.

'I'm looking forward to hearing all about it tonight at the end of year class dinner. You haven't forgotten, have you?'

I shook my head. 'Of course not.' Of course, I had. It was still November. Too early for an end of year get-together.

'I'll pick you up in an hour.'

She clicked off and I mentally cursed myself for volunteering to be a class mum, a duty I'd neglected well before I had a job to blame. Apart from organising the weekly reading roster, I hadn't done much at all. Oh, we'd had a half-hearted morning tea at the beginning of this term, a 'how's everything going' affair. Eight mothers turned up at the park, several with fertile dogs and noisy toddlers in tow.

It ended up being a screaming, crying, barking fest lasting two interminable hours before we all politely retreated to our own lives, exhausted and having learned very little about each other or the other children in Year Three. Rupert had a ball though. Got to sniff a few new dogs' bottoms, wee on some recently planted bottlebrushes and have me follow him around cleaning up after him.

At least toddlers and dogs weren't invited tonight.

❄

Diane and I sat at one end of a very long table at Bruce's BBQ Bistro sipping Prosecco.

I picked up the bottle. 'Since when did everyone start drinking this?'

Diane shrugged. 'So, how did you feel after our little walk the other day?'

'Exhausted. Tired. Crabby.'

'Diddums! My heart bleeds. I work a full-time job, Kate, and I still make time to exercise.'

'Yes, yes, how's David? Over his little op?' Diane's husband David had recently had a vasectomy.

'I'm never going to hear the end of it. One tiny snip. That's all it was. We agreed before we got married that we had enough children between us, and he was the one who suggested the operation. But now, the poor baby's tender. And now he can't take out the garbage, can't drive the kids to school or help with the end of year activities. He doesn't want to talk about Christmas, like, when will he see his children for Christmas? Christmas Day? Christmas Eve? Boxing Day? These things need to be worked out but he says it's too stressful. He's a wimp. That's all there is to it.' We clinked glasses.

'How are all the kids?' Diane has four – two of her own plus David's two.

'Feral. Fighting. Blended families, hey? Then there are the exes. This will be our second Christmas together.' She sipped her wine. 'I can't face another disaster like last year, so we need to clarify exactly when the six of us can celebrate together.'

The disaster in question happened when David's kids turned up unexpectedly on Christmas Eve when Diane was in the middle of glazing a ham. No presents wrapped and zero food prepared. Miscommunication meant that his children stayed Christmas Eve and were picked up the following morning.

'I often have moments when I wonder whether David and I will go the distance. I felt so sure when I said *I do* again, but now I'm not so certain. Passion doesn't endure. Aptitude in the kitchen, however—'

'Is a skill for life,' I chimed in. 'I'm sure he's learnt from his mistake last year.'

'You'd think, but so far, he's studiously avoided the topic. But enough about me. Still admiring the soccer coach from afar?'

I laughed, thinking again about Arnaud's thighs. He was fit, no doubt about it. Yes, Arnaud was my number one fantasy guy. It probably had a lot to do with the fact he's French and ever since I was little, I'd dreamt of living in France... or at least visiting Paris. When I was sixteen, we even planned a European family holiday: me, Robyn, Mum and Dad. For months, I researched everything about Paris and immersed myself in French lessons. I couldn't wait to stand under the Eiffel Tower and explore the city's art galleries and museums. But it didn't work out. Our family never made it to Paris. We never even made it as far as the airport.

Gradually, the table filled with latecomers and their excuses, greetings were exchanged, and we got down to the crux of the night – one-upmanship in the parenting stakes. Diane and I played a little game whenever someone spoke about parenting duties. We'd add a silent *Because I'm a perfect mother* to the end of their sentences. It amused us no end.

So, who was the best mother at the table?

Esther, (vibrant, flame-haired, and toothy grin to rival Julia Roberts) with two boys at school and another at preschool started. 'I gave up my career to care for my boys full-time. And I love it. I love being there for them whenever they need me.' *Because I'm a perfect mother.*

'I know what you mean,' Karin (perky breasts) agreed. 'My whole life is spent ferrying the kids around making sure they're looked after and pursuing their dreams. Karate on Monday, piano Tuesday—'

'Sounds exhausting,' I said.

'With my Ben,' Mardi (conservative, opinionated) piped up, 'I make sure he gets at least two hours of Mummy time every day.' She held up two fingers and waved them in the air, like we were imbeciles. 'Not the token ten minutes some mothers spend with their children.' *Because I'm a perfect mother.*

Mardi has one child, plus a live-in maid, a full-time gardener and an accommodating husband who spends several months of the year overseas.

'Our only real hiccup this term has been summer soccer,' Mardi, the milestone monitor continued. 'It's criminal the way Ben's being treated. Arnaud isn't allowing him to shine the way he should. Ben's a star. He's also brilliant academically...' Whether it was about soccer, reading groups, maths groups or class groups in general, Mardi had an opinion. A loud one. Once, when a few of us were discussing our children's lack of reading progress, she proudly announced brilliant Benjamin had been reading *National Geographic* since he was four. Milestones indeed.

'That, and he should have been given a solo at the upcoming Christmas concert. He has an amazing voice. God's gift.'

Diatribe about the unfairness of Ben's outstanding, but as yet uncelebrated academic career and vocal prowess exhausted, Mardi drew breath. For a moment. 'I'm no Instagram fan, but I did notice Robyn's hysterical post a few days back.' Pause. 'Given she's not yet a parent...'

I knew what Mardi was referring to: Robyn's seeming embrace of baby formulas if her baby failed to 'latch'. (And it wasn't hysterical, but hopefully Robyn wouldn't endorse a brand any time soon. Or later.)

Mardi continued. 'Surely even she knows breast is best.'

I put my hand up. 'I'm not my sister's keeper.'

Diane shifted in her seat. 'Let's talk about something interesting.' She exhaled. 'Kate's doing some photography at *Delicious Bites* magazine.'

'With Mara Milton?' Esther piped up. 'I absolutely loved her restaurant. Can't believe she closed it to work for a magazine.'

'No doubt the hours are a lot better,' Diane quipped.

Karin clapped her hands. 'Phwoar! Graeme Grafton's something, isn't he? No wonder Mara gave up *Milton* to work with him. Gorgeous. And his smile! Bachelor of the Year, wasn't he? Have you met him, Kate?'

I nodded.

Karin was practically swooning. 'Lucky you. Can you get me his autograph?'

CHAPTER 6

Two hours later, I arrived home to a shambolic kitchen and Rupert lying on the good sofa (forest-green velvet – an impractical choice, given my homelife) chewing my half-read Anita Heiss novel. And though the kids and Matthew were asleep, every light in the house was shining. Dimmers and off switches be damned.

Matthew hadn't waited up to ask how my first day had gone. We'd barely nodded to each other earlier this evening as he arrived home just as I was leaving.

I was so hyped I knew I wouldn't sleep – though tonight's conversation had been boring enough to put most people into a coma – so I wandered into the study, and pulled out a collection of prints I'd taken in New York the summer I won the scholarship. My favourite was a black-and-white photo of an elderly couple sitting on a park bench. I thought back to that day. Central Park had been frantic with activity. Roller bladers zigzagged between bike riders, kids played tag, and dogs barked and chased squirrels. Through it all, the couple had sat together holding hands and smiling, oblivious to the bustle around them. They were gorgeous. And content. Satisfied. Together.

In bed forty minutes later, I studied Matthew, who was crashed out and snoring, and wondered if we'd be like them in our old age – content? I hoped so, but right now, we were like two icebergs slowly drifting apart.

When I first met Matthew, I didn't need to indulge in fantasies about other men. Matthew was my real-life fantasy man, my escape. And now? Well, he was still handsome, clever and hard-working. But he wasn't the man I married. The man I married was wild, gregarious and funny. These days, Matthew was too busy working to have fun.

But he was also thoughtful, kind and great with the kids. All things considered, Matthew was solid. So I didn't know why I lay awake at two in the morning most nights agonising over inconsequential stuff like the lack of sex and laughter. We had a great marriage, except... for the loneliness. I guess as the years had sailed by, life had become predictable – busy but mundane. And there was never enough time for the two of us. Sometimes it occurred to me Matthew might not be in love with me anymore, that he no longer desired me. Perhaps that part of our lives was over. If so, what were we? Flatmates who shared a bed? The thought was so depressing at times I could barely look at him.

Finally asleep, I dreamed I was hosing the garden, lost in reverie, enjoying the sun, the water, the quiet. My hands moved along the rubbery hose, almost caressing it. Suddenly Arnaud appeared behind me, grasped my waist and murmured in my ear in his so-sexy French accent he couldn't wait to have me. He wanted me now, here.

The children! Matthew!

My protests were weak. He laughed and kissed me behind my ear, savouring the sweat that had collected there, told me I tasted of the sea, then wrapped a blindfold around my eyes, warning me not to make a sound. He picked me up in his arms. I struggled, but didn't mean it, and he laughed again, low and throaty.

He carried me into the house and up the stairs and lay me on the bed.

Don't move, he warned, stripping off my clothes. I tried to turn away. He shouldn't be here! This was wrong! What if the kids came home? What about Matthew? Arnaud held my arms above my head, pinning me to the bed, and lowered himself over me, kissing my neck, my nipples, my ribs. He smelled of the mountains, woodsy, fresh and more than a bit dangerous. His tongue left blazing trails of fire as he held me immobile.

I gave myself over to wanting him, needing him, demanding him. As he entered me, I arched up to meet him. I was deep within the throes of ecstasy when I woke, exhausted, hot and sweaty in a mess of tangled sheets.

CHAPTER 7

When I walked into the studio on my second day, Graeme was in full flight with Mara.

'I asked for green grapes and sparkling frigging mineral water, Mara. Not green grapes and still frigging mineral water. There's a difference, you know. The assistants are imbeciles. I won't shoot until I have the right water.'

'Yes sirree, captain.' Mara saluted, and Graeme stalked out of the room.

'You'll get used to working with Graeme,' she said, noticing me creeping behind her.

'Will I?'

'Probably not but do as I do and ignore him... and when that fails, ignore him anyway. With Simone injured and several others on annual holidays, I'm all about multi-tasking and doing what I can to ensure a seamless flow. Graeme's a pain, but unfortunately, necessary.'

I nodded.

'And a word of warning about napkin colours: always agree with him. It'll make your life easier. In addition to being a pain, Graeme's completely obsessive.'

'He's got a certain way about him.'

'Thinks he's a world conqueror.'

'I don't *think*, Mara, dear, I know.' Graeme appeared out of nowhere. 'Kate, where did you study?'

'Sydney College of the Arts with Jacques Miller.'

'Should have guessed. His methods don't work in the magazine industry. Banging on about natural light – what a joke. Dead now, isn't he?'

I couldn't tell whether he was joking or serious. 'I don't think so,' I said, though I couldn't be sure; I'd been out of the loop for years.

'Really?' Graeme said, glaring at me. 'Are you only interested in photographing in natural light, too?'

'If there's a choice, I'd prefer not to use artificial lighting, but in a studio, you have to.'

'And the work that comes out of a studio, Kate,' Mara said, 'would you agree it's not exceptional to see every shot well done?'

I hesitated. 'I'm... I'm not sure.'

'Technically at least,' Mara continued, 'once the lighting's been determined and the camera's positioned on the tripod—'

'So anyone can do it?' Graeme's cheeks were blazing. 'A monkey, for example?'

Mara smiled. 'Oh, Graeme, you might need to train the monkey for an hour.' She paused. 'Maybe two.'

To be fair, with food photography, lighting was everything, or almost. Making a two-dimensional image look as three-dimensional as humanly possible usually came down to lighting.

Fern whizzed into the studio, phone to ear, smiling. 'All getting along, are we?'

'Great,' I sparkled, feeling anything but. However, I could

take inspiration from her, a woman who had it all. The confidence. The enthusiasm for life.

She handed Graeme an invoice to sign and breezed out again.

Don't go, I inwardly shouted. I felt safe when Fern was around because, truthfully, I wasn't sure I was cut out for this.

Exhaling, I took in my surroundings. Concrete floors, stainless-steel benches, and the smooth white walls upon which Graeme's huge and vibrant canvases hung. Rustic bowls bursting with vivid multicoloured tomatoes hung on one wall, a five-metre fried egg covered a back wall, and a bright orange cut butternut pumpkin dominated another. The images were striking.

At the fried egg end of the studio, Mara arranged several desserts. While the preparation and cooking took place in the kitchen down the corridor, the finishing touches were added here. At the other end, the all white end, Graeme muttered as he set about hooking up the Hasselblad to a Mac – way beyond my experience, but I was trying not to let it show. Several cameras lay nearby. A darkroom for monochrome printing was off to one side near a bank of computers and huge colour printers.

Near Graeme, I spied the infamous wobbly ladder, the whole reason I was here in the first place. I happened to be at the right (or wrong) place – the swimming pool – at the right (or wrong) time, when Simone, the assistant photographer, fell off that exact wobbly ladder and broke her ankle.

Fern knew I had no experience with food photography – an ex-newspaper photographer taking mostly outdoor shots, filling shadows and dodging reflections, making the transition to stylised food photography? A huge leap. Not only was lighting an issue, but it was hard work. Cooking shows had a lot to answer for. Regardless of how appetising the cuisine looked on *MasterChef*, you barely had minutes before food (any food) looked like yesterday's garbage – fried food became greasy, ice cream melted, sauces congealed. It's a nightmare.

But Fern was obviously desperate, and now, here I was, desperate to prove I could photograph anything thrown at me. That is, when finally given a chance to pick up a camera, whenever that might be.

I aspired to be like Fern. She seemed to breeze through most things, and I bet she didn't have to contend with her adolescent daughter's boyfriend wearing pornographic T-shirts. She wouldn't lie awake at night agonising over the spreading cellulite on her buttocks, the multiplying crow's feet, or her sagging breasts.

'So, are you up for it, Mara?' Graeme asked.

Her eyes visibly protruded. 'Up for what?'

'Some slap and tickle under the table. What do you think? It's Friday, for Christ's sake. Let's shoot this frigging shit so I can get the hell outta here. You may not have a life, my dear, but I certainly do.'

'You have no idea how truly charming you are, Graeme.' Mara slammed several plates on the bench and walked out of the room.

He threw back his head and laughed before following her. I stood in the middle of the stark silent room and considered whether their little show had been for my benefit.

'Hey, I know you,' came the voice of my dreams, interrupting my worries that the pavlova's whipped cream would start to melt. 'What are you doing here?'

'Arnaud? I didn't recognise you without your soccer shorts on,' I said, then blushed.

With wild curly black hair, and sporting a three-day growth, Arnaud was wearing a black polo shirt with dark faded jeans and black work boots. He looked rather bohemian and had a rugged sexuality about him – nothing like the soccer coach I knew. But he was definitely the man I went to bed with last night. My body shivered at the memory.

'And, in answer to your question, it's my second day as a photography assistant on *Delicious Bites*. Just a couple of weeks, helping a friend.'

'Graeme Grafton?'

'Yes, well no. His boss, Fern McLeod. And to tell you the truth, I have no idea what I'm supposed to do. Food photography is new to me. All I seem to be doing is running errands and putting out fires. There's been no camerawork so far.'

'Ah, join the club. I write for *Action Sports*. I know how to play soccer but writing about it, in English? Well, this is new for me, too.'

This day was getting odder by the minute. Arnaud was working here, in this very building, as a writer and resident football pro? I hadn't realised how privileged Angus's team was. No wonder the parents took the club games so seriously.

Still, I wasn't sure if having Arnaud so close was such a good idea.

CHAPTER 8

I arrived home, shook off my shoes and went in search of Angus and Mum. I found them playing chess in the living room adjacent to the kitchen, a plate of Christmas sugar cookies in front of them.

Bugs, our favourite bunny, was draped around Angus's neck, Rupert lounged in the corner on a cushion –my favourite Designers Guild emerald-green velvet fringe cushion (yeah, I was asking for trouble – and yes, have a penchant for green and velvet) – and Cleo was swinging on a nearby fly-screen in search of an elusive fly. I glanced over at the fish swimming in their tank. At least they were behaving themselves.

I clapped. 'Cleopatra!'

All eyes turned to me, startled. Cleo dropped to the floor and slunk into the pantry.

'Thanks for picking Angus up from school today, Mum.' I bent over Angus and kissed the top of his head. 'How was your day, darling?'

'Okay,' he replied vaguely, before taking Mum's queen with his bishop.

'More to the point, how was your day?' Mum asked, standing to hug me. 'Two days on the job. All good?'

'I guess.'

'Well, you certainly *look* glamorous.' Glamorous? Only a mother would say that. She held up the plate. 'Candy cane or Christmas tree?'

'Yum.' I took a cane-shaped biscuit with red icing and white sprinkles. 'But a bit early, don't you think?'

'Less than five weeks, Katie, and it's never too early for festive treats.'

Inwardly, I groaned. There was so much to do before then.

'When are we putting up the tree?' Angus asked.

I turned to him. 'Excellent question, darling. Maybe tomorrow.'

Angus beamed.

It was almost six o'clock. 'Any sign of Lexi?' She played netball Friday afternoons but was usually home by now.

Mum shook her head and peered back at the chessboard, tutting. 'I'm as confused as a goat on Astroturf.'

Poor woman. A king and three motley pawns were not going to win the game for her.

Lexi didn't answer her mobile, so I texted:

Where are you?

In the kitchen, I opened a bottle of Sauv Blanc and poured a couple of glasses. I handed one to Mum and waved a takeaway menu. 'Pizza?'

'Sure.' Robyn wafted through the laundry door at the side of the kitchen. Immediately, she eyed my wine. 'I'll have one of those, too.'

I shrugged and poured her half a glass. Who was I to be the pregnancy police with my single, soon-to-be-a-mother, sister?

As well as being a pregnant social influencer, Robyn's a tad neurotic. I guess I'd be anxious, too, if I was facing parenthood alone. But I'm here for her. I go to her antenatal classes, I'm her birth partner (God help us both), and I listen to her with sisterly interest when she chatters incessantly about her Insta posts and likes.

In recent months I'd shot:

1. Beach scenes – Robyn glowing in full sun, (yes, SPF 50 applied), Robyn smiling through high winds, pounding surf, and torrential rain, most complete with seagulls and pelicans.
2. Fashion – Robyn dressed in body-hugging knits and huge flowing caftans (bell-shaped sleeves, the whole bit) in swirling tutti-frutti colours, a flattering cross-section of ALL maternity fashion, most showing her growing baby bump.
3. Hair – platinum updo, sleek auburn bob, shaggy blonde wet-beach, don't-care hair. (All wigs.)
4. Miscellaneous. Too extensive to list.

'How was your day, Robyn?' Robyn said loudly as I handed her a drink. 'Thanks for asking, family.'

'Give me half a chance,' I replied. 'I've only just arrived home.'

She sipped her drink. Grimaced. 'Yuck.' She set the glass down on the kitchen bench. 'I'll tell you: I was up painting the baby's shoebox until three this morning. Three! It's now fluorescent lime.'

My eyebrows raised. 'Lime! I thought you were going for canary?'

'Thank you, I was. But because you were so mean about it, I switched colours.'

'Lime?'

'I know. It's awful.' Robyn's eyes welled with tears.

Mum wrapped her arms around Robyn. 'I'm sure it's lovely.'

'No, it's not. It's foul! A sickly apple green. Definitely not Insta perfect.' She turned to me. 'All your fault.'

'What did *I* do?'

Mum raised a warning finger at me. 'Katie, why don't you like canaries?'

Robyn eased herself into a chair at the kitchen nook. 'I wasted all my time painting and now there are baby things all over the apartment.' She took a breath. 'I can't breathe. The tabloids are saying Kylie Jenner is pregnant – again! Another yummy mummy social media influencer to compete with.'

Compete? I almost choked on my wine.

'It's hard enough being pregnant without seeing celebrities strutting around in their third trimester wearing Jimmy Choos... let alone bikinis two weeks after their baby's birth.'

'Scrummy mummies?'

'Exactly. Why can't there be more women like me who eat pizza and chocolate cake?'

'Slummy mummies?'

'Shut up.' Robyn closed her eyes and rubbed her stomach.

I set my glass down on the bench. 'You can talk. What about your Insta posts showcasing your perfect pregnancy? Hashtag LivingMyBestLife. Hashtag Blessed.' My neck ached and I rolled it from side to side while breathing deeply. 'Your latest post...'

She glared at me. 'What about it?'

'Do you think it's wise advertising baby formula before you've actually given birth?'

Robyn waved me away. 'I wasn't advertising a brand. I was simply putting it out to the universe that I'm open to the idea of a formula-sponsored post or two. I need the money.' She clutched her stomach and yelped. 'I'm having the baby.'

I groaned. 'You're not having the baby.'

'How would you know? It'd be better to have it now than on Christmas Day.'

'You're not due until after New Year,' Mum soothed.

'At least then I wouldn't have women in shopping centres coming up and touching my stomach,' Robyn continued, as if Mum hadn't spoken. 'They're freaking me out. I was walking through the cosmetics department and three women attacked me, spraying perfume, patting my stomach. Invading my personal space. Why can't they leave me alone?'

'Hang on. You're the one putting yourself out there for the world to see and comment, like with the baby formula.'

Robyn glared at me. 'Sometimes I turn off the comments section. Anyway, I was so overcome with fumes and panic, I almost fainted.'

'Poor love,' Mum said.

'But I couldn't faint. I had to pull myself together and head to the baby department to buy extra coat hangers. I don't have enough baby coat hangers.'

Robyn's apartment is full of baby coat hangers.

CHAPTER 9

I left the conversation to read a note that had been pushed under our front door by our – in my opinion – insane neighbours, Margaret and Peter.

Despite hanging their festive multi-coloured fairy lights every year in mid-October – too many to be counted – draped on hedges and shrubs, wrapped around their veranda balustrades, dangling from windowsills, dressing up their letter box as Frosty (adorned with white lights), and positioning five reindeer (red lights) prominently on the verge, the couple didn't ooze Christmas spirit.

So, to the note. Margaret and Peter have tree issues. Specifically, hedge-height issues. Apparently, our conifer hedge is growing too tall and blocking their 'right to light'.

I read in a magazine recently the top five things that aggravate neighbours. In no particular order, they are:

1. Pet noise and pets fouling neighbours' gardens.
2. Noisy, late-night parties.
3. Boundary disputes.
4. Garden trespass.

5. High hedges.

Yes, high hedges.

The note requested an urgent ('urgent' underlined) meeting ('meeting' followed by several exclamation marks – four, to be precise) to resolve the aforementioned hedge concerns.

I walked back into the kitchen, crumpled up this latest communiqué, and threw it into the bin under the sink. Maybe we could have a meeting about their festering work shed, decrepit clothesline and the growing pile of bricks in the middle of the junk depot they call a backyard – an eyesore if ever there was one. The whole reason we let the conifers grow untrimmed is so we wouldn't have to look at them or hear them and Muffy and Midget. Highland terriers, they fling themselves at our fence whenever we step outside. Woof, woof, scurry, scurry, thud – over and over again. It was amusing at first. But now? Tiresome.

'How are *you*, Mum?' I was hoping she'd forgotten about running into Dad earlier in the week.

'Your dad and I had a lovely evening last night. Champagne, music. Just like old times.'

'Last night? You went out with him? What old times precisely? I don't remember them.'

'I thought I'd be as nervous as a fly in a paint pot, but it felt so right. So easy.'

'Okay. You're scaring me.' What was she thinking, having dinner with him? Was she a masochist, setting herself up for further pain and heartbreak? What was Dad playing at, anyway? We hadn't heard from him in years and suddenly he's hanging around, taking Mum out to dinner?

I glanced at Robyn, who was scrolling through her phone. 'What do you have to say about this?'

She looked up. 'Yeah, I missed him for a long time.'

I rolled my eyes.

'What? He's my dad. Then I got used to him not being around. It's what men do. They impregnate you, then run off as soon as the going gets tough.' Robyn patted her stomach.

Mum sipped her wine. 'Dad suggested the family get-together for dinner tomorrow night.'

'Excuse me? What family exactly?' I asked.

'Don't be like that, Katie. We can eat at my house – Robyn, you, Matthew, Angus and Lexi—'

'Are you mad? Not in this lifetime.'

We gave up the idea of ordering pizza and agreed to cook. Soon, the three of us were standing around the kitchen island. I took assorted meats, tomatoes, capers and olives from the fridge and handed a block of cheddar to Robyn. 'Grate this.'

As kids, Robyn and I spent whole Sundays in the kitchen making coconut ice, rocky road – always sweet, sugary treats – leaving messy trails of flour, coconut and sugar on the floor. The afternoons usually ended with one of us in tears, but it was still fun. Warm and comforting.

'You're going to have to see your father sooner or later,' Mum said, as she chopped tomatoes. 'He's very keen to catch up.'

Robyn shrugged. 'Sure. All fodder for Insta. I haven't posted a food pic for a while. In fact, we could do one now. My fans would love this. The three of us in the kitchen preparing dinner together. We could get Bugs in on the action too. Chowing down on lettuce. Brilliant.'

'I'm not sure,' Mum replied. 'You've said yourself, there are weirdos out there.'

'No one's out to get you, Mum. It'll be fun. Bugs'll love it.' Robyn turned to me. 'We could tie it in with your new job at *Delicious Bites*.'

I shook my head. 'Let's not bring the magazine into this.'

'Cross-promotion.' Robyn brightened. 'What's not to love?'

She paused. 'Maybe you're right. The less said about Graeme Grafton, the better.'

My phone pinged with a text message from Lexi:

c u soon.

That was it. It didn't tell me much except she was alive.

Angus sidled up beside me. '*The Flintstones* is finished.'

Robyn raised a brow. 'Pardon?'

'Nostalgia cartoons,' I answered.

'What's for dinner?' Angus continued. 'Where's Dad?'

'At the golf club, remember? Why don't you watch another episode and then we'll eat.'

'Cool. Love you, Mum.' He vanished back to the TV.

Mum cleared her throat. 'I wish you'd change your mind about your father, Kate.'

'Dad abandoned us... destroyed our lives.'

'You're exaggerating.'

'He left us years ago and you want to welcome him back with open arms?'

'Water under the bridge,' Mum replied matter-of-factly, as if it was a spilt cup of tea that could be mopped up and forgotten. 'Life goes on.'

'Yes, but not with him. Why his sudden interest in you, anyway?'

'You can ask him yourself at dinner.'

'I'd rather drink mud. You tell me. What happened to Lovely Legs?'

'Wasn't so lovely it turns out. They divorced—'

'Surprise. Surprise.'

'Dad moved back to Sydney some months ago. Anyway, we went out for dinner, then returned to my home for a nightcap. The attention was very flattering, I must say.'

'Mum, don't!'

'Why shouldn't I? It was like old times. He was sweet—'

'Please don't say sweeter than stolen honey.'

'But he was.' She drew breath. 'Don't be such a prude, Kate. Most men my age aren't looking my way. They're looking at women twenty years younger.'

'Perverts,' Robyn chimed in.

I rubbed the back of my neck to ease the knot of tension. 'Mum, I don't want you to get hurt again.'

'I'm a big girl, Kate. I can look after myself. It's not as if I'm going to do anything silly. We were catching up, that's all.'

Catching up? Was Mum completely missing the point? The point being Dad walked out on her without so much as a backward glance. But Mum was blind to it, locked in a fantasy world. As the universe knows, I wasn't opposed to a spot of escapism now and then. Arnaud flashed before my eyes. I shuddered. Now wasn't the time.

I reached for my phone and turned to Robyn. 'Okay, how do you want to pose?'

CHAPTER 10

Outside, the early morning crows squawked. Beside me, Matthew's heavy breathing was regular and steady. Apart from that? Silence. It was six forty-five on Saturday morning and I was savouring snuggling under the blankets before attending to the daily routine.

A hundred years ago, before Lexi and Angus were born, Matthew and I could stay in bed all weekend, making love, reading the papers in the pre-digital age, and drinking champagne. Okay, it didn't happen often, but when it did, it was amazing.

Banishing erotic Arnaud daydreams from my mind, I rolled over and wrapped my arms around Matthew's stomach, then decided a back massage might be a more direct way to gain his attention. He rolled over to face me, my arms still around him, and I thought about suggesting I blindfold him or tie him up with scarves like I used to do in the old days. When Matthew and I first started dating, I owned an amazing Celtic wrought-iron bed. That bed was now languishing in our garage, covered in a mountain of grime and dust, but I couldn't bring myself to part with it. Just the thought of Matt being tied up in bed excited me.

'I've missed this,' he murmured, then kissed me. I could feel him pressing into my thigh as his kissing became more urgent.

'Me too,' I whispered when we took a break. All right. We might get to see some action after all.

But Matthew had barely put his hand on my right breast when I heard Angus, stomping down the corridor to our room. 'Where are my soccer boots?'

Matthew groaned. 'Don't go. Stay with me, pretend you didn't hear him.'

It was very tempting.

'Mum, are you *ever* getting out of bed?' This time, the cry from outside our door was more insistent.

Maybe we could borrow Angus's handcuffs tonight and take up from where we left off, I thought as I slipped out of our queen-sized ensemble. Though it'd be a challenge tying Matt to the Sealy Posturepedic.

'You're a good mother,' Matthew muttered. That would be the hangover talking and his not-so-subtle way of asking if I could take Angus to his soccer game this morning.

I left Matthew to sleep and, on autopilot, swept through the household chores. I threw Coco Pops at Angus (what would the perfect school mums say about that?), biscuits to the pets, put on a load of washing, took the clean clothes out of the dryer, unloaded the dishwasher, and swept the floors, all while Angus followed me around, telling me to hurry up because we were going to be late. (And I found his boots. They were in the laundry cupboard where I'd put them two days ago after soccer training.)

'About tonight,' Mum started after I answered my mobile in the car.

'Not a chance.'

'Your dad really wants to see you, Katie.'

'He can have a viewing at my funeral.' I pressed end as I parked at the Dragons home ground.

Barely eight o'clock and the sun was already warm. I discarded my denim jacket. (Why hadn't I brought my camera? The light was perfect.) I knew the drill. After all, I'd taken Angus to most of his games this year. And, let me say, it's a very long soccer season, like ten months. This year, I swore it would be different – that Matthew would appear at least fifty per cent of the time. It's not so much that I dislike the game; it's that some of the parents get caught up in the win-at-all-costs frenzy. The soccer mafioso.

Yes, I want Angus to play well and kick *all* of his team's goals and win, but sometimes it's excruciating – the frivolous chatter with parents, the heckling and the booing. *Tackle him! Get him! Kill him!*

At an under-nines game earlier this year, a mother from Angus's school (normally a sane, level-headed woman, I've been told) ran onto the field shouting abuse at the ref. She ended up chasing him into the car park with her umbrella. She didn't show her face at the school gate for several weeks afterwards.

Seeing Arnaud, I briefly wondered what it would be like to wake up to his French face in the morning, his dark hair, tanned skin, wide green eyes... Then I shook myself and walked over. Fantasies aside, my instinct was to dump Angus and take off, but seeing Arnaud with eleven swarming boys, soccer shirts in one arm, juggling balls, oranges and a mountain of papers in the other hand, I stayed.

'Give me those.' I took the oranges from him and regretted my ill-fitting jeans and threadbare blue sweater. Meanwhile, Angus and several boys chased a soccer ball around the dewy field. How these kids could run around in skimpy shorts, get knocked down, eat a mouthful of dirt, get up smiling and do it all again, staggered me.

'How's everything with you?'

I blushed.

'Here we go.' Arnaud leaned in and nudged me. Mardi, mother of Ben, was marching towards us.

'Not happy, Arnaud.' Mardi was, in fact, scowling.

'Mardi,' Arnaud said in a big bright voice. 'You know Katie?'

'We're old friends,' I said quickly.

She glanced at me and then back at Arnaud. 'No offence, but Benjamin shouldn't be playing in your team.' Mardi was clearly meaning to offend. 'He played for the A's in the winter season, and I assumed he'd automatically be put in the same team for the summer.'

Arnaud coaches the B team.

'*Oui*, but I have no control. They were chosen according to how they performed on grading day.'

'That's not fair. In netball, once you're put in a team, you stay there.'

'Hang on,' I said. 'This isn't netball. Soccer grading is supposed to be fair and the teams fluid.'

'But Benjamin had a cold, he wasn't kicking his best. He should be in the A's.' She huffed loudly. 'It's embarrassing. I won't have him playing in your team.' Meanwhile, Ben was running around and laughing with Angus and the others. He didn't look the slightest bit embarrassed. 'If he's not moved up, I'll take him to another club.'

'Talk to him, the one wearing the red shirt.' Arnaud pointed to a small man surrounded by several irate parents, all posturing and puffing themselves up, no doubt demanding to know why their sons had not been selected for the A team. Meanwhile, the A team parents were looking mightily pleased with themselves as they smiled smugly into their morning lattes.

'The B's.' Mardi sighed. 'Playing with the likes of Billy with the wandering eye and Marcus with the learning disorder.'

My eyes widened. 'Pardon?'

Mardi waved me away. 'You can tell when a child's not up to speed. Have you met his father? And his mother? Don't get me started. She should have been playing Mozart while Marcus was in the womb. Instead, she was probably gobbling white bread and drinking cask wine.' I hated to think what Mardi said about me when I wasn't around.

'Have you thought about offering Red Shirt an expensive Christmas gift? Wine? Restaurant voucher? BMW?' I suggested.

'Ha. Don't think I haven't considered it. I'm sure it's how half of them got in the top team. It certainly wasn't through talent.'

CHAPTER 11

With the game underway, I checked Robyn's Instagram feed. To think she'd stumbled upon the site six years ago and now, all of a sudden, was an influencer. I don't know when Robyn went from being my everyday, girl-next-door, sister, to becoming semi-famous. She wasn't especially pretty or tall or anything, really. But maybe that was her appeal. Perhaps whatever Robyn had or aspired to have, *could* be attained by mere mortals. Maybe that was her charm. Her allure.

In her latest post, Robyn was looking polished and fresh-faced, holding a perky Bugs in her arms, with a wide practised smile and sparkling eyes. *#familytime #bunnytime #33weeksandcounting #blessed #happylife #adoptdontshop*

Yes, I'd smoothed out her slight skin imperfections, transformed her flat hair into glossy and bouncy curls and enhanced her lips, but everyone knew Instagram posts were photoshopped.

And here she was, twelve hours later, having gathered over a quarter of a million likes and too many comments to read.

Robyn was a someone.

From what I could scan, most were in the realm of *Goddess, I love you. I love your style. Life goals.*

But there were a few negative ones – *Who do you think you're kidding? Get a life? Who's the father? Bet you're ugly on the inside.* Chill86.

I put my phone away and focused on the field as lots of little legs ran in a pack after a ball.

Chase the ball, you've got to want it!

Well in. Attack!

Harry, what the fork! You big girl.

At the end of the game, I caught up with Arnaud again.

'We should get together for a drink so I can fill you in on the office gossip,' he said.

A drink? Yes please. 'Sure. Great.' Harmless flirting, I told myself. Harmless.

I hummed all the way home, not even the parched landscape keeping the smile from my face. The once-leafy vistas were now little more than shrivelled and dying trees. Brown and desolate. But the humming stopped when I arrived home and fell straight into a crisis meeting with Matthew and the neighbours, who were standing in our backyard.

Matthew appeared dazed, silently appealing for help. I could have pretended I didn't see him with Margaret and Peter and snuck up the stairs. What I really wanted to do was give him the middle finger and say, 'That's what you get for not going to your son's soccer game – where they were soundly beaten, incidentally, four goals to one.' But this was my life, and I had to accept it: a flaccid suburban existence. A life that involved squabbling with neighbours over petty plant issues.

A long time ago, I was a hip inner-city dweller living on the edge. Well, perhaps not on the edge exactly, but I had better things to do with my time than bicker with the neighbours.

'Roots, Kate,' Margaret wailed as I approached. 'Your hedges are encroaching on our property, and I think you'll agree our back garden is suffering from a severe lack of sunlight. In summers past, sun streamed in.'

I nodded sympathetically.

'We may need to consult an arborist. I've checked. With roots, anything extending into a neighbour's garden is considered trespass.'

'Not that we're saying you and Matthew are trespassing,' Peter added.

No, of course not.

'But if falling branches waving around in the wind cause damage to our property, it could be considered negligence for which you might be liable.' Margaret's smile was saccharine.

Despite his hangover, and under the watchful eye of Margaret and her stream of instructions – *Careful of my zinnias. Watch out for Muffy* – Matthew, defeated, dutifully began trimming hedges.

Lexi shouted to me from the back door. 'Mum, I've got nothing to wear.'

'Coming.' I was glad for an opportunity to escape, even if it was to sort out Lexi's latest emergency.

I followed her upstairs. Clothes littered the floor, her bed, in fact every square inch of my daughter's room where cute kitten posters had been replaced by shirtless tattooed men in suggestive poses. At least fairy lights still decorated her pink bed frame.

'Goodness, Lex, what are you doing?'

'Throwing everything out.'

'I can see. Your clothes are everywhere.'

'I've only got two passable outfits and the rest are so childish only a five-year-old would wear them.' She took a pair of scissors to her favourite black T-shirt. 'If I rip the sleeves off, then cut the bottom to make it a midriff singlet, maybe I can get away with it.'

'Hey! Stop tearing your clothes to pieces.'

'I told you. I've nothing to wear. Everything sucks.'

'So you're hacking the clothes you do have?'

'You don't understand.' Lexi finished cutting her new singlet in half. A singlet that would barely fit a toddler.

'Try me.' My heart ached for her. 'Anyway, why do you need something to wear? Where are you going?'

'To the movies with Jazz and Issie. You promised.'

I'd totally forgotten. 'Which movie?'

'*The F**k-It List.*'

I turned to walk out. It seemed like every conversation Lexi and I had, Lexi pushed my buttons, trying to pick fights. In the space of months, we'd gone from best friends to strangers who shared a kitchen and, occasionally, Netflix.

'Joking! We're seeing *Barbie.*'

Again! How was that movie still on at the cinemas when it was streaming on TV? No denying Margot Robbie was cute and witty, but still.

I started picking clothes up off the carpet. 'What about this?' I said over and over as I held up dresses, skirts, jeans and shirts for Lexi's inspection. She dismissed each suggestion with an eyeroll and insolent headshake.

'If I get caught wearing the same top twice, it'll be social suicide.'

Suicide. I flinched. Bullies had moved from the playground to online chat rooms and beyond. I regularly received emails from Angus and Lexi's schools advising us to collect our children's mobiles at night before bed and monitor their non-school-related computer usage, along with tips on how to recognise signs they're being cyber-bullied, developing toxic friendships, and/or having mental health issues.

I held up a black-and-white polka-dot shirt, her favourite only weeks ago. 'This?'

Lexi visibly gagged. 'As if!'

I briefly remembered my own angst regarding a flouncy pink gingham peasant skirt and frilled halter-neck top. I must have been about fifteen at the time. Mum thought the combo was the prettiest thing this side of Kansas. It was hideous. I shuddered at the memory.

'I was saving this,' I said over my shoulder as I walked to the hallway cupboard and removed a brown paper bag from the top shelf.

I returned to Lexi's room and handed it to her. On a generous whim a few weeks back, I'd bought a jacket on sale to give to her at Christmas. But needs must.

'Mum!' She squealed and looked inside to find a black cropped leather jacket. 'Thanks heaps.'

Best not to dwell on the fact I was buying my daughter's affection.

Lexi settled on wearing a pair of low-rider jeans – slightly too tight – and her new jacket worn over the mutilated black singlet which exposed her flat tanned midriff. She completed the outfit with oversized pink sunglasses.

'Now then, do you think you could stop using so much make-up? You wear more mascara and eyeliner than the guys from KISS. You have beautiful eyes.'

'Okay, Boomer.'

'Lexi…'

She hugged me. 'Come on, Mum, you've got to admit, you're too old to know. But if you really want me to, I'll smudge it down.'

I knew Lexi was desperate to grow up and, in my calmer moments, I sympathised. Lexi was trying to find herself, to fit in, and to figure out who she was in an unforgiving world. Still, she was maturing much faster than I could cope with. Thirteen going on twenty-three.

❄

As I drove Lexi and her friends to the movies, I was pleased I'd remained firm on not allowing her to buy a push-up bra like the one her friend Issie was wearing under her pink crop top. Lexi's other two friends, all black eyeliner and heavy mascara, resembled adolescent raccoons. Their conversations – littered with words like 'Hunter', 'sucks', 'random' and 'totally hot' – were worrying, mostly because I couldn't get a clear fix on what they were talking about. The radio was too loud. But I had an uneasy feeling. I needed to pay more attention to how my daughter was occupying her spare time, especially with summer holidays fast approaching.

'She. Is. So. Thirsty. Desperate for attention. Who wears *that* anymore?' This coming from a person wearing a pink sequinned boob tube over a singlet, a denim miniskirt and knee-high pink platform boots.

'I so know what you're saying, Jazz. A freak.'

'Like, pure psycho skank. Whatever! Sewing sequins on her no-name jeans. Can you believe it? And she slashed her no-name T-shirt as well, as if we couldn't tell.'

I glanced at Lexi. Her own T-shirt was nowhere to be seen. She'd zipped up her jacket.

CHAPTER 12

'I wish you'd change your mind,' Mum said to me later as we walked in the garden enjoying the late-afternoon sun with Robyn. She was trying, unsuccessfully, to convince me to have dinner with Dad.

It was unusually quiet. Issie's mum was dropping Lexi home later – a big tick for car-pooling. Matthew was inside, working on his laptop, exhausted from a self-inflicted hangover and excessive hedge trimming. And Angus was lying on the outdoor day bed, playing his Nintendo Switch and muttering, surrounded by Rupert, Cleo and Bugs. His little empire. Sure, he should have been building his science project (the water cycle in 3D?!), but he was happy and wasn't asking for food. I knew if I said anything to disturb him, the food issue would rear its ravenous head within seconds.

Besides discovering kids may want pets but will accept no responsibility beyond rolling around on the floor with them, during my seven months' experience as the mother of an eight-year-old boy, I have learned:

1. It's all about food – and M&M's are a sound nutritional meal.
2. When it's not about food, it's about the NS, PS4, PS5 (but life is definitely not worth living without a Nintendo Switch).
3. Life's about fun – and getting filthy – and refusing to bathe or shower.
4. Homework? What's homework?

I deadheaded a daisy. 'Lexi's pulling away from me, she's not my little girl anymore. She's only interested in hanging out with her friends.' I threw the dead daisy onto nearby mulch. 'She's not telling me everything going on in her life.'

Robyn snorted. 'Of course she's not telling you! She's a teenager.'

'Just. She's not seventeen.'

'She looks it.'

I felt helpless. Even if I got the chance to eavesdrop, I couldn't understand most of Lexi's conversations. The other day, when Lexi walked away from her laptop long enough for me to snoop at her Snapchat page, I was dumbfounded. It was all smiley icons and incomprehensible abbreviations. Whether it was talking or texting, Lexi and her friends had their own vernacular.

'I remember not so long ago Lexi always wanted to be with me, shop with me, hug me—'

Robyn coughed. 'How many years back are you going?'

I deadhead a purple hydrangea. The garden was dry, very dry. There'd been no rain for months. No grass to speak of. Most of the leaves had fallen from the trees. The only plants still thriving were the conifers. It seemed cruel to slash them. I looked over at the mountain of cut branches piled against the fence.

'She did. She was hugging and cuddling me up until—'

'She discovered boys?'

'I guess. Now she wants to do things on her own or with her friends. She has secrets. I try to pick up on the signals, the snatched ten minutes in the car in the morning, bonding when we're walking Rupert, or sharing chocolates. But really, she thinks I'm a know-nothing nuisance, a source of aggravation. A Boomer, even though I'm Gen X.'

Mum clicked her tongue. 'Welcome to my world. I know what it's like to be considered an irritation. I was in the supermarket checkout line this morning and the cashier, a mere child, asked through her bubblegum if I was carrying my senior citizen's discount card! The whole store heard. I was mortified. I said, "Certainly not!". She assumed I was over sixty-five. *Me!* And then she snapped a bubble under my nose.'

I patted her back in solidarity.

'As if it's not humiliating enough going to the supermarket these days,' she continued. 'There are cereals pitched exclusively at women like me who are over a certain age. The cereal makers have decided Weet-Bix isn't good enough for me anymore. It's outrageous. I know what I need, thank you very much, and it's not a lecture from a cereal company or a pimply youth.'

I poked Robyn on her shoulder. 'Thoughts?'

She waved her hand. 'I know you think I'm part of the problem.'

'You're selling an idyllic lifestyle that doesn't exist.' I held up two fingers in a V sign. 'Hashtag blessed. Ordinary people can't keep up with the hashtag happy life, hashtag living my best life.' I exhaled. 'We feel lost, alone and desperate. Hashtag tired and worn out.'

'Are you talking on behalf of a generation of women or specifically yourself?' Mum chimed in.

I rolled my eyes. 'I'm generalising.'

'Yes, you are,' Robyn said, patting her stomach. 'It's all right for you, Katie. You have the perfect home, the perfect husband, and two great kids. I'm pregnant. A fat little butterball...'

'I'd hardly call you little' – I ducked out of the way before Mum could whack me on the arm – 'but your Instagram devotees wouldn't know that, would they? And I don't have a perfect life. But your fans think you do.'

'It's how I make money, Kate. Back pimples and chaffed nipples aren't going to get many likes.'

'No, but is selling a perfect, blessed alternate reality sustainable? Also, that baby formula post is getting a lot of vitriolic push-back.'

She clenched her jaw. 'Who says formula isn't better? Jeez.'

Maybe I was being too hard on her. It was how Robyn earned a living. In addition to happy snaps, she advertised vitamins, honey, and recently prams, nappies and toys.

Robyn's mouth wobbled and she looked as if she was about to cry. 'I'm having nightmares about the attacks.'

'You know not to read the comments. It's not healthy.' Some of the ones I'd read this morning were vicious. 'Don't let it get to you.'

'How can I not when people tell me I'm ugly on the inside. I need a safe space.'

I pointed upwards. 'Mars is looking good.'

'Thanks.' Robyn rubbed her belly. 'I'll get run out of BabyCo if I advertise pacifiers.'

Or formulas. 'Are you thinking about it?'

'There's a possible offer in the works for baby formulas' – I knew it – 'and I need the money.' Robyn breathed deeply. 'It might all end tomorrow.'

'What will end, love?' Mum asked, walking up beside us with a handful of weeds.

'The endorsements, Mum. Keep up. Anyway, I'm not sure I'm up to the task.'

I frowned. 'Of parenthood?'

'Yep. My vision board's not inspiring me. Most food makes me gag. I have reflux, sciatica. You name it. A baby means the end of my youth, the end of freedom, and the end of life as I know it.'

'You're right,' I said, taking the weeds from Mum. 'Your followers don't want reality posts.'

Robyn nodded. 'Don't you ever feel like packing it in, that it's all too much? Do you ever feel like taking a holiday, a long holiday to... oh, I don't know, the Mediterranean? Or the Maldives? The Maldives would be perfect this time of year.'

'I think about it every day, Robbie, but I can't.' I glimpsed me trembling on a tightrope. 'I have responsibilities, and so do you.'

❄

Despite dreaming about being chased by land-dwelling sharks, I walked into the kitchen Sunday morning feeling refreshed, mainly because Matthew and the kids had let me have a sleep-in. Now, they were laughing, and I felt truly happy.

I grabbed a handful of berries and sat. 'What's the joke?'

'Lexi and I were remembering the mix-up with the Americans,' Matthew replied.

My sunny mood dimmed. 'I worked very hard to make the evening a success, and Lexi's theatrics didn't help the situation. Yet I'm the person who ruined the dinner party?'

Matthew held up his hands. 'I didn't say that. You always work hard to manage tough situations and you always pull through. You must admit, though, you're a bit of a control freak.' He winked at Lexi and she nodded in agreement.

'I hate it when you call me that.' Even though it was true.

'And anyway, why am I a freak to want to be in control of my life?'

The more they giggled, the more I fumed.

I didn't make a fuss though. My family didn't need additional fodder upon which to graze. Instead, I made myself a strong cup of Earl Grey and retreated outside to sit in the sunshine, determined to let the incident wash over me.

Besides, it was only a few days till my birthday. I didn't want to argue with Matthew. In fact, I fancied rekindling some semblance of romance with him before then, with or without handcuffs, because if he hadn't yet bought me a present, I wanted to make sure he was in a generous mood when the time came.

The day passed without further blow-ups, and late in the evening after the kids had gone to bed, I whipped on my sheer black negligée and gave myself a once-over in the bathroom mirror. Passable, passable.

Wrapping myself in a matching black robe, I glided down the hall and into the office. 'Matt,' I purred, letting the robe fall open. 'Let's go to bed.'

He barely glanced my way before closing his laptop. 'Sounds like a plan but let me pack first.' He stood and started walking towards our bedroom, me trailing behind.

'Pack?'

Matthew stopped mid-stride and turned. 'Sorry sweetheart, didn't I say I'd be in the Melbourne office this week?'

I shook my head. 'No.'

Eyes finally clocking my attire, he grinned. 'You look absolutely gorgeous by the way.'

Despite his words, desire drained from my blood. 'But the kids? The magazine? How will I manage?'

He kissed me lightly on the lips. 'Your mum'll help.'

In the bedroom walk-in wardrobe, Matthew puckered his brow. 'Have you seen my navy chinos? They're here somewhere.'

'There.' I pointed to the pants directly in front of him.

'I know you're disappointed. I promise to take you out for your birthday and to celebrate landing the magazine gig as soon as I get back. A double celebration.'

My birthday. Reality dawned. 'You're away for my birthday?'

'Till Friday, hon. Sorry. I thought I'd told you.'

No, you didn't. But no point arguing about it now. Matthew's mind wasn't focused on me. Work worries occupied all his brain space. Still, if I was ever to return to regular employment, we'd need to renegotiate the whole parenting pact.

'Sorry. The timing's not ideal given it's your birthday week. But I need to sort out ongoing issues with the Melbourne branch before the end of the year.'

'I guess,' I started.

'You know work is always hectic in the lead up to the holidays.' He paused. 'And you did spring this photography gig on me. It came out of nowhere.'

I nodded. 'True, but I didn't want to pass up the opportunity.'

'I know.' He took me in his arms and kissed me.

'Guess I'll have takeaway with the kids on my birthday,' I said, returning from the bathroom some minutes later, after I'd changed out of my cold, impractical negligée into comfy flannel pyjamas and slipped into bed.

Matthew didn't answer. He was asleep well before I turned out the bedside light.

CHAPTER 13

It wasn't until I heard my phone beeping on Monday morning that I remembered Diane. It was five fifteen and surprisingly chilly.

'What kept you?' she asked after I finally emerged from the house.

'Sleep. Shut up and walk.' I hated walking but did it anyway, though not with great enthusiasm – perhaps because, despite getting up before dawn and walking briskly for sixty minutes, the exercise wasn't having the desired effect.

'Come on, Katie, it's all about fitness; the weight will fall off, trust me,' Diane said as we pounded the pavement and nodded to other idiotic early morning walkers and joggers.

'Ha!' I moaned. 'It's so depressing.'

But Di kept me motivated – to a point. She was a very fast walker and intimate with all the hills in the neighbourhood. Just when I'd get used to a new one, she'd giddily chirp, 'Guess what? I found a more interesting route. If we turn up here...' And sure enough there'd be another Mount Everest staring at me.

'It's either this or swimming,' Di threatened when I shied away from yet another mountain.

'No way. Last time I swam laps, people grabbed at my feet because I was moving too slowly.'

'Pool rage. It's getting worse.'

'Bloody lap dictators. People passing me with swimming paddles...'

'Exactly.' Diane dragged me forward. 'Keep walking. It's only a slight hill. Distract yourself by telling me about Arnaud.' She snapped her fingers in my face. 'Hel-lo!'

'Yes, sorry. You could have knocked me over when I ran into him at the magazine.' I suddenly found a spring in my step.

'Could be dangerous.'

'But he's gorgeous. Ar-naud. I've always loved the name Arnaud.'

'Since when? Besides, Arnie's a pet's name, suitable only for dogs and muscle-men actors parading as politicians.'

'It's harmless flirting. Although he did invite me out for a drink.'

'Please don't have drinks with him. I don't need to remind you what happened to me when I embarked on an office affair. Disaster. An absolute disaster right from the word go.'

'What are you talking about? You married David.'

'Yes, but remember, I was married to Paul before David came along. And really, I don't think Nina' – Di's sixteen-year-old daughter – 'is handling the situation well at all. She fights with David all the time, and with school exams and Christmas looming, well, tensions are intensifying. It doesn't help that he lets Sam' – David's sixteen-year-old son – 'come and go as he pleases. They're the same age. Same rights. I keep telling David and Nina to cool it. They're like two rabid dogs at each other's throats.'

'Okay, you've convinced me.'

'Besides, you only want Arnaud because he's French and handsome.'

'You're supposed to be convincing me an affair's wrong, right? Not that I would ever consider one.'

'Let me tell you, real life is no *Brady Bunch*. Nina and Sam get on well, but he barely speaks to me. I'm dreading the holidays.'

This ignited a twenty-minute conversation about the secret lives of teenagers, the seemingly endless summer school holidays of squabbles, boredom and sunburn, and the fact that neither of us were any closer to sorting out Christmas plans. After venting mutual frustrations, I arrived home with leg cramps but felt remarkably unburdened.

I was determined to have a great day... until Lexi locked herself in the bathroom and refused to come out.

She'd been normal at breakfast. Sullen. Rude. Then, when I was dressed and ready to leave the house, she wouldn't come out of the bathroom. She'd been in there for over half an hour. Lexi was going to miss the first bell and I was already running late for the magazine.

'Is everything okay?' I wondered whether she was attempting to recolour her hair.

'Go away.'

I took that as a no.

In the meantime, Matthew's taxi arrived, he kissed my forehead and left with a breezy 'Have a great week. I'll call.'

'Dear Lord, no,' I yelped minutes later when I walked past Lexi's bedroom. Her hair was practically a crew cut. 'What possessed you?'

'The devil, Mum. The devil.' She glared at me. 'And before you say anything more, it's got nothing to do with Hunter. I couldn't get the black out, so it was easier to cut my hair. It'll grow back.'

CHAPTER 14

Replaying my earlier conversation with Lexi in my head, I accidentally shouted 'Grow back!' in Graeme Grafton's surprised face as we read the set-up sheets together.

'Pardon?'

'Sorry, I was thinking about something else.'

I was sure Graeme assumed I got the job because Fern couldn't find anyone else, which was probably true. No time to interview and hire someone more qualified and suited to the job.

'Mara wants this revolting turducken shot,' he bellowed for Mara's benefit, who was on the far side of the studio. 'Succumbing once again to Americanisms. Thanksgiving no less. These mutant fowls have got nothing to do with antipodean Christmases.'

I looked at the sausage-stuffed turducken, which had been cut into quarters to show the internal layers. Though roasted, it was pale, almost colourless, and sitting on the large white platter, looked unappetising.

'Maybe we could photograph it on a red plate,' I suggested.

'To add Christmas *joie de vivre*.' I immediately shrunk into myself. Why had I said that out loud?

'*Joie de* fucking *vivre*?' Graeme stared, smirked and shook his head. 'Kate, I don't know how much food experience you have, but here at *Delicious Bites* we only use white plates for photo shoots. The colour comes from the napkins, accoutrements and food. Even at fucking Christmas,' he bellowed. 'The plates, my dear, are always white.'

'What about the red plate right there by your shoulder?' I asked.

I shouldn't have.

Without a word, Graeme picked up the plate and hurled it across the room. It shattered on the floor millimetres from where Mara was standing.

'We only use white plates. It's our signature. White. Plates. White. Background.'

Stepping away from the broken crockery, Mara stared at us before going back to her mixing bowl. Not a word.

'Yes, of course.' I nodded. 'Baby rocket leaves, maybe?'

Graeme looked as if he might punch me at any moment. Photographing food was hell. Who could take a good shot of peppers? Turnips? Turducken?

Graeme said nothing, eyes clearly focused on Mara, who was silently preparing several desserts. 'Mara,' he shouted. 'My notes say turducken – nothing else. I'm not shooting lumps of several dead fowls by themselves.' He looked directly at me and then at my vibrating phone on the table. 'Either answer that thing or turn it off.'

'Sorry.' I picked up the phone.

'How could you let her do this to her hair?' Matthew was shouting down the line.

'Aren't you supposed to be on a flight to Melbourne?'

'I forgot my phone. What's Lexi doing at home at eleven o'clock on a Monday morning anyway?'

'I don't know. I dropped her off at school hours ago.' I really needed to invest in one of those bracelet tracking devices with GPS technology – one which could be securely welded to her wrist. Or at the very least glue an Apple AirTag to the back of her neck.

'How could you let her? Lexi said you thought it was a good idea.'

'To cut her hair? Yeah. Just like I gave her permission to punch four holes in each ear.' Graeme looked up from his schedule and shook his head. 'Can I call you back? I'm in a meeting. There's nothing I can do about it now. Lexi cut her hair. She's probably at home because she's too mortified to show her face at school.' A wave of sadness washed over me. I'd never want to be thirteen again.

I ended the call.

Back to the poultry.

'Graeme, you should have told me you were ready to unleash your brilliance.' Mara used tongs to pick up braised Brussels sprouts and positioned them on the platter, followed by baby carrots and red onions.

Graeme tapped his fingers silently on the table and watched as Mara walked the few metres to another table, and quickly returned with a green bean salad in a white serving dish and placed it beside the platter.

'Now for the salad leaves and cherry tomatoes.' Mara expertly retrieved the ingredients from an adjacent bowl. 'A drizzle of extra-virgin olive oil, some lemon zest, and we're ready to fly.' She beamed.

As Graeme turned away, she trilled, 'Let's not forget the cranberry chutney! Delicious cuisine at *Delicious Bites*!'

'What is this before me?' Graeme had moved to the

makeshift Christmas dining table where cutlery had been laid out for the photographs. Talk about dramatic. He should have been on stage.

'Knives, forks, serving spoons,' Mara said matter-of-factly. I admired her patience – to work with Graeme full time without having stabbed a bread knife into his back or at least his lower leg, made her a saint in my eyes.

'Ugly gold cutlery. So crass.' With one quick sweep of his arm, the utensils crashed to the floor.

'I'm not picking them up.' Mara walked past him and out the door.

'Well?' Graeme said to me before he, too, stalked out.

Alone in the studio, I bent down and picked up the crass cutlery. I busied myself wiping down benchtops and stacking the dishwasher, rather like I did at home. All I needed was a broom and I'd be on truly familiar ground.

After ten minutes, Mara returned. 'Sorry you had to see that, but I won't put up with bullying. Truthfully, he belongs in an asylum, heavily sedated.'

'Why do you stay?' I was genuinely puzzled.

'Because I love this job. I'm the editor, the public face. Before this, I briefly worked on the programme, *Fabulous Foods*. It was only for a few months after I closed Milton. But still too hectic. I have cardiovascular disease.' She massaged her heart. 'As much as I love cooking, I needed to reduce stress and work less hours.' She stared around the studio. 'Fern found out, and here I am, still finding my way.'

'You've been here a year?'

'Eleven months. When Fern poached me, she made it clear Graeme Grafton was part of the package, especially after he won the ridiculous Bachelor competition. He's a fat-head, no doubt about it. But I can handle him. I'm used to working with lunatics. My aim is to make *Delicious Bites* the number one food magazine in the country, digital and print, and I will, despite Graeme's theatrics. I'll leave when I'm ready. Open another restaurant and run my own game, but for now...' Mara paused. 'Besides, I'm not about to walk out on three hundred thousand a year.'

Three hundred thousand dollars? No wonder Mara oozed confidence.

❄

It was early afternoon, and I was tired. We'd limped through the turducken shoot, and were setting up another composition, but Graeme wasn't happy with the napkin colour an assistant had chosen. I was dispatched to the props department in search of the perfect green napkin.

I rummaged through the endless drawers of rags – forest green, bottle green, lime green – but nothing matched the green Texta I was holding. No point putting off the inevitable, I decided after I'd gathered every green napkin I could find. I left the props room and started the long walk back up the stairs to hell.

'Graeme put on quite a performance earlier, *non*?' It was Arnaud. To think today was the day I'd decided to surrender my infatuation.

I giggled foolishly.

'With all the knives and blunt objects, you'd think there'd be more violence in the studio.'

I tittered. Again.

'Kate, you laugh, but I'm deadly serious. I 'ave seen Graeme, in fury, leap across a kitchen table, clamp his teeth onto a stylist's ear and shake her like a fluffy poodle. His charming way of saying he didn't like her choice of napkin colour.'

I believed him for a nanosecond. 'Oh, ha-ha,' I said, looking down at my full hands.

'*Oui*. You must take it easy.' He smiled and continued on his way.

Strangely, the idea of Graeme biting an underling didn't surprise me. Illegal and certifiable, but not surprising.

Back in the studio, I showed Graeme the napkins. Eventually, after much huffing, he settled on a green that matched the green of the basil leaves on the plate. Relief.

It took over two hours, but Graeme finally got the look he was after. This time, it was rice-and-fetta-stuffed pumpkin, chargrilled eggplant, and some sort of tomato, ricotta and olive tart with basil: all served on white plates with silver cutlery and basil-green napkins.

'What do you think?' Graeme asked after we'd finished taking several hundred digital shots and were sitting at the computer scrutinising images.

Panic set in, but I steeled myself, and with close and steady eyes, picked out several I particularly liked. In real life, the food looked absolutely disgusting, totally inedible, but on-screen, it looked simple, fresh and appetising.

He peered over his glasses at me and nodded. 'Decent choices, K.'

CHAPTER 15

'You'll need to rub it out and start again,' I said to Angus absent-mindedly as he scrawled his maths homework at the kitchen table. I was thinking about Mum, who was staying for a few days while Matthew was interstate. She was upstairs preparing for her meeting with Dad. That's how I chose to see it, anyway. It certainly couldn't be a date. My palms were sweaty. My head ached. And I felt somewhat delirious. Sick with worry.

'But I don't have a rubber.'

'Ask Lexi.' I continued chopping tomatoes and contemplated a glass of wine. Resisting the urge, I was chopping cucumbers by the time he came back.

'Mum, do you ever think about cutting your fingers?'

'What? By accident?'

'No, just because.'

'No, Gus. Why would I?'

'Dunno.'

'The way your mind works...' I shook my head. Maybe *The Flintstones* wasn't the only programme Angus was watching. I thought back to *The Banshees of Inisherin*, the movie where

Brendan Gleeson's character cuts off his fingers. Horrible. I shuddered and continued slicing vegetables, paying close attention to the position of my digits.

'So did you find a rubber?'

'Yeah.' Angus rubbed a hole in his *Maths Mentals* book. 'But it's not working.'

I sighed. 'Show me.' I picked up the eraser. 'What the?' – A condom – 'Where did you get this?'

'Lexi's pencil case. It fell out yesterday, and she said it was a rubber, so I went to her room and borrowed it.'

'Lexi!' I shouted up the stairs. 'Get down here now!'

Puzzled, Angus said, 'She's in the bathroom.'

Mum came rushing into the kitchen. I held up my open hand. 'Don't ask.'

She took Angus by the hand and moments later, I heard *Twinkle, Twinkle* playing on the piano in the lounge room.

Lexi sauntered in, eyed me and scanned the condom clenched tightly in my hand.

'It's a joke, Mum.'

'Really? I'm not laughing.'

'Susie put it in my pencil case.'

'Do you think it's funny? Does it make you feel grown-up? Clever?' I stared at her long and hard, choosing not to focus on the small purplish bruise on her neck that looked suspiciously like a love bite.

Lexi's expression was unforgiving. Defiant. 'Some of my friends have competitions to see who can get a condom on a banana the fastest... with their lips.'

'What's that supposed to mean? Which friends exactly? Lexi, come back here now,' I ordered as she walked out of the kitchen. Who was Susie? Where had she come from? Had my daughter fallen in with a bad crowd? As far as I knew, she still had the same girlfriends including Jazz and Issie since she was six or seven. My mind went into overdrive as a grainy video of Lexi messing around with boys played in my head. I didn't want my daughter to be the type of girl boys treated badly and whispered about in school halls or online... My daughter, Lexi, the subject of toilet walls – make that cyber – and discussions about bananas and God knows what other fruits.

I marched upstairs and banged on her locked bedroom door. 'Lexi, open the door. Now!' She didn't answer. Music blared from inside her bedroom. I waited outside. Eventually, she'd have to come out and when she did... well, the first thing I'd do was take the stupid lock off her door.

As I walked down the stairs, I passed Angus, who was singing along to her music, then I heard Lexi bellow, 'Can you tell dumbo the lyrics are about *single ladies* not *wanna see my legs?*'

'Mum, I don't want you to see him again,' I said unreasonably as I poured Chardonnay. I'd promised myself I wouldn't drink alcohol from Sunday to Thursday, but I couldn't manage it, not this week at least – Mum and Dad; Lexi and the condom (not to mention her neck); Graeme and the red plate; Arnaud and those green eyes. Matt's absence.

I handed Mum a glass. 'You look very nice by the way.' And she did. At least ten years younger. I shuddered at the thought her flushed cheeks were because of the sex she was anticipating having with Dad at some stage.

'Katie, I can take care of myself. Stop worrying.'

'I can't, it's all too much. I can't get my head around the fact you're' – I dared not say dating – 'seeing Dad again.' There was a time, after the blackness, a good time – a time that lasted many years – when Mum had hated Dad. I missed those years.

'But it's not just that. It's Lexi and her hair, the condom. She's locked herself in her room. I don't know what to do anymore.'

'You were like that once.'

'I never cut my hair and never had condoms in my pencil case. She's thirteen.'

'True, but it's only hair, sweetheart. It'll grow back.'

'And the condom?'

'A silly joke.'

'If I'd done that...'

'Different standards. Times have changed. She's testing boundaries.'

'Understatement.' I rolled my eyes and swigged my wine. I couldn't believe fourteen years ago I'd looked into Matthew's loving eyes (as they were at the time) and said, 'Let's make a baby' in the overly optimistic naive voice of a woman in lust. Bingo! Nine months later I was in labour. Fool! A couple of minutes thinking about the consequences of such a rash decision would have made all the difference.

I jumped when the doorbell rang. 'You said you were meeting *him* at the restaurant.'

Mum placed her glass on the table. 'I thought we were.' She picked up her coat and handbag and we stood for a moment listening to the sound of the front door being opened. Then voices and laughter. Bloody Lexi!

'Hurry up then.' I pushed her into the hallway. I'd seen Dad infrequently over the past twenty-five years, the most recent occasion being three years ago, by accident, at a relative's funeral. I'd only agreed to go as the family representative because I assumed he wouldn't be there. For the excruciating five and a half minutes I spent talking to him at the wake, my stomach had been in knots. I'd felt so disloyal to Mum.

When Dad left all those years ago, I blamed myself for the break-up. Mum was a mess, and because I was the eldest child, I took it upon myself to remove every photo of Dad in the house. I no longer considered him part of our family. It took me hours –

we were a very snap-happy clan. I thought I was doing the right thing, but it backfired.

Mum flew into a rage when she finally crawled out of bed. *What did you do that for*? she demanded. *Where are all the family photos?* I remember the scene like it was yesterday. *I put them away to protect you, us*, I told her. *Well, put them back exactly where they were*, she said. *He's still your father*. After everything he'd done, she still wanted photos of him on mantelpieces, sideboards and hanging in the entrance hall. It took two years before his pictures were permanently removed from sight.

Who'd have thought more than two decades later, Dad would be in my home calling to take Mum out to dinner? My stomach was in knots again. I could see my father standing in the doorway with Lexi. They were still laughing.

'Grandpa says I look exactly like you when you were my age,' Lexi said to me as I crept behind Mum. I was trying to hide behind her and not doing a very good job of it.

Dad walked over and held out his arms to me. 'Darling, it's been too long.'

'Mmmm.' I looked at him but refused to relax. Maybe his hair was thinner. At least it was greyer. Yet he still looked like my father – tall, fit and strong. The deserter. I pulled away.

When he embraced Mum, I couldn't decide whether I was more repulsed or embarrassed. I was definitely horrified. Lexi giggled.

'I see you've met Lexi.'

'Last time I saw you, you were barely walking, Lexi,' Dad said.

I frowned. 'Whose fault is that?'

Mum glowered. 'Katie!'

'Please join us for dinner.' Dad acted as if we were one big happy family who saw each other twice a week. 'We'd like that, wouldn't we, Pip?'

'We can't,' I said quickly. 'Lexi has homework.'

'Mu-u-m,' Lexi whined.

'Besides, Angus is already asleep.'

'No, I'm not,' Angus called from the top of the stairs.

'Gussy, come down and meet Grandpa,' Mum said.

Angus bounded down the stairs.

'Let me look at you.' Dad stretched out his arms.

'How come I haven't seen you before?' Angus asked as Dad engulfed him in a bear hug. 'Mum said we've only got one grandpa and he lives in Adelaide.'

'Later, Gus,' I said, waving him away.

'Katie, I tried to stay in your life—'

'Now's not the time,' I said as Mum took hold of Dad's hand. I needed a Scotch. A large one. And I don't drink Scotch.

Suddenly I was a teenager again, watching as my parents prepared to leave for a neighbour's dinner party.

Mum kissed me on the forehead. 'Have a great night.'

I didn't like the way Dad touched the small of her back as they were leaving. I shut the door and watched them through the window as I'd done many years earlier. In those days, Mum was always immaculately dressed, never without her pearls and high heels. Dad was always charming.

I watched as he opened the car door for Mum and held her hand as she climbed in. They were laughing. Tears streamed down my cheeks until long after they'd driven away.

Angus tapped me on the shoulder. 'Butch is dead.' He took my hand, and we walked over to the fish tank.

He was right. Butch was floating on his back, quite dead. I scooped him out of the water, and Angus and I carried him to the laundry toilet, where I conducted a quick but heartfelt funeral. After Angus played a few off-notes on his trumpet, we flushed the toilet together. Before leaving the room, I double-checked to make sure Butch really had flushed away.

'Come on, Angus, let's change the fish-tank water together.' A longer activity than anticipated. For the next hour, Angus and I changed fishy water, adjusted filters and cleaned plastic seaweed. It kept my mind off Mum, Dad and Lexi. Almost. By the time we'd finished, the remaining five fish looked happy. At least they showed no visible signs of disease or despair.

At bedtime, I resisted the urge to correct Angus's pronunciation as he read aloud from a book on dinosaurs and then, when I could resist no more, we started an audio book, *The Mapmaker Chronicles: Race To The End Of The World.*

'Mum, do you think there's a fish heaven?'

'Probably.' I kissed him and turned out his light. 'Love you, Gussy.'

Then I knocked on my daughter's door. 'Lexi, you're going to have to come out and talk to me sooner or later.'

'Yeah…'

'So when will you?'

'Tomorrow.'

'I love you – You know you can talk to me about anything. Don't you?' Silence. 'Lexi?'

'Yeah.'

'Anything at all – sex, drugs, TikTok…' But it was no use. Lexi refused to step out of her room. Even though I was angry, part of me envied her. She was free. Unburdened by responsibilities and worries about the future. She was free to express herself, regardless of whom she offended.

But then, was she? Maybe Lexi wasn't as free as I wished she was. Cyber-bullying, boyfriend worries, and the general school and friendship angst that few teens could escape. So much worse now that iPhones could record a person's every move and upload a video within seconds for the world to view. A permanent recording. I briefly thought about Robyn. No one was immune.

CHAPTER 16

I was still awake when Mum arrived home after midnight, so I ambushed her as she walked out of the bathroom in her dressing gown.

Mum jumped. 'Katie, you frightened me.'

'How was your night?'

'Lovely. This old girl's still got some snap in her garters. And yours?' Mum was grinning like a love-struck teenager, as if the last twenty plus years had been wiped away.

I ignored the question. 'Why now, Mum? Why? You're happy. Why do you need *him* back in your life?'

'That's the whole point – I don't need him. He makes me laugh.'

'Watch the Comedy Channel.'

'Bob makes me feel young again. Sexy.'

'Mum!'

'What? He does. He makes me feel like a woman – not just a mother or a grandmother or a friend. He makes me feel like a desirable, attractive woman. Think about it.'

That was something I really didn't want to do.

'Apart from a few short-lived friendships here and there, I've been alone all this time. Night after night, by myself. I need more for myself and to share my life with someone again.'

'With someone, yes, but surely not with him?'

'What happened between your dad and me is ancient history,' she barked. 'It's time to move on. Put the past behind us. Right now, he makes me happy. End of story.'

I hugged and kissed her goodnight then walked into my bedroom. Blanche's book was lying on the dressing table, so I picked it up. I wonder if she wrote a companion title, *Don'ts for Husbands and Fathers*?

I climbed into bed and curled myself into a ball, then unstretched and pulled the duvet up over my head. Dad was going to break Mum's heart all over again, and there was nothing I could do to stop it. I knew he would because I'd been there the first time. I'd lived through it.

I was the sixteen-year-old who'd helped Mum through the dark months of her breakdown. Made sure there was food in the house because she couldn't get out of bed to go to the shops herself. I was the one who made sure Robyn had clean uniforms to wear to school. I was the one who insisted Mum see a doctor. I made her take the prescribed sedatives so she could sleep through the night for the first excruciating six months after he left. Sometimes, I didn't know how to keep myself going, but I did. I had to look after Mum and Robyn.

No. I loathed the thought of meeting Dad, and I certainly didn't want Mum seeing him either – let alone dating the man again! I didn't want her world to fall apart again.

When I became too tired to analyse that looming disaster, my panicked mind latched on to Lexi. She was frantically trying to discard her childhood and pushing me away in the process.

Then there was Matthew. It wasn't that I had fallen out of love with him. I was in love with Matthew, or at least I could be again if we could revive the romance. I read an article advising the way to keep a marriage alive was to treat your spouse like a lover. Fine in theory, but difficult when you had two children and one of those was a teenage girl.

Besides, lovers were simply that, weren't they? People with whom you scoffed champagne and had amazing sex, but who were removed from the everyday reality and fights over whose turn it was to clean up the dog turds in the backyard.

It got me thinking back to how Matthew and I met – at Fern's twenty-fifth birthday party. Fern and I were housemates, and our apartment was full of Annie Leibovitz prints. I was holding court, explaining to anybody who would listen why her portraits were amateurish.

Matthew walked up to me and introduced himself. He especially liked the idea I was on the verge of becoming *the next hot young thing who was going to turn the photography world on its proverbial ear*. My words, not his.

When Matthew finally did manage to get a word in, he said Annie Leibovitz was *so last century* and my photography was *so right now* – not that he'd seen any of my work, given he'd just met me. I was charmed in turn. I said if he stuck with me there'd be nothing but good times ahead for him. He said he'd never leave my side. And that was pretty much it. I fell passionately in love with him on the spot.

It wasn't only that Matthew bore more than a passing resemblance to a young Paul Rudd and had a curl in the middle of his forehead. I wasn't so pathetic I'd fall in love with Matthew because he had movie star looks and great hair. My attraction for him was based on something extra.

Matthew was a computer whiz at Microsoft with ambition to burn. 'The internet's the way of the future,' he told me. 'And I'm determined to be the best in the business.' He knew where he was headed, and so did I. We both had dreams and determination.

Even better, Matthew liked photography, even if it was photography that leaned towards the *arty* end of the scale – *Playboy* photos that celebrated breasts, thighs and other female body parts. But I was willing to overlook it. We were young. We were in love. We got engaged quickly. We married quickly.

In hindsight, I think my speedy marriage was a gross overreaction to my parents' divorce, which spurred an urgent need to find lasting security and comfort.

When I married Matthew, I knew these things about him:

1. He was gorgeous, and he had great hair (unlike me).
2. He liked photography (it takes all types).
3. He made me laugh.
4. He was ambitious for us both to succeed.
5. He truly loved me and promised he would forever (he said so in his wedding vows).

Yep! Back then, we couldn't keep our hands or tongues off each other. I guess it was natural that after all this time we wouldn't still be lusting after each other all minutes of the day. After so long together, our physical intimacy blew hot and cold. These days it was decidedly cold. There was no desire in Matthew's eyes or even a great expression of happiness on his face when I greeted him in the evenings. Maybe he'd stopped looking at me altogether. One thing was certain though: the longer we remained intimately inactive, the more unsure and anxious I became. Truthfully, I was almost embarrassed to appear naked with him.

At least with Matthew away this week, I could pretend we were still happy together.

CHAPTER 17

At breakfast, before I'd managed even one sip of coffee, Mum launched in with, 'Please have dinner with Bob and me – you, Matthew, the kids, Robyn. How about Friday night when Matthew's back from Melbourne? It'll be nice. You'll see.'

But I knew it was more than dinner. I didn't want to see *him* again, and I was especially averse to explaining Dad's sudden appearance to Lexi and Angus. I couldn't even explain it to myself.

'Why do you want to get hurt all over again? Reopen old wounds?'

'People change. Your father's mellowed.'

'People don't change, Mum.'

She shot me her 'you're breaking my heart' look. And I probably was. I'd tried the same look on Lexi and Angus many times. It used to work. It doesn't anymore. There may be a time in the future when I can bring my heartbroken parental face back into circulation, but for the moment, it's tucked away until I can be sure my real daughter has returned from Planet Teen.

When Angus bounded into the kitchen, I busied myself

going over (and over) the seven times tables with him. Pure agony. How could I make it any clearer? Six lots of seven was the same as the seven lots of six we memorised ad nauseum for his six times tables. Giving up, we switched to his news item: *My Favourite Australian Animal*, due yesterday and which *absolutely must be presented in class today, Mrs Lombardy said so.* I found a moth-eaten toy koala lurking in a box under Gus's bed and told him to improvise.

'Sometimes I think I'm just a slave to this family,' I said to the kitchen wall as I washed my mug in the sink and mentally wrote my to-do list: take Cleo to the vet for her yearly vaccination; worm Rupert; buy Bugs a new collar and harness. He chewed through his last one a few days ago, as I unfortunately discovered when I found him several houses away cavorting with several rabbits. I also needed to buy Lexi new sneakers. Not that she'd worn out her previous ones. The girl had bigger feet than me. As for Christmas, we still hadn't put up the tree or decorated the house. Tick. Tick. Tick.

'No, love, you're the one who has it all,' my mother chimed in, interrupting my thoughts. 'You have choices. I was a slave to the family, remember. I had nothing to offer but my homemaking skills.'

'Well, could you use them now and help me with this?' I pointed at Angus who was throwing the stuffed koala at Rupert.

'There's no way I'm ever going to be a slave,' Lexi said before licking Vegemite off her toast.

'Lex, that's disgusting. And besides, sometimes you have no choice. When you get married, you change, give up things—'

'You don't have to.' Lexi was indignant.

You do, I thought to myself as I glanced at an ancient print of mine hanging in the hall, but I wasn't prepared to have another stand-up fight with my daughter. She'd learn soon enough.

'You need to get a life, Mum,' she said.

What? Other than the one I've been living for the last forty odd years? I resisted the urge to reply. Little wonder some animals eat their young.

'I do have a life, Lex, and *Delicious Bites*–'

She laughed. 'You don't even like food photography. How could you?'

'Excuse me?'

'Even after watching every reality cooking show in the world, *Lessons in Chemistry*, and two seasons of *Julia*, you hate all culinary activities. Why don't you do something you really want to do?'

Because, I thought to myself, when you have children, sometimes you need to make sacrifices – bow out of the world as you know it to raise a family. Unfortunately, when you're ready to re-enter the world of the living, sometimes the living doesn't want you anymore. Anyway, I know I can't have it all – not all at once. It's not possible. When I was younger, I assumed when I reached adulthood, I'd no longer have to answer to anybody. I'd finally be able to please myself. But unless you live alone on a deserted island, you quickly discover real life's not like that. Life's full of compromise.

'Lexi,' I said, choosing my words carefully, 'the magazine's a stepping stone, an opportunity to further my skills and get paid for it.'

Mum nodded. 'I gave up tech after I married Bob and look where it got me. I didn't get my first paying job until after Bob and I split.'

Lexi glared at me and Mum. 'You're both crazy. When I'm older, I'm going to be free. Free to do exactly what I want, whenever I want.'

'I hope you are free, Lexi, but life is about choices. You make certain choices, and you live with them. For example, right now you could choose to take yourself upstairs and make your—'

'I know the drill.' She put up her hand to silence me. 'I can make my bed or stay here and get nagged.'

Still, she stayed. In the three minutes it took to go through Angus's times tables again, Lexi and Mum had moved on to Mum's date, chattering excitedly. I lived in hope her enthusiasm for Dad would wear off once reality set in. In the meantime, I had to put up with Mum cooing like a lovesick teenager. Just what I needed – two adolescents in the house.

❄

All this meant I arrived at work on Tuesday morning feeling no better than I had at midnight. Probably because I'd barely managed three hours' sleep.

'You look like you need this.' Arnaud bent down and handed me a coffee. 'Thought I'd drop in to see how you're getting along.'

I was in the studio measuring distances between the floor camera and the dining table, which I'd already set according to Graeme's specific instructions. It was number five on my menial list. In fact, I'd spent the morning doing all sorts of dogsbody jobs: loading film into some of the Hasselblads and digital backs onto others. There were several cameras, ranging from the digital SLRs, small enough to fit into the palm of my hand, to the huge floor camera resting on a three-metre-high tripod.

Earlier, I'd put some test prints on Graeme's desk. Mercifully he hadn't been there. It was the first time I'd been into his office and had a moment to look around. Sixty Thunderbirds were lined up in a huge side cabinet, staring out across the room.

Right now, I was involved in focus pulling, measuring the distance from the camera to the dining table. Well, as involved as I could be given Arnaud was hovering above me and I was on the verge of having a full-blown anxiety attack.

Inappropriate thoughts raced through my head. My breathing was shallow. What if I dropped a camera? The tripod? What if I got the distances wrong or tripped over the electrical cables, stepped on a laptop and broke my ankle... or neck? What if Graeme, Fern and Arnaud realised I was an incompetent fraud?

Arnaud was staring at me.

'Thanks.' I took the cup from him. 'That obvious?'

'Not to the untrained eye.'

'What are you doing up here anyway?'

'After yesterday's excitement, I need to inspect the damage myself. Rumour has it Graeme overturned the utilities table, *non*? And trashed the pots and pans and kicked an enormous hole in the wall.'

'Really?'

'*Oui*. And you, Katie, lived to tell the tale. How is it?'

'Graeme's got the whole tortured-artist gig down to a fine art. He's like no one I've ever met before. Fern likes him though – says he could be working in London or New York but stays here out of loyalty to her. Mara lets his nonsense wash over her. Meanwhile, everyone else walks around on eggshells, trying not to upset him. Is it normal for people to throw dinner plates around?'

'Define normal. Wait till you get to know him better.' Arnaud's French accent was becoming sexier with each word.

'He gets better?'

'No, but at least you won't feel so bad about calling him tortured.'

I sipped my coffee. 'Graeme's not too bad in small doses. He's very clever with an extended zoom and does some innovative moves with angles and lighting.' I took a deep breath and changed the subject. 'How did things work out with Mardi?'

'Ah, Mardi... still networking to get Benjamin into the A's, complaining most of the boys are big for their age because they're being fed steroid-filled battery chickens for dinner.'

'Kate!' Graeme shouted from outside the studio.

Startled, I completely missed my mouth with my coffee. Excellent. A stain blossomed on my pale-pink shirt. I already felt insignificant and frazzled in Graeme's company. Now he was going to think I was a klutz as well.

'You all right?' Arnaud fossicked around the bench and produced a dripping, grey dishcloth.

'These stills are okay.' Graeme was waving a print sheet in the air and leering at the breast with the coffee stain. 'The lighting needs fine-tuning and the colours are all wrong but the essence of what I'm after is here.' He threw the prints on the table and kept walking.

I was relieved because everyone sees things differently through the lens. It wasn't a given Graeme would automatically see what I saw or vice versa. It often took years of working closely with someone before you were in sync – even then, there were no guarantees. You couldn't *get* every picture, you miss things... looking through the viewfinder, as in real life, no one sees exactly the same image, even when it's staring you in the face.

Arnaud picked up one of the contact sheets. 'But where is the food? This is a picture of two wooden blocks and a pink napkin.'

'The blocks are just a stand-in to fix the viewpoint. The food will come later. And the napkin's not pink, it's cherry.'

'Photographers!'

After Arnaud left, I thought about what Graeme had said and couldn't wipe the smile from my face. For the first time since starting here, he'd made me feel like I was a *real* photographer.

CHAPTER 18

The sheets, usually so soft, were scratchy, prickly. I felt itchy all over. I tossed, turned, couldn't get comfortable. Sleep hovered, out of reach. I closed my eyes, determined to relax, but instead, images of Arnaud rose. Arnaud with his cat-like green eyes, his perfect hard body. I touched my breast, and the T-shirt I was wearing became a black push-up bra. Then I added black silk stockings attached to a garter belt and thigh-high black boots with stiletto heels. Where was I? Where were we?

For now, Arnaud is with me, here in a fabulous Turkish bathhouse, water all around, velvet draperies, and the smell of incense. He reaches for me, caresses my naked belly, lingering over my navel, and I feel hot stirrings. He pulls me to him, his mouth seeking mine, his tongue thrusting deeply into my mouth, my own tongue responding greedily. He pulls away and – wait! Oh my God! It isn't Arnaud at all! It's Graeme, with his rich blue eyes, laughing at my surprise.

He commands me to stand perfectly still, not to move. He kneels before me and begins to kiss my inner thighs, his tongue tracing the tops of my boots, exploring the region with the skill of a veteran climber. Then I feel hands on my shoulders, tracing down my spine, unhooking my bra, reaching around to cup my aching, hungry breasts. Arnaud! Here, too! I am swept with waves of passion unlike I ever imagined. I am like a person lost in the desert, parched and alone, who finds an oasis. I drink in all the fiery, wet, pulsing sensations as these two men stroke, lick, touch, tease and thrust themselves into me, and I give myself over completely to the uninhibited delight of being worshipped and adored.

How amazingly dangerous, how frightfully decadent, how perfectly wonderful.

'Mum.'

Angus's voice was in the distance, but what about Arnaud? Graeme? I can't quite pull myself away—

'Mum! Wake up. It's your birthday.'

I opened one eye. Angus was standing beside my bed with a tray bearing breakfast and scattered with several pink hydrangeas from the garden.

'Angus, thank you.' I sat up and dismissed the dream from my mind. His smile was almost as big as his face. There was Vegemite toast, tea and a glass of orange juice. 'Thank you so much, beautiful boy.' I reached over to kiss him.

Mum walked into the room with Lexi trailing behind. 'We know you have to work, but we didn't want you to leave on an empty stomach, especially on your birthday.'

I wolfed down the toast and tea, and within minutes, was showered and dressed and standing in the kitchen with my loved ones and their gifts of chocolate (Angus), lipstick (Lexi) and flowers and a pair of Royal Albert pink vintage teacups and tea caddy from Mum.

'Thank you. They're beautiful gifts,' I said before rushing out the door.

❄

It was after midday when Matthew called. 'I'm sorry I can't be with you. I'll make it up to you, I promise. And I'm sorry I forgot to organise flowers and a card—'

'That's okay. Mum did.'

'I'm also sorry about our argument. I was just so shocked at Lexi's hair.'

'Yeah.'

'Why don't you go out with Diane tonight to celebrate?'

'It's midweek. She has kids to look after.'

'I promise I'll make it up to you. Love you.'

❄

Throughout the day, Robyn and several friends, including Diane, called. It wasn't like I didn't feel special, but I missed Matthew.

As I was packing up to go home, Arnaud popped his head in. 'We're going out for drinks. Join us?'

'Better not. It's my birthday and—'

'All the more reason.'

'But Matthew's away…'

'I insist.'

I hesitated all of ten seconds before calling Mum.

After assuring me everything was under control at home – 'There's a casserole in the oven, Gus is doing his homework and Lexi's home from netball practice' – she insisted I go out. 'It's your birthday. Enjoy yourself. Lexi wants to have friends over to watch a documentary regarding penguins on the Discovery Channel. Something about a final biology assignment…'

'As long as you don't mind,' I said, hoping she wouldn't. It'd be nice for Lexi to have some old friends over, maybe even do a bit of adolescent bonding by remembering when they used to dress up and dance to Hi-5. Back when she had hair.

'It's fine, but I do have a request.'

'Anything,' I heard myself say. Then crossed my fingers.

'Dinner, my house, Friday night. You, Matthew, the kids – and Dad. A belated birthday celebration for you.'

Friday night! God! The pain! How would I survive it? But until I agreed, I knew she'd continue to pester me about dinner with Dad. There was nothing to be gained by further resistance except heartache. It was better to get it over and done with.

'Okay. Deal. Can you make sure the girls go home at a reasonable hour? I won't be late. Thanks, Mum.'

I was tired. Tired – and nervous about going out for drinks with my colleagues.

Every place I'd ever worked had staff politics, whether it was a small magazine or the photographic department of a large newspaper. It was part of the culture, like leaving dirty coffee cups in the kitchen sink when no one was watching and whispering on your mobile to friends when you thought no one was within hearing distance.

But after-work drinks were usually where it all happened. My ancient experience revealed:

1. Staff always jockeyed for position, trying to get the boss's attention in a vain attempt to get ahead.
2. Everyone from the receptionist to the managing director worked their agenda, hidden or not.
3. Sooner or later, chatter got round to gossip.
4. Inevitably, wine would be spilled.
5. By the end of the night, someone's harmless flirting and/or gossip would have turned into something more sinister.

6. And it was always a lot worse once silly season kicked in, a month before Christmas, which happened to be today!

CHAPTER 19

I was at the bar, drinking cheap wine and getting to know my co-workers. Much to my disappointment, I couldn't see Arnaud, so I settled down next to Coco, a redhead with a penchant for black, high-heeled, pointy-toed boots and tight-fitting vests. She was one of the staff writers, bubbly, friendly and always ready for a chat. Coco was young, about twenty-two years old, and I envied her enthusiasm, her *she'll be right* attitude. She also prided herself on using unusual words in conversation.

'My birth name is Karen, can you believe?' Coco's drawl was exaggerated. 'Too prosaic. Coco is much more enchanting, don't you think?'

'Absolutely,' I said, wondering whether I should change my name.

'So, how are things working out with Graeme? You know' – she leaned in close – 'he's made all the women on staff shriek at some stage. I'm over him now, water off a duck's back, but I'm flabbergasted he hasn't procured you yet. You've been hither a week.'

'Hmm,' I said as I spied Arnaud walking in.

'Yeah, beware, Kate. Graeme can be a real satyr.'

I laughed, not only at Coco's use of satyr. 'I'm sure there are more interesting people for him to sleaze onto than me. I'm a mother.'

'Hasn't stopped him before, trust me.'

What? Did Graeme shag anything with a pulse?

'Does he have a wife? Kids? A dog?'

'The Bachelor of the Year? Hardly! No wife. No kids – none I know of, anyway. He isn't a commitment sort of guy. He works, he drinks, and he has girlfriends from time to time, often a couple at once. He's a cad, really.'

Arnaud came over with a drink in hand to toast my birthday.

'Hip, hip, hooray,' the assembled crowd sang. I felt rather chuffed.

As Arnaud and I talked, I noticed Fern chatting easily with Graeme at the end of the table. An enigma. On the one hand, Graeme was short-tempered, aggressive, violent, arrogant and rude. On the other, he could be gracious and social. I could see why some women fell for his charms.

He was saying, 'Fern, you know me. I explode, storm out, then come back five minutes later. Really, I'm a pussycat and easy to work with.'

Fern threw her head back and laughed.

Yes, Graeme had a certain danger, and he was handsome when he wasn't hurling cooking implements.

All too soon, Arnaud was standing up to leave, helmet in hand. 'Want a lift?'

I looked at my watch. Seven o'clock. I could go home, eat dinner, read Gus a story, then have an amicable chat with Lexi and her girlfriends. It sounded like a plan. A sensible plan. But my head was buzzing, and I liked it. It had been a long time since I had been out with work colleagues.

Over eight years.

And it was my birthday.

I swayed, happy to discard my familial responsibilities. I could do without watching a documentary on the mating habits of penguins. And I doubted my ability to remain upright on his bike.

'No, I'll stay for a bit longer.'

'Make sure you leave your car then, *oui*?'

Arnaud! Such concern. A true gentleman. I held on to his arm a little longer than I needed to when I said, 'I'm glad you're here. You make my days here at Image Ink fun.'

'*Merci*... Take it easy and 'appy birthday.'

A minute later he was gone, and I wondered why I hadn't left as well. I didn't need the fresh glass of wine Coco handed me. It would have to be my last. Then I'd catch a cab home. But just then, a waiter delivered my seared salmon and salad.

'I guess you were shocked at Graeme and Mara's antics this morning?' Fern said, when I pulled a chair up beside her to eat.

'You mean when Graeme and Mara argued violently over the Boxing Day degustation menu and lobbed fruit and pans at each other, while I cowered in the studio corner?'

'That's the one.'

'Not at all.' I smiled. 'Though I was grateful no knives were thrown.'

'Don't take it to heart. They both like to think they're creative geniuses and I guess they both are. With Mara appearing on *MasterChef*, Graeme's on edge, worried her celebrity will eclipse his.'

'You're amazingly rational and calm. I'm on guard whenever I'm with them both.'

Fern picked at her lettuce. 'They're the talent, I'm the manager. Both want to be in control, to take the opportunity to showcase their creativity. Unfortunately, it leads to clashes, which I do my best to manage. Not always successfully...'

'Clashes? They fight like animals.' I put down my fork. 'Exactly what is acceptable behaviour between creatives? I mean besides bullying, harassment, and victimisation?'

Fern ran her fingers through her hair and glanced at Graeme. 'It's not that bad, though there's definitely a link between creativity and negative moods. Also, poor impulse control.'

I smiled. 'You don't say?'

'As Nietzsche once noted: "One must have chaos in oneself to be able to give birth to a dancing star". Eventually Graeme and Mara always calm down and compromise. It's all for show. Graeme's really quite gifted.'

'So you keep telling me.'

'Truly. And not only is he a brilliant photographer and visionary, but he brings the hip, cool factor to the magazine. Graeme's the one who cruises the social circuit... always networking in the hottest clubs. He gets the magazine noticed big time.'

'I'll say.' Graeme swaggered over to join us. 'If you're not impressed by me by now, I don't know what else I can do. I am, after all, me.' He took off his glasses and sat down without breaking eye contact with me. I blinked and turned away, unnerved.

I was drinking too much wine. I'd hardly touched my salmon. Soon after our conversation, plates were cleared, and Fern left, citing personal commitments. I moved back to Coco who filled me in on staff dynamics. The gossip. The scandal. The lowdown. The skinny. I was far too intoxicated to take the moral high ground and stop her. And even if I hadn't been drinking, I doubt I'd have stopped her unless the gossip had been about me.

Though I didn't know most of the people Coco mentioned, her anecdotes and words were compelling. I was hooked.

'Do you know *how* Simone – the person you superseded – shattered her talocrural joint?' Coco asked me.

'Her–'

Coco rolled her eyes. 'Ankle. Keep up.'

I nodded. 'Fell off a wonky ladder?'

'Sort of. I wasn't in attendance, but ostensibly Simone was so incensed by a malicious comment Graeme made about her camera angle she disremembered she was positioned on a two-metre ladder and vaulted to abuse him. Boom! Shattered her talocrural joint when she smacked the floor.'

Took me several moments to disentangle Coco's terminologies… I was drunk and starting to think like her. (Except I didn't think terminologies was the right word.)

It was around this time everyone left the pub except Coco, Graeme and me.

The more I talked to Graeme, the more entertaining he seemed, witty and charming – all the things that make someone fun to be with. Of course, after all the wine I'd consumed, I was easily entertained. And distracted. I'd never noticed his perfect skin, strong hands and deep, throaty laugh. Until now.

I listened attentively as Graeme told me the *real* story about Simone and her broken ankle. 'It was her vile temper and impulsiveness that led to her broken ankle, K. I had nothing to do with it. Simone can't stand to be told anything. I made a simple suggestion about the camera angle, and she flew off the plank, so to speak.'

'Get out!' I was fascinated.

Soon after, Coco answered a telephone call and left. Alarm bells were ringing in the back of my head, but I didn't listen. Instead, I stayed for one more drink.

But I'd had so many *one-more-drinks* I'd lost count.

'Not only that,' Graeme continued, 'but Simone's a dobber – and no one likes a dobber, do they, K? She runs to Mara whenever she doesn't agree with me. I'm her boss, for fuck's sake. Since when do you argue with your boss? Or tattle-tale?'

As I listened to Graeme talk, I kept repeating the mantra in my head: *I am not going to get drunk and kiss this man. I am not going to get drunk and kiss this man.*

Unfortunately, I was already drunk.

I think.

Anyway, I kissed that man.

CHAPTER 20

'Katie, it's after seven,' Mum's voice called from behind the closed door.

'I'll be right out.' My head hurt. I vaguely remembered arriving home. It was after...

'Okay, love?' Mum opened my bedroom door a little. 'I've brought you a cup of tea. Lexi's much better, but—'

'But what? What's up with Lexi?'

'I thought it was harmless. How was I to know they were adding vodka to their orange juice?'

'What?' I was developing a migraine behind my right eye.

'I told you last night. Lexi, the vodka... her friends... vomiting on the carpet.'

I had to think for a moment. Was I the one who vomited on the carpet or was Mum talking about Lexi?

'And the chillies! Why on earth Susie fed Lexi chillies, I'll never know.'

I was confused, with a very dry mouth, and had lost several hours. 'Hang on. Back up a minute. What chillies?'

'And, Katie, I kept calling your mobile, but you didn't answer. I didn't want to bother Matthew...'

I stared ahead vacantly. 'You didn't call Matt, did you?' Focus was problematic, difficult given my head was split in shattered shards.

'No, silly, I told you. I made Lexi drink lots of water, threw her in the shower, made her drink more water and finally put her to bed... just before you came home in the wee hours.'

'What about her friends?' I had visions of her friends arriving at their respective homes drunk.

'Luckily, they didn't drink it. They certainly didn't seem intoxicated. Apparently, Lexi was the only one brave enough to gulp the glass in one go.'

'Brave or incredibly stupid?'

'I think she might have learned her lesson. She was very ill.'

'She's thirteen!' I rested my aching head in my hands.

'And you're forty. You look sicker than a three-legged dog at a rubbish tip.'

'Thanks,' I groaned.

'What happened?'

'Nothing. A few birthday drinks.'

'A few?'

'Mother, I'm fine.' I sounded superior, but guilty, exactly how Lexi did when *she'd* done something wrong.

'If fine is looking half dead, puffy and flushed. You were so worried about not driving your car home. But if you're sure everything's okay...' She trailed off and walked out of the room.

I slowly drank my tea and seriously contemplated not going into work. How much longer was my contract? I'd only been there a week. Whatever, it was too long. I showered, dressed and staggered downstairs.

Lexi had her head bowed when I entered the kitchen.

'You look awful.'

She looked up. 'Where were you last night? I needed you.'

I swallowed the urge to cry. Lexi finally needed me, and I

wasn't home for her. Okay, I wouldn't have been much use, in fact it would have been disastrous had she woken when I'd arrived home. But I'd missed an opportunity to be with my girl. I'd failed her.

'I'm sorry, Lex.' I rubbed her back. 'I shouldn't have gone out after work.'

'Maybe I wouldn't have done something so dumb if you'd been here.'

I attempted a smile. 'When has that ever stopped you?'

'I was really scared. And when Susie gave me chillies, I thought I was dead... and then I puked—'

'Yes, I get the picture, Lexi.' I clutched my forehead. I'd been out drinking while my thirteen-year-old daughter was at home doing the same thing. Clearly, my mothering skills left a lot to be desired.

'You gonna tell Dad?'

'You've done a very silly thing to yourself, not to mention what you've put Nanna through—'

Lexi started to cry.

'It's all right. We can handle this together... can't we?' I bent down and put my arms around her. 'But I don't ever want to hear about you spiking your orange juice again. Ever. Even when you're twenty-five!'

Lexi dried her eyes, shrugged, and with a mouthful of egg said, 'Yeah.'

I watched as she ate the remainder of her breakfast. At least she didn't appear to be suffering any after-effects. I leaned against the kitchen bench in a daze, my legs barely able to support me, until Lexi swished out of the room.

'Mum, how do you spell *ignoramus*?' Angus was beside me with an open exercise book in his hand.

My mind was blank.

'For school,' he prompted.

I closed my eyes and confidently rattled off the letters, baffled at my ability, given my mind was mush. I was thinking about Lexi, my car, Graeme and my acute embarrassment. I'd kissed Graeme. How could I have, especially when my little girl was at home being force-fed chillies in a foolish attempt to sober her up? And what about Matthew?

'I guess I need to order a cab.'

'I can drive you, Kate,' Mum said.

Lexi had strolled back into the kitchen at the same time as Mum. 'Where's your car?'

'At work. Engine trouble,' I lied. 'Have you apologised to Nanna?'

'Sorry, Nan.'

Mum kissed Lexi softly on her forehead. 'I know you are, sweetie. You had me worried, that's all.'

That's all! If I'd have done that, I'd have been whipped off to boarding school, quick smart. Was this the same woman who'd grounded me for a month when I was fourteen because I drank half a glass of spumante at a cousin's wedding?

After Lexi left the room, I said to Mum, 'Thanks for the offer of a lift, but I'll catch a cab if you can take the kids to school. And thanks for being here these last few days. I'll pick Angus up from soccer this afternoon.'

Mum opened the dishwasher and began filling it with used breakfast plates. 'Remember, you've got Robyn's antenatal class tonight.'

I stopped wiping the kitchen bench. 'Do I?' I vaguely remembered her having to reschedule but my recollection was hazy.

'I can take her if you're not up for it.'

I touched Mum's hand. 'Thanks, but I'll be fine.' Except I wasn't. I felt like crying. I didn't want to work in a business surrounded by people all day, every day. It was hard always thinking about what to say next. Making sure you sounded intelligent, knowledgeable.

Being on your best behaviour at all times.

Being careful not to offend anyone, ever.

Toeing the company line, no exceptions.

Saying no to after-work drinks, not getting drunk or kissing your boss.

I wasn't cut out for it. My head was spinning. I was hungover, embarrassed. But the sooner I saw Graeme and cleared the air, the sooner I'd feel better.

Better was probably not the right word... less wretched.

CHAPTER 21

So far so good, I thought, as I stepped into the foyer. I'd taken several Nurofen and was holding a large skinny cappuccino. It was eight forty-five am, a perfectly respectable hour to arrive at work. I walked up the stairs, past the offices and into the studio.

'Hey.' Mara handed me a job sheet. 'Watch out. Graeme's on the warpath, *again*.'

'Really? Is he here?'

'No, he called from the car. So much for our bonding session last night.'

Inwardly, I cringed as I tried to remember. My recollection was Mara stayed for dinner and then went home.

'Good night?'

Confident my behaviour was acceptable up to that point, I said, 'Yeah. It was fun.'

'It's just the next morning you have to worry about, hey?'

What did she mean? Did Mara know? Had Graeme told her?

I looked at the list as I walked out of the studio and into the kitchen ready to complete my first job of the day: preparing Graeme's coffee for when he arrived. I was a bloody chore whore, that's all I was! I knew my job revolved around saving Graeme time, but why couldn't he buy his own coffee from Tribeca across the street like everyone else or, better yet, plunge his own? Maybe he wouldn't still expect it after... Maybe from now on, I'd be relieved of coffee-making responsibilities.

'Mademoiselle.' I swung around. Coco. 'You and the fiend were certainly flourishing when I vamoosed last night.'

My eyes widened and my palms were suddenly itchy. I was too hungover to decipher her words. 'Pardon?'

'Did you have a courteous spell? It vexed me to abandon you with the ogre, but you and Graeme were having a right old hootenanny without the folk music. I told you he had a way with the ladies.'

Without waiting for a reply, she walked out, the happy click of her high heels echoing down the corridor.

It was going to be okay. It wasn't yet nine o'clock but at least I'd seen Coco and Mara. They appeared normal. It wasn't like I'd taken my clothes off and tap danced on tabletops. I sipped my coffee, rubbed my aching head and walked back into the studio.

I sat at the utilities bench and reread Graeme's job sheet instructions. Curt. Short. No niceties to indicate last night had meant anything to him. Excellent. I didn't want our relationship to change. Excuse me, was I still drunk? What relationship?!

'Kate, you okay?'

I looked up to see Fern's furrowed brow.

'Sorry I left when you were in the middle of everything, but I had to be home by eight. You know how it is.'

Everything?

'I'm sorry if I chewed your ear, Fern. I didn't mean anything by it. Birthday anxiety, I guess.' I hoped I sounded plausible because I couldn't exactly remember our conversation. 'And Christmas,' I added, as an afterthought.

'Still, I'm worried about the extra pressure I've put on you, especially at this time of year. If it's all too much, I'll understand. I know how difficult it is to juggle work and family.'

This coming from Superwoman. My temples throbbed and my eyelids felt heavy. I shrank inside myself. Fern could manage *Delicious Bites* and Graeme, as well as several other magazines and two extra children. What had I said to her over dinner?

'And working with Graeme? He is prone to brain explosions...'

Understatement, I thought, recalling our chat about creatives and negative moods.

'But don't worry about upsetting him. I meant what I said about the digital Christmas campaign. I should have spoken with you about it on your first day, but—' She shook her head. 'You've gathered life at Image Ink is chaotic at best? You'll be in charge. That is, if you still want it?'

'Yes. Great.' I had no idea what she was talking about.

'Cool. Four weeks until the big day. We kick off next Tuesday, December first.' She laughed. 'Remember, food doesn't need to be the star. I've assigned Chef Dana to support with the Christmas cuisine you require and accompanying easy-to-follow reader recipes. She's an absolute breeze. And so long as your daily nativity calendar screams Christmas and summer sunshine, it'll be a smash.' Beaming, with a thumbs up gesture of approval, Fern turned to leave, then stopped. 'And we're still on for Saturday night?'

My mind was blank.

'You, me, Terry and Matthew? Dinner? My house?'

I vaguely remembered making dinner plans.

I nodded and Fern departed.

What the hell was the digital nativity calendar I'd agreed to shoot and post every day? Every day up to, and including Christmas? Lordy!

Deep breaths. I'd worry about that tomorrow. Right now, I

needed to let go of whatever embarrassment happened last night with Graeme and move on from this unfortunate business. I busied myself checking the white balance and aimlessly waved around the exposure meter, frequently glancing at the doorway, waiting for Graeme to arrive.

Despite my hangover and my insides quivering, I felt a growing sense of excitement. For now, I was assisting Graeme, doing the set-ups and taking test shots, but next week, I'd also be the genius snapping the pivotal frames.

Finally, I heard his voice.

Adjusting my clothes, I hurried into the kitchen, turned the kettle on and watched, willing the water to boil faster. Checking his cup was clean (for the tenth time) and the sugar cubes had not dissolved, I turned to the plunger. Were exactly three level tablespoons of ground coffee sitting at the bottom? Check. I tapped the kettle.

He walked straight past the kitchen and into the studio, where he said something to Mara. I couldn't distinguish the words.

Carelessly, I sloshed two and a half cups of boiling water into the plunger and was away. I arrived at the studio as Mara was departing.

'Hey.' I placed his coffee before him.

He grunted and continued inspecting test images.

Excuse me? Was he ignoring me?

I waited a bit longer. 'I've finished everything on the list.' Nothing. He didn't even look at me. What exactly did he have to be ashamed about? It's not as if he had a wife and two children. 'Everything okay?' I persisted.

'Listen, babe, I know you want me and hey, I wish I felt the same, really. If I could help you out I would, but it's not happening for me. Plus, there's the whole Robyn saga.'

'But—' I was outraged. Wanting him to *help me out* was absolutely the last thing on my mind. And what Robyn saga?

'Easy, tiger. You won't get me to change my mind by throwing a tantrum and pouting. It's not going to happen. You're nice enough, but not my type. What's the line from that movie? Oh yeah: *I'm just not that into you*. So how about you sparkle those lenses?' He pointed to several on a nearby bench.

'Thanks, but I'd rather hammer nails into my skull,' I said, except no sound came out. Humiliation pulsed through every vein in my body. I felt worthless and pathetic. Not to mention mortified Graeme could think that (a) I was attracted to him, and (b) I planned to sleep with him. I was the one who'd made the mistake. I was the one who'd responded to the inappropriate attention he'd paid me.

Twenty minutes later, I'd finished cleaning all but one lens when Matthew called. 'I left you messages. Did you end up having a fun birthday? Pip said you went out with people from the magazine.'

'Fern,' I replied.

'How's Lexi?'

'Lexi?'

'Yes, Lexi... our daughter.'

Mum told. He knew something.

'Kate, what's the matter with you? Pip said Lexi was too sick to come to the phone last night. Did you take her to the doctor? Is she all right?'

'She's fine. A slight tummy bug. She went to school happily enough this morning.'

'Nothing else?'

If you really want to know, I got pissed and made an idiot of myself while Lexi was at home showing off to her friends by skolling vodka and orange. 'Nothing else. We miss you.'

CHAPTER 22

By three o'clock, I'd had enough of fixing viewpoints, arranging lights and positioning props like eucalyptus wreaths, snowflake confetti, and reindeer tealight candle holders. I had an involuntary twitch. All day I'd avoided being alone with Graeme, but as I was leaving, he walked in.

'The fucking fluorescent lights are tinting the set with a vomitus shade of green.'

I spent the next hour sniffing back tears and lugging huge plastic diffusers into place to create an even light.

By the time I left the studio, I was exhausted. Matthew was coming home tomorrow, and I needed to pull myself together. I rubbed my tired eyes and yawned. An uninterrupted eight-hour sleep would hopefully fix it. But first I had to pick Angus up from soccer practice and make it through dinner and homework tantrums. And Robyn's antenatal class.

'Hey, buddy, what did you get up to at school?' I quizzed Angus as we drove home from the soccer grounds.

'Stuff.'

'Any advance on *stuff*?'

'Nup.'

'Good day, then?'

He shrugged. 'Random.'

That little catch-up went well.

At home, Mum was in the kitchen sprinkling grated cheese over a vegetarian lasagne. She popped it in the oven and grinned. 'Ready in forty minutes. I've also made apple crumble.'

'You're too fabulous.' I hugged her then glanced at my watch. 'Lexi'll be home soon, so I should—'

'She's in the garden with her friend.'

Friend? Garden? Scooting outside, I discovered Lexi and Hunter kissing enthusiastically near the mutilated conifers. She was supposed to be at the library finishing an assignment on Shakespearean tragedies.

Teenage girls are sneaky. Sneaky, obnoxious and devious.

'I hate you, Mum,' Lexi screamed after I asked, or rather demanded, Hunter go home.

'Thank you, darling. I'm thinking of installing video monitors in strategic locations around the house and garden.'

'You would do something evil like that, wouldn't you? If only to make my life more miserable than it already is.'

I wouldn't actually. Far too expensive.

'How could you embarrass me like that? I hate you!'

'So you've told me. Twice.'

'Everyone will laugh at me.'

'What do you mean?' She didn't answer me. 'Lexi, you're too young to be kissing boys.'

'You don't understand. Hunter's my boyfriend. The *right* kind of boyfriend.'

'He's your boyfriend now? A week ago, he was only a friend.'

'When I'm with Hunter, the girls don't treat me badly.'

'Who's treating you badly?'

'No one. Leave me alone.'

'Last night you got drunk, and this afternoon I find you kissing Hunter. What next? You're a choir girl, for God's sake!'

'What's wrong with kissing? Juliet was only thirteen.'

'Lexi! I don't care about the other girls in your class. This is about you.'

'Juliet, as in *Romeo and Juliet*.'

My daughter had dibs on being superior. *Romeo and Juliet*! For goodness' sake, that relationship was a complete and utter tragedy, all because some adolescent infatuation was elevated to the status of sacred love. I racked my brain. Surely Juliet was older. Though, from memory, she was only thirteen, albeit two weeks shy of her fourteenth birthday.

'And look where immature, blind passion led her! Didn't turn out too well, did it?'

'They were in love!'

I focused on remembering the Serenity Prayer Mum used to repeat... *God, grant me the serenity to accept the things I cannot change, courage to change the things I can, and wisdom to know the difference.*

CHAPTER 23

'You look like shit. What's up?' Robyn asked as I battled the evening traffic on the way to her antenatal class.

'Nothing. I mean late night. Birthday drinks.' I exhaled. 'Lexi. Mum.'

'Backtrack. Late night?' Robyn caressed her stomach. 'Please don't tell me you were hanging out with Graeme Grafton.'

'No. Well, yes, but with loads of other people from the company. Anyway, I had one too many drinks. Feel like death.'

Robyn nodded. 'Stay away from him.'

I turned to look at her. 'Because?'

'Keep your eyes on the road. He's a jerk.'

'True. Anyway, I'm more worried about Lexi.' I told Robyn about Lexi's misadventures the previous night, then, 'She looks different. It's not just her hair. It's obvious her brand-new body parts are influencing her – and her boyfriend. It's all happening so quickly.'

'What does Matthew say?'

'You think I'd talk to Matthew about this? Are you crazy?'

'Sometimes.'

'I'm serious. I don't think it'd be wise to tell Matthew. Besides, he'd blame me.'

'He wouldn't blame you. It's not your fault. Lexi's different to you.'

'You can say that again. She and her friends know how to whip a condom onto a banana. Imagine doing those things when you were thirteen!'

'Me, sure, but you? Never.'

'Everything's changed, Rob. I'm falling behind. I wasn't even at the head of the pack to start with. Lex can learn the finer points about foreplay and sexual intercourse within three seconds on the internet.'

'She'll find out anyway. I got a lesson on anal sex last week thanks to *Sex and the City* repeats.'

❄

At the hospital, Robyn and I sat with eight other couples in the conference room waiting for our session to begin. Tonight's focus? Breasts.

In previous sessions, we'd visited waiting rooms, labour rooms, maternity rooms, bathrooms and nurseries. We'd seen stirrups and rubber boots. Robyn had stuffed plastic babies through plastic pelvic bones and almost fainted. We'd watched birthing videos where she *had* fainted. We'd done breathing exercises, back massages, squatted, flopped into beanbags, crawled about like dogs and learned about alternative pain relief. And that's where I drew the line.

'My advice is drugs. Take lots of drugs,' I told her.

But Robyn hadn't been a fan of the drug option. Right up until she caught sight of the vacuum cleaner with the toilet-plunger attachment in class four. Afterwards, she was close to agreeing with me. It took most of the two hours in class five, however, to convince her when push came to shove, so to speak, a little epidural probably never hurt anyone. Which was nothing compared to Robyn's reaction when she saw the forceps.

'I'm going to be ripped apart!'

'Most probably.'

Robyn and I had bonded early on with the group, most of them cornering one or both of us over shortbread and herbal tea sessions, telling us the ups and downs of their relationships. Mostly downs.

'Sometimes I think it might be easier being a lesbian,' Adele had confided conspiratorially.

'I guess,' I'd replied blithely.

'Because you get it, don't you? The mood swings, the cravings. It must be so much easier.'

What? 'Pardon?'

'You and Robyn, the two of you together.'

'What? No!' I shuddered. 'We're sisters.'

After that, we weren't treated any differently. We were run-of-the-mill members of the group. That is until they found out about Robyn and her Insta fame.

'Group photo,' she was squealing now. 'Come on, Nurse Julie, you too.' Robyn pulled our facilitator in beside her.

I positioned the squad before a backdrop of stock pregnancy and toddler care posters. All expectant mothers sat obediently in almost comfortable pale-blue armchairs (cushions positioned behind their backs for maximum relief) holding various props including plastic newborns, forceps, and a stethoscope. Birth partners stood at the side or sat on the floor in front of the chairs.

'Katie,' Robyn boomed. 'Stop fussing. Hurry up and take the photos. One of us is going to drop any minute.'

❄

At home, Angus and Lexi were asleep and Mum was in a hurry to get back to her own house. I didn't ask why.

After perfecting Robyn's group photo for Insta and sending it to her, I took myself off for a long hot bath and immersed myself in bubbles. It was several minutes before I realised there were tears streaming down my face due to the Graeme fiasco, my marriage... and Lexi and the venom in her voice.

Lexi was three years old the first time she told me she hated me. It was the middle of the night, and she'd staggered into our bed half asleep, warm and smelling of strawberry shampoo. She crawled in under the blankets and as I reached out to pull her close, she pushed me away, yelling, '*Get away, Mummy, I hate you.*' She kicked her legs into my stomach and threw herself on top of Matthew. He didn't stir, but I'll never forget that night.

I had to face facts. I was getting older. My little girl was no longer little. She stood at one hundred and sixty-four centimetres, only two centimetres shorter than me... okay, we were the same height.

She was no longer mine. Not saying I ever owned her, but she used to look at me with a modicum of love and respect; now there was only distaste, distrust and anger. What happened to the girl in pink leotards with pigtails and pink ribbons?

Then there was Matthew. What used to be a slow creeping distance between us was fast becoming a gaping chasm.

I lay in the bath wondering what I could do to leave everything behind and escape. If I lived to be eighty – and I was optimistic enough, on a good day, to believe I would – then I had already lived half of my life. If I was ever to win awards for my photography, publish said award-winning photos, trek the Himalayas, or own a fabulous gallery full of my award-winning photos, I needed to get on with it.

Instead, I was still dreaming the dreams I had long ago. They weren't coming true, and I doubted they ever would. They were the dreams of a young idealistic woman who imagined living her life in a perfect bubble of happiness with her husband and children, pursuing her creative ambitions, cocooned from life's harsh realities and disappointments.

Fifteen minutes later, in bed, teeth cleaned and body sufficiently moisturised, I checked Robyn's Instagram feed. She'd posted the pic.

#antenatalclass #mytribe #pregnant #34weeks #blessed #lovinglife #babybump

My first thought was that I hoped Robyn had permission from everyone to post it. My second was that there were plenty of wackos trolling her.

We lost our baby at 34 weeks. Thanks for the reminder, bitch Chill86

You're huge. Ready to split. Sure it's not triplets?

I can see your back acne from here (That one made no sense.)

Get over yourself husbandless whore

CHAPTER 24

I was awake most of the night worrying about Robyn, and just as I dozed again, the alarm woke me. Climbing out of bed, I felt an overwhelming sense of dread that this was the beginning of the end of my life. I was having a mid-life crisis. I was sure of it. I felt unattractive, had zero energy, couldn't jog thirty metres without my legs aching, my kids hated me... *I* hated me.

I'd recently read about the five signs of a mid-life crisis:

1. Uncharacteristic thoughts, including feelings of entrapment, anger, depression, boredom, anxiety and dissatisfaction – all of the above, thanks. I dreamt of running away and starting a new life. I felt like a prisoner, a caged animal. Don't get me started on anger – the neighbours, their dogs, our hedges, the plumbing. There was a long list.
2. Constant inner questions, such as, *What do I yearn to do for the rest of my life?* and *Who am I?* – another tick. I was always having those thoughts except I asked them with several expletives thrown in.

3. Difficulties with work and relationships. Another thumbs up.
4. Emotional outbursts. Hell, yes!
5. Showy behaviours, such as flirting and affairs. *EEK!*

Thankfully, I had the prospect of a brisk morning walk to distract me. I even took off my pyjamas and dressed in appropriate exercise attire. By the time Diane opened my front gate, I was already outside the house and jogging on the spot. Well, perhaps not jogging but at least I was awake and upright.

'It pains me to do this, but I will.' I forced a smile in the dark. 'I'm here for you.'

'Great,' Di replied flatly as we walked out my front gate and trekked up the street.

'I don't know how you do it, Di, working full time, four kids. I'm barely coping with work and mine's only a temp job. Plus, I made the mistake of getting drunk on Wednesday night…' I hesitated, unsure whether to tell her about Graeme and the kiss but decided to keep it to myself. Diane had her head down and was walking at a frightening pace. 'And the politics! But at least I get to see the gorgeous Arnaud.'

'Nice.' Diane's tone was subdued.

'Then last night, at Robyn's antenatal class—'

'David and I are splitting up.'

'Shit.' I stopped in the middle of the street and faced her. 'Really?'

'Yes. No. Maybe.' Di started walking again. 'The upcoming school holidays, Christmas arrangements. It's all so stressful. David wants me to negotiate with his ex. Me! I've got my own ex to negotiate with. Then Oliver said he doesn't want to have Christmas with us. So, I jokingly said to David, "Great, one less problem to deal with". He was furious. "Are you calling my son a problem?".'

'Yikes.'

Diane sniffed. 'It's a monumental fuck-up.'

We walked the final four kilometres in companionable silence.

'I'll ring you,' I called as she opened her front door.

Back home, there were beds to make, animals to feed, children to find and finally a shower.

My mid-life crisis could wait. Kissing Graeme wasn't the smartest thing I'd done but neither was drunkenly mooning a police officer when I was twenty-two. At the time I was mortified – once the hangover kicked in and I woke to find myself inside a police station holding cell. I never thought I'd live that one down, but I did. You move on. Life's crap one minute and then not so crap an hour later.

I believe it takes roughly six weeks for the horror of a crisis to work its way through and pass. I can't remember what I was worrying about six weeks ago, but I'll bet I was having dramas. Now, six weeks on, those old dramas have been forgotten and I've got new ones to work with. In time, these current dramas will fade. Though I'll admit the kissing incident was a major departure from my normal daily activities.

'Mum, Angus is hitting me.' Lexi's voice could pierce a balloon. I heard a whack, then a thud, a shrill squeal, associated crying and a door slam.

I climbed out of the shower, wrapped a towel around myself and walked down the stairs to the sound of someone banging on the kitchen door. Lexi was nowhere to be seen. I opened the door to Angus, shivering and crying.

'She punched me,' Angus shouted, then picked up a punnet of dahlias and flung them across the patio, narrowly missing Cleo.

What parallel universe was I living in? Since when had my normally good-natured son turned into a snarling, two-headed monster? I thought that honour was exclusively reserved for Lexi.

'Angus, leave the plants alone. Tell me what happened. Did you hit her first?'

'No.' I could tell Angus was fibbing because he's a very bad liar. His whole face twitched, convulsing, as he desperately tried to think of a way out of it. Sensing trouble, he took off down the backyard, yelling, 'I hate this horrible family.'

Cheers. Why had I let my mother leave?

Moments later, Lexi appeared. 'Tell me he was adopted at birth. He really can't be my brother, seriously.'

'Seriously, Lexi, he is your brother, and you're old enough to know better. Why don't you walk away when he annoys you?'

'Because I'd be in London by now, that's why. He's such a baby!'

'You're such a baby!' Angus roared as he stripped leaves off the gardenias.

Next door, the two dogs were going ballistic, throwing themselves at the fence, which was going to come crashing down any second.

'Everything all right over there?' Great. Meddlesome Margaret. 'That's an awful lot of noise for so early in the morning. Peter and I are trying to enjoy a quiet cup of tea, and we can't hear ourselves think over the racket.'

'Everything's fine, Margaret.' I grabbed Angus by the hand. 'Get. In. Side. NOW!' I hissed through gritted teeth. I pushed him inside, following close behind, and slammed the door. 'As if I haven't got better things to do than pander to you two every second of every day.'

'Where are my shoes?' Lexi demanded, ignoring me. She pointed to the middle of the kitchen floor. 'They were there yesterday.'

'Freezer.'

'What?'

'I've told you before. You leave things lying around and I'll put them in the freezer.'

She stomped to the fridge, opened the freezer drawer, and retrieved her shoes. 'Mum, your joke is old and embarrassing. Just like you!'

I reached for my teacup. 'But motivational!'

CHAPTER 25

At work, the conversational buzz in the kitchen was deafening.

'What's up?' I asked Coco.

'Mara's taken trauma sabbatical. No one knows when she'll be revisiting.'

Sharp as a needle, deciphering all of Coco's words, I responded. 'Really? Why?'

'Well, inmates are cogitating, as you do,' Coco said, toying with me. 'Graeme. Who else could it be? The intimidation, the skirmishes, the perpetual petty piddling.' She took a breath, possibly exhausted by her words. 'Something might have happened at the pub the other night.'

'Really?' Panic set in. This wasn't going well at all. It was one thing to gossip. It was an entirely different story if the gossip involved me. I feared the worst.

'Yeah. There's a whisper going about but it can't be factual. It just can't.'

'What? Tell me!' As the words left my mouth, I attempted to remove the end of sentence exclamation to salvage a calm I didn't feel.

'Scuttlebutt, but some of us think Graeme and Mara are having a liaison, and the combat's part of their insane fervour.'

'What? Graeme and Mara are having an affair?'

Coco hesitated. 'Could be. But I reckon something happened to change all that. We'll find out soon enough. Meanwhile, I'll keep my investigative ear to the ground. Let me know if you hear anything.'

'Sure, okay.'

In the studio, I stood at my table, staring at the blinding white wall. Thinking. Coco had spilled the speculative beans on Mara and Graeme, and those beans didn't include me, so was I obliged to report to her anything new I heard? Was I in gossip debt?

Fern stopped by the studio barely five minutes later.

'HaveyouseenGraemethismorning?' she asked without taking a breath.

I shook my head.

'Well, that's great. I suppose you've heard.'

'Mara's taken stress leave? Is it true?'

Fern nodded. 'Those spats I thought were all part of the flow of creative energy are apparently real. They hate each other.'

'But I heard...'

'What? What did you hear?'

'Nothing. Just that Graeme and Mara...'

'Oh, the affair? Graeme assures me they're not. Besides, he'd be stupid to do it, here of all places. He told me there's nothing going on between them, and I believed him. But now I think... well, I guess it could be true. Regardless, we're in trouble. I need Mara. Almost as much as I need Graeme.'

It occurred to me that maybe Mara and Graeme could be having an affair, and Mara had seen Graeme and me together at the pub. There was something about the night I couldn't put my finger on. It was at the back of my head hiding in an alcohol-induced haze. Or was it? My real and fantasy lives seemed to be colliding. One minute, I'm imagining cavorting with Arnaud in the Turkish bathhouse down the corridor, the next I'm remembering kissing Graeme at the pub.

'Graeme. Thank God.' Fern grabbed Graeme's arm as he arrived beside us.

'Whoa, easy girl.' Grinning, he shook himself free.

'Haven't you heard?'

'About Mara?' He shrugged. 'She's pissed at me. She'll come around. Always does.'

'Maybe not this time. I think you've pushed her too far.'

'So? Get another editor.'

'Hell, Graeme, it's not that easy. Mara is more than an editor. She's as beloved as Steve Irwin and Dame Edna.'

Graeme coughed. 'Both dead.'

'People adore her, Graeme. She has cachet. We can't just replace her.' Fern snapped her fingers and looked genuinely concerned. She was flappable after all. 'Besides, Mara's scheduled to appear on *MasterChef* in February.'

'How could I forget? You bang on about it all the time,' Graeme huffed.

'Think of the publicity!'

'The magazine gets enough publicity because of who *I* am.'

I took a tape measure and checked the distance from the bowls to the camera and the edge of the carpet to the tripod, then looked at them through the viewfinder in the hope I would magically disappear. Then I stared out the window across the road to the entrance of Tribeca café at the only greenery I could see – a lone rubber plant, spindly and in desperate need of water.

'Kate,' Fern said, jolting me to attention. 'Graeme and I were going over the preliminary shots for February's print issue last night.'

He held up several proof sheets in his hands. 'I don't often compliment anyone, but I couldn't think of anything negative to say about these.'

'You're a natural. Always have been, Kate.' Fern looked over to where Mara was normally stationed and shook her head. 'Some problems are more easily solved than others.' She turned and walked out of the studio with Graeme trailing close behind.

A while later, Coco asked me again if I'd heard anything new. I told her I hadn't.

'I still can't credit she's nailing him.'

I winced. 'It might not be true.'

'So how do you elucidate the aggro?'

'Maybe they really do hate each other.'

'Conjecture,' Coco replied, eyeing me suspiciously.

❄

What had happened to the woman who used to be Kate Cavendish? The woman who was strong, independent, feisty and determined?

There was a time when I aspired to rule the world with my great photography, the exhilaration of holding a camera, focusing in on my subject... the freedom. Elation. I might have only been in my early twenties, but I was ready to take on the world. Even after Lexi was born, I was gung-ho.

There was no doubt in my young mind I was on track to becoming one of the few independently successful photographers in the country. I had all the prerequisites. I'd completed my degree at the right institution, and I was fearless and fast.

The old me would never have put up with Graeme; I'd have knocked him out at our first meeting. But I hadn't been in the workplace for eight years. I'd forgotten the rules and now I was beginning to remember them, I didn't have the nerve.

What I needed to do was take some astounding shots, get my confidence back and leave *Delicious Bites* on a high note. *That Katie Cavendish, now there's a genius. A whiz with the camera, truly breathtaking. Have you ever met anyone like her? And the magic she can weave with potatoes? Brilliant.* Something along those lines anyway.

But the main problem with food photography was the food. We're talking groceries – pumpkins, risotto, pears. How did anyone expect to get mind-blowing shots working solely with foodstuff? *Thank God Katie Cavendish's gone. You should have seen her behaviour at the pub. We were all watching her, such a slut. And her photos? Ugh!*

'Kate!' I blinked; Fern's loud voice pulling me from my daydream. 'Meet Dana. Dana, Kate,' Fern enthused, as she and Dana arrived at my workbench. 'The plan is to showcase a themed festive photo montage, say ten pics, on the digital edition every day of December. With me so far?'

Dana and I nodded.

'Cool. I'm thinking it will be a combo of archive photos and new photos that Kate—' Fern looked at me. 'You'll snap, using your distinct flair and creativity. Every day, there should be several cuisine items incorporated into the theme. So, while food will feature, it doesn't have to be the focus. Okay?'

'Great,' I said.

'Good,' Fern continued. 'Kate, you've access to our complete photo library from past editions, so use them where you see fit rather than take photos of the same scenes. Dana, regarding the accompanying food items, please include recipes so readers can recreate your delicious biscuits, desserts and such. You know the drill.'

Dana smiled. 'It'll be fun.'

'I know you guys will work well together.' Fern checked her watch. 'And now, I'll leave you both to it.'

'I don't know how she does it,' I said, watching as Fern flew down the corridor.

'Yep, she's a dynamo.'

'I've thought about the first few days,' I said cautiously.

Dana grinned. 'Glad to hear. I'm totally happy for you to tell me what to do. I'm very good at following orders!'

'And an excellent chef by all accounts.' Dazzle her with flattery, Kate. 'I thought that day one could simply be *Tis the season*. I can take the best ten photos from the first Christmas edition of *Delicious Bites*.'

'Fabulous. I can add simple but universal festive treats like chocolate-dipped marshmallow pops, Christmas balls, coconut ice, and maybe some gingerbread reindeer faces and stars?'

I nodded. 'For day two's theme, I thought *Red*?'

Dana clapped. 'Candy canes, toffee apples, cherries, that sort of thing?'

'This really is going to be fun,' I said. 'Day three, *Summer Fun* featuring beaches, surf—'

'Prawns and sausages on the barbie,' Dana finished.

'And the great part about the digital magazine is you can take the food home after it's been shot.'

'Really?' My eyes widened. 'Won't I have to inject everything with artificial dye and lacquer?'

'The rules for online spreads are much more relaxed. We don't tamper with the food too much.'

We chatted animatedly for the next fifteen minutes, before Dana left for her next meeting, and I promised to email her the final four themes for the first week of December, by the end of the day.

I searched the archives, selecting photos, and placing them in appropriately named files. Day four's theme would be

Favourite Ornaments, including edible Yuletide shortbreads. Day five, *Gold*; day six, *Festive Drinks*; and day seven, *Pets in Christmas Sweaters*. I'd rope Cleo, Bugs and Rupert into posing.

It was three o'clock before I remembered today was Angus's athletics carnival. I made it in time to hear the team war cries and school song. But I took lots of photos. In years to come, Angus would believe I was there for the whole day. I congratulated him on his two second-place ribbons.

'Did you see me, Mum? I rocked.'

'Sure did, sweetheart,' I lied. 'You were brilliant.'

CHAPTER 26

I kissed Matthew as he walked inside that evening. 'Welcome home.' Now things could return to normal.

'Thanks, hon. Big week.' He sighed and flopped on the sofa.

My eyes scanned the room. Papers scattered across the floor, empty chip packet on the coffee table, milk carton on the kitchen bench. Lid off. All the animals in the house, lounging around. Yep, normal. Normal everyday chaos.

'How was it?' I asked, trying to engage him as his eyes practically rolled to the back of his head.

'The Melbourne branch is a mess. Took me three days to sort out the overdue tenders. I had performance review meetings with all the staff. They still don't get it. You'd think they'd never heard of Covid and rising interest rates. I didn't finish half of what I needed to. But I did manage to book a restaurant for us tomorrow night to celebrate your birthday and new job.'

My birthday. I'd forgotten. At least I'd tried to.

'Thank you.' I edged closer towards him. 'Sweetheart, Fern's invited us over tomorrow night.' Matthew seemed to have dozed off. I nudged him slightly. 'If you're so busy, why don't you create another position? Divide your workload?'

He shook his head. 'Have you seen the latest inflation figures? Business is tight. Besides, I don't mind the work most of the time.'

What could I expect from a man who had a sign hanging on his office wall saying *I love Mondays*.

'But I'm exhausted. I've had a headache ever since our argument the other day.' He rubbed his temple. 'Hope it's nothing more serious, but you never know.'

I sat down beside him and massaged his head. When it came to illnesses, Matthew leant to the hypochondriac side of the swing. To Matthew, having a headache was code for, *I have an inoperable brain tumour and less than three months to live.*

Once, I rushed him to hospital in the middle of the night because he was in agony, wailing he was dying of stomach cancer. Turned out, it was constipation. Then there were times, usually around this time of year, when Matthew whipped himself into a frenzy over melanomas. God give me strength when he turns fifty and conversation turns to prostate ailments.

I hoped he didn't develop a sniffle – one sneeze and he'd convince himself he was dying from Covid, though he's up to date with his boosters.

'How's Lexi?' he asked, eyes searching the room.

'We're coping.' I neglected to mention the binge-drinking session and the kissing incident.

'She's settled down?'

I nodded.

'At least we can stay home tonight and watch the cricket, maybe order in curries – just what I need.'

'I'd like nothing better.' Watching five hours of cricket would be heaven. 'But I promised we'd go to Mum's for a belated birthday dinner.'

'Haven't you spent the whole week with her?'

'I'd rather not go either, but I promised. Dad will be there.'

Matthew's eyes widened. 'Your father? I thought you said they'd have to cart you away in a wooden box before you'd agree to see him again?'

Matthew and I had been together fifteen years, and he'd never met my father. I guess he thought he'd escaped that family introduction forever.

'I did, but it's complicated. It's easier to get on with it. See him, and then come home.'

Matthew stared at me with a look that said, *Honey, your family's really peculiar. Is your mum really seeing your dad again after all these years? And if so, do I really have to witness it?*

Well, yes, you do. If I have to suffer through this evening, so do you.

'But the Aussies are batting.'

CHAPTER 27

We arrived at Mum's promptly at seven without too much squawking. Even Lexi, who never normally wants to go anywhere with the family because it's *lame and embarrassing*, was thrilled – and dressed inappropriately for the occasion in a black midriff-baring creation. Angus wasn't overly keen, but Nintendo Switch in hand, he figured being at Nanna's was almost the same as being at home, except with a different fridge and furniture.

Obviously, Matthew would rather have been at home snuffling through sports tweets and preparing himself for tonight's viewing, but he'd stepped up and even showered.

And I was feeling relaxed from the glass of wine I'd had in preparation. As luck would have it, I'd read an article online about new research published by academics in London. They'd found *people who drink wine have significantly sharper thought processes than teetotallers.* That's the spirit!

On the strength of that, I was determined to be pleasant to everyone. I felt the week had been dramatic enough without me becoming hysterical about seeing my father again for the second time in less than a week. It would be hideous, but after some awkward pleasantries and dinner, we could all go home and resume our respective lives. Eventually, Mum would see Dad hadn't changed and would chalk it up to experience. Maybe Christmas two years from now, we'd all sit around eating prawns and laughing about it while each drinking our medicinal wine.

Despite my bravado, I was nervous. My legs could barely carry me when I stepped out of the car. Mum and Dad must have been watching through the sheer curtains, because with several metres still to walk, the front door opened and Mum hurried out, looking gorgeous in a cerulean 1960s-inspired pantsuit complete with beading and fringe work. She'd even been to the hairdressers and was sporting highlights. Mum hadn't had highlights since the early noughties. They'd done a great job.

'Hello, everyone!' Mum rushed to hug us all together at the same time. Somewhat difficult, but she managed, even though she was desperately nervous and shaking.

Then I saw him.

'Katie.' He hugged me tightly.

Mum and Dad, together as a couple, were welcoming us to dinner. It was surreal, like I was caught in some weird *Father Knows Best* television programme.

I stepped back from his embrace and introduced Dad to Matthew. Once inside the house, he handed Matthew a beer and said, 'Been watching the Ashes? The Aussies are batting tonight.'

Hey presto! Matthew and my father instantly bonded over cricket. And I was sure once cricket chatter had been exhausted (which wouldn't be for months), there'd be the state of the economy and lack of rain to discuss. And football. Men!

We were midway through a glass of wine when Robyn walked in, dressed in a red caftan with a yellow hibiscus print.

'What's this?' I asked, staring at her multicoloured hair. 'A wig?'

'All mine,' she said, twirling blue strands around her index finger. 'Got bored. Needed a change.'

I poked her rotund belly. 'This not a big enough change for you? And what's with the bare feet?'

'If you must know, none of my shoes fit. Not only is my stomach bulging but my feet are getting fatter by the minute.'

'Should I shoot them for an Insta post, *reality versus postcard perfect* and all that?'

Robyn's left eye twitched. 'I'm really not in the mood, Kate.' She rubbed her brow. 'But speaking of which, my antenatal post is getting thousands of likes.'

'I noticed, but aren't you worried about the trolls?'

'Trolls?' Mum interrupted. 'I've read some nasty stories. People getting shot and worse,' she tut-tutted.

'What could be worse than being shot?' I muttered.

'Enough of that,' Mum continued. 'Bob, Robyn's here.'

Dad appeared and he and Robyn embraced and started babbling over each other.

I followed Mum into the kitchen.

'Everything okay?' she asked. 'Recovered from birthday drinks? I didn't know what to think when you arrived home in tears. You were in a real state.'

That didn't sound right, but then, memories of that night were hazy, especially towards the end. I only vaguely remembered seeing Mum before falling into bed.

I glanced into the dining room. 'Mum!' The table looked like something out of *Vogue*. On top of a soft sage linen tablecloth, sat iconic green cabbage plates, (definitely new purchases) white linen napkins, and elegant old-fashioned pale-pink wine and water glasses. (More recent purchases?) A magnificent display of greenery, pink wildflowers, and white daisies graced the centre.

'Thoughts?' she asked.

'Stunning, though the candelabras might be overkill,' I said, spying the elaborate pieces with three arms hosting tapered pale-green candles, at each end of the table.

'Nothing like soft candlelight to set the mood,' she trilled.

I ignored her remark.

'And the cabbageware?' Mum continued.

'You've always loved Bordallo Pinheiro. I don't know why you waited so long to buy them.'

She put an arm around me. 'Waiting for the right occasion.'

Together, we carried roast chicken, crispy baked potatoes and sides including green beans, cauliflower and carrots.

Robyn and Dad composed themselves, and we all sat down.

'I almost forgot the gravy.' Mum disappeared into the kitchen and returned moments later with a silver gravy boat. 'And for you, my darling,' she said, stopping behind Lexi, 'my famous vege kebabs.' She placed a small platter in front of her.

Lexi grinned. 'Best nanna ever.'

Dad poured the wine and water, and between us, Mum and I served everyone.

'Mum told me you left Nanna and ran off with another woman,' Lexi said to Dad after she'd polished off two kebabs. 'Where is she now?'

'Enough, Lexi,' I warned.

'What? You asked Nanna and she didn't know either. I'm only trying to help.'

'It's okay, Lexi,' Dad soothed. 'I've always loved your nanna. In fact, we weren't much older than you when we met. Only fourteen.'

'See, Mum,' Lexi beamed. 'Nanna and Pop fell in love just like Romeo and Juliet.'

Matthew gulped his beer and looked at me. 'I'm definitely out of this conversation loop.'

Robyn held up her hand. 'Ditto.'

'But you and Mum didn't start dating until you were at least sixteen, did you, Dad?' I said firmly.

His face pinched in confusion. 'No, we—'

'That's right, love,' Mum cut in. 'Sixteen, but still children. In hindsight, perhaps we rushed into a relationship and marriage too young.'

'I've always loved you, Pip,' Dad declared, eyes misty. 'We just went our separate ways for a time.'

And? I itched to say. *Did Miss Inspirational die? Did she get a better job and eclipse you? What?* But that conversation didn't go anywhere.

Lexi turned to me. 'How come you're not freaking out about Auntie Robyn's hair?'

'I did not freak out about your hair. It's actually growing on me now I've had time to adjust.'

'A pixie cut suits you,' Matthew agreed.

'Did you know babies can be born with teeth?' Robyn spluttered. 'What's the story with that? I'm not showcasing my baby on Insta if they have teeth.'

'So, you're a social influencer, Robbie?' Dad put his knife and fork down. 'What exactly does that mean?'

Mum cleared her throat. 'It means Robyn has a reputation for being an expert in certain areas and can pressure people.' She sipped her wine. 'Isn't that right, love? You post photos of yourself on the internet?'

Robyn frowned. 'It's not just photos of me, and I don't pressure people.'

Mum nodded. 'You're trendy though?'

'You mean she's a trendsetter,' I said. 'Robyn can sway followers to buy the products she endorses.'

Lexi sniggered. 'Trendsetter? How old are you, Mum? Auntie Robyn's an innovator.'

Dad looked to Robyn, bewildered. 'That's your job?'

She nodded. 'I get paid to promote vitamins, honey, picnic rugs. It's lucrative *and* fun.'

'Except for the trolling,' Mum added.

Robyn clenched her jaw. 'Except for the trolling.'

Dad smiled and turned to Mum. 'It's lovely being here tonight with everyone, Pippin-Poodle.'

'Sure is, Bobby-Boy.' Mum had a faraway look in her eye.

Who were they talking to? Their pet dogs? They weren't holding hands but still did a great impression of lovesick teenagers. Every time Dad opened his mouth, Mum giggled and flirted.

Then it was Lexi's turn to hold court. 'I want to be taken seriously at school.' She'd managed to charm both Dad and Matthew into believing she had cut her hair only to avoid being mistaken for an airhead. 'And, Pop, you wouldn't believe the random school sport colours. I mean seriously, who ever made up the colour yellow needs a bullet. It's *so* unflattering.'

'Yellow's better than lime!' Robyn chimed in.

I sat at the table dumbfounded while Lexi explained to the table the hardships of peer group pressure. Mum guffawed like a fool. At least Angus had the sense to put his head down and play his NS.

Meanwhile, Matthew ate another helping of chicken and vegetables. 'Beautiful dinner, Pip,' he said. 'You've outdone yourself tonight.'

Mum smiled and reached to hold Dad's hand.

Yes, it was a lovely meal, but I felt uneasy. Mum was blissfully unaware of the fate that was to befall her when Dad left her a second time. For the moment though, they were simply merry morons. Sure, they'd been divorced a hundred years and were virtual strangers, but that didn't stop them.

Then their lips smacked. Shuddering, I felt my hand reach

for the table jug, compelled by the urge to pour cold water over them. I sighed loudly instead.

After an eternity, they disengaged and beamed contentedly.

Dad clinked his glass against Mum's, like in countless American movies where the father, as head of the family, says he has an important, life-changing announcement to make. Then Dad actually said, 'Thanks for coming tonight. Your mother and I would like to say—' and when he looked at Mum, I knew.

Finally, I realised what this evening was about.

'—we're getting married.'

'Pardon?'

'Katie, your father and I are remarrying. What do you think?'

I couldn't believe my ears. 'So you're not dying? Of cancer?'

Dad threw me a strange look. 'No.'

'It might sound sudden,' Mum continued. 'But we'd like to get married before Christmas—'

'What?' I said, spitting the word out.

'Before Christmas,' Mum repeated.

'Stop saying that.' I pushed my plate forward and leapt up out of my chair, almost pulling the tablecloth and one of the candelabras with me. 'Of all the ridiculous things to do, Mum, why do you have to get married again?' I was circling the table, pacing. 'It didn't work out the first time, remember?' I glared at Robyn. 'Say something.'

She shrugged.

'It did,' Mum insisted. 'We were married eighteen years.'

'Yes, eighteen years – twenty-five years ago,' I fumed. 'You've been divorced longer than you were married. Why do you want to tie yourself down again?'

'The past is the past. We can't change what we've done but we can change what we do now. We're mature adults now and I love your father, and he loves me. We're getting married, Kate, whether you agree or not.'

Strangely, as I was having this conversation with Mum, I imagined the exact same scenario being played out with Lexi in a matter of years – Lexi defiantly standing before me, saying, *I'm in love with Spike/Luke/Hunter (insert appropriate name). We want to be together. We are getting married.* It gave me chills.

I eased myself back into the dining chair. 'Only a week ago, Mum, you said, and I quote, "It's not as if I'm going to do anything silly" and yet here we are. Married before Christmas? How is that even possible?'

Matthew raised his glass. 'Congratulations.'

'Stop,' I shouted, suddenly feeling nauseous. I couldn't see any reason for Mum to marry again. What did she have in mind? A minister? A reception at the local town hall? Speeches? Bridesmaids? The whole shebang?

Then, to my horror, I quickly found out.

'Lexi, darling, I'd love for you to be my bridesmaid.' The words were out there, hanging, for the entire world to hear before I could catch them, put my hand over Mum's mouth and shoot her, or at least kick her very hard in the shins or head. I was numb.

Seconds later Dad said, 'Angus, your nanna and I would like you to be our ring bearer.'

'Ring bearer?' I spluttered.

'Can I choose my own dress, Nanna?' Lexi purred.

'Yes, darling, you can wear whatever you like.'

No. No. No. Why was she saying this? To torment me? I looked around for hidden cameras because surely this was a joke.

I gulped for air. 'This has gone far enough.'

Clearly impatient, Mum's voice was sharp. 'I really don't see what all the fuss is about. Your father and I are getting married – accept it.'

I scowled at Mum, then Dad. 'Be reasonable. It's Christmas.

For starters, you'll never find a venue or celebrant at such short notice.'

'Kate has a point,' Robyn chimed in.

I turned to her. 'At last!'

'Oohh, I'm going to be a bridesmaid, I'm going to be a bridesmaid,' Lexi sang.

'Lex, you're not going to be a bridesmaid because there isn't going to be a wedding. Full stop. End of story. Now, please be quiet. I have a headache.' Which I did. Of all the absurd... my parents remarrying.

'And I get a ring,' Angus said. 'What's a ring bearer? Do I get lollies?'

I was about to explode. 'Shush, Gus.'

'Katie,' Dad said finally, 'if you and Robyn are truly against it, we won't get married.'

'Bob!' Mum shrieked.

'No, love. If it's going to upset everybody, it's not right. The whole idea of us remarrying is to bring the family closer together, not tear us further apart.'

'The most sensible opinion I've heard all night,' I said. 'Why don't you live together and see how it goes? Then, if it works out, maybe in a year or ten, you can think about getting married.'

'Actually, I think it's wonderful,' Robyn said, her eyes sparkling. 'A Christmas wedding. Think of the posts. It will be ah-maaa-zing!'

CHAPTER 28

'I want to talk to you about something,' Matthew said later that night in bed.

I put down my book and turned to face him. 'Please not about my parents.'

'No, but really it's up to them if they want to get married again.'

I shook my head. 'No.'

'You're being very one-eyed, Kate. As Pip said, they're adults. Anyway, it's about the business. An opportunity's come up in Auckland.'

'An opportunity? What kind of opportunity?'

'A contract for a couple of years... give or take.'

'For you to work there? Leave us?'

'Of course not! We'd all go.'

'What?' I blinked. 'Auckland?'

Relocating abroad reared its ugly head every couple of years. I always managed to beat it off with a heavy thick stick. This time would be no different.

'Not now, Matt, especially after the night we've endured. I

can't believe you're even bringing it up. There's the kids' schooling, Mum, Robyn.'

He sighed. 'You're always putting other people first. Always. Except me. You never put me first. I'm always way down on your list of priorities.'

'You, Matthew? What about me? When do I get a look-in? It's not as if I'm swinging from the chandeliers having the time of my life. I'm barely hanging on.' Wobbling on a tightrope without a safety net below.

'No matter what I say, you always manage to turn the conversation back to you. Your needs. Your family. What about me? You won't even listen.'

I pushed my back up further against the bedhead. 'I am listening. Go to New Zealand. Stay there for all I care. It's not like I'll miss the sex.'

'Very mature, Kate. Very mature.' He exhaled. 'What sex?'

'Exactly! You want me to uproot the family, move overseas and we don't even sleep together anymore.'

He raised an eyebrow. 'Wow, this conversation escalated quickly.'

'It's not a joke, Matt.'

'I know. But why would we have sex? You're always angry.'

'Not true. I'd call it politely indifferent. Anyway, what about you? You're never here, and when you are you're only interested in the cricket, or tennis, or whatever sport is on TV.'

'And you're always on about your mother or Robyn or the kids.'

'Ah, that would be because they're my family. But you pay no attention. And if you haven't noticed, Angus is developing a temper, Lexi has a strange boyfriend, Mum's remarrying my father, and as for Robyn... It's too much. And it's fucking Christmas! We don't have fairy lights. Or a tree. And you...

you've not even asked about the magazine. I don't remember the last time you told me you loved—'

'You're ranting. Again.' Matthew rolled over as far away and quickly as he could.

And I lay thinking. Thinking about how it had come to this.

❄

Saturday morning was no better. Matthew wasn't talking to me because of my ranting; Lexi wasn't talking to me because, once again, I'd destroyed her life – this time by not letting her be my mother's bridesmaid; and Angus thought somewhere along the line, he'd been diddled out of sweets.

But even though I was the wife/mother/daughter/sister from hell, it was still up to me to find clean clothes for everyone and tidy the house. I also had to get Angus to soccer on time. Matthew couldn't take him – again. Why? A Christmas charity golf tournament with clients. Convenient? I think so.

Cups of tea and juice were banged down on the table and toast was flung in the general direction of plates. The only ones oblivious to the hostility were the marauding animals awaiting whatever scraps fell their way.

'Angus, don't feed Rupert under the table.'

He glared at me and kept passing crusts to the panting dog.

'So, you're playing the Cowboys today? I'm sure you'll beat them,' I said, hoping to win back his love.

'I'll come to soccer this morning, Mum,' Lexi said.

'Pardon?'

'Soccer. I'll come. That's okay, isn't it?'

I regarded her suspiciously. Normally on a weekend, she was never out of bed before ten, yet here she was, dressed and at the breakfast table at seven fifteen.

'She only wants to because Hunter's brother plays for the

Cowboys and we're playing at their home ground,' Angus said. 'Lexi and Hunter kissing in a tree—'

'Angus!' Lexi and I shrieked at the same time.

Dressed in lurid checked golfing trousers, Matthew silently got up from the table, kissed Lexi and Angus and stalked off.

I headed upstairs and walked past Lexi's room. A piggery. Past Angus's room. Ditto. I wandered into our bedroom, made the bed, picked up Matthew's wet towel and clothes, then showered. My mind was racing like I was on speed. Not that I'd ever taken speed. I didn't even know where to buy speed. I'm sure Lexi would know. And Hunter.

Driving to soccer, Lexi studied her phone, Angus played with his Nintendo and I had time to think. Like it or not, Mum and Dad would probably get married again. Mum was determined. But why so soon? And at Christmas when there was so much else going on, not that I'd planned anything.

And Matthew? I wondered if he was serious about the move. Perhaps he was saying it to wind me up further. Theoretically, he could commute. In hindsight, maybe last night wasn't the best time to mention our non-existent sex life.

And on top of that we were having dinner at Fern's. I wondered whether Matthew would even come. He might have already booked his flight to Auckland, leaving me alone to deal with the kids and pets. So much for a pleasant weekend. Yep! Old dramas moved down the list of importance as new ones took their place.

CHAPTER 29

'A bit dramatic, don't you think?' Robyn barked into my mobile as I drove into the car park.

'Pardon?'

'Your exit last night? Dramatic. After Mum had gone to so much effort, too.'

'I was choking.'

'On raspberry cheesecake?'

'I had to leave. Don't you think it's odd? Mum and Dad have been divorced all this time and suddenly they're remarrying?' I turned to Lexi and Angus. They'd pulled out their earphones and were hitting each other. 'Would you two please stop? I can't hear myself think.' I sounded like my mother. My mother when Robyn and I were teens, and she was still married to Dad.

Grunting, they reconnected their earphones, moved as far as possible away from each other and resumed their solo immersive entertainment experience.

'Each to his own,' Robyn persisted.

'How can you be so blasé? They were grinning, giggling and holding hands like a pair of love-struck fools. Obscene. Finishing each other's sentences. The nicknames... ugh. Nasty. It's like the last twenty-five years didn't happen. But they did, Rob. He's broken her heart before. What's to stop him from doing it again?'

'I have my own dramas.'

'These are our parents.'

'I know, but I have other things on my mind.'

'Like what? Your next Instagram post?'

'Steady! I'm pregnant. Besides, not just any old post. I've been offered a sponsorship deal for baby formula.'

'Robyn!'

'What?'

'It'll be controversial. You've already had backlash over even hinting new parents embrace formula.'

'I never said they *should* embrace it.'

'But you didn't say they shouldn't.'

'It's not my place.'

'Exactly. Besides, you haven't even had the baby yet.'

My patience with Robyn was wearing thin. 'We'll talk about this later.' I put the phone back in my bag and stepped out of the car. Lexi and Angus quickly disappeared into a sea of children. Then I saw Arnaud.

Despite everything, a wave of relief washed over me as soon as I saw him. I dropped my shoulders, the stress disappeared, and I smiled. With his three-day (maybe more) growth, he looked especially rugged and outdoorsy.

'Hey,' I said, waving.

'What's happening with you?' he asked, as he pumped up soccer balls.

'You really don't want to know.'

Arnaud threw a ball at me. 'Try me.'

'Okay... My parents are getting married again. To each other.' I bounced the firm ball on the barren oval.

'But this is wonderful news! The whole family can be reunited.'

'No, it's a nightmare. I want to die.'

'There must be an easier solution?'

'I guess I could kill them, but then there's the whole prison thing...'

'*Oui.* The food, exercise yard and non-parole period. I do not think it would be so great.' Arnaud paused. 'So maybe you could accept it?'

'Pooh to that. They've seen each other like three times in twenty-five years and now they're getting married. *Married*, for God's sake! Before Christmas!'

He put his hand on my shoulder. 'Maybe, but sometimes you just know.'

'Sorry, Arnaud. I shouldn't be dumping this on you, but you did ask.'

'Please. I am 'appy for you to dump.' He went back to pumping air into the black-and-white balls.

'Mum's normally so sensible, so together. Yet when she's with Dad... well, the thing is, they look like a couple. A very happy couple, unfortunately,' I said, mesmerised by Arnaud's muscleman arms and hands.

He stopped mid-pump. 'If it makes you feel better, their euphoria probably won't last more than six months. They too, will soon be immersed in the unpleasantness of everyday life like everyone else.'

'I guess...'

Arnaud smiled. 'Tell me what happened after I left the pub.'

I recoiled at the memory. 'The party fizzed once you left.'

'You looked to be enjoying yourself. What 'appened?'

'Nothing.'

Arnaud put his hands on his hips.

'Why? What did you hear?'

'There was a scuffle between Mara and Graeme, and she walked out, never to return to *Delicious Bites* again.'

'Well, if they scuffled, I didn't see it.'

'But?'

'But, yes, Mara's taken stress leave and Fern's worried.'

'And?'

'And nothing. Honestly. That's all I know. At the pub everyone seemed to be getting along. You'd never have known Graeme and Mara had been fighting earlier in the day, and I'd never have suspected they were having an affair. At least that's the rumour.'

'Mara? I thought she'd have more style than to make music with 'im.'

'It's gossip.'

'*Oui*, but some truth, maybe? Grafton has been through most women at Image Ink. Has he not tried with you?'

'I'm a mother.' I tittered nervously. Time to change the subject. 'You know enough about me and my dysfunctional family to write a book, and I know practically nothing about you.'

He stared at me. 'I am boring and now I must warm up the boys.'

'Okey-doke,' I said as he walked away. Who says okey-doke, dingbat? (Or dingbat, for that matter?)

I turned. Lexi was beside me. 'You look weird.'

'Lexi! I was wondering where you were.' A straight-out lie.

'You were looking at Angus's coach the same way the girls at school look at Hunter.'

'I certainly was not.'

'You had the faraway look in your eyes of girls in love.'

'Don't be silly.'

'Gross, Mum. You're married.'

'You have no idea what you are talking about.' I didn't need Lexi telling me I was gross. Or pathetic. I already knew that.

'I wondered why you got so dressed up this morning.'

'Nonsense.' I glanced down at myself, shocked to find I was wearing ludicrously inappropriate blue suede sandals. Come to think of it, I had spent several extra minutes blow-drying my hair and applying mascara and lipstick. I hadn't even realised. Looking around, I noticed all the other mothers were wearing sneakers. 'Did you find Hunter?'

'Nope.'

Had I really dressed up for Arnaud? I hadn't gone out of my way to wear heels and apply make-up this morning. It wasn't something I'd consciously thought about and conspired to do. But there was no denying the effort. I put it down to the fact I was working every day. It had become a habit. That was my excuse, and I was sticking to it.

CHAPTER 30

'Welcome, welcome!' Fern ushered Matthew and me into her home. 'It's been too long.'

I'd only met Terry a couple of times, years ago, and barely recognised him when Fern reintroduced her 'devilishly handsome' husband to me, mainly because he had stacked on at least twenty kilos since I'd last seen him.

Her house was picture perfect. I felt like I'd stepped into a *Vogue Living* French provincial – no, Hamptons – feature. I couldn't imagine her children getting messy and spilling chocolate milkshake on the oriental rugs, or dog hairs littering the cream suede lounge.

In fact, apart from the photos and artwork on the fridge, it was impossible to believe four children lived here – until they appeared in person wearing gorgeous designer pyjamas. After the introductions, Lily, Rose, Thorn and Leaf (a flora obsession, obviously) disappeared with quiet orderliness. Lily, the eldest, carried baby Leaf in her arms.

If it were my house, Angus and Lexi would have been interrupting every few minutes with tears and tales of torture.

We settled on the beautiful cream sofa. In the corner of the room stood a magnificent floor-to-ceiling green Christmas tree, festooned with fairy lights and sparkling baubles in pastel shades of sage and pink. At least twenty perfectly wrapped presents sat on the floor around it.

'Your tree looks stunning,' I said.

Terry passed me a glass of wine. 'We like to put it up early in the hope the kids will embrace the festive spirit and be kind to each other.'

Fern rubbed his arm and smiled.

'Ah, so that's what we need to do, Matt.' I sipped my drink. 'Our two are constantly snarking at each other.'

'End of year snarkiness gets to everyone,' Fern sympathised.

'Yeah, but the tree might temper it down.'

As I reached to take a cracker and cheese from the table, I spied a glossy photography book, *My Eye, My Lens*. Not just any photography book, however. The photographer was Sarah Stanthorpe – a woman who'd been in my year at college. We weren't friends.

'What's this?' I pointed to the publication.

'Thought you'd like that,' Fern answered.

Like was unquestionably the wrong word. Having a collection of my photographs published – in full colour, no less – had been my dream. My heart sank further with each passing second. It was agony. And Sarah? She'd thought she was better than everyone else in the course and didn't shy away from telling us. She'd undermined my confidence with snide remarks like, *Kate, don't you know anything about film or shutter speeds? Why are you wasting your time and everyone else's?*

I couldn't believe those same feelings of inadequacy were resurfacing now, years later. I wished it was my book sitting on Fern's coffee table.

'I've been meaning to tell you about Sarah.' Fern halted

briefly. 'I was at her book launch recently. Her publisher, Venus, is in the same building as Image Ink, sixth floor.'

I felt ill. Gulped my Shiraz.

'She's certainly hit the big time.' Fern exhaled. 'Was overseas for a few years. These photos are a compilation of her wildlife photography. I think she's planning a themed series – wildlife, beaches, babies...'

Matthew picked it up. 'Isn't that what you've always wanted to do, Kate?'

I shrugged. He was right, of course. I was sick with envy.

'Sarah's married and has kids,' Fern continued.

I smiled. Yet another superwoman who could do it all and have it all.

'But just before the launch, she left her husband. She's dating a twenty-two-year-old landscaper.' Fern giggled. 'Can you believe it?'

Terry grinned. 'Some people!'

I wrenched the book from Matthew's hands. 'Not that I'm bitter and twisted.'

'Not at all,' Matthew agreed.

I was desperate to run off to the bathroom and examine it in all its gory detail, but three sets of eyes were upon me, waiting for me to speak. I opened the first page and quickly snapped it shut. I couldn't do it to myself. Not here. Not with Fern watching.

'Take it home if you like,' she encouraged. 'Have a close look. You'll be surprised.'

'It's okay.' I put it back on the table.

'Go on,' Matthew urged. 'Maybe it will inspire you.'

I glared at him, signalling the end of that conversation.

Sarah and Fern were living the dream. Terry obviously doted on Fern. From where I sat, they were the perfect couple living in the perfect home with perfect (and quiet) children. And an impressive Christmas tree to boot. So, Terry had love handles, it was clear Fern adored him.

'Tell me how you're getting along at *Delicious Bites*?' Fern asked as we dined on yellowfin tuna in white bean sauce. 'It's hectic, I know. Sorry I haven't been more available. How was your meeting with Dana yesterday?'

'Great. We've worked out the first seven days of the nativity calendar.'

'The what?' Matthew asked.

Fern turned to him. 'Hasn't Kate told you? Every day in December, she'll be responsible for posting a different festive photo montage on our online magazine.'

'Like what?' Terry asked.

'Anything Kate wants,' Fern replied. 'It's her baby.'

'Will you be working on weekends and Christmas Day?' Matthew asked me, sounding confused.

I shook my head. 'I'll take photos in advance and schedule publication for the same time every day. Not as time consuming as it sounds. Much of it will be research... putting photos together in an ordered sequence. The online calendar is a side project for when I'm not trailing Graeme around.' To Fern, I asked, 'Speaking of which, how does he feel about it?'

She rubbed her nose. 'I haven't told him.'

'Fern!'

'The nativity calendar is my brainwave, an add-on for Christmas. Graeme rarely checks the online magazine. He has a vague idea, but is so busy...' She trailed off. 'Besides, what he doesn't know, can't hurt him.' She flashed me a smile. 'Or you.'

I wasn't so sure.

Fern cleared her throat. 'I know how impressive your photography is, Kate, but the truth is, Graeme doesn't want the competition. He can be a bit precious.'

'A *bit*? And don't you think he's a little demented as well?'

'Don't know about demented. He's demanding...' Fern took a moment. 'And he can be unstable at times.'

Terry smirked. 'Doesn't it make you feel proud to work in an industry where unstable nutcases can still be respected and succeed?'

'I guess.' The flashback... why had I allowed Graeme to kiss me? Why hadn't I listened to my inner voice? I'd been wary of Graeme from the start. His superior attitude, his arrogant manner.

Table conversations continued as I searched the deepest recesses of my mind to figure out exactly what had gone on between Graeme and me, but I couldn't remember anything more than a rushed kiss.

I tuned in as Terry and Matthew talked cricket. 'What about that batting debacle last night?' and then the economy: 'What's the government doing?' I listened but felt outside the moment, like one of those people who have near-death experiences and find themselves hovering above their body. My head was spinning.

CHAPTER 31

Once home, Matthew was keen to prove we were capable of a sex life, but I felt too guilty to take advantage of his new-found libido. I massaged his back and neck, and he was asleep within minutes. Meanwhile, I was wide awake.

Graeme! Technically, if I'm to be honest, I kissed him as much as he kissed me. I lunged for him in the pub as all those horrible insecure feelings of loneliness and unattractiveness bubbled to the surface. I'd felt especially alone because it was my birthday and Matthew was away. But that's no excuse. It's pathetic to think after a few wines I could be swept along and end up kissing and groping him in the back seat of my car.

Or was it a taxi?

Where had that memory sprung from? What car? When? Oh God, was it so much worse than I'd first thought?

I climbed out of bed and began pacing, walking from room to room, picking up toys, dog biscuits, sweeping up rabbit droppings – anything to avoid going back to bed and thinking about the inevitable: Sarah's book, and the Graeme/car combo desperate to dance back into my head. For some reason, I'd been in the back seat of a car with Graeme, and we were... well, I can't exactly remember what we were doing. Suddenly, I was very worried...

In the study, I turned on the computer. It had been three days since I'd checked my emails. There were thirty-four new messages. Without reading them, I deleted twenty-eight dubious ones. The rest were from friends. One was from Matthew.

Katie, hi gorgeous. Sorry I'm away for your birthday. I love you so much. I hate leaving you. It's tough, I know it's not easy on you either. Sorry I blew it about Lexi's hair. You couldn't have done anything to stop her. She's a teenager and not always going to behave the way we want her to. Looking forward to spending the whole weekend with you – hope it's not booked out with social engagements. Love you, hon. xx

I stared at Matthew's email, tears running down my cheeks, feeling like the biggest arse ever. I closed the laptop.

Back in bed, I wriggled over to Matthew and snuggled up to him. He didn't respond. Sound asleep. But his warmth felt lovely.

The next thing I knew it was morning and Matthew was walking into the bedroom holding a cup of tea for me. He sat down on the edge of the bed. 'I hate it when we fight. I know you're upset, and I haven't been around much lately, but I do love you.'

'I read your email, Matt. I am a cold-hearted bitch. I'm sorry.'

'You're not cold-hearted.' He leaned over and kissed me. 'Or a bitch. But we don't get enough time alone. It'd be nice to have a conversation without being interrupted all the time.'

Matthew kissed me again. 'I think' – the landline started ringing – 'Just a sec.' He picked it up. 'Hello... yep.' He passed the phone to me. 'Pip.'

'Hi, Mum.'

'Don't *hi Mum* me, Katie. Your behaviour the other night was appalling. I expected an apology from you yesterday.'

'I was in shock. I'm still in shock. I can't believe you're going through with this.'

'Is it so wrong of me to want to marry your father again? Is it? You're breaking my heart.'

I tried to imagine myself in the same position, if Matthew and I were to reunite, years after our divorce. Would I marry Matthew again? Would he marry me?

❄

'Let it go,' Matthew said to me later at breakfast. 'You're upset, but it's her life.'

'Mum was doing well on her own. She has it all: independence, financial freedom; a free spirit living the life she wants.'

'But *she* wants Bob.'

'I get that, Matthew! I just can't understand it. She has everything she wants already.'

'Obviously not.'

'Well, if that's true then why not live with the man? Why go through the hoopla of a wedding?'

'It's not about us. It's about your parents.'

'Forget it. You wouldn't understand.'

'And you say Lexi doesn't talk anymore. I wonder where she gets it from.'

'Has she thought about the fact she's leaving her perfectly acceptable life behind and starting who knows what kind of life? I hate it. It'll all end in tears.' I stifled a cry.

'It might.' Matthew's voice was soft. 'But then again, maybe it won't. Who knows?'

'I do. I've lived through their marriage before.'

'They're adults,' Matthew reminded me. 'They know what they're doing.'

'Do they? Do they really know what they're doing? I wonder.'

❄

Later as I sorted several loads of dirty washing, I smelled something unfamiliar. It was more than the combination of dirty soccer socks, perspiration and the general unclean smell the clothes basket usually offered. Definitely a fragrance. Not mine. Probably Lexi's. I pulled out her school shirt and sniffed. No, her shirt smelled of the citrus orange scent Lexi always wore. I piled the clothes into the washing machine and stopped when I reached one of Matthew's business shirts. Aha! I sniffed and an overwhelming aroma hit me.

Was I was imagining it? No. A flowery scent had definitely attached itself to Matthew's clothing. Perfume. I recoiled. I took a step back and slumped against the washing machine. I could almost feel my heart breaking as a tsunami of sadness washed over me. I thought about Mum and her feelings of emptiness and despair after Dad left. Then I thought about Matthew and me. Despite making a commitment to love and stay with me forever, if he was involved with another woman, it meant he'd given up.

What was I thinking? I'd kissed Graeme or Graeme had kissed me. Either way, it's not as if I was a paragon of virtue. Talk about double standards.

Still, when I saw Matthew relaxing in the lounge room with his feet up on the coffee table, eating Pringles and watching cricket, I wanted to destroy him; to rant about the perfume on his shirt, to fling it at him and accuse him of having an affair. But I was being irrational. Instead, I picked a dirty sock up off the floor and threw it at him.

'Steady.' He looked up at me, picking up the Pringles that had fallen out of his hand. 'You want me to do the washing?'

'No. I want...' *I want to know whose perfume is on your shirt and ask if you're having an affair.* 'Nothing.'

'What's up? Is this about Pip? I'm guessing it can't be about me. I never get a look-in.'

'Matt...' I couldn't fight anymore. I had no energy left. 'Let's not.'

'I know, I know. You don't need me causing trouble as well. I can't help wondering if you wouldn't be happier on your own, and that when you talk about Pip losing her independence, you're really speaking about yourself.'

He paused, then found his voice again. 'Why do you go to the ends of the earth for others but not for us?'

'What about you? Purposely cutting yourself off from me so when you leave it will be easier on the family.'

'You're not making any sense. Is this about Auckland?'

Auckland! As if! I was kind of hoping it would disappear, like many things in my life: the kiss with Graeme, Sarah's book, Mum, Robyn... my flabby thighs. 'My mind's been on other things.'

'Always is.'

'Okay... If you want the truth, I think it's a stupid idea. There, I've thought about it. I'm not going to live in New Zealand, and neither are the children.'

'That's it? No discussion? A straight-out no?'

'Yes, a straight-out no,' I yelled.

He shook his head. 'There's no pleasing you, is there?'

'Are you getting a divorce?' Angus had wandered into the room, one hand fiddling with his Nintendo, one hand fiddling with something down the front of his pants.

'Divorce? We're having a discussion, Angus.' I picked up Cleopatra and hugged her close. 'Grown-ups quarrel sometimes, just like you and Lexi do.'

'And on that note...' Matthew gathered up his Pringles and iPad and vanished.

Surprisingly, we didn't talk for the remainder of the evening. I had washing to hang, clothes to iron, year three homework to correct, the usual.

Finally, I curled up with Angus and fell asleep listening to *The Mapmaker Chronicles*. I managed to wake up long enough to crawl into the marital bed around two in the morning. Another weekend closer to Christmas and we still hadn't put up the tree or decorated the house.

CHAPTER 32

Divorce was still on Angus's mind when I dropped him at school Monday morning.

'I don't mind,' he said. 'Jack thinks it's great. He has lots more toys, lollies and everything. Are you coming in to see Mrs Lombardy?'

'No, Angus, why—' And then I remembered the note she'd sent home last week requesting a meeting with me about the Christmas concert. 'Yes, of course.' I hesitated at the kiss-and-drop zone before deciding it would be social suicide to stop. I whizzed around the corner, narrowly missing three chattering children jaywalking, and parked.

At the school gate, I was blocked by eager year six students raising money for the school band excursion. I bought five raffle tickets then put in an order for two dozen Christmas crackers – fundraiser for covered walkways – and quickly made my way down to Mrs Lombardy's class before any other children could nab me. I had no more cash in my wallet.

The classroom door was locked. As there were still a few minutes before school started, I waited and watched as Angus kicked pebbles with his shoes.

'Don't do that, Gus.' It made no difference. He continued kicking stones.

I walked towards the administration building. Turns out Mrs Lombardy was away today. I left a note with the school's executive assistant and noticed a pile of *Living Christmas Tree* brochures on his desk.

'Interested?' he asked. 'We're raising money for new after-school care equipment.'

'Why not?' I slipped a brochure into my bag and scooted out the door. 'Angus, remember you're going to after-school care this afternoon.' I have no idea whether he heard me or not, but five other Anguses in the playground turned to look at me.

❄

Sarah's book was waiting for me on the workbench in the studio, along with a Post-it note from Fern: *K, Look. Later, F.* I pushed it aside and got on with preparing the set for Graeme's next shoot, '*Bush Magic: An Outback Christmas*'.

After I'd completed my to-do list, and with Graeme and Mara still missing, I played with the tripod and Hasselblad. Having the cameras hooked up to a computer made the shots instant and accessible.

I arranged watermelon pieces with blueberries and strawberries on a white plate and snapped off several photos. Then I got creative with chilled beetroot soup. But I didn't stop there. The all-white paper lanterns, damask napkins, elegant glassware and delicate porcelain, was begging for attention. I just needed to throw in splashes of red – Christmas bush, flowering gum, and bottlebrush. Next, I retrieved the white Christmas tree (meringue tower) and white chocolate cake from the cold room to complete the picture.

Three hours later, having taken too many photos to count, I was feeling inspired and confident.

At my workbench, I ran a hand over the cover of Sarah's book. I opened it and stared at the acknowledgements page. A hint of a smile crossed my lips. No mention of friends, only colleagues and several editors at Venus Publishing. At least I had friends. I glanced at my watch. How did it get to two o'clock already? I didn't have time to look at Sarah's vanity project now. I needed to chase up print details with Fern.

She wasn't in, so I popped the best of my test shots for Graeme's shoot on her desk and headed across the street to buy a sandwich.

In the queue, I recognised a voice I hadn't heard in years: Sarah Stanthorpe.

'Kate, after all this time.'

Too stunned to respond, I said nothing.

'I was shocked to hear you were working for Fern. I'd have thought she'd have called me first. After all, her magazines are prized for their consistent high quality. I'm not suggesting you're not up to it, Kate, but I *am* published. Of course, I wouldn't have accepted such a lowly position.' She paused. 'How are you, by the way? You look tired.'

Cool and calm, I finally answered. 'Sarah, nice to see you again.' Though Fern had told me Sarah's publishers occupied the same building, I never imagined I'd be standing face to face with her.

'Having lunch with my editor.' Sarah waved to a nondescript, middle-aged man with a goatee sitting at a window table. 'Did Fern tell you I have a three-book deal?'

A solid kick in the guts. Three books! 'I'm pleased for you,' I lied through gritted teeth. The queue was very long. There were still four people ahead of me.

'You had dreams of publishing a book, didn't you? Or was it a gallery you wanted to open?'

'I can't quite remember.' I felt numb. Numb with humiliation. Sarah used to accuse me of having *delusions of grandeur* back when we were at college. She was implying much the same now.

'I thought you'd abandoned your photographic aspirations for a life of domestic bliss – or should that be drudgery?'

Sarah was still acting like a queen bee, fifteen years later.

'And now here you are.' She coughed. 'Food photography, so dreary, don't you agree?'

I was saved by my ringing mobile. 'Excuse me.' I reached inside my bag.

'Mrs Cavendish? It's Tania Westley from Lexi's school.'

'Mrs Westley?' I cupped my hand over the phone. 'My daughter's school,' I told Sarah.

'Enjoy.' She flapped a hand and sauntered to her table.

'Everything okay?' I asked.

'Mrs Cavendish, I'm calling to ask you the same. From what Lexi tells me, on the very rare occasion she attends school, you are very ill. Almost dead, in fact.'

'Really?'

'Yes, and she's been taking rather a lot of time off to care for you. Lexi was about to leave school again when I suggested we call you first. But Lexi assures me she needs to leave right now to give you a sponge bath and change your bedclothes.'

'Is that so?' I walked out of the café so I could hear properly. I cringed, wondering who else was listening on the other side of the line. All the teachers in the staffroom were no doubt having a great giggle. The least of my concerns. 'What else has Lexi told you?'

'After your affair with the gardener—'

'We don't have a gardener!'

'Lexi's father left, and you had a mental and physical breakdown.'

'Hence why she needs to change my bedclothes?' Patrons at an outside table looked up from their lunch in surprise.

'Exactly.'

'This won't happen again I can assure you. Lexi won't be taking any more time off for at least a few years. I'll be there in thirty minutes.'

I'd kill her, that's what I'd do – as soon as I recovered from the shock of Lexi telling her principal I was having sex with our non-existent gardener.

Back inside, I ran up the stairs two steps at a time.

'Kate, have you got a moment?' It was Fern.

'Not really. Lexi's pulled a prank at school. I have to leave.'

'You will be back, won't you?' It was Graeme. 'We have a shoot at Palm Beach tomorrow, and I know how much you're looking forward to it – natural light and all.'

'Ignore him, Kate. Everything okay with Lexi?'

'Yes, though she'll be grounded till she's twenty-five.' I fiddled with my shoulder bag and keys while Graeme conspicuously checked his watch at the studio door.

I hurried past him, impatient to sort out my wayward daughter.

CHAPTER 33

Half an hour later, I was face to face with Lexi's principal.

'It's not only about Lexi skipping school, Mrs Cavendish. It's a combination of several things, I'm afraid. Her hair, her uniform, her general attitude.'

Lexi was sitting outside Mrs Westley's office. She had spiked what little hair she had left with what looked like an entire jar of gel, her uniform was two sizes too small, and her expression? Well, let's just say I wasn't going to be receiving flowers from my only daughter any time soon.

'Lexi, please go back to class while I chat with your mum,' Mrs Westley instructed.

'But there's only half an hour left,' Lexi moaned.

'Lexi, manners! I'll be waiting for you after school's finished,' I said.

Without a backward glance, she sauntered down the corridor.

'Lexi started as one of our brighter students,' Mrs Westley said as she ushered me into her office and closed the door, 'but this term her grades have slipped significantly.'

Sitting on a bright-red chair in front of her desk, I peered out the window across a grassed courtyard with benches and towering jacaranda trees, then at the huge floor-to-ceiling bookshelves which took up an entire side wall. So many books.

I listened as Mrs Westley spoke, ashamed I hadn't kept a closer eye on my daughter. Mortified Lexi had told her teachers – and who knew who else – I'd had an affair with the gardener and was now in the throes of a breakdown. Of course, no one believed her (I hoped) but that's how rumours started.

'Is anything happening at home that might help us understand Lexi's behaviour?'

'No. Nothing's changed in Lexi's home life. All much the same as it has been. Her grandmother is getting married to her grandfather again, which is slightly unusual, but Lexi seems happy about it. She doesn't tell me much anymore. Keeps to herself when she's at home.'

Taking a breath, I glanced around the room. Mrs Westley's desk was pleasantly cluttered, but not chaotic: lots of handwritten foolscap pages and several Post-it notes on one side, together with several educational tomes; an open laptop, two coffee mugs, a small vase of colourful garden flowers, and an apple. There were also several brightly coloured stress balls in a blue ceramic bowl, and one of those fabulous pin-art toys where you use your hands (or face) to create instant 3D art. (I wonder where the one Santa had given Lexi a few years ago had gone.)

'And?' She looked at me expectantly.

'Lexi talks to her friends mostly, and she's been seeing a boy, boyfriend maybe? Even though I think she's too young. And then there's her mobile. She's always on the phone, talking or texting.'

'In the past month alone,' Mrs Westley read from notes, 'Lexi has missed in excess of nine complete days of school.'

'Goodness.' Was that the best I could come up with? Goodness.

'I must say, I'm surprised you haven't noticed.'

'Well, I work during the day. I've started this new job and—'

'I see.'

'But I try to keep tabs on her.'

'She's got schoolwork to catch up on. Several missed assignments need to be completed if she's to have any chance of passing this term, which is less than three weeks away.'

Avoiding eye contact, I replied, 'I'll see Lexi completes them all. Definitely.'

Mrs Westley handed me several reams of paper. 'I'll email you the rest. Lexi's teachers will make sure she doesn't leave school before home time unless she has a valid excuse, but you need to establish firm house rules as well.'

'Yes,' I said quietly. 'I don't seem to connect with her anymore. She's got new friends... her schoolwork is slipping. It was so easy before—'

'Before she turned thirteen and was a tangle of hormones, rebellious compulsions, social anxieties and academic pressures?'

'That about sums it up.' I forced a smile. 'I feel like I'm walking a tightrope with her the whole time. Nothing I say or do is ever right.'

'My advice? Listen to her. Try to remain calm and open-minded. Walk beside her when you can and try to remember the teenage years are a phase. Sooner or later we all outgrow them. They wouldn't be kids if they didn't give their parents and teachers hell. In my experience, girls rebel because they either want more or less parental control over their lives. The key is understanding their behaviour *before* trying to change it.'

I stood up, nodded and bit my bottom lip. As I turned to go, my gaze was drawn to a large purple ball in the corner near the door. 'Is that a... fitball?'

Mrs Westley clasped her hands together. 'Yes, and in answer to your unasked question, I do sit on it. But not during school hours.' She paused, then whispered, 'At least, not anymore. Fitballs require a certain level of stability and alertness. I've been caught off guard in the past.'

I smiled weakly.

'Take care. Don't worry too much.' She rested her hand on my shoulder. 'Lexi's not the first teenager who's skipped school... or imagined her mother was having an affair. Think back to your own adolescence—'

I stared out the window and sighed.

'Remember both the positive and negative messages you received from your parents and strive not to repeat their mistakes or to share their unhealthy attitudes.'

'I'll try,' I replied, my voice cracking with emotion.

'Mrs Cavendish, be as healthy a role model as best you can—'

What? Did she have hidden cameras on me, twenty-four-seven?

'Get to know Lexi's new friends. Invite them over—'

Minus the vodka.

'—Be honest with her. And remember,' she encouraged, 'when all else fails, breathe.'

❄

It was three twenty. I had a few minutes before Lexi was due out of class. I rang Matthew but was immediately diverted to voicemail. I tried him on his mobile. Same response. I tried again. I was persistent if nothing else.

He finally answered with, 'Yes!' Clearly distracted.

'Lexi's been skipping school. I've just finished meeting with her principal.'

I could hear Matthew tapping a pen. 'Has Lexi said why?'

'Nope.'

'I'm about to go into a meeting. Take her home and talk—'

'It's the middle of the afternoon. I need to get back to work.'

'Kate, where are your priorities? You can't possibly think taking photos of salad is more important than sorting Lexi out.' There was a moment of silence followed by, 'What happens to Gus when you can't pick him up from school?'

Had Matthew been living under a rock? 'If he doesn't have an after-school activity and Mum can't pick him up, he goes into after-school care, and I pick him up on the way home. And after-school care is where he's headed today. Silence. 'Matt? You know all this. Don't make me feel guiltier than I already am.'

'Sorry. Yes. My mind's been elsewhere. Work's hectic.'

'Auckland?'

'Maybe. Kate, things are stressful for us right now, and with the two of us employed full time as well, Lexi and Gus are being overlooked.'

'So it's my fault?'

'I didn't say that, but I earn enough for the family. You don't have to work, at least not full time.'

'But I want to. I want to feel productive again. Maybe even proud of myself. Besides, it's only until Christmas. Maybe you could cut your hours?'

Matthew sighed and we ended our unsettling conversation.

I set off in search of Lexi and spotted her minutes later: the attitude, slouched shoulders. Silently, I bundled her into the car.

'This is *so* embarrassing, Mother.' She huffed, then huffed some more. 'Are we going home?'

'Not yet. You'll have to come into *Delicious Bites* with me.'

Lexi rolled her eyes. 'Really?'

'Yes!' I couldn't trust Lexi at home by herself, so that's all there was to it. 'Are you wearing your retainer?' I knew she wasn't.

She unzipped her backpack, retrieved it and loudly pushed it inside her mouth. 'Happy?'

'Why on earth would you tell your teachers I'm having an affair with the gardener?'

'Gives them a rev… Do you know how boring geometry is?'

'I don't care!' I counted to ten in my head. I remember a similar conversation with my own parents. '*I'm going to be a photographer. Why do I need to pass maths?*' It was right before Mum and Dad split. I had a horrible feeling history was about to repeat itself. Not that she was responsible for the problems Matthew and I were having, but the whole scenario seemed too familiar. Too close to home.

I thought about Blanche Ebbutt's advice in *Don'ts for Wives* – yes, I'd been reading it. How could I not? It's such a stupid book, it forces you to take notice. In fact, I'd come to consider Blanche rather like my own personal Dalai Lama. During those moments when I knew I truly wanted to become a better person, a more rational and loving human, I thought to myself, what would Blanche do in this situation? I knew for a fact in this case, she'd say, silence is the best answer. Still, I was furious.

'That's no reason to invent lies or skip school. And last week with the drinking… You don't get it, do you? Wake up to yourself. You're not a baby anymore.'

She smirked. 'Okay.'

But I wasn't finished. 'I've had it, Lexi. I'm not your nursemaid.'

'So stop treating me like a child.'

'I'll stop treating you like a child when you start acting responsibly.' I breathed deeply, exhaled and pivoted. 'Lex, is there something else going on? Are you being bullied? At school? Online? You can tell me. I overheard you and your friends.'

'Huh?'

'When I drove you to the movies.'

She blinked. 'You shouldn't have been eavesdropping.'

'You haven't answered my question.'

'No, I'm not being bullied.' She shook her head. 'Drop it, okay? You've got no idea about the pressure. The anxiety and stress to make sure everything you do is perfect. The perfect clothes. The perfect hair. Having the best assignment no matter what the subject because everyone is using Canva, CapCut or ChatGPT to make theirs perfect too. It's exhausting and terrifying, especially when you have to share in class. I'm always anxious that my best effort isn't good enough. So why try?'

I dipped my head. Lexi was experiencing the exact pressure I was at the magazine because I wasn't up to date with current photography wizardry.

I'm always anxious that my best effort isn't good enough. So why try? I absolutely got it.

'Lexi—' At that moment the nauseating ad about erectile dysfunction boomed through the speakers. I snapped the radio off.

'Mum, you don't need to be embarrassed—'

'Don't start—'

'What? You look really tired by the way.'

Instead of biting, my mind focused on Mrs Westley's comments. *'Lexi's not the first teenager who's imagined her mother was having an affair.'*

Where did Lexi get that idea? Of course I wasn't, but had I inadvertently let something slip?

'You were looking at Angus's coach the same way the girls at school look at Hunter... Gross, Mum. You're married.'

Did Lexi think I was involved with Arnaud? What a mess. What an absolute bloody disaster.

'Think back to your own adolescence—'

Back then, my father actually was having an affair. I didn't want history repeating itself. I needed to focus on unifying our family and regaining my daughter's trust.

CHAPTER 34

By the time we'd crawled through the afternoon city traffic and parked at Image Ink, it was after four o'clock.

'What do you do here?' Lexi asked once we were in the studio, and she was seated at my workstation.

'Look after the photography side of things.' I swiftly moved Sarah's book to a dusty corner of the room and walked back to Lexi with several sample photos I'd taken for *Bush Magic*.

'What happens to the food afterwards? Why don't you bring it home?'

I smiled. 'It gets tossed because it's inedible – we use food colouring and sometimes paint and hairspray to get the food looking appetising and appealing.'

'But not edible?' Lexi peered at several photos. 'You'd never know.'

'Thanks, I'll take it as a compliment.' I thought back to what Dana had said about the standards being more relaxed for the online edition and wondered whether there might be a few perks of the job after all.

'Are you still going to make a book of photos for Robyn to give her when her baby's born?'

I nodded. 'Let's do it together. You can help me choose the photos.'

Lexi scrolled through her phone while I pulled out cameras and extra equipment, I needed for tomorrow's location shoot at Palm Beach. I was looking forward to shooting outdoors and being at the mercy of the elements. You never quite knew how the wind, sun and clouds would shape the photographs. There was a degree of unpredictability when it came to photographing in natural light. It would be fun. I gathered all the cases and began hauling them downstairs to the company van in the garage.

'Did you pack the tripod?' Graeme barked as I tiptoed past his office, hoping to avoid him.

'Yes.' Thanks for helping me load up. No, I don't mind at all. Three downstairs trips to the garage so far. Good exercise. Loving it. I thought for a moment. 'I've packed the small one. Do you want the larger as well?'

Graeme huffed loudly and followed me to the doorway of the studio. 'Fuck's sake! Of course I need the other one. If you want something done right... Jesus. I don't know what we're paying you for, Kate. Running off in the middle of the day... you did remember the reflectors, didn't you?'

Lexi looked at me, puzzled. Dana glanced up from her pastry bowl, caught my eye, winked, and quickly went back to kneading dough. I crouched down and opened a cupboard to retrieve them.

'Yep,' I called, my voice cheerful.

'No need to bellow. I'm right here.' Beside me, Graeme leered, then turned toward Lexi. 'This must be the wayward daughter you're always talking about.'

God, I hated him. I should have quit right then. But I didn't because I wanted to show Fern I was up to the challenge of the online nativity venture. Screw Graeme Grafton. I would succeed. I refused to fail.

❄

'Is that man your boss?' Lexi asked after we left Image Ink and were driving to pick up Angus.

I nodded.

'He kinda looks like Ryan Reynolds, and he's kinda loud.'

'Yes, he is loud.' I laughed and Lexi grinned. 'The good news is it's only for a couple of weeks.'

'Then what?'

'Don't know.' I slowed to change lanes. 'After Christmas, I go back to being your mum full time.'

'You're working up to Christmas? What about decorating the house and organising Nanna's wedding? There's so much to do.'

'Yeah, there is. And most importantly, you need to catch up on all your missed classes and assignments so you can move up to the next grade in the new year.'

Lexi bowed her head.

'Sweetheart, why do you wag school?'

She looked up. 'Because it's boring.'

'That doesn't mean you can stop going. Is everything okay? I mean with Hunter? Your friends?'

'I guess. Yes and No.'

'How are Jazz and Issie?'

'Mum, it's not about friends anymore. *I'm thirteen.*' It was all in the tone. The way Lexi spoke, she could have been saying, *I have leprosy* or *I'm an alien*. 'It's about your clothes and your boyfriend, and only if you've got those, do you get to have friends. Friends on TikTok, Insta... Do you know how many girls have got me as one of their "top friends" on TikTok?'

I shook my head.

'Six hundred and twenty-eight! Do you think I'd have that many if Hunter wasn't my boyfriend? Susie says it's not important what kind of person you are, so long as you're the *right* sort of person.'

'Why would she say that?'

'Because she knows *everything*! And I'm trying to fit in. Get a life.' I wasn't sure whether Lexi was telling *me* to 'get a life' or whether she herself was trying to 'get a life'.

'Lex,' I said in my most sympathetic, motherly voice, 'you can tell me anything, darling, and I'll understand. Really, sweetheart, anything at all. I'm always here for you.'

'Great, Mum... I'm thinking about having sex with Hunter.'

I almost crashed the car.

'Joking.' Lexi laughed. 'See? Things could be a lot worse.'

We cruised to a stop at the traffic lights, and I breathed deeply, trying to regroup. I looked around.

I loved this area, the artisan cottages, the community feel. I could easily set up a studio here. A couple of weeks before Fern's call, I'd even inquired about renting space and setting up a photography studio. But I thought it too indulgent, my skills being what they are. However, now I had a renewed passion for the craft, it was certainly worth keeping in mind.

I glanced across the street and saw Matthew standing outside a café. I was about to honk when I noticed he wasn't alone. He was with a blonde, shapely woman. What was Matthew doing with an attractive woman several suburbs away from our home when he was supposed to be so damned busy at work?

CHAPTER 35

I swung by after-school care and picked up Angus at exactly five fifty-five pm. Matthew's car was in the garage when the three of us arrived home.

'Home early, Matt?'

'You sound surprised. I told you I'd be home so you could go to the class mothers' end of year dinner.'

'Dinner? It was more than a week ago. Your mind really has been elsewhere. Still, it's nice you're home.' *Anything else you'd care to mention?*

Matthew shook his head. 'You told me it was tonight, I'm sure you did.' He turned to Lexi. 'What have you got to say for yourself?'

'Not much.' Lexi tossed her school bag down in the doorway where we could all trip over it and disappeared upstairs. Angus threw his bag on top of Lexi's and then proceeded to roll around on the floor with Rupert.

'Angus!' I was tired. My legs felt like lead. 'Kids, please take your bags to your rooms. But take any uneaten lunch out first and throw it in the bin, okay?' No response.

'What's going on with Lexi?' Matthew asked.

'*What's going on?* You make it sound like it's my fault.'

'Jeez, it's not your fault. I'm just surprised she can miss so much school without you noticing.'

Funny both Matthew and Lexi's principal should think the same thing – and say it out loud.

'I knew this would happen when you started at the magazine, Kate. You can't run a house, look after the kids and have a career as well.'

'Really? It's not even been two weeks!'

'You know what I mean. Something's got to give and right now it seems like it's the family.' Matthew opened the fridge and pulled out a beer.

Keep it civil, I told myself, even though instinct told me to punch him. Hard. 'So, it's my fault because I'm not monitoring Lexi's every waking moment. You're saying I can only pursue my interests, even if I'm being paid, strictly in accordance with the mum shift? Because the reality is I do ninety-nine per cent of the work around the home and that's exactly where you want me to be, at everyone's beck and call. I never get a break.'

'Sorry,' Matthew snapped. 'I guess it's all on me.'

'It's not, but I need a life as well.'

'Don't start. I'm not in the mood.'

This wasn't going well. At all. Angus picked up his bag, glanced at me and bolted upstairs.

I took a deep breath. 'I'm sorry. Is everything okay?' I tried to put my arm around him, but he pushed me away.

'What do you mean? As if you'd notice if everything wasn't! You can't keep blaming me for not pursuing your dreams. I'm not the one who's held you back from taking photos all these years.'

'I gave up my life to marry you and have children!'

'No, Kate, you gave up because you were scared – scared of the new technology, scared of being rejected. The kids and I became a convenient excuse for you because you'd rather shut yourself away in a darkroom than get out and embrace life.'

'We don't use darkrooms anymore.' Silently, I counted to ten.

'Stop hiding,' Matthew grunted. 'You've been given an opportunity, don't collapse and say it's too hard. Go for it.'

'Hang on.' I wasn't letting him off that easy. 'What about what you said about not being able to run a house, look after the kids and have a career?'

Matthew shook his head. 'I'm not the enemy here. I'm doing the best I can.'

'Yeah, well, so am I.'

Matthew threw his hands up in the air. 'I'm sick of everything – Lexi, you... I never get a moment's peace. I feel trapped.'

'You? *Trapped?* You're not confined to a cage, Matthew. And you're not running around after the kids, helping with their homework, driving to soccer and all the rest of it. What if I'm sick of things as well? Does it ever occur to you I might be fed up or at my wits' end?'

'You're their mother! You can't be fed up. It's your job. Besides, what have you got to be fed up about?' Without waiting for a reply, Matthew walked out of the kitchen and into the living room and turned on the television.

'Matthew, is there something you want to tell me?' Like about the woman I saw you with at the coffee shop. 'Is there... someone else?'

He spun round and shook his head. 'No. I'm not about to run off with the twenty-year-old au pair down the road, if that's what you're asking. As if I don't have enough financial commitments as it is.'

On the verge on tears, I rummaged through the pantry. 'It'll have to be puttanesca pasta tonight.'

Matthew ignored me and turned up the volume on the TV. The sports news had started.

I walked upstairs, sat down on the edge of the bath and listened to the five voicemails on my mobile.

One: '*Kate, it's your mother. Please call me. We need to discuss the wedding.*'

Two: '*Hello, Katie? Are you there? This is your dad speaking. I'll call you this evening.*'

Three: '*We're walking tomorrow. No excuses. Yes, it's humid but it's my mental health we're talking about. I won't take no for an answer so don't bother ringing back with a lame excuse. Come on, porky, you know you want to. I'll be outside at the usual time.*' *Pause.* '*You're not porky, but you will be if you don't walk.*'

I snorted. Diane!

Four: '*I need a new Insta post. I've run out of ideas. Call me.*' I'd run out of ideas too. Maybe one of Robyn hugging a gum tree in the botanical gardens, captioned: '*Can't wait to play with my beautiful bub in this magnificent park, surrounded by butterflies and flowers all the colours of the rainbow.*' Ugh, what a cliché. I swallowed hard and pinched my lips together.

Five: '*I'm in labour. It's the real thing this time, I'm sure of it.*'

Nothing that couldn't wait. I ran a bath for Angus, and then, in my bedroom, changed into track pants and a black T-shirt.

'Mum, Pop wants to talk,' Angus said, appearing beside me with my phone in his outstretched hand. Grr. I'd obviously left it in the bathroom. He handed it over and ran down the hall after Rupert.

'Katie, it's about the wedding,' Dad started. 'I haven't been around much for the last few years' – understatement of the century – 'but your mum and I love each other. We want to start over again… Are you there?'

I nodded. 'Uh-huh.'

'We've got a lot of catching up to do and all this seems rather sudden, so if you are strongly against it... what I'm trying to say is, if we don't have your full support, I won't marry Pip.'

'Okay.'

'Okay, what?'

'I'm strongly against it and I don't think the two of you should get married. At least not before Christmas. Why the rush?'

'Because we want to. Will you at least think about it, for your mother's sake if not for mine?'

'That's what I'm doing... thinking about Mum. I have her best interests at heart, which is why I'd prefer she didn't go through the misery and disappointment of being married to you again.'

'It's not like that. I love your mother very much, and I love you and Robyn. I'm hoping we can be a family again.'

'You can't wipe away a quarter of a century, Dad. This is real life. What's to say you won't leave again?'

'Pip knows I never wanted to leave her in the first place. It's – you need to talk to your mum, okay?'

'I'm busy dealing with my own family dramas.'

I hung up.

'Why did you do that?'

I turned and saw Lexi, Cleopatra in her arms. 'Do what?'

'Say you didn't want Nanna and Pop to get married?'

'Lexi, you wouldn't understand. They've been married before. It didn't work the first time.'

'But they're in love and getting married again and it would make Nanna happy.'

'Lexi, enough.'

'You're so mean you make a wasp look cuddly.'

'Stop with the Nannaisms.' I clenched my jaw. Unclenched. Spoke. 'Trust me, it's for her own good.'

'That's all you ever say: *it's for your own good*. Are you going to punish Nanna for the rest of her life like you're trying to punish me?'

CHAPTER 36

Dinner was bleak. Lexi didn't speak, Matthew didn't speak. The bland pasta didn't help. Angus talked a lot about the kids in his class whose parents had divorced. He was still very much of the opinion divorce was great because of the higher lolly count. I retreated outside to watch the sunset.

'Mum, Nanna's on the phone,' Angus said, when he found me surrounded by chocolate wrappers. She must have rung the landline when I wouldn't answer my mobile.

'Tell her I'll call her back, Gussy.' My mouth was full of mini Mars bars.

'She says she needs to talk to you right now. I think she's crying. Can I have one of those?'

I took the phone and handed Angus two chocolates. 'Give one to your sister,' I called as he skipped into the house. 'Hello?'

'Katie, this can't go on.'

'What—'

'I know about the conversation with Dad. The wedding... I'm not a child. Your dad's the only man I've ever loved. Will ever love. Don't interfere. It's none of your business.'

'It *is* my business. I'm your daughter.'

'Yes, you are, and I'm telling you to back off. You don't see me interfering in your home life. I keep my thoughts to myself.' Mum stopped talking and I heard nose blowing. 'Don't you see? I'm trying to right the past. Make up for all the wrongs—'

'What do you mean?'

'Katie, you're young. You have your whole life ahead of you. Me? I'm old and want to enjoy my remaining years with Bob. I need my husband back and I am going to marry him whether you approve or not.'

'Dad asked for my opinion, and I told him,' I said, defending myself.

'Butt out! We're getting married. If you don't like it, don't come.'

❄

It was after eight thirty by the time Angus was settled in bed. I turned on *The Mapmaker Chronicles* – book two, *Prisoner of the Black Hawk* – and lay beside him. Though I tried to concentrate on the story, I kept thinking about Mum. I thought she was happy with her life, at least she was, until Dad waltzed back into it. Now, she couldn't live without him.

And as if I had *my whole life ahead of me.*

Twenty minutes later when I checked on Lexi, she was propped up in bed, Cleo beside her and laptop open, seemingly doing homework.

'Want to talk?'

She shook her head. Lexi didn't want to continue the conversation we'd had with Mrs Westley, but at least she promised – reluctantly – she wouldn't leave school again without my permission. I needed to believe her.

I almost wanted to go to bed unwashed, mascara caked on, foundation, or what remained of it, left to rub off onto my pillow, teeth unbrushed. A crumbling wreck. But then I thought, *Katie, what if your husband is having an affair and is about to leave you? What if your kids run away from home and you're left all alone? Do you really want to add blotchy skin and decaying teeth to your list of worries?*

I scrubbed my face until it was taut and shiny, and cleaned my teeth until my gums ached and the enamel was worn. After the eye, face and neck cream, I examined myself critically in the mirror. What was Mum banging on about? Okay, I didn't have one foot in the grave, but I certainly wasn't getting any younger. On the plus side, at least I didn't have raccoon eyes and bad breath.

By the time I crawled into bed, Matthew was asleep, legs spread and snoring. I was restless. Restless and wide awake, thinking about the perfume on Matthew's shirt. Was I focusing on that so I didn't have to take responsibility for my own adulterous actions? Perhaps trying to convince myself if he'd been unfaithful as well, I'd be in the clear?

I picked up my iPad, completed Wordle, then scanned the day's headlines followed by feature articles. A sex survey popped up.

According to latest research, thirty per cent of thirteen-year-old girls have engaged in deep kissing. *Deep kissing.* I courageously continued reading to find ten per cent of them have had sex. I stopped reading and closed my eyes. That meant two in Lexi's class were...

Thanks for enlightening me! Now, not only did I have my imagination to deal with, but I also had cold hard facts. It dawned on me that I could easily be a grandmother before I was forty-one! I contemplated discussing the scenario with Matthew but mentally slapped myself instead.

CHAPTER 37

Tuesdays: you're over the hurdle of Monday but Friday is still a distant prize. All things considered, there's not much to like about Tuesdays except tacos and cut-price movie tickets.

The alarm buzzed and I hit the snooze button... until I heard my phone vibrating. Diane! I dragged myself out of bed, took my pyjama top off, slipped on a bra and put the top back on. Okay, I was a lazy walker. I threw on my pale-blue hoodie and track pants, scrunched my hair into a ponytail, pulled on my sneakers and was out the door within four minutes of waking.

Before Diane arrived, I confirmed that my *Tis the Season* story had dropped on the magazine's website. It had. Perfect!

'Are you sure these hills aren't getting steeper?' I wheezed, hot and desperate to peel off my hoodie, thus revealing my very pink pyjamas. 'How's everything with David?'

'Shit.'

'What's going on?'

'My daughter and stepson. I can't even...' Diane stopped and sat on the kerb. 'I walked in on them kissing in Nina's bedroom.' She sniffed back tears. 'They said they were mucking around, and when I asked Nina about it in private, she said it was no big deal and that Sam has a girlfriend.'

'So, maybe they were having fun?'

'I guess.' Di blew her nose. 'Except I panicked and told David.'

I grimaced. 'Not good.'

'No. He's ballistic, accusing Nina of all sorts of things. Of course, he's not saying a word against his own son. It's too much.'

'I can't believe David would do that.'

'He said, "Boys will be boys".'

'Maybe they need some time apart?'

'Of course. Just before Christmas.'

'Summer boarding school?'

'I'm thinking about it.'

Composing herself, Diane stood and started walking. 'Enough about me and David. 'What's happening with you?'

I exhaled. 'Got called in to see Lexi's principal yesterday. She's been skipping school and told her teachers I'm having an affair with the gardener and having a nervous breakdown.' I pulled my hoodie down and increased my step to match Diane's.

❄

After my walk, though worried for Diane, I felt invigorated and full of energy. Before Matthew left for work, we made peace, sort of. Well, we grunted civilly. In all honesty, we might as well have been living on opposite sides of the planet such was our emotional distance.

'This isn't your battle,' Matthew said, referring to my parents after he kissed me goodbye. 'Trust them. They'll sort it out.'

'Dad's right,' Lexi said, as the front door closed behind Matthew.

I chewed my inner cheek. 'It's complicated.'

'But they were married for like a gazillion years.'

I gritted my teeth. 'As I said, complicated.'

'You don't want any of us to be happy, do you?' Lexi's voice thundered. 'You're not happy, so you don't want anyone else to be happy. You don't like Grandpa. You don't like Hunter. No one's ever good enough for you.'

'Not true. When you're older, you'll understand.'

'How old do I have to be? I understand plenty. But you won't listen.'

No. I declined to explain to my daughter why her grandfather was a shit. As for Hunter... Well, he wore pornographic T-shirts.

Changing the subject, I said, 'Could your skirt be any shorter?' She glared at me, eyes on fire. 'Don't you find it draughty when you sit down?'

Ignoring me, she peered into her lunch bag. 'I can't eat this.'

'Why? It's—'

'Meat, Mum. I refuse to eat Bambi or her farm friends.' Lexi's mobile was in one hand and her other was making a stop sign in my face.

I was so furious I could have choked her. Ingrate. 'Fine! I'll eat it.' I snatched the ham roll she'd set on the bench. 'Angus, we're leaving.'

Lexi scowled, took a Granny Smith from the fruit bowl and stalked towards the door.

I dropped Lexi off at her school and waited until she walked through the school gates before leaving. Common sense told me she could easily skip out again minutes after I drove away, but I had high hopes of her making it through a full day.

'I'm not supposed to be at school until eight thirty, the teachers said so,' Angus complained as we pulled up at the kiss-and-drop zone shortly after eight o'clock. 'I'll get a detention.'

'No, you won't. Can't you go to the library or kick a football on the oval until then? It's only this once.' I knew full well I'd dropped him before eight thirty several times in the past two weeks. I kissed him and pushed him out the door. 'Best of luck with your eight times tables today. Love you.'

Guilt stabbed as I watched him walk into the school grounds. My darling boy. Choking back tears. I drove to Image Ink.

CHAPTER 38

At the beach sometime later, the birds were singing, the sky was blue, and happily, I arranged the set – the lights, sandbags, tripods and backdrops. The fresh air was wonderful. I felt more awake and motivated than I had in weeks. And it was shaping up to be a relatively easy shoot despite the breeze. Even Graeme appeared happy. There'd been no squabbles with the stylist or Dana, who, in addition to running the food section of the online Christmas campaign, had been doing most of the heavy lifting, or at least cooking, since Mara had taken leave. The set was downright cheery. My best day at *Delicious Bites* by far.

'We need some more lemon and rocket, Kate,' Graeme said as I dusted specks of sand from the duck-egg blue napkins.

I walked back up the beach to the restaurant we were using as a base. In the cold room, I pottered around, retrieving rocket and lemons before walking out and opening a door leading to the function room. You just needed to pull open the bi-fold doors to reveal the enormous deck, and *voila,* breathtaking views of sand and beach as far as the eye could see.

Hearing a noise, I turned. 'Graeme, you startled me.'

'I was about to send out a search party.'

'Admiring the view. It's incredible.'

'You've been ignoring me, Kate. But then again, we don't want anyone getting the wrong idea, do we?'

'Wrong idea about what?'

'You and me, babe.' Graeme stopped beside me. 'The other night... sorry I was offhand the next morning. But we have to be careful, the walls have ears and eyes – and you know how jealous girlfriends can be. It was too bad we were interrupted. But I've got time now. Everything's under control outside. Let's...' He leaned in towards me, and I backed away.

'I was drunk. I'm sorry if I led you on.'

'You didn't lead me on, Tiger, you were mighty feisty. And frisky.' He laughed. 'You married chicks really want it, don't you?'

'No. No. I really don't.'

'Not what you said the other night.'

Noticing a suspicious bulge through his pants, I felt ill. What had I been thinking? I must have been more smashed than I thought. There's no way I'd ever consider anything intimate with this pathetic excuse for a man, ever.

'Graeme, you've got the wrong idea.' He grabbed my hand as I swung away to the door. 'Let me go!'

Dana's voice sung out from the other side. 'Kate, are you in there?'

Graeme reluctantly let me pass. 'Later.'

Unfortunately, he appeared beside me on the beach soon after. He glanced through the test shots I'd taken before the rocket misstep. 'So, are we shooting these dead octopi or not?'

All the props were in place. Dana was putting the finishing touches to the plate, the lighting was good, and the Hasselblad was firmly mounted on the tripod. All Graeme had to do was click one button and then bask in the accolades that would inevitably follow extolling his extraordinary vision.

'Ready to go,' I announced.

Seconds after he took the photo, he turned on me, furious. 'That reflector, there' – he pointed – 'is in completely the wrong position.'

Frustratingly, Graeme was right. The wind had blown it slightly and the new angle meant the lighting was totally wrong. All that hard work for nothing. I set about fixing it while Graeme barked instructions. He must have said 'I fucking hate working outside' at least a dozen times in the space of ten minutes.

Confident the set was once more perfect, I called him over. 'I can take the photos if you'd prefer,' I said, eager to get behind the camera.

'If I'd prefer?' he repeated loudly enough for bystanders to stop and stare. 'Let's get this straight, Kate. I am the photographer; you are the proverbial dogsbody. I take the photographs; you lug the furniture.'

CHAPTER 39

After a horrendous finish to the day, I drove straight to Mum's to apologise for acting like a six-year-old spoilt brat. I'd assumed the role of dutiful daughter for so long I'd stopped considering her feelings. Maybe I hadn't wanted to acknowledge Mum was a sexual woman who had desires and fantasies of her own. If they included my father, then so be it.

My marriage? Daughter? That drunken kiss with Graeme? It wasn't like I was doing a bang-up job with my own life. Who was I to say how she should be living?

'Mum,' I said when she opened her front door, 'I'm sorry. I don't want to argue with you. It's just... I always thought you were happy.'

Mum led me inside, we hugged, then sat at the dining-room table. This time minus the cabbage plates. Candelabras were still in position.

'I am happy,' she said, 'but your father's been missing from my life for too long. I've done things in my time I haven't been proud of. And it's rare in life you get a second chance, an opportunity to right wrongs. I'm doing that now.'

'I don't understand, but I'm not going to stand in your way. I want you to be happy.'

'I am, darling. Happier than I've been in a long time. Your father loves me very much. Always has. And I love him, too.'

'That's all that matters. But if he hurts you again—'

'He's not going to.'

'I guess you've had long enough to find someone else, and you haven't. So, if you're really sure...'

'I am. Now, what about you? You look terrible. Has something happened? Did you tell Matthew about—'

'About what?'

'Your late night last week? Lexi?'

'No. I feel so guilty about Lex. What if—'

'Guilt's a wasted emotion. There's no point feeling guilty about the past, you're only hurting yourself. Besides, Lexi's okay. Probably won't go near chillies or orange juice for some time though.'

'How could I have deserted her when she needed me most?'

'You weren't to know what she was about to get up to. Teenagers can be sly.'

Understatement. 'And she's been skipping school.'

Mum exhaled. 'That's unacceptable. Do you want me to talk to her?'

I shook my head.

'Lexi's crying out for your guidance and support.' She kissed the top of my head. 'And you? The trick is to learn from our mistakes and move on. We all have to. Kate, you'll come through this. I know you will. Forgive yourself. Vow to become a better, stronger and wiser person as a result. That's what life is about. None of us is perfect.'

'I saw Matthew standing outside a coffee shop with someone... a woman... yesterday.'

'With her or beside her? I'm assuming it wasn't just the two of them on the street?'

I frowned. 'And I smelled perfume on his shirt last week. I think he's having an affair.'

'Goodness, he's not having an affair. He loves you. Are you sure it's not wishful thinking on your part?'

'How could you say that? Of course it's not. I genuinely think he's unhappy and is looking for an escape.'

'And you, Katie?'

'I don't know. I'm always checking to see how I feel about my life and my marriage. I'm constantly asking myself, is it good enough? Am I good enough? Is everything as perfect as it can be?'

'That's what I mean, love. Listen to yourself – it's exhausting. You put yourself under so much pressure all the time, it's not surprising to see you collapsing despite your best efforts not to. There is no perfect. Perfection doesn't exist. Slow down and start enjoying yourself. All that worrying and fretting isn't helping.'

'But everything's a mess. Lexi's skipping school. She says I don't understand and don't trust her, but how can I when she's lying to me? She's out there, desperate to live some kind of adventurous life, a mini-Robyn, and it scares me.'

'She's growing up. We all have to at some stage. It's not easy, but Lexi will grow out of it. You and Robyn did.'

I stared at the candelabras. They were rather stunning.

'Well, you did, at least. Lexi's a good girl at heart. You might be in for five years of hell now, but eventually she'll pull through. You both will.'

'Lexi thinks I'm the most boring, unexciting—'

'All daughters think their mothers are boring and unexciting and have no life to speak of.'

'Touché. I'm sorry. But Lexi is too...'

'Young? And I'm too old?'

'Mum!' I cleared my throat. 'That's not what I'm saying. I remember being thirteen. The lure of the cool group. Falling out of favour because you weren't wearing the right brand of jeans. I know being good is boring and being rebellious and naughty is exciting and fun. I get it, but it breaks my heart.'

'You skipped school too.'

'Not at thirteen!'

'Maybe not then, but you did years later. You obsessed over boys, fought with girlfriends. If memory serves, there was a new drama every day. And hey, we survived, didn't we? Lexi has to find her own way, within reason. You can't stop her getting into trouble, but you can be there to pick up the pieces when she falls. It's what mothers do – and daughters, sometimes.' She sniffed. 'I'm sorry I wasn't a better role model for you and Robyn after your father left.'

'Mum, you've always been there for me. That hasn't changed.'

'I did the best I could, but—'

'But nothing.'

Mum composed herself. 'Let's do something to take our minds off our troubles. We need to plan my wedding.'

I smiled. 'Okay, but please remember apricot is a colour that should only be used to describe a fruit.'

❄

Later that night when I arrived at Robyn's apartment, she was in tears.

'I've made a terrible mistake.'

I glanced inside the baby's bedroom. 'No, the colour looks great.' Thankfully, Mum had hired a painter. The baby's room was now the canary yellow Robyn had wanted in the first place.

Downside? Baby clothes were strewn in piles over the

bedroom floor and spilled out into the hallway. 'How about we put these clothes back in the cupboards?'

'Have you seen my latest Insta?' Robyn made no attempt to pick up the clothes, instead mesmerised by her phone. 'Look.' She thrust the device into my hand.

An image of Robyn beaming and rubbing her swollen belly with one hand and holding a huge can of baby formula in the other stared back at me with the words: *If I can't breastfeed, my baby will still have the very best with Very Breast XX. #verybreastxx #verybreastformulaxx #loveverybreastxx #breastisbest #happybabyhappymum #lovemybaby #babylove*

I stopped reading. 'You're advertising Very Breast XX?' My voice was higher than a beach kite. 'Who took the photo?'

'Company photo shoot.' She shook her head. 'It doesn't matter.'

'It does, and we talked about this. You haven't even given birth.'

Robyn blinked tears. 'I know, but when I do—'

'You have no idea what you'll do once your baby arrives.'

'Read the comments,' she wailed.

I scanned several.

All women can breastfeed.

Too busy with your career to pump?

Invest in a wet nurse. You obvs have the money but not the boobs.

How many babies will die because you don't want saggy tits? Chill86.

Die, motherfucker, die.

#verybreastxxsucks #verybreastformulaxxisdeath #fuckverybreastxx #fuckyou #wetnurse #formulaispoison #yourepoison #hatingonrealmums #breastforever #breastordeath

Robyn slumped in a chair, sobbing.

Momentarily, I was too stunned to speak.

When I found my voice, I wished I hadn't. 'It's not great.' Silence. 'I did warn you.'

'Shut up. Just shut the fuck up.' Robyn wiped her nose with her shirtsleeve. 'I've missed several calls from the company.'

My focus sharpened. 'What were they thinking, getting you to advertise baby formula?' I shook my head, furious. 'Not to overstate the obvious—'

She looked up. 'Which is?'

'Jesus, Robyn, there are no guarantees in life, especially when it comes to giving birth to a healthy, might I add, living, baby.'

Robyn's head collapsed into her open palms. 'What have I done?'

CHAPTER 40

First thing Wednesday morning, I checked that my second Christmas post, *Red*, had gone live. Tick. Thank you publish scheduling.

'Mum, can Hunter come over this afternoon?' Lexi asked as I drove her to school.

'You've got several assignments to complete before the school year finishes. Remember what Mrs Westley said.'

'I'm doing them, I promise.' She pinched my thigh. 'Please, Mummy? I've promised to stay at school, and today I'll come home straight after netball, so can he come over? Please?'

I nodded. 'But I don't want the two of you at home alone.'

She removed her hand. 'Gross! We're just hanging out.'

'Can he come for dinner instead?'

'Dinner?' Lexi snorted. 'You're joking, right?'

'What's wrong with sharing a meal with us?'

'Because you're not normal.'

'I'm a mother. I'll never be normal again.'

'Exactly. If he comes for dinner, you might bring out the lame *Family Conversation Starters* cards.'

I grinned. 'They're a great way of getting to know people.'

'This afternoon?' Lexi persisted. 'For an hour?'

On Wednesdays, Lexi had netball practice until four thirty, and Arnaud had changed soccer practice this week to today. Theoretically, I could swing by and pick Angus up from the oval and still be home by five. 'Okay, but I'm going to be keeping my eye on you both.'

Angus wasn't happy when I dropped him at school at ten minutes after eight.

'The clock's slow,' I lied. 'It's closer to twenty past eight. Love you, sweetheart.'

He smiled. 'Love you too, Mummy.'

'Jack's mum's picking you up from school and taking you to soccer practice. Remember your manners and wipe your feet before you climb into her car. And don't forget to bring home two reading books. Proper reading books, Angus. Books that have more than six words of two syllables on each page, okay? I'll be at the oval before five.'

Angus's lips puckered. 'I miss walking Rupert with you. We used to do that all the time.'

My heart swelled. 'Let's do that tonight before dinner.'

He beamed. 'Yay.' Moments later, he was inside the school gates. Shoelaces undone. Shirt hanging out.

❄

Entering the Image Ink offices, cappuccino in hand, I tried to recall the previous night's dream. It annoyed me that I couldn't quite remember, interrupted by Rupert's pre-dawn barking. Eventually, it'd come to me.

Walking towards the studio, I heard raised voices booming from Graeme's office. Door wide open, I stopped and peered in. Fern was blasting him.

'This little problem, as you call it, won't disappear by itself.

You caused it, remember, so you need to fix it. Today.' Way to go, Fern. The woman had style. She didn't let Graeme bully her. She was all action.

Graeme pushed his chair out from behind his desk and stood. 'No, Fern. Christ! Didn't I make myself clear?'

'Yes, but—'

'You're not listening to me.'

I quickly stepped out of sight, mesmerised, struck by their fury. Surely, the entire floor could hear Graeme's raging voice. He was a seething mass of anger about to explode.

Fern, master of control, dropped her voice so low I could only hear snatches. 'Graeme, we need Mara... *MasterChef*...'

'Either she goes, or I do,' Graeme thundered.

'Be reasonable. We're committed to a Wednesday deadline – one week! The only way that's going to happen is if Mara's here.' Fern's voice softened and I couldn't hear what she said next. I edged closer, worried I'd get caught gawking. Still, I was amazed crowds hadn't gathered in the hallway.

Graeme's door slammed. Fern imprisoned inside. I hovered a moment longer, but Graeme was obviously aware his raised voice had reverberated throughout the building because I could only hear muffled sounds.

Arriving at the studio, I opened the door, stepped inside and turned on the lights.

'Hey,' Coco trilled. I jumped and spilled my coffee. 'Ascertained Fern's locus?'

'She was with Graeme a moment ago. Maybe they've gone downstairs.'

'Whatevs,' Coco said. 'I require blueprint endorsement. And since there's no Mara, I need Fern.'

'Need Fern for what?' Fern was standing in the doorway.

'Layout approval.' Coco hesitated. 'Graeme as well.'

'Graeme's left for the day.' Fern's tone was sharp, not to be messed with. 'Go on, Coco, I'll be right with you. Kate, about the *Bush Magic Christmas* photos?'

'Those? Playing around—'

'They're fantastic. Fresh, light. I'm using one for the front cover of the special edition coming out Thursday week. I was going to use Graeme's, the one with the exotic feathers, sequins and black satin, but yours are so much more innovative and sophisticated, not to mention, Christmassy. Let's not tell him though, he'll find out soon enough.' Fern clicked her tongue and sighed. 'That's why I'm the boss. I make the hard decisions.'

'Fern... Thank you.'

'No, thank *you*. I wouldn't use them if they weren't brilliant. I'm loving the online festive advent posts too. Very good. Getting lots of likes and comments. Well done.'

'I'm having fun.' I paused. 'If Graeme's out for the day, I'll make the most of my time and meet with Dana to discuss the food for the next round of nativity releases.'

My recent dream flashed before me as Fern walked out of the studio. I was in the back seat of a car with Graeme doing something... and we stopped. Then we were in a taxi, again in the back seat with Graeme, and we were heading... to his apartment.

Dismissing my unreliable memories, I got on with the *Delicious Bites* online nativity calendar. Day eight: *Christmas Trees*. Day nine: *Traditional Christmas Baking*. Day ten: *Music*. Day eleven: *Everything's Green*. Day twelve: *Family*. Day thirteen: *Sweet Treats*. Day fourteen: *Festive Flowers*.

❄

'Kate,' Fern said later when we crossed paths in the corridor. 'Come with me.'

I followed her into her office. Fern's walls were painted a

calming pale green. We sat in comfortable burgundy lounge chairs opposite a glass coffee table and floor-to-ceiling windows which overlooked scruffy bush. To the side, Fern's oak desk was uncluttered but for a vase of colourful dahlias, photos of her family and a computer. I glanced at Sarah's book and a selection of Image Ink's magazines scattered on the table.

'Would you mind heading back up to the beach on Friday and taking more location shots? We don't have enough.'

'Sure. Any news about Mara? Or Simone?'

'The good news is Simone will hopefully return in two weeks, but Mara's still AWOL.'

'And if Mara doesn't come back?'

'Not an option. She's the driving force of the magazine. If she doesn't...' Fern shook her head. 'She must. That's all there is to it.'

'I saw Sarah at the café across the street earlier this week. She hasn't changed since college. There's no humility about her at all.'

'Look at her book.'

'She doesn't need any more glory.'

'Stop! Graeme's not here, you'll have no interruptions. Take it and go.' Fern reached across her coffee table, picked up Sarah's tribute to herself, and handed it to me. Again.

❄

In the studio, I sat at my workbench, eyeing the book. What was it that scared me so

much? First, there was the cover with the words SARAH STANTHORPE, INTERNATIONALLY ACCLAIMED PHOTOGRAPHER, plastered across the front. *Internationally acclaimed photographer!*

Her smug face was on the very first page, her superior self-righteous expression looking at me as if to say, 'Ha-ha. My photography's better than yours. I have a three-book publishing deal. You've got nothing. Nothing but envy, you talentless no-good piece of trash.'

Maybe not. Maybe Sarah was simply smiling a happy smile, but it looked like she was speaking directly to me, and I didn't like it. I couldn't turn the pages. My hand hovered over the acknowledgements page, frozen. Fear of what I'd see on the next page, I guess. The fear of finding Sarah was so much more talented than me and always had been. I had stomach cramps, a looming headache and was sweating profusely. Why did I care so much? So scared her photography would be so poignant, so meaningful, so soul-crushingly perfect that I'd never want to pick up a camera again in my life?

Absolutely.

Quietly, I flicked through several pages, then several pages more, until I reached the double-page spread in the middle of the book: a stunning portrait of three lions, two adults and a cub, basking in the sun on a flat rock surrounded by lush green grass. The adult female was licking the cub, her eyes wide open. Beautiful. Their upper bodies were perfectly framed – the photo taken at the precise moment the sunlight hit the back of their heads.

The accompanying caption read: *Words cannot express the exhilaration I felt being up close and personal with these magnificent animals as they watched over their cub in the late afternoon sun. Image taken at Kruger National Park, South Africa, Spring, 2019: Nikon N90s/600m lens and Kodachrome 64 film.*

Tears rolled down my cheeks.

I felt a hand on my shoulder. Fern. 'Beautiful, isn't it? I remember the day that photo was taken.'

'October fourteen, 2009.'

'Your photos, Kate. Part of your final assessment portfolio.'

My breath hitched.

I almost laughed through my tears. 'I waited hours to get that bloody shot. Waiting for the right moment. Africa, hey? At least she got the lens and film details right.'

'I bet Sarah's publisher would be very interested to know it was you who took this photo at Taronga Zoo, Sydney, not Sarah at Kruger National Park, South Africa. And you know what, Kate? Your photo is by far the best. No matter how many times I look through the collection, yours stands out.'

'Why didn't you tell me?'

'I wanted you to see it for yourself.'

'But she stole my photo.'

'Yep. What are you going to do about it?'

I shrugged, too stunned to speak.

'Why are you here?'

'Because you asked me, and when you asked, it hit me: I realised what my life had been missing all these years. I love taking photographs, bursting to shoot everything I see. I'm so angry with myself for giving up. I feel like I've wasted so much time, lost so many opportunities.'

She nodded. 'Kate, you have to get out there. You're an artist. Don't get me wrong, I'd love you to stay at *Delicious Bites* permanently, but you have real talent. Use it.'

CHAPTER 41

Still reeling from the knowledge Sarah Stanthorpe had stolen at least one of my photographs, I arrived at the oval to pick up Angus from soccer training. Eleven filthy little boys, half of whom were shirtless (including my son), were running around the oval screaming.

'Put your shirt back on,' I yelled at Angus.

He glanced at me, then ran in the opposite direction towards the bush.

Arnaud approached me. 'I know what you are thinking.' He couldn't possibly have known, but I still blushed. 'Why has Arnaud let them take their shirts off? I didn't, but they don't listen to me when they're running with the pack.'

'Angus never listens to me either, so don't take it personally.'

Too suddenly, Angus was beside me, covered in mud from head to foot and jogging up and down on the spot holding his penis. 'Mum, I'm busting.' Several boys looked on, laughing.

He ran to the toilet and by the time I'd found various shirts, school shoes, bags and uneaten scraps of lunch, Angus was back and I hurried four filthy kids into my now filthy car and left.

I delivered the J's (Jack and Josh) to their respective homes, and when I stopped to let out Tom, Diane called, 'We're walking on Friday.'

I drove home to the sound of Angus's Nintendo buzzing in my ear.

Thinking about Arnaud. Thinking about him walking into the studio and locking the door behind him. He'd lean against the door and look at me, smiling. Daring me to make the next move. And I'd take the bait. Saunter over to him and drag my fingernails around the collar of his shirt. He'd be too startled to say anything.

I'd loosen his shirt, blow softly in his ear, and put my finger to his lips, and say, *Shhhh. You don't want anyone to hear, right?*

Breathing more heavily, not really daring to believe what was happening to him, Arnaud would reach for me, pulling my skirt higher, exposing my thighs, and I'd let him. Let him caress my breasts through my sheer blouse.

Kate! I couldn't be thinking about this now with Angus in the car, in the middle of peak-hour traffic! It was nonsense. I was on a collision course to hell. If I wasn't careful, my world would come crashing down around me and I'd have no one to blame but myself.

Anyway, what would happen after the first seduction? After Arnaud and I had fucked for forty days straight? Being a man, Arnaud would catch up on some much-needed shut-eye, but what about me? Women liked to analyse...

The thing about affairs or at least the fantasy of affairs, is it's all about the build-up. The temptation, the flirting, the first kiss, Arnaud's tongue. But what happened when the fantasy became reality? While the sex might be incredible, new and exciting, eventually we'd still arrive at *What's for dinner?* And, *Have you seen my other black sock?*

Life goes on and on. School, homework, tears and tantrums – those things wouldn't disappear. Maybe they did in other people's lives, but I was sure they wouldn't in mine. Even if I was with Arnaud and his magical tongue.

I blinked, suddenly overwhelmed by guilt and sadness – the guilt I was feeling about having kissed Graeme. And the sadness I felt about Matthew and how our life together had effortlessly careered off course.

❄

'Lexi, I'm home,' I called as Angus and I stepped through the front door. I couldn't face walking in on Lexi and Hunter doing... whatever. The last time I'd seen Hunter, I'd practically thrown him out of the house. I was hoping it wouldn't come to that this time.

When I entered the kitchen, they were sitting at the bench, Lexi looking a picture of sweet innocence, even with two buttons of her shirt undone.

'Hi, Hunter, nice to see you again. Have you eaten?' I said in a pleasant, *I-want-to-be-your-friend* tone. (Ignoring what I'd seen on his T-shirt two weeks ago.)

'Mother,' Lexi said, in the voice of irritation she'd recently adopted. 'We're going upstairs.' Hunter followed her as she strode away.

'Lexi,' I called her back. 'Keep your door open, okay?'

She glared at me and rolled her eyes.

Breathing deeply, I turned my attention to Cleopatra who was jumping at flies. Lexi was home at least, not out in a deserted car park in the back seat of someone's car – I cringed as the thought crossed my mind.

I was amazed by Lexi's confidence in herself and her future, whatever it might hold. Notwithstanding my ongoing dramas with her, I had to admit I was envious of her youth, her *I-don't-*

give-a-shit attitude and her blossoming sexuality. Not that I'd ever admit that to her. Or Matthew.

It's not that I wished to be a teenager again and relive all those adolescent torments and raging hormones. I didn't. But Lexi was on the brink of an amazing adventure; her whole life was ahead of her, there for the taking. Lexi would make plans, chart her own destiny and barrel head first into her future.

And her mother? No doubt Lexi saw me as a meddlesome middle-aged woman living a tedious, conventional life in the suburbs. No wonder she rebelled. Rebelled against the predictable boredom of good girlhood and beyond... everything her mother embodied. If only she knew I was dying to break free as well.

Still, I was conveniently overlooking the honour I had of being a parent. Not only a parent, but one who was living a comfortable life with healthy children. While I might not have anticipated the enormity of parenthood, the responsibility I accepted the moment I decided to proceed with my pregnancy hadn't completely eluded me.

Motherhood was a privilege, but so was pursuing my dream. Photography. I had to make it work. Me, a housewife, living in suburbia?

Yep! So what? Onward and upward. I could do it.

CHAPTER 42

'That's atrocious; you need to do something about it. Can you sue her?' Matthew said when I told him about Sarah's book.

'Not sure. I think copyright laws have changed. Besides…'

'Besides what?'

'What's done is done. The photo's in her book now.'

'I can't believe you're saying that. Where's your fighting spirit?'

'Mostly in the laundry.'

'The woman I fell in love with would have ripped her to shreds.'

'The woman you fell in love with also weighed eight kilos less and didn't have wrinkles.'

'Stop being melodramatic.'

'Thanks. Exactly what I need. Another lecture.' I walked away to answer the door. 'Lordy!' I said to Robyn as she and her blonde shag and nose ring toddled inside. 'I didn't know you were coming over.'

She waved me away. 'You like? I got a trim. Again. And colour. Again. Instaperfect, babes.'

'Indeed.' Hairdressers say critical times for hairstyle changes are after the demise of a relationship and after the birth of a baby. Full points to Robyn for being ahead of the curve.

Though Robyn's cut was cute, it reminded me of the time I got a spiral perm just after Mum and Dad's divorce. I looked like a startled poodle. Even before I left the salon it was ugly, but it was truly frightful once I was required to manage it myself. Days later, I shuffled back to the hairdressers and demanded they cut it off. For free. They did. Another disaster. I contemplated getting hair extensions but, in the end decided it was more economical to wear a beret (a nod to the French) for the next two years. Since then, I've kept it permanently shoulder-length and brown, and trim it myself when needed.

Funny how I'd forgotten about that. Even more reason to kick myself for not empathising with Lexi's recent shock experiment.

'Hey, Matt.' Robyn waved to him as she walked through the kitchen to the fridge and opened it. 'Any wine?'

Matthew glanced up from his phone in Robyn's direction, opened his mouth to say something but changed his mind and went back to scrolling.

I closed the fridge door and turned on the kettle. 'Peppermint tea, I think.'

Once we had our drinks, Robyn and I moved to the living room. 'You're chipper,' I said. 'Last night you were in tears.'

'Fake it till you make it.'

'So what's happening?'

'Well, as of ten minutes ago, at' – she checked her Fitbit – 'seven pm, that post has accumulated over 300,000 likes, so I'll receive a hefty payment from Very Breast XX. Any additional likes and we're talking serious bonus territory.'

'What?' I spluttered through my tea.

'Yeah, it's not all doom and gloom. Plus, there were heaps of positive comments. At least there were until I turned off the comments function.'

'You're going to keep advertising with them?'

Robyn rubbed her belly. 'Of course, but probably no more until after bub is born.' She pulled out a colourful pale-green bunny blanket (as in decorated with white rabbits) from her backpack. 'Onward. Let's take some snaps.'

'Of that blanket?' I'd seen hundreds of these before and couldn't see that this one was any different.

'It's not a blanket. It's a one hundred per cent certified, bamboo cotton no-wrap baby wrap.' She handed me a pamphlet. 'To swaddle the baby and strap him/her/they to your chest. Or back. Perfect for baby and Mum, or baby and Dad, or baby and non-binary caregiver... you know. Perfect for all sorts.'

'Please don't write that in your post.'

She poked out her tongue. 'Photos please? And make me look like the goddess I'm destined to become.'

While Robyn applied lipstick and arranged herself into an almost comfortable position, I retrieved my camera from the kitchen. I returned with the camera, Bugs, and a couple of carrots.

'Bugs!' Robyn squealed. 'We meet again, gorgeous boy.'

'Props,' I replied, sitting Bugs and his carrots beside her.

She prodded him. 'Stacking on the pounds, fella.'

I frowned. 'Pot. Kettle.'

After taking upwards of thirty photos of the same pose, I put my camera down. 'Enough. I'll fiddle with the best ones and send them to you in the morning.'

'Thanks.'

'Are you sure you're feeling okay about the online remarks? It'd wear me down.'

'Nah, I've got the hide of a rhino.' Robyn sipped her tea. 'Though sometimes—'

The doorbell rang. 'Hold that thought.' I stood. 'What's going on? It's a school night.'

Mum and Dad were standing at the front door, and I ushered them inside. 'This is unexpected,' I said, because it was.

Mum smiled eagerly. 'Hope we're not intruding, we wanted to show you the wedding invitations.'

No, why would you think that? 'Robyn's here.'

'Darling, how are you?' Mum said, walking over to her. Surprisingly, she didn't react to Robyn's hair or nose ring. Dad seemed oblivious, just like the old days.

'Excellent.' Robyn beamed.

'Nanna!' Lexi rushed down the stairs. 'I've got some great ideas for my dress.'

'Me too,' Angus said.

'Lex, have you done your homework?' Hunter had left less than an hour ago and Lexi had only just finished dinner. There was no way she could have completed all her study. 'Including the extra assignments?'

'Mum!'

'How are you, sweetheart?' Mum moved towards Lexi. 'I hear you've been giving your teachers a hard time.'

'Katie and Robyn used to run away from school when they were about your age, Lexi,' Dad chimed in.

'Thanks, Dad.' I scowled. 'Not helpful.'

Matthew walked in with a beer for Dad and a wine for Mum, and we shouted around him.

Robyn pouted.

'Really?' Lexi was enthralled. 'Mum didn't tell me. She always pretends she was such a goody-goody.'

'Oh no.' Dad smiled. 'Far from it.'

'I was good,' I countered. 'Especially when I was thirteen.'

'I wasn't.' Robyn chortled.

'Robbie, your hair!' Lexi squealed. 'Awesome.'

'Yeah, nice hair, Rob.' Matthew gave Robyn two thumbs up, then he looked at me.

I didn't comment.

'Says he who hasn't changed his hairstyle in fifteen years,' Robyn snorted. 'As for your straggly mane, Kate...'

'What? What's wrong with it?' I flipped my head from side to side. 'I can whack it in a ponytail and it looks great. Short hair requires constant maintenance, styling products, buckets of grooming time.'

'Don't listen to her, Robbie, your hair's cool,' Lexi said. 'As for the nose ring, I'm busting. Can I get one, Mum?'

'Of course you can. When you're thirty-five.'

'You never let me do anything. You know, Nanna, Mum doesn't want you and Pop to marry again. Isn't she the worst mother ever? She's so mean.'

'Lexi,' Mum said, 'that's not true. Besides, your mother and I have spoken about the wedding and she's very happy about it now. Aren't you, Kate?'

'Of course,' I lied. 'Speaking of which, we need to talk about the wedding plans and Christmas with Nanna, so you two finish your homework and then, Lexi, you can talk about your dress, and, Angus, you can find out all about being the ring bearer.'

He scrunched his nose. 'What about the lollies?'

Dad tried to ruffle Angus's spiky hair. 'There'll be plenty of lollies on the day, sport.'

Mum pulled an invitation from her bag. 'It's only a draft but what do you think?'

I snatched the card from her and examined it. Printed on the front was a photo of the four of us taken at a beach thirty years ago – Mum and Dad holding hands and looking incredibly young and gorgeous. Each was holding a child with their free arm. My head was leaning on Dad's shoulder. I'd forgotten I was such a daddy's girl.

'I remember that. We were staying at the old beach house... we built sandcastles all day.' I stopped and caught my breath. They were good times. 'It's a great photo,' I managed, and wondered why it had to come to an end all those years ago. 'But, Mum, you're really getting married on Christmas Eve?'

'It's short notice but we only want family and a few friends. Fifteen at most.'

'I'm the fifteenth I guess,' Robyn said. 'The only person without a partner.'

'Not if you count Lexi and Angus,' I chimed in.

Mum rubbed her temples. 'I've called everyone, including Carol and Bernard. The invitation's merely a formality.'

'Thanks for inviting my Mum and Dad,' Matthew replied. 'They're looking forward to it.' He glanced at me, knowing we hadn't discussed it. He shrugged. 'They're staying for Christmas week.' I could hardly complain.

'Again, Christmas Eve.' I held the invitation in my hand, feeling myself tearing up. 'Tell me what you've decided.'

'We were going to have the wedding at Bob's apartment, or my home.' Mum glanced at Dad. 'But then we thought it would be much nicer to have the party at a restaurant. No worrying about the weather...'

Dad grinned. 'Or cleaning up after.'

Robyn grunted. 'Cramps. The baby's coming.'

Mum clucked sympathetically and continued. 'We've organised the celebrant and chosen flowers. But stuck for a venue.'

'Aren't you supposed to give one month and one day's notice for a marriage licence?' I asked.

'Yes.' Dad beamed. 'We organised it after our first night together.'

Right! I knew when I was beat. Best to smile and embrace the chaos.

'I might have a place for you,' I said, scrolling on my phone. 'I did a photo shoot on the northern beaches the other day and there was this gorgeous restaurant, Jonah's by the Sea. It's got a stunning outlook and there's a private function room. If it's not booked, you could be in luck. It would be in keeping with the invitation, too. But again, Christmas Eve.'

Overcoming the almost-grope by Graeme that darkened my memories of that room, I pushed past and showed them an image of the restaurant and surrounds.

'Perfect,' Dad said.

I opened notes on my phone and started typing. 'If we're going to do this bloody wedding, let's do it properly.'

Matthew stood up and left the room. Okay, so perhaps he wasn't up for another family celebration, despite his parents being included. I sometimes forgot how hard it must be for him having my family living in the same city as us. We hardly ever saw his family. But mine! Like tonight, rarely a day went by when Mum or Robyn didn't pop in. Usually unannounced.

I'd finished writing *1. Ring Jonah's by the Sea, tomorrow am*, when Matthew returned with a bottle of Moët and five flutes.

'This calls for a celebratory drink!'

'I'm sorry,' I whispered as I stood to join him. I loved Matthew, no doubt about it. But I still felt we were both going through the motions and our emotional connection was seriously lacking. We needed to work things out, but the hugeness of our problems overwhelmed me, especially when surrounded by family. Like now. Also, there was my very real concern Matthew was indulging in extramarital activities, and as for me, I still couldn't remember why the hell I was in a taxi heading to Graeme's apartment that night. The memory remained just out of reach, and it scared me.

After squeezing my hand and kissing my cheek, Matthew popped the cork and poured everyone a glass. 'To Pip and Bob.'

It was a true Kodak moment. I should have taken photos, but I wasn't quite there yet.

Dad stroked Mum's arm while she talked. 'White, red and pink roses for the ceremony, and bouquets of white roses and hydrangeas for the tables. What do you think?'

Looking at them together again, I almost recognised the father who'd cooked us Sunday roasts when we were growing up; the father who'd taken us on family beach holidays; and the father who'd stroked my arm, like he was doing now with Mum, whenever I fell over or was troubled... Pity he ducked out just as I was having serious growing pains, boyfriend hassles and exam pressures.

'Are you writing this down, Katie?' Mum asked, pulling me back to the present.

'Sorry, I missed that.'

'I said, do you want me to call the restaurant?'

'No, I'll call first and see if it's available.'

Mum nodded. 'Then I'll print the invitations and email them.'

'What about music?' Robyn asked, after Matthew and Dad had drifted into the TV room to watch cricket.

'Yes, music, although...' I hesitated.

'Although what?' Mum asked.

'Are you going to have a bridal waltz?'

'I haven't thought that far ahead.'

'Well, Mother, remember mine and be warned.' Flashbacks of Joe Cocker came scuttling back. 'Remember "You Are So Beautiful"?'

'Good in theory,' Robyn agreed, 'but it was way too slow and Joe's voice!'

'Sounded like he was having a convulsion.' I shivered. 'Horrible.'

'Everything makes sense in hindsight,' Robyn muttered.

'What about Kirsty's, "I Will Always Love You"? Ha! What a joke that turned out to be.' Kirsty and Ian had divorced four months later.

Mum grimaced. 'I'll make sure I ask your advice before your father and I choose the wedding song, if we have one.'

'Nanna, when are we going to talk about *my* dress?' Lexi's hurt voice came from the top of the stairs.

'Right now, love.' Mum stood, champagne in hand. 'Wish me luck,' she whispered.

We watched as she climbed the stairs to join Lexi.

Eyeing Dad in the living room with Matt, I picked up the wedding invitation again. 'What do you think about all of this?'

'I was shocked at first,' Robyn started. 'But after the few months I've had, I realise anything can happen.'

'I never would have thought Mum and Dad... I mean, imagine getting back together again after all this time apart.'

'Can't have been easy for Dad, separated from us for all those years. It's so sad.' Robyn gingerly sipped her champagne. 'I remember one night before he moved out, Dad crying, begging Mum to let him stay, pleading with her. He said he could change, that he'd do anything to keep the family together and the marriage alive. Mum was so cruel, adamant their marriage was dead.'

I sprang to Mum's defence. 'What did he expect? He had an affair with Miss Inspirational, and then married her, remember. Let's not forget the facts, Robbie.'

'I know, but that night he looked like he'd lost his best friend. He stayed in the spare room next to mine and cried all night.' Robyn shook her head. 'Heartbreaking.'

CHAPTER 43

'Guesstimate this!' Coco beamed as she stood in the doorway of the studio the next morning. 'Opinion has it Graeme and Mara rendezvoused yesterday.'

'Really?' I took a bite of banana bread and a swig of my skinny cappuccino, trying not to think about my encounter with Graeme earlier when I'd given him his coffee. 'So nice to be waited on, Katie. While you're here, I have a couple of other *jobs* I know you'll be interested in performing.' Instead of tipping the plunger of boiling coffee over his head, I backed out of his office without saying a word.

'He's here today.'

'Not surprised. I earwigged Fern on the phone to him yesterday afternoon. She was not happy. There was lots of *Well, we'll see about that* and *You're not the only photographer around who can do this job*, that sort of thing. So, I estimate Mara's smashed Graeme and he's trying to woo her back for the sake of his occupation. Whether or not it's succeeded... Anyway, let me know if you gather more intelligence.'

'Will do.'

Coco strolled towards the open-plan office where the computer heads worked.

I answered my ringing phone. 'What did the restaurant say?' My mother's tone was anxious. 'You haven't phoned yet, have you?' I glanced at my watch. It had just gone ten thirty.

'No, but I was about to.'

After ending the call with Mum, I dialled the restaurant, hoping for a miracle. And what do you know? It didn't happen. I called Mum straight back. She picked up her phone in less than half a ring.

'Completely booked until early February,' I told her.

'No!' Mum's voice quavered.

'There are other venues on the beach, but really, Mum—'

'I know, Christmas Eve.'

Despondent, she hung up. Moved by how unhappy she sounded, I resolved to secure a venue and make sure Mum had the second wedding with Dad she wanted.

I checked my Instagram feed. As expected, Robyn's bunny post was garnering thousands of likes. Two hundred and seventy-six thousand so far.

Picture perfect, Robyn was wide-eyed and smiling, her hair and skin extra shiny. She was draped in the no-wrap baby wrap, with a hand on Bugs, wide red eyes, nonchalantly reclining beside her, chewing on a carrot. *Can't wait for my bubba to be snuggled in this gorgeous 100% certified bamboo organic cotton wrap – a cuddly second skin for both of us. #nowrapbabywrap #baby #cruelfreepregnancy #dreampregnancy #babyove #bunnies #adoptdontshop #vegan #crueltyfree #cutenessoverload*

Eldest sister wields her magic!

I was exhausted, surprised by how tired my legs felt – and I hadn't even been walking this morning. My whole body felt like it was about to shut down. I put my head on the desk and closed my eyes.

'Dreaming of me again, huh?' Graeme leaned across the desk until his face was barely five centimetres from mine. 'Go on. Tell me you were. Please.'

I jerked my head away and stood. 'Get a grip.'

'Well, if you're going to behave like a bad-tempered child, K…'

'Me? Who do you think you're speaking to?'

He pushed his glasses up onto his head and stared down at me. 'Last time I checked, darling, I was your boss. It wasn't so long ago you were happy I was making you squirm – with delight, I might add.'

'You should be reported.'

'Be my guest, honey. But remember our little secret? It doesn't have to be a secret, not if you don't want it to be.'

'I'm glad you're both here,' Fern said, walking into the studio. 'Has Graeme told you, Kate? We've solved our Mara issue. She's coming back.'

'That's great but—'

'It is, isn't it? We can all be one big happy team again – and make this month's deadline. Speaking of which, Graeme, I'm going to use one of Katie's photos from the *Bush Magic* shoot for the cover of next week's special Yuletide print edition.'

Graeme shot me a filthy look. 'Hang on. What—'

'You heard,' Fern replied. 'I may even use one of her beach snaps for our February front cover, to coincide with Mara's *MasterChef* debut. Great publicity for you, Kate. It'll be hard deciding which photo, though. They're all brilliant. Must dash.' She headed for the door.

'If you think for one minute,' Graeme hissed, 'Kate's getting front cover credits, let me tell you something, that will happen over my dead body!' He followed Fern out the door, shouting, 'Wait up.'

The fame was nice while it lasted. Although she was goading

him, I couldn't see Fern stepping out on a limb for me if it meant upsetting Graeme – not with all the upheaval this place had seen since I'd been here.

❄

'How about that drink?' Arnaud suggested as I was contemplating leaving the office for the day.

Truth be told, I wanted to go home. I glanced at my watch. It was only four thirty. 'I guess so,' I replied, suddenly feeling bright. 'A quick one.'

'*Très bien!* I am very lucky to be having drinks with the woman who has upset Graeme, *non*?'

'How?' I asked, suddenly feeling very guilty.

'Everyone knows Fern's using your photo for next month's front cover. That's never 'appened before. It's always been Graeme's baby. Meet you at the bar in ten.' He smiled and held up ten fingers.

I dashed to the bathroom to spruce myself up. Some lipstick here, a shake of the head and hairspray there. A spray of perfume. A dab of powder.

A few minutes later, Arnaud and I were sitting at a booth two tables away from where Graeme and I had kissed barely a week ago. He was knocking back a Heineken. I was sipping an Adelaide Hills Chardonnay.

'How is everything?' Arnaud asked. 'The wedding…'

'The wedding…' I said vaguely, clutching my wine as though someone might try to steal it from me. 'I'm sorry I chewed your ear off last week. I overreacted. Mum and Dad will be okay. It's not for me to interfere.'

'From where I'm sitting, Kate, you have it all – you're beautiful, you have two gorgeous children…'

I shut my eyes and listened as Arnaud talked. I imagined him reaching over, taking my wrist, placing his hand over mine... but that's not really what I desired. I wished I was with my husband and—

'I thought I might find you here, Arnie.' I looked up to see a woman – and judging by the greeting, Arnaud's significant other.

Arnaud quickly stood. 'Ze love of my life.'

'Darling,' the woman's voice purred. 'Who's this?'

'Kate... Kate Cavendish.' My hands were clammy, and I could feel perspiration forming on my top lip.

'Where are my manners?' Arnaud drawled. 'Kate, this is Sophie, my girlfriend. Sophie, Kate is a colleague at Image Ink.'

'Charmed.' Sophie's smile was ice.

'Lovely to meet you.' I felt like I was trapped in a nightmare – or a very bad B-grade movie.

Sophie sat down opposite me while Arnaud went to the bar.

'Arnaud is a great coach. That's how we met, through my son, Angus, his soccer team.' I was babbling but couldn't stop. 'Angus is learning a lot from him. Then when I started at the magazine a few weeks back, Arnaud was one of the first people I bumped into.'

'Goodness. He gets around.'

'Yeah, the boys love him.'

'Arnaud is a great person, full stop. Great with kids, adults – women especially.' Sophie looked me straight in the eye. 'I bet he lays on his accent a bit thick at the office though, right?'

'No!'

'I'm sure he does. Arnie's been living in Australia for years, but he tends to overdo the French bit, especially when he's trying to be cute.' She snorted. 'Cute! He's a thirty-four-year-old man.'

We watched in silence as Arnaud walked back to the table with a tray of drinks.

'How are you finding life at Image Ink, Kate?' Sophie asked, once Arnaud was seated.

'Okay,' I croaked. 'I'm only there until Christmas.'

'Why's that?' Sophie questioned.

'Because of Graeme?' Arnaud turned to Sophie. 'Graeme is Kate's boss.'

'Poor thing. I've only met him the once. Remember, darling?' Sophie was rubbing Arnaud's thigh with her slender hand. 'At last year's Christmas in July party? He was pawing anyone with a vagina. Such unattractive behaviour. Men who think they're God's gift, they never seem to learn.'

'Graeme's not too bad,' I lied, growing more uncomfortable by the second.

Arnaud sipped his beer. 'Really?'

'Okay, he is bad. He's one of the most appalling men I've ever met. I don't know how the staff put up with him. At least my time there is finite.'

I checked my watch. I'd been in Sophie's company for an excruciating seventeen minutes – I figured I had needed to stay at least that long so as not to appear rude... or uneasy. I stood. I couldn't bear it any longer. Arnaud and Sophie were nuzzling and talking excitedly about their plans – plans for the weekend, plans for their holidays, how they'd spend the next fifty years of their lives together.

'If you'll excuse me, I really do need to get home to my family. They're expecting me.'

The object of my affection, make that my *wasted* affection, for the last however many weeks, was a happily attached man. A man who'd no sooner run off with me to a deserted island than fly backwards on a broomstick to the South Pole.

I studied my reflection in the rear-view mirror of my car.

Tragic. I took a tissue and wiped the lipstick away. Too much colour. I flattened my hair. Too much hairspray. I sat in my car for ten minutes with my head resting against the steering wheel, thinking... thinking about nothing.

Nothing apart from my own stupidity.

CHAPTER 44

'Di, you look terrible,' I said. 'Even in the dark.'

'Don't ask, just walk.'

'Is there anything—'

'NO! Tell me what's been happening in your life.'

'My life is one long series of humiliations, but you already know that. I met Arnaud's girlfriend last night.'

Diane turned and stared.

'Arnaud and I were having a drink at this bar after work. Anyway, she practically accused me of having an affair with him. It was awful. I felt lower than an ant.'

'What did I tell you? These so-called harmless flirtations...'

'Why do I keep messing up my life? I seem to do it so well.'

'Kate, your life isn't messy. Are you getting divorced?'

'Not yet.' I paused. 'How about I take Tom for the weekend. Gus would love it.'

'Thanks, but after soccer tomorrow, David and I are taking Nina and Tom up the coast for the night to David's parents' home. Family bonding. Talking about Christmas.'

'No Sam and Oliver?'

'Nope, they'll be with their mother. I'm dreading the next couple of days. His parents aren't fans.'

I thought of giving her my *Conversation Starters* cards but stopped myself. 'Good luck.'

'I'll need it. The only good news is that they live two hours north, one block from the beach.' She exhaled. 'I saw my therapist yesterday, and she advised me to look at my life like it was a pie.'

'What kind? Apple, cherry?'

Diane was not amused.

I completed our walk thinking about what Di's therapist had told her and trying to picture my life as though it were a pie. I visualised serving up slices – for the kids, Matthew, my photography, other family members. Pretty soon I ran out of pie. Perhaps the fact I had no pie left for myself was the reason I was cranky and a bad mother. Surely there had to be some pie for me. But then I imagined explaining to Matthew – *honey, there's not enough pie for me.* He'd tell me to buy another one. (He knew I'd never bake it.)

Still, there was never enough pie to go around.

❄

'Katie, how much longer are you staying at the magazine?' Matthew asked at breakfast.

'Until Christmas week. Why?' I was sipping coffee, not paying attention. 'You never know, I might be offered a permanent position.'

'You hate food photography.'

'Food photography is better than no photography, Matt. And it's a way back into the industry.'

'I wish you'd make up your mind.'

For the briefest of moments, I thought he might be going to

say something more. Confess something. He looked distraught. What did he want to tell me? Nothing, as it happened. He turned and the moment was lost.

❄

'Morning,' Coco said when I walked into the building.

Was it still only morning? Friday seemed to have stretched for hours already.

'Mara's back,' Coco continued. 'Behind closed doors in the meeting room with Fern and Graeme.'

No embellishments or clever speak.

I spent the morning preparing for the extra shots Fern wanted photographed at Palm Beach and thinking about how I needed to get my life in order, but felt lost… alone. Still, as Kurt Cobain once said, wanting to be someone else is a waste of the person you are.

I needed to accept that and find my spirit again, my passion for life and family. But where to start? Matthew believed I was unloving and uncompromising; Lexi insisted I was out to ruin her life; and my friends? Well, they used to think I was fun, or at least had a hint of a personality. But now, who knew? Apart from Di, who I walked with, I didn't have time for friends.

Sometimes, I coveted a complete change to my life, to become a new person, but most of the time, I just wanted to be satisfied with the life I was living… the life I had. Happy with my husband and children, and take great photos, that's what I really wanted. To reclaim my passion. But then photography made me think about Sarah and her bogus book.

Fern had asked me what action I was taking against Sarah. Matthew had asked the same question. But I didn't know. Sarah's book was out there, published for the world to see. I knew the photo was mine and was furious she'd stolen it from me, but I didn't have the energy to battle yet another person. But I knew I needed to find my fighting spirit because I was damn sure I wasn't going to let Sarah get away with stealing my work.

I sat at the utilities desk drinking lukewarm coffee and staring out the window at the city street activity below: a world full of street eaters and coffee carriers, scurrying to work, to catch a bus or to eat at a café. Where I lived, no one scurried anywhere except at five thirty in the morning when they power-walked with dogs and friends. Suburbia. A place where people eked out an existence once they acquired two or more children. And once there, were locked in until the kids left home or you died. Whichever came first.

'Heard anything?' I asked Coco on my way out. There was still no sign of the three of them despite Coco hovering around the closed door with an empty glass and a very red ear.

'Not a peep,' she said. 'It's vexatious! I hate missing out.'

I smiled. Vexing indeed.

CHAPTER 45

That Friday at the beach, double-checking Fern's instructions, I marked off each picture as I photographed it. Close-up of water lapping at the pier. Tick. Seagull in mid-flight against cloudless blue sky. Tick. Seagull perched on a white post in foreground, ocean in the background. Tick. This was more like it. I had a camera and was in my element. This was what I loved. Taking photos of living, breathing things. Things that showed expression and blew in the breeze, not pumpkins, ceramic dishes and napkins. (Actually, napkins do blow in the breeze, so perhaps not the best example.)

I was engrossed in taking photos of couples strolling along the beach and kids squealing in the park when I noticed Mum and Dad walking toward me.

I put down my camera. 'Any success finding a venue?'

From the look on Mum's face, I knew the answer.

She shook her head. 'We've made dozens of calls, checked online. Nothing.'

Dad wrapped his arms around her. 'We can have the wedding at my apartment, Pip.'

'That's not going to work,' she replied. 'We'll do it at mine, but if we can't have a view, I was hoping at least for a garden wedding.'

'Wherever it's held, it will be perfect,' I said. 'No one will mind, as long as you're both happy. Lexi and Angus are so excited. Not many kids get to be at their own grandparents' wedding.'

'We'll sort out something. I've still got a few calls to make.' Dad moved away slightly and punched numbers into his mobile.

'What's next?' I said to Mum. 'Invitations?'

She grimaced. 'Until we decide on a venue, they're on hold.'

I nodded. 'True. But as you said, you've asked everyone verbally, so they've saved the date.'

'The only interstate guests besides Matthew's parents, are Aunt Lucy and Nick.'

Auntie Lucy being Mum's older sister. Obviously, my favourite aunt. And Nick, my favourite uncle.

'There's no way they'll miss this, free drinks and all.' Mum linked her arm through mine. 'How are you doing, Katie?'

'Busy. Stressed.'

'I'm not surprised, love. Working at the magazine can't be helping your state of mind.'

'What do you mean, *my state of mind*?' I asked, unlinking my arm and turning towards her. 'I'm fine.'

As if I could fool Mum. Wasn't it only a few days ago I'd thought I was having a breakdown? I couldn't keep up with my state of mind. In the past twenty-four hours alone, my emotional well-being had run the gamut of feelings from desolate to euphoric. Perhaps euphoric was too strong a word. It had run the gamut of emotions from desolate to hopeful.

'I think you'd feel finer if you weren't there, especially around *that man*.' Mum said *that man* as if... well... as if she knew things she shouldn't know.

Dad touched Mum's shoulder and shook his head. 'We're out of options as far as restaurants go.'

'We'll organise something,' I said brightly. 'And then you'll be married again.'

'Forever this time,' Dad said, hugging Mum.

She swooned. 'Yes, forever.'

'Who's up for fish and chips?' Dad asked.

Not long after, the three of us sat on the beach drinking ginger beer and eating battered fish and potato scallops.

'What do you want to do with yourself, Katie, after your stint at the magazine?' Dad asked. 'I've seen all your albums at Mum's house and the portraits on the walls. You're very talented.'

'Thanks. I'm putting a collection together of Robyn's pregnancy photos to give to her when she has the baby.'

'Wonderful – but I'm sure there's a lot more you can do, like setting up your own studio.' Dad paused. 'It's a crime to waste your gift, Katie.'

'Speaking of crimes, a woman I was at college with has published a book of photos, and she included one of mine.'

Mum popped a chip into her mouth. 'Well done to you.'

'No, I mean she stole it from me and is claiming it's *her* photo.'

'That's outrageous! What are you going to do?' Dad asked.

'Seek legal advice and contact the publishers.'

'What can we do to help?' Dad asked. 'She can't get away with that nonsense.'

I almost smiled. 'No, you're right. She can't get away with that nonsense. As for me, I'm determined to take photographs professionally, but I couldn't handle the magazine industry full time. Been there, done that. I'm too old—'

'Pardon?' Mum and Dad said together.

'I'm not cut out for corporate life, office politics. It's all about following other people's directions, their rules, their way of doing things.' I chewed on some fish. 'Speaking of corporate, Matthew's company has offered him the opportunity to live in Auckland for a couple of years.'

Mum gulped. 'I'll miss you.'

'Thank you, but I'm not moving. I don't think Matthew is either. I think he was after a reaction from me.' And he certainly got it.

'Do you want him to go?' Dad asked.

'I guess if it advances his career. He could always commute. Lots of people do.'

'Forget the business side of things for a moment,' Dad said, 'do you really want Matthew to live in Auckland for the foreseeable future?'

Mum gathered up scraps and walked to nearby bins. Several seagulls trailed behind.

'Because I've lived through it,' Dad went on. 'I know first hand what it's like when a family splits. It's not good. There are no winners.'

Had I heard him correctly? He was hardly able to offer me advice, especially when it came to my family responsibilities.

'Are you forgetting I lived through it, too?' I tried to remain calm. 'Look, I'm fine with the marriage thing – though why you must do it so quickly is beyond me. But that's between the two of you. You're both adults. I'll kill you if you break Mum's heart but I'm willing to trust you again because she does. But don't ever preach to me about family life and family values. They certainly didn't mean a lot to you when you ran off and married—'

'Katie,' Mum yelled. 'Enough! You have no idea what you're talking about. You of all people should know that some things in life are more complicated than they appear.'

'I should have tried harder to be a part of your life and my grandchildren's lives,' Dad said. 'I'll always regret I wasn't there for you, but if you give me a chance now, I'll do my best to make amends.'

'Haven't you ever done something foolish?' Mum said, knowing full well I had, many times over. 'Something selfish? That you regret?'

'I don't want to interfere in your home life,' Dad continued. 'And I have no right to. I'm only saying decisions made in haste sometimes backfire. Things don't always work out for the best.'

We sat in silence for several minutes.

Dad was the one who spoke first. When I was little, he was always the one to initiate a peace plan, especially as Robbie, Mum and I preferred to sulk in separate corners of the house.

'This reminds me of the time you sang in the school concert. You must have been nine, maybe ten. After the concert, we drove to the coast as a treat, and we all sat in silence looking out at the waves. Do you remember why?'

I thought for a moment. 'I didn't think you were at that concert.'

'Your dad was always there, Kate,' Mum said. 'At every concert, every award night, and every parent-teacher meeting.'

Mum was certainly remembering our family life through rose-tinted glasses.

As for me, I couldn't recall. 'Sorry, I don't remember.'

'Your hair had been curled in ringlets specially,' Dad said. 'You always wanted curly hair' – maybe that's why I got that horrid spiral perm – 'and I said you were our own little Shirley Temple up there on stage. Well, you didn't like it. *I'm not a baby*, you said. *I'm not Shirley Temple.* Then Robyn and Mum started singing, *I'm Shirley Temple and I've got curly hair...*'

'You're right. I cried and you asked them to stop singing. Said it was no way to treat a star like me. You stood up for me.' I hadn't thought about that concert in years, yet now I was reminded, I clearly remembered the singing, the sand, and the tears. And it *was* Dad who'd looked after me.

'Another time when the four of us were at the beach' – Dad poured sand from one hand to the other – 'you were about four, and learning to swim. The waves were crashing around, the wind was blowing. But you were determined. Determined to dive into the water just like your dad. *I can do it, Daddy, I can do it. Let me swim. I'll show you,* you said. And you flung yourself into the water and by gosh, you swam, darling. Your head dipped under a wave and just as quickly it bobbed right back up again. Mum almost had a heart attack, but I knew you could do it. Determination and faith, Katie, you've always had it. I wish I had that moment on tape. I wish we could always live in that moment. But sadly, time waits for no man. Or woman.'

I nodded. 'Hence why I love taking photos, capturing a moment in time – that's what Nanna used to say.'

'Ah, Nanna.' Dad stared out to sea. 'My dear old mum. Bless her soul. Nanna loved you so much, Katie.'

'I know.' I sniffed, fighting back tears.

'You have your whole life ahead of you, sweetheart.' He put his arm around me. 'And you have to live it with the same determination and spirit you had in your youth. Things aren't always going to go your way, in fact, they hardly ever do – but you have to keep trying.'

As I sat and listened to him, I realised things in Dad's life probably hadn't worked out the way he wanted them to either.

'Never give up your dream,' Dad continued. 'I never gave up hope that one day your mum and I would be together again. We were meant to be.'

I longed to love him again. To feel the closeness we'd had when I was a child, to recapture all the time we'd lost because of what he did, how he'd hurt Mum and almost destroyed her spirit and will to live.

'Why did you do it, Dad?' Why did you cheat on Mum and ruin it all? Destroy our happy life?'

He didn't answer.

❄

I waved goodbye to them and climbed into my car, watching as Dad walked Mum to the passenger side of his car and opened the door for her, both with smiles so wide their happiness was impossible to disguise.

Mum had said that when she saw Dad weeks ago, it was as if time had stood still. The last twenty-five years simply vanished and now they were starting afresh. She knew at the art gallery she wanted to be with Dad forever and realised she had to take a chance and find the courage to step up and tell Dad she still loved him, even though he'd left her for someone else all those years ago.

Katie, I keep going over all the reasons why Bob and I married in the first place, she'd said. Mum was willing to risk being hurt all over again for the sake of having the love of her life back in her arms once again.

And it seemed to have paid off. So far.

On the drive home, I stopped at the two-dollar shop and bought several celebratory pet sweaters that were decidedly more than two dollars apiece. Then Lexi and Angus helped me dress Rupert, Cleo and Bugs ahead of Monday's pet montage. Rupert loved it, Bugs was indifferent or maybe confused, and Cleopatra was furious. No matter how I tried to attach it, she refused the red angel headband. The other two were far more compliant.

Using the edible Christmas pet treats Dana had couriered to the house that afternoon, naturally coloured with hard yogurt, and beautifully decorated with dog- and cat-friendly green, red, and white icing, I managed to photograph the three animals perched in the garden, surrounded by red flowers and greenery. Tick. Then I found more photos of animals dressed in Christmas garments to complete my medley of ten pictures. Done!!

I spent a busy evening answering emails, returning phone calls and catching up on the week's news. I didn't learn a lot apart from the fact that new research out of London claimed women were angrier in the home than men. Who'd have thought? The article went on to say women were more angry because they struggled to combine paid work with running a household. I could have told them that for free! At least now I had a valid scientific reason for my anger.

CHAPTER 46

I woke up on Saturday morning feeling hungry and wretched. Hungry because I was craving pie, and wretched because I didn't want to get out of bed. I desperately wanted to gaze into a crystal ball and see that a week, a month, a year, ten years from now, all would be okay.

I closed my eyes and visualised Matthew and me together, years from now, happy and in love. Matthew's gorgeous Paul Rudd looks have survived, as has his full head of hair, though now it's in shades of salt and pepper. I'm beside him, looking pretty much as I do now, maybe a few kilos lighter. Obviously in later years I join a gym and take to Botox with gusto!

I got up, showered, then stood in my walk-in wardrobe – it wasn't big but there was enough room to turn around – looking at racks of unsuitable clothes. I had nothing to wear. I know it's what all women say but it was true. I literally had nothing to wear. My jeans sagged around my backside; my shirts revealed unflattering bulges. As for my jumpers and coats, most were misshapen or faded. I really hadn't paid much attention to fashion these past few years.

'Mum, where are you?'

'In here, Lexi,' I said. 'I have nothing to wear.'

'That's my line. Besides, it's only a soccer game. Please don't get dressed up like you did last week. It was *so* embarrassing.'

I winced at the memory. 'I didn't dress up.'

Lexi pretended to belch. 'Sure. Don't wear heels. Black boots and jeans. That'll do. Dad said he's ready to go.'

'What? I'm still in a towel, no make-up and my hair—'

'Mum, I've got my own issues. I'm just passing on the message.'

I stood in the cupboard for a few minutes longer before deciding on black pants and a plain navy sweater. It wasn't going to set the world on fire but at least I felt comfortable.

❄

I waved to Arnaud when we arrived at the soccer field. 'Hey.' I hadn't seen him since the night with Sophie and was determined to act naturally, even though I was still mortified.

'I've got to tell you' – Arnaud shook his head – 'the kids are way easier to deal with than the parents.'

'Mardi giving you a hard time already?'

'And the rest. Two parents have already complained their boys were rested too long last week. Then Mardi pipes up, *I don't want my Ben pulled off the field at all. He's the best player.* Which he is, but I'm not going to agree with her.'

'What did you say?'

'I said it is a team game and every player needs to be rotated throughout the match.'

'Bet they were happy about that.'

'Not at all. I felt like handing over my whistle and saying, "Here, guys. Go for it." I don't get paid for this. I do it because I love the sport, to teach young kids the art, the skills. I don't have to come here week after week to coach and ref.'

'Feel better now you've got that off your chest?'

'*Oui – merci.*'

'Good for you. I think you do a great job—'

'Mum,' Lexi said, 'you are *so* sad.'

Arnaud looked embarrassed.

'Lexi, I didn't mean it like that,' I said, my face turning an unattractive shade of beetroot. 'I meant Arnaud is a great coach.'

'Yeah, right.'

Arnaud blew his whistle and began rounding up the kids for the start of the match.

'Dad's right there, you know.' Lexi pointed towards Matthew.

I looked to see him wolfing down a sausage sandwich and walking towards us, smiling. He looked kind of cute. He offered me a bite of his sandwich, which I accepted, and the game began.

I was fiddling with my camera, getting ready to take a few action shots, when, barely three minutes into the match, the standard shouting started. Fathers from the opposing team gave instructions like, *Tackle him, Tommy!* and *Ryan, get forward or get off the field*, to their sons as they paced like caged lions, up and down the sideline, air-punching and roaring.

Did these people really have so little in their lives that the highlight of their weekend was stamping their feet and beating their chests every Saturday morning at their eight-year-old's soccer game? And then I remembered. I was one of those parents. I wanted my child to win. I wasn't any better because I kept those feelings to myself, though I hoped I never got so worked up I'd attack a ref with an umbrella.

Seeing a couple of overbearing dads push aside two reserves from our team to get a closer look at their sporting progeny, Matthew walked up, tapped one of them on the shoulder and said, 'Guys, settle down. They're only kids.'

They ignored him and continued yelling.

Just then, a boy from the other team accidentally tripped and fell beside Angus.

I grabbed Matthew's arm. 'Is he okay?'

The boy stood, seemingly unhurt, but his father, one of the screamers, yelled, 'Oi, ref, you fuckin' tool, my son's been kicked to the ground. Whatcha gonna do about it?'

Within seconds, the fracas escalated. Arnaud stopped the game, checked on the child, made sure Angus was okay and then walked over to the father who was wildly gesticulating and sweating profusely. Arnaud had barely reached the guy before he punched Arnaud in the face. He fell to the ground, hard.

'Matthew, help him,' I yelled as parents and kids began screaming.

Matthew almost tripped over himself to get to Arnaud and, as he reached him, more punches were thrown.

It was verging on an all-in brawl. Hang on – it *was* an all-in brawl. Parents and officials exchanged blows as mums, dads and grandparents hurled insults across the field while their children looked on in shock. It took over twenty minutes to halt the fight and that was only because someone had the sense to turn on the oval's automatic sprinklers.

A nose was broken, a cheek shattered, and two wrists fractured. The black eyes and bruised egos were too numerous to count.

'This is sport, is it?' Lexi remarked on the drive home.

I brushed the wet hair from Matthew's forehead. 'You're going to have a black eye.'

'Yeah, probably.'

'I'm very proud you didn't hit anyone, though. You only helped Arnaud.'

'And got punched in the process.'

'But you did the right thing, Matt. Really, you did.'

In the back seat, Lexi and Angus made up rude songs about

soccer hooligans and I stared out the window wondering. Wondering where the distance between me and Matthew had come from. Why *did* we argue so much? Usually our fights were petty and pointless.

Me: *Pick your clothes up off the floor, hang your wet towel back on the rack.*

Him: *Jeez, Kate, let it go for once, will you? The house doesn't need to be perfect. The world isn't going to end because there are wet towels on the floor.*

And, of course, he was right. The world wasn't going to end because the house resembled a tip. But it mattered to me. Once upon a time it didn't matter so much. Once, I loved Matthew more than anything in the world. More than a tidy house. But grocery shopping, toilet cleaning and changing nappies would get in the way of even the greatest romance, I'm sure.

I didn't want Matthew to leave. And I didn't want to leave Matthew either – fighting over visitation rights and whose turn it was to spend Christmas with our kids. I didn't want it to come to that. And I certainly didn't want to end up divorced like Mum and Dad, even if it meant we'd remarry later down the track when the messiness of raising our children was behind us. I didn't want to win that badly. Maybe he had a point when he said I shut him out and didn't listen to him anymore.

Sitting across from Matt in the car, I thought about all the things we had in common, starting with Angus and Lexi. We both loved spaghetti vongole, Italian being Matthew's favourite cuisine. Okay, it wasn't going to sustain a life together but there was more. We both loved hiking, gardening and watching old black-and-white movies. How long had it been since we'd done any of those things? Between work and running around after the kids and making sure there was enough milk in the fridge, it didn't leave time for frivolity. And it was something I needed to change.

We were stopped at the traffic lights when Matthew turned to me. 'I look pretty bad, don't I?'

'Not at all.' I smiled. 'You look rugged, lived in. Does it hurt?'

'A bit.'

'I'm so sorry.'

Matthew reached over and held my hand. 'It's going to be all right. Everything's going to be okay.'

From the back seat Angus piped up with, 'Why do grown-ups do stupid things?'

'I have no idea, darling, no idea at all,' I answered truthfully.

At home nursing his black eye with frozen peas, Matthew said, 'I've been thinking about your parents' nuptial dilemma.'

'Please tell me you've come up with a brilliant plan.'

'I think so. Why don't we have the wedding here?'

'Here, as in our house here?'

'Sure. Why not?'

'How can we? The garden's a mess. Who'd do the catering? Imagine all the furniture we'd need to hire.'

He sat the peas on the coffee table, stood and walked over to join me on the sofa. 'It's a few phone calls and would mean the world to Pip. We're talking about fifteen guests. If you discount Pip, Bob, Robyn, you, me, Lexi, Angus, and my parents, that's an extra six people. Definitely manageable if we agree that on Christmas Day, we'll eat leftovers and watch *Die Hard*.'

'Really?' I hugged him. 'Sounds perfect. You're really fine with it?'

Matthew took my hand and kissed it. 'More than fine. Let's do it.'

CHAPTER 47

In the shower on Sunday morning, I thought back to Mum's reaction when I told her Matthew and I would host the wedding on Christmas Eve. She burst into tears. 'Really, Kate? Really?' She was overjoyed and so was I. Until panic set in. There was so much to organise.

Deep breaths. How hard could it be?

All I needed was a plan, one I could stick to.

1. Make sure all aspects of the wedding were covered: tables, flowers, menu, crockery, etc. It was a very long list.
2. Get into the festive spirit by erecting the Christmas tree, hanging fairy lights, etc.
3. Eradicate Graeme from my life.

Reminiscent of yesterday morning, I walked into my wardrobe, wrapped in a towel. Still nothing to wear. That was another thing. I needed to buy new clothes. I opened my enormous underwear drawers – three of them. They were overflowing with ill-fitting greying knickers with frayed elastic.

All the ugly underwear I'd ever owned in my life had come to live out their final days in my drawers. There were countless bras that didn't fit. They were either too big, too small or had wonky wires which speared me. And all because I refused to get professionally fitted. For years, I'd guessed my size rather than suffer the embarrassment of having an elderly bespectacled lady with a tape measure draped around her neck fit me. I glanced at the beautiful black lacy lingerie Matthew had bought me last Christmas and persisted in asking me to wear for the next two months. I didn't have the heart to tell him the set was two sizes too small.

I dumped the contents of my drawers on the bed and walked downstairs in search of a plastic garbage bag. One normally reserved for garden waste.

'What's going on?' Lexi asked as she watched me throw piece after piece in the bag, including several sets of maternity knickers and bras.

'Spring clean.'

'It's summer.'

'I'm a bit late. Come and sit on the bed and watch me toss everything out.' I wanted Lexi to join me. To chat. Or not. For her to sit on my bed and watch me the way she used to when she was four years old. Back when she was little and adored me. We adored each other.

'No, thank you!' Lexi was clearly repulsed at the suggestion.

'Come on, stay with me. And for goodness' sake, put in your retainer and stop grinding your teeth.' I tried not to nag, but I was her mother, after all. When she was older, she'd thank me. No adult ever complained about having straight teeth.

'I do it to stay in control, like you do.'

'Pardon? If I grind my teeth – do I really grind my teeth? Anyway, it's got nothing to do with control. It's because I feel overwhelmed. Grinding my teeth is a diversion. It's not something I use to get your attention.'

'Really? Because it works.' Lexi stood and walked out.

Half an hour later, I was left with two reasonable bras – at least they could be worn without cutting off circulation – and only three pairs of briefs. It was oddly satisfying staring into a full plastic bag of garments I'd never have to look at again. And then there were the empty drawers. The possibilities, the expectation… I peeked into my wardrobe, at a battle waiting to be fought… but one step at a time.

Besides, it was almost time to meet Mum and Robyn. We were going wedding shopping.

I called out to Lexi and surprisingly she responded.

'What do you think?' I asked her as I stood before the mirror, deliberating over my black spotted dress from three seasons ago. 'Does this look okay?'

'I guess.' She paused. 'You need one of those True Mirrors.'

'A what?'

'A mirror that has lots of different angles, so you get a three-dimensional view. You know, so you can see yourself as other people do.'

Truth: I wasn't sure I really wanted to know how others saw me.

❄

'Before we meet Nanna, I'm buying new underwear,' I said, after we'd parked. I was in search of gorgeous lingerie. Undergarments that would transform and inspire me. Give me the confidence I was seeking. And I knew just the place, a gorgeous lingerie shop. 'Down this arcade,' I said to Lexi, who was dragging her feet.

'This doesn't look like your kind of shop,' Lexi remarked

when we stopped.

Probably because the window display featured slim models in various suggestive poses, wearing skimpy black lingerie and tiny peek-a-boo bras and crotchless knickers.

'Nonsense!'

We stepped inside. A petite strawberry-blonde stopped picking at her fingernails for a microsecond and glanced over. She looked incredibly bored. Bored or haughty, I couldn't tell, but I could see her black push-up bra through her thin chiffon top. No doubt she was wearing a thong as well. Lexi was right. I felt immediately intimidated. I mumbled something about a black bra and scurried out of the shop.

Lexi followed. 'Told you.'

Next stop, an upscale department store. Lexi wandered off in search of the computer section and I headed towards women's underwear. The area was huge. Vast tracts of land featuring a multitude of bras and undies in every conceivable style and colour. Hipsters, G's, boy leg, Wonder bras... on and on. Racks as far as the eye could see.

A woman in her late fifties approached me. Pearl, her silver badge informed me. I tried hiding behind a sheer black teddy, but she found me. Before I knew it, we were in a tiny changing room together, Pearl, myself and the twelve wall-to-wall mirrors. I took off one of the two bras I owned.

'Hmm,' she said, examining my shoddy worn bra. 'Formfit haven't made this model for over a decade.'

'Really?' I crossed my arms over my chest while trying not to appear precious or uncomfortable about my nakedness. 'I thought it might have been eight years old, but ten? Really?'

'When was the previous time madam was fitted?' Without waiting for an answer, she pushed my arms away and hooped her tape measure across my back and around my front, over my embarrassed nipples.

'Fitted?' I repeated. 'A couple of years.' I had never been measured before and as I stood in the cubicle, shivering and exposed, I understood why.

'Thirty-eight C, I think. I'll bring you some samples.' She disappeared from the closet, and I stood alone with the mirrors and my naked chest. Maybe it hadn't been such a great idea to turf out all my underwear.

I forced myself to look in the mirror. At least I still had my skirt on. No doubt Pearl would collapse if she saw the state of my cottontails. Moments later, she was back, fitting a new black bra to my reluctant body.

'Here, I'll fasten the snaps,' she said, turning me around. 'There. Now bend over, that's right. Cup your breasts with your hands. No, inside the bra, so that your breasts feel comfortable and fill out the material. Now stand up. Straight up. Excellent. Now with both of your index fingers, separate your breasts.'

I did as I was told.

'Let me look at them. See. Standing up at attention, not squashed and hidden from view. You have lovely breasts.' Pearl was practically floating with joy. 'You should show them off. How do they feel?'

'Good. Great...' And they did. No wires cut into me. And my boobs actually looked bigger, rounder, bouncier. The bra was pretty, too. It wasn't a ridiculous slip of material a teenager would wear, but it was fetching, nonetheless. I was sold.

I bought three bras in black, white and nude, all with matching knickers. At the counter I spied a book, *What Not To Wear*, and added it to my booty. My clothes needed a complete overhaul and I had to start somewhere. I put it all on my American Express card without looking at the total. After ten years of wearing the same bra, I was entitled.

Even so, I choked slightly as I punched in my password.

CHAPTER 48

Lexi and I found Mum and Robyn bickering in a nearby French-inspired café, and picking at rockmelon, prosciutto, basil bites, and lemon crêpes.

'Odd combination,' I said, sitting. 'What happened to old-fashioned chocolate cake?'

Robyn shushed me. 'I'm pregnant.' She paused. 'So the wedding's at your house, Kate?'

I nodded. 'We didn't have many options. In fact, we had no options.'

Lexi hugged her nanna before sitting. 'It's going to be epic. I can't wait.'

'Yes, it will,' Mum replied.

'Although, remember what happened to Samantha before her wedding? She had a chemical peel. Her face was one giant red peeling pus ball. Gross,' Robyn stated.

'Thanks, Robyn.' Mum sighed. 'I'll remember not to book a facial peel.'

'And don't get your teeth bleached, either. You'll blind the guests.'

'What are you two talking about?' Lexi asked, after she and I had settled and ordered drinks.

'Robyn's telling me about all the things that can go wrong on my wedding day.' Mum sipped her Earl Grey.

'Not *on* your wedding day, Mum, before it,' Robyn corrected her.

'Like getting one of those spray-on fake tans and coming out looking like an orange monster?' I asked. 'By the way, do I grind my teeth? Lexi says I do but—'

'God, you always grind your teeth,' Robyn barked. 'I'm surprised you've got any left.'

Lexi smirked. 'You need to get one of the mouth guards you force me to wear.'

'Anyway,' Robyn continued. 'What was I saying? Oh yeah, that's right, the list of potential wedding disasters is endless. And then there's the wedding itself.'

'Robyn!' I sensed Mum was close to tears.

Robyn turned to me. 'What? You have to prepare for these things. What if the caterer serves prawns that have been sitting in the sun too long? And someone vomits on Mum's dress? Or worse, mine? Or—'

'Or you say something wildly insensitive to upset me?' Mum snapped. 'Give it a rest. Please?'

'What?' Robyn huffed. 'What did I say?'

'Enough.' Mum banged her cup on the table. I thought I might be able to rely on my daughters to help me, and for once, just this one time, put me first. Is that too much to ask?'

'Sorry,' I mumbled.

'Me too,' Robyn muttered. 'It's the foetus talking. I wish he'd keep quiet.'

Lexi regarded the three of us and coughed. 'Dr Thom hosted a wedding special last week—'

'Who?' Mum looked confused.

'Relationship guru,' Robyn replied. 'Netflix. You wouldn't know him.'

'And he said when somebody's getting married,' Lexi resumed, 'everybody needs to say, *It's their day, and if I need to step to the side and give them this day, then it's a gift I'm going to give them.*' She took a breath and, in a tone that suggested superiority, said, 'I think Nanna would like us to do that.'

Mum smiled. 'Thank you, Lexi. The calm voice of reason from my granddaughter.'

I resisted asking Lexi exactly when she'd been watching *Dr Thom*, given how much homework and extra assignments she had, but I didn't want more arguing. Instead, I reached into my bag and pulled out some paper. 'I've got a checklist. Let's see. Venue, check. And I think the caterers have been confirmed too, Mum?'

'Yes, and menu selected, apart from dessert. I'll do that.'

'Good.' I crossed a couple of items off the list. 'Prenup? Signed?'

'I beg your pardon?' Mum warned.

'Kidding. I've emailed a party hire site and we can bundle furniture and crockery together from the one spot. Flowers?'

'Ordered.'

'Cake?' Lexi asked.

'I've already made a plum pudding for Christmas,' Mum replied. 'Why don't we have that together with a traditional festive pavlova and berries?'

Lexi clapped. 'Yes please.'

Robyn nodded. 'I'm happy with that. Wedding attire?'

'At home hanging in my wardrobe.' Mum's dress was a secret. She wouldn't budge on details no matter how hard we pressed her.

'Hints?' I asked. 'At least tell us the colour.'

'Is it ruched?' Robyn said.

'Are you wearing a mini?' Lexi probed.

'My lips are sealed,' Mum replied.

'You're very good at keeping secrets,' I said.

'I've had decades of practice.'

'Next on the list – hair, make-up, et cetera?' I asked.

'Booked for you, me, Robyn and Lexi. I just need to confirm the time.'

'What about special effects?' Robyn asked. 'To give your wedding the *wow* factor... like disco lighting? Or maybe professional entertainers?'

'What?' I asked. 'Like jugglers? A circus act?'

'Maybe, or a wedding stripogram. Something to lighten the mood.'

'Implying the mood won't be light on its own?' Mum was fierce. 'How about a string quartet?'

'Lovely, but Christmas Eve.' I sounded like a broken record.

'Yes,' Robyn agreed and pinched me. 'I can see the Insta posts now.'

Fearful of any more café flare-ups, I paid the bill. It was time to get down to business: searching for appropriate wedding attire for Lexi.

'Robyn's wearing black. Why can't I?' Lexi grumbled.

'Just because Robyn's decided on a black chiffon muumuu doesn't mean you have to,' I told her. 'Any other colour, Lex.'

'That'd be right. Because I choose to wear black, you're telling me I can't.'

'It's not that, darling,' Mum soothed. 'But it's a wedding... it's festive. And there are so many great colours in the shops. You can choose any one of them.'

'To be fair,' Robyn chimed in, 'I haven't made up my mind. I might wear aubergine. Or scarlet. Maybe a polka-dot pant suit.'

We walked into a boutique where every piece of clothing was size zero (size zero being the equivalent of an adult having an eight-year-old girl's waist measurement, but let's not get me started) and exposed plenty of skin.

'I... I don't know.' Mum gazed at Lexi as she paraded a form-fitting, hot-pink halter-top complete with diamantés. It was more like a very revealing bra. The calf-length skirt sat on Lexi's hips, or rather her pubic bone. Very low cut. Everything Lexi picked out was tight, backless, frontless, slashed to the thigh, or a combination of the above.

'Here,' I said to Robyn, having picked up a perfume from the counter. 'Let me squirt this on you in case it's revolting.'

'For goodness' sake!' Robyn dutifully extended her arm and I sprayed. Ten seconds later we both took a deep breath and wrinkled our noses. 'Yuck!'

So much for perfume taking my mind off Lexi's clothing. After much deliberation, we compromised. Sort of. Lexi chose a pale-pink silk backless ankle-length dress.

'I adore the colour,' Mum said. 'Soft and romantic.'

'Lovely,' I agreed. Some outrageously priced silver sparkly sandals completed her outfit. And everyone was still on speaking terms. Bonus.

As we walked out of the shop and into the central courtyard, 'I Saw Mummy Kissing Santa Claus' was blaring from the surround-sound speakers.

'The two worst things about Christmas,' Robyn explained. 'Festive songs and crowds. Ugh.'

'You can't really sing about your mother kissing Santa anymore,' Lexi chirped. 'It's subjecting minors like me to softcore porn.'

Mum blinked.

'As for Rudolph,' Robyn said. 'He was bullied.'

'Thank you both. Let's hoof it to the next shop.' I'd researched online and had my eye on an emerald-green number, so I led the way to the boutique to see it for real. Being the new confident me, I marched straight over to where it was hanging and picked a dress off the rack. Happily, it was in my size.

As I entered the changing room, a chirpy shop assistant wearing antler ears said, 'We have other colours if this one's not to your taste.'

Was there something people weren't telling me? Did I look like a bag lady? Did green look hideous on me?

'No, I love this colour,' I told her, as she critically examined me, head to toe.

I hurriedly closed the curtain. Once on, the dress was far from perfect. But if I wore a super-tight body stocking underneath it and draped a black wrap strategically around my shoulders and across my mid-section – and didn't eat or drink anything at the reception or the day before – I could possibly get away with it, once my hair was professionally washed and styled, my make-up professionally applied, and I stood in flattering, forgiving candlelight. Out of the wind.

Sold!

Lexi and I arrived home to find Matthew and Angus admiring a huge pine tree in the family room, upright and looking stunning even without decorations.

'Wow,' I said, walking up to Matthew and kissing him. 'You've outdone yourselves. Scout hall? *Living Christmas Tree* fundraiser?'

'Where else? And before you ask,' Matthew said proudly, 'we sprayed for spiders and insects outside before we brought it in. It's been denuded of crawling creatures.'

'Thank you, darling. No one wants to wake up on Christmas morning and find a family of arachnids living inside their presents.'

CHAPTER 49

The first three days of the week passed relatively uneventfully. Graeme was occupied in Melbourne with a Bachelor of the Year Christmas reunion and photo shoot, so I was happily left to get on with my nativity montage.

Head down, I pounded through the subject matter. Day fifteen: *Holiday Cards*; Day sixteen: *Something Silver*; Day seventeen: *School Holidays*; Day eighteen: *Grateful*; Day nineteen: *Wreaths*; Day twenty: *Traditions.*

As I ticked off each day closer to December twenty-fifth, it got harder finding photos and food ideas, but I was determined. Day twenty-one: *Self-portraits*; Day twenty-two: *Wrapped*; Day twenty-three: *Christmas Eve Eve*; Day twenty-four: *The Night Before Christmas*; Day twenty-five: *Christmas Day!*

Fussing with my online picture boards, I put together believable holiday story ideas, then emailed Fern for approval, and Dana for the few food items I'd need to accompany the shoots. I was organised and pleased with what I'd achieved.

The plans for the wedding were coming together too. With Mum and Dad having organised the celebrant, caterer, menu, flowers, and make-up people, I hired extra tables and chairs, crockery and several potted hydrangeas and poinsettias to decorate the garden. Wedding attire was also sorted, so I was relaxed (sort of) about Mum's big day. There was nothing I could do if there was a disruptive summer thunderstorm at the precise time of nuptials, so I had to stop worrying about it.

Still to discuss: string quartet and other music. DJ or video Christmas-themed? I brushed thoughts of inappropriate bridal songs to the back of my mind when I met up with Diane, Thursday morning.

'I guess David told you all about the soccer fiasco on Saturday,' I said as we walked together in the early morning sunshine. 'It was terrible. Punches were thrown, kids were crying, Matthew got smacked in the eye. Dreadful.'

'I heard.'

'The kids'll have interesting memories of their final game of the year, but I'm sure they'll all play again after Christmas break. We just have to be more vigilant about sideline bullies.'

We walked in silence for a moment before Diane spoke. 'Nina confessed she and Sam had been drinking beer and spritzers before they kissed. She promised that was all they did and said she was super embarrassed when I caught them.'

'I bet.'

'And that after she'd sobered up and thought about it, she knew it was dumb.'

'Nina's level-headed. I'm sure she really does think it was silly.'

'Yeah, but David's being a real dick about it. Saying Nina's ruined Christmas and Sam won't be allowed to stay with us anymore. Because, of course, he told Sam's mum.'

'Escalation?'

'Yep. The weekend was a disaster, made worse by having to spend it with David's family. In hindsight, we should've stayed at a hotel alone instead of taking Nina and Tom to his parents, but it was my weekend to have them stay. What a mess.'

I thought about how I'd feel if I had to divide parenting duties with Matthew. I didn't envy Di's position. I'd struggle as well.

Then I thought about Lexi having sex with Hunter, or some other boy who wasn't related to her. I'd freak. It's not like I expected her to wait until she was married, but I didn't want her having to deal with all the ramifications of a physical relationship until she was mature enough to deal with it. Imagine if she got pregnant! It didn't bear thinking about. Besides, Lexi might not have children until her thirties, or not at all. If that happened, I wondered if I'd become one of those irritating mothers who talked about 'ticking' and 'biological' in the same sentence.

❄

Graeme would be back in the office today, so I'd steeled myself to talk with Fern about leaving, given I'd been at *Delicious Bites* three weeks and Simone was returning next week. All that was left was for me to complete the nativity calendar which I could do remotely.

'Mumbling to yourself,' Arnaud said as he passed me in the corridor.

'Something like that.' Working out my battle plan. 'How are you? You don't look so good.' Arnaud had plaster taped across his nose and his cheeks were swollen.

'Broken nose. Under-nines soccer, a rough game.' He forced a smile. 'Don't say anything funny. I can't laugh. God 'elp me if I catch a cold.'

'Can I get you anything? Coffee?'

'You are sweet, but no, it's—'

'Yes, she is sweet, isn't she?' Graeme sneered at us. 'I notice you haven't made my coffee – yet.' He turned to Arnaud. 'What happened to you? Girlfriend found out about you and the K, hey?'

'See you later, Kate.' Arnaud dismissed Graeme with a shake of the head.

'You still coach next year?' I called after him.

'*Oui*, of course, hopefully healed so as to not scare the boys.' Too soon, he disappeared round the corner.

'Sweet on lover boy, are we? Is that why you rejected me?'

'Leave me alone.' Number three on my to-do list: rid my life of Graeme.

'What makes you think you're so great? I've seen the way you look at Arnaud. You want him, don't you? You come across all prim and proper, but you forget, I've seen you in action. I've seen how you behave when you let your guard down. You're an animal.'

'And you're a bully. You shouldn't be allowed to work with people.'

'Sticks and stones.' Graeme moved closer, backing me against the wall.

'Kate,' Fern said, entering the room.

Graeme jumped. I kept my facial expression blank.

'Your animal montage from Monday is blowing up. People love your pets. You must respond.'

'What's this about?' Graeme asked. 'Have you gone behind my back—'

'How dare you?' Fern's voice was ice. 'Have you forgotten, I'm your boss, Graeme? Kate's doing a special online Christmas photography project. Nothing to do with you.'

Graeme went to argue, his face flushed beetroot.

'Don't,' Fern replied.

Ignoring them, I fossicked in my bag and pulled out my ringing mobile.

'Mrs Cavendish?' a vaguely familiar voice said.

'Yes?' I sniffed, wiping my eyes and nose with a scrap of tissue.

Graeme glared at me before stalking away.

'It's Tania Westley.'

'Yes, Mrs Westley,' I said apprehensively. What on earth had Lexi done this time? It wasn't even nine thirty.

'Lexi's had an accident.'

'Oh my—'

'We've called an ambulance.'

CHAPTER 50

On the drive to hospital, after I rang Matthew, I kept going over what I'd said to Lexi when I'd dropped her off that morning. *I love you. Stay at school all day. Promise?*

This week had been relatively calm. She was well on her way to catching up with her assignments, and I had faith she'd move up to the next grade in the new year. Last night, Matthew, Lexi, Angus and I had spent two hours after dinner doing normal family activities including decorating the Christmas tree and hanging fairy lights.

Barely an hour ago, she'd waved me away without a backward glance.

We've called an ambulance. Mrs Westley's words rang in my ears.

My nightmares were getting worse. The worst being something terrible would happen to Lexi and I'd be powerless to stop it. Powerless to help her. Save her. Keep her from harm. It was my job to protect her. I'd failed two weeks ago... and I'd failed again this morning.

As a teenager, I said things to my mother like:

1. You don't understand. It's not like in the old days, times have changed.
2. I hate you. I wish you were dead.
3. I hate myself. I wish I was dead.
4. Stop worrying about me. I'm fine. I don't need you to protect me.

I'm fine. Funnily enough these were the very same words Lexi said to me. On a regular basis. And I knew how untrue they were.

Fine!

She wasn't fine and neither was I.

❄

Hours later, Lexi lay in a hospital bed with her arm in plaster. Her body was a mass of bruises, scratches and cuts, the most severe covered in bandages.

'What happened?' I asked after the sedatives had worn off.

She looked at me, then her father and finally turned away, closing her eyes. 'You wouldn't understand.'

'Please, Lexi.' I stroked her hair. 'Try me.'

'Do you really want to know, Mum?'

I nodded. But did I really? Was I ready for what my daughter was about to tell me?

Some things in life are certain. Like there'll always be a mountain of dirty clothes to be cleaned even though you did three loads yesterday and the washing basket was empty this morning.

But some things were more puzzling. I wasn't prepared for Lexi's need to grow up so quickly. She was still a young child, at least in my eyes. She was thirteen. Logically, I shouldn't have been mystified. I'd lived through being that age. And yes, there was barely sunshine.

Lexi had changed so much in the last six months she was almost unrecognisable to me. I wiped my tears. Seeing her lying in a hospital bed, distressed and shattered, broke me.

'What were you doing up a tree?' I asked gently.

'Spying on Hunter.'

'How?' My voice became a little more strained. 'You were both at school.'

'He was talking to Susie outside the school gates. I needed to get a closer look.'

'I'll go and find us some coffee.' Matthew bent down, kissed Lexi's forehead and walked out of the room and into the corridor, hesitating before turning left towards the nurses' station.

Focusing, I asked, 'Why were you spying on them?'

'God, Mum, because I was. All right?' Lexi was crying. 'I knew you wouldn't understand.'

'Lex, all I know is you fell three metres from a tree, and now have concussion and a badly broken arm. 'Why were you spying on Hunter?'

'He dumped me, okay.' Lexi's sobs became louder. 'Now all my friends are going to dump me. I'll be deleted from Facebook, TikTok, Snapchat. Removed from everyone's "top friends" list.' She gulped in a lungful of air. 'I've probably already been replaced. All because I don't have Hunter anymore.'

My darling girl. I closed my eyes for a moment. 'Sweetheart, I'm so sorry to hear that. I really am.' I stroked her hair some more. 'How can I make things better?'

'You can't. Everyone's making fun of me. I'm worthless, a nobody. My life's over.'

'Don't say that.'

'Why? It's the truth.' She turned her head away. 'I knew you wouldn't understand.'

'I do, Lex. We'll get through this together.' I was trying to be positive even as I imagined her being endlessly bullied and then cast aside by her so-called friends. 'Thank goodness it's only your arm that's broken. It could have been much worse.'

'How?' She turned to face me, her voice cool. 'How could it have been worse? Now I have no friends. I wish I was dead.'

I tried to gather my words, to say something that would reach and resonate with how she was feeling. 'Lexi, I remember—'

'Please don't. You're old. You have no idea.'

I bit my lip. Thinking. 'Yes, I'm old,' I said slowly, 'and I have no idea how you're feeling.' I breathed deeply. 'I hate seeing you like this, Lex. I love you, darling.' An overwhelming urge to wrap Lexi in my arms and never let her go, struck me. 'I'll help you get through this. We'll do it together. Trust me.'

'Why?' Her voice was pure venom. 'Why would I trust you? I don't need you telling me what to do anymore. You hate me, too!'

As the tired, confused mother of a teenage daughter, I wanted to tell Lexi I did understand her. Times hadn't changed so much. I worried about her. That would never change. Even if she became a mother herself, I'd sit up late at night worrying about her. Lexi's happiness would always be uppermost in my mind. I didn't want her shutting me out of her life. I'd always love Lexi more than she could ever know. And if she ever had her own child, she'd understand. But how to explain that? I couldn't. It was impossible.

'I don't hate you. I love you.'

'Go away and leave me alone. This is absolutely the worst thing that's ever happened to me.'

I nodded and held her good hand. Yes, it probably was the

worst thing that had happened to Lexi in her short life. What I found so sad was she didn't realise this was only the beginning. Mum was right. There'd be many more times like this ahead for Lexi. Her journey had only begun.

Still, I held her hand so tightly that she cried out. 'Mum!'

'Sorry.' Reluctantly, I eased my hold, and caught my breath as I blinked away more tears. I wanted her to feel that closeness between us. For Lexi to come back to me. Trust me. Feel secure in my arms once again.

She wiped her eyes with tissues. 'It's okay. I'm fine.'

She wasn't. She'd said it to make both of us feel better.

Once more, Lexi was the calm but jaded teenager who insisted everything was okay.

Fine!

❄

'Everything will be brighter in the morning,' I assured Lexi after we'd arrived home and I'd helped her into her pyjamas, pumped her full of medicine and tucked her into bed. Even though it was only four in the afternoon, the excellent drugs the doctor had given her had taken effect. He'd told us she'd probably sleep for the next eighteen hours, waking only for toilet breaks and pain relief every four to five hours.

'It won't. My life's over.' Lexi's bravado slumped as exhaustion took over. 'And, Mum,' she said, sniffling, 'I lost my retainer. It fell out when I hit the ground.'

'Shh, it's okay. Don't worry about that now. Guess how much I love you?' I said, referring to the title of her favourite childhood book.

'Dunno. Not much.'

'This much.' I stretched out my arms as wide as they would go. 'I love you right up to the moon, darling.' I kissed her forehead before she turned away. I hesitated a moment and walked towards her door.

'Mum,' she said in a tiny voice, 'I love you to the moon as well.'

'And back,' I croaked, rushing back into her room and squeezing her tight.

'My arm!'

CHAPTER 51

'Are you sure about this?' Robyn asked, when we met at hospital for her penultimate antenatal class.

'Of course.' I was shocked Robyn was thinking about someone other than herself. 'Lexi's asleep and sitting in a room full of pregnant women will help take my mind off her troubles for a couple of hours.'

Five minutes before the class started, we settled ourselves. We weren't with our regular group and decided there was little point trying to bond with strangers. Besides, we were both too exhausted to make new friends.

Robyn appeared drained and pale. Maybe because she was wearing a flowing orange and brown creation. At least she was calm.

'Insta snap?' she asked.

I nodded and looked her up and down. 'Though there are more flattering clothes.'

Robyn grinned and stroked the fabric. 'This ensemble was made for beach holidays and endless sunshine.'

She had no idea how abruptly her life was about to change. 'At least you're wearing shoes again. Sensible flats too.'

'Yes.' She looked about the room. 'Check all the no-nonsense shoes here tonight. Please edit mine from any photos.'

Twenty minutes into the session about what to expect during labour, Robyn announced, 'No epidural for me. Why would I fancy a needle stuck in my back?' She made a stabbing motion with her right hand. It was effective because the woman next to her grimaced and shied away.

I sniggered. 'Why don't we do a post about that?'

'Ha. Ha. Seriously, I'm going to have a water birth, pure and simple. No gas. No drugs and no bloody great needle jabbed in my back. A massage with oils and soothing classical music is all the stimulant I'll need.'

Robyn had obviously forgotten our recent forceps conversation.

A couple of pregnant women nodded their heads in approval. Others, like the woman next to Robyn, looked at her in horror and covered her mouth with her hand.

Men shifted uncomfortably in their seats. I knew what they were thinking because I was thinking the same thing: *Who is this insane woman? Water birth, baby, blood, red bloody water. Is there still time to escape?* From my experience, any way you chose to do it, childbirth was not for the faint-hearted.

Eyes swung from Robyn to me. That's right, hello! I'm her birth partner. I sunk lower into my chair.

❄

'Really, Robyn,' I said, after we staggered out later, 'I thought that guy was going to bop you over the head when you started banging on about how all men are only in it for the good times, that none of them would ever stick by their partners once the baby was born so they might as well leave tonight.'

'It's true. They're only prolonging the inevitable.'

'Some of those men looked genuinely excited about imminent parenthood.'

'Yeah, right. What about you? Telling the lank haired woman she should rent an explicit childbirth video and watch it repeatedly – on a large widescreen TV in the freezing cold, naked, on the loudest volume setting, and with all the lights on, preferably fluorescent. "And even then," you said, she "couldn't begin to imagine the agony of childbirth." What about that?'

'Obviously, I was being mean. I didn't expect her to vomit on her partner.'

'Lucky we were already at hospital.'

'She never should have eaten nachos before class anyway.'

While the rest of the class fussed over the vomiter, Robyn and I plonked down our peppermint teas and half-eaten McVitie's and bolted out the door.

According to my calculations, Robyn was approximately three and a half weeks away from giving birth and I was pretty sure neither of us was adequately prepared.

❄

At home, I raced upstairs to Lexi's room. Matthew was sitting beside her in the darkness, stroking her good arm. Cleo and Rupert were curled up together at the foot of her bed, asleep.

I squatted beside Matthew, my hand resting on his shoulder. 'How is she?'

'Not bad. I've given her more medicine. Saying weird things, mumbling mostly.'

We both stood and walked away from Lexi's bed.

'How's Robyn?'

'Still Robyn. She's in for a huge shock... I feel like this is my fault, Matthew. If I was looking after her—'

'You can't always be there for her. She's an adult. She has to stand on her own two feet.'

'I was talking about Lexi, not Robyn.'

'Honey, Lexi was at school. There's nothing you could have done to stop her from climbing a tree and falling.'

'But I didn't know about Hunter, that he'd broken up with her.'

'Neither did I. She told me he wasn't even her boyfriend.'

'Dads aren't supposed to be in the loop. Mothers are.'

'I thought we were co-parents, equal responsibility and all that.'

I bit my tongue. *When it suits you*, I grumbled to myself, thinking back to my first day at *Delicious Bites*.

'Anyway, the main thing is Lexi's safe.'

'But what if she'd fallen on her head and broken her neck? I've failed her as a parent.'

'It's not a test, Kate.'

'What do you mean, *not a test*? Every day's a test and every day I either pass or fail. Most days I fail spectacularly, especially where Lexi is concerned.'

Matthew took my hand. 'You haven't failed. *We* haven't failed.'

'Mum?' Lexi squinted into the semi-darkness, her voice weak. 'Are you there?'

'Hello, darling,' I called. 'I'm here.'

Matthew let my hand go. 'I'll leave you two to talk.' He walked out of the room, and I sat on Lexi's bed beside her.

She winced. 'My arm hurts.'

'I know it does, sweetie, but it'll be better soon.' I'm thinking six weeks. Everything takes six weeks.

'How soon? I've ruined Nanna's wedding, haven't I?'

Mum's wedding! I hadn't given it a thought. 'No, of course you haven't. Why would you say such a thing?'

'Look at me. I'm ugly. I can't be Nanna's bridesmaid looking like this.'

'Looking like what? You've got a couple of scratches. You're still gorgeous. And when you smile, you light up the room, bruises or no bruises.'

'You have to say that. You're my mother. If you don't say it, no one will.'

'You *are* gorgeous, Lexi.'

Rupert and Cleo edged their way further up the bed in search of hands to pat them. I pushed them both onto the floor and, without so much as a sideways glance, they jumped back up onto the bed again.

'Let them stay, please.'

'I don't know how much sleep you'll get with these two snoring beside you.'

'I'll be okay.' She patted them as they settled. 'Mum, do I have to go back to school?'

'Eventually.'

'I just want to fit in, but nothing's working.' She started crying again. 'I thought Susie was my friend, and now I'm scared of getting my head flushed down the toilet.'

Hearing the words *head* and *flushed* in the same sentence brought back agonising memories from year eight at high school. Twisted flashbacks. I kept as far away from the girls' toilets as I could. At the time, there were rumours the school cat, Sox, had been flushed and hence why he was deaf in one ear, but they were never substantiated. Still, I don't think I used a school bathroom for three years.

Twenty-five years later, my daughter held the same fears. What was Lexi's school doing to protect students like her? She shouldn't be worried about being unable to use the bathroom. And as for falling out of a tree on school grounds, where had the playground supervisors been at that time?

'But worse,' Lexi wept, pulling me back into the conversation, 'they'll post rumours about me on TikTok.'

This was a whole new world to me. I massaged her spiky scalp. 'I'm sure it's just talk.'

'It's not. Girls post rumours on Insta and Snapchat all the time. TikTok mostly.'

'All bullies are gutless cowards. Cyberbullies are no different. We'll get through this together, I promise.'

'So I don't have to go to school tomorrow?'

'No, not tomorrow, and you'll have the weekend before school on Monday.'

I stroked Cleo and she purred contentedly. 'Then, you've only got another four days of classes before you break up for the holidays, assuming you finish your assignments.'

She grunted. 'Do you sometimes wish I was never born?'

'Never, Lexi. How could you think such a thing? You're the daughter I've wished for all my life. I can't imagine how empty my world would be without you in it. You're my angel.' I looked down to where my tears had fallen on her cheek.

Even with her bruises, cuts and rough hair, Lexi *was* gorgeous. Man-boy posters adorned her walls, her floor was strewn with clothes, books and other paraphernalia, but that was Lexi. And as frustrating and difficult as she could be, I loved her more than ever.

I picked up her school jacket and hung it in the closet. Stuffed out of sight beside her clothes were all the cuddly toys Lexi had been collecting since birth. Hidden, but not out of reach. Whenever I broached the subject of donating them to charity, she'd shut me down. How bad a kid could she be if she refused to part with her teddies? I placed several of them between her, Cleo and Rupert.

Matthew was dozing when I crawled into bed. 'Lexi okay?' he mumbled, rubbing his eyes.

'She will be. She's worried about getting her head flushed at school.'

Matthew rolled over and sat up. 'What?' He sounded genuinely shocked.

'Apparently there are some spirited older girls who make it their business to make the other girls' lives miserable. Lexi thinks she's on their hit list.'

'Why?'

'Because of what happened with Hunter, and now with her broken arm and bruises, well, she thinks she's ugly. She thinks she'll never have another boyfriend and she's got no friends. She's miserable trying to keep up with the cool kids. I wish I could protect her from it all. The thing is it's probably going to get worse. She's barely six months into being a teenager.'

'She wouldn't have time to be miserable if she was kicking a football around the oval with friends.'

'I'll remind you of that when Angus is thirteen. Besides, you know what girls are like.'

'No, no I don't. I'm beginning to realise I really don't know much at all.'

CHAPTER 52

Friday morning, it was like the night before had never happened. Matthew scurried out of the house at daybreak to his other life, and I showered, fed the animals, acknowledged the psycho dogs next door, put on a load of washing and made a cup of tea. All before the clock struck seven.

When Lexi unexpectedly came down the stairs at seven thirty, I was full of love, sadness and hope for her. And Lexi? She was full of... well, Lexi was clearly full of cynical youthful anger.

'How are you feeling, darling?'

'Mum, I'm fine,' she said in a bored, *don't mess with me* voice. 'Did you come into my room last night?'

'After I got back from Robyn's? Yes.'

'I don't remember. How is she?'

'Still pregnant. Rampaging about men at antenatal class.'

Lexi held up her good hand and made a fist. 'Girl power. Why do guys even exist? When we can clone ourselves, women will take over and men will survive solely to serve as our slaves.'

'Maybe not in our lifetime, Lex.'

'Maybe not in yours, but mine? It's a given.'

After Lexi had eaten some Vegemite toast, I tucked her up in bed with her iPad, a pile of magazines and chocolate biscuits.

'What's this?' Lexi asked as she rummaged through the magazines. 'You hate me reading these.' Her wide eyes stared at *Who* and *Girlfriend*.

'I know, so don't ever say I don't do anything nice for you. I stopped by the supermarket last night after Aunty Robyn's class.'

'You know I can read them all online, right?'

Lexi and I would be okay. I wasn't so naive as to think there wouldn't be many more times like this, some even more trying than the last few weeks had been – and I hadn't entirely given up on the idea of fixing an AirTag to her neck – but generations of women before me had survived motherhood. I was in with a chance.

'I'll be home early, then if you feel like it, you can come to Christmas carols at Gus's school tonight.'

'Sure, whatever.' She scowled at a *House & Garden* magazine. 'Not reading this!'

'Fair call. I was a bit delirious when I bought them.'

She reached for her phone.

'Please don't spend time scrolling. Read a book or better yet, complete your biology and English assignments.'

She held up her arm. 'Broken.'

'Thankfully, your right arm. You write with your left.'

By the time I reached school to drop off Angus, the final bell was ringing.

'You'll have to come into the office to sign me in. I'm late. All the kids are in class.'

'You're not late.' I pushed him out the door. 'The bell's only just rung.'

'Principal Jordan said if we're late, our mums have to go to the office to sign us in.'

'But not the dads?'

'What?'

'Never mind. Tell Principal Jordan you caught the bus today.'

'That's lying.'

'I'll be home early so we can be at school by six tonight. Love you, darling.'

I sped out of the kiss-and-drop zone and waved to Mardi and a couple more soccer mums. I could almost hear them gossiping. *Kate Cavendish! She's either dropping her boy off at daybreak or he's getting to school so late it's practically not worth him coming at all. And have you heard about her daughter...*

I caught up with Dana late in the morning as she bustled around her work kitchen, pulling out trays from the fridge, oven and pantry.

'I know I'm cutting it fine,' she said. 'Here's the selection of sweet treats for Sunday's nativity layout.'

I suffered sugar overload just looking at the white Christmas slices, cherry-choc cheesecake bites, chocolate rum-ball truffles, white chocolate and raspberry fudge, rocky road, and choc peppermint brownies. 'You're amazing. Thank you. I'll snap these in your kitchen if you don't mind?'

'Not at all. I've got meetings the rest of the day. Make yourself at home.'

I didn't need to ask if Dana had prepared the recipes to match the photos, because she said, 'I've emailed you the files. Again' – she grimaced – 'sorry it's all last minute. It's been a tough week.'

'You're a superstar.' I thought for a moment. 'I don't have any food for my holiday cards spread, so I might split the sweet treats: half in Sunday's spread and half for that.'

'Great. All sorted for the family montage tomorrow?'

I nodded. 'Glazed ham; prawns and sausages on the barbecue; mango, avocado and lobster salad; pavlova, champagne and beer. Obviously, active beach-cricket snaps as well. Maybe a twenty-second video?'

'Absolutely.' She raised a brow. 'If only all our Christmases could be that idyllic.'

For the next couple of hours, I fiddled with Christmas napery, Santa ornaments and other paraphernalia.

All done

I texted her when finished. She worked across several titles, so I was never sure which magazine meeting room she was in. Even the sporting magazines carried features such as *What to eat when training for a half marathon*. Dana was the go-to chef, especially when Mara was unavailable.

Her response was immediate.

Too easy. Please take them home with you.

What? No.

LOL! They'll go to waste here. Also, don't you have your son's Christmas concert tonight? Hand them out. You'll be adored forever more.

Doubt it. You sure you're sure?

Get outta here.

Armed with a truckload of goodies, I arrived home at two. Lexi was asleep, Rupert and Cleo vying for prime position on her head. Not wanting to wake her, I did some house chores, watered the garden and then picked up Angus from school.

She was still asleep when Matthew arrived home. I gently nudged her. 'Sweetheart, we're about to leave for Angus's concert. You up for it? Aunty Robyn's coming.'

She rubbed her eyes, momentarily confused. 'How long have I been asleep?'

'The better part of the afternoon.' I handed her two pills. 'You're due for these.'

She swallowed them with water. 'I'll come.'

Gus, Lexi, Matthew and I arrived at school promptly at six. Gus looked adorable decked out in red shorts, a green Christmas tree printed on a white T-shirt and red sandals.

Matthew, as school security monitor, clutched his torch, brows furrowed. 'Is this necessary? It won't be dark until eight thirty, and by then, we'll be heading home.'

Lexi sighed. 'Dad, kids in bushes... they get up to all kinds of mischief.'

He gently elbowed her. 'Speaking from experience, champ?'

I dropped off most of the Christmas-inspired treats to the sausage sizzle station (yes, I held a few back), much to the bemusement of the staff, and then tried to hand over twenty dollars for four sausage sandwiches.

'Are you kidding?' Mardi said, kindly. 'Get out of here. You've contributed more than your share.'

Angus disappeared to find his tribe, and when Robyn arrived, we went to take our seats in the hall.

Matthew, suddenly relishing his role, halted. 'I'll stay outside. According to Lexi, I need to be vigilant.'

Robyn chortled. 'Alert but not alarmed.'

'Here's a tip, Dad,' Lexi said. 'Look up. Vapers climb trees.'

'Vapers?'

Robyn huffed. 'Kids who vape.'

'To avoid detection,' Lexi added.

Moments later we were seated, and twenty-five minutes after that, Angus's class performed a stilted but amusing four-minute skit about Rudolph saving Christmas, ending with a rousing rendition of 'Rudolph the Red-Nosed Reindeer'. Intermission was called.

Lexi rolled her eyes. 'I'm starting a petition about that song.'

'Please, not tonight,' I implored as we all stood and clapped.

'I want an Insta post with all those little munchkins,' Robyn squealed. 'Angus in front with me. Hashtag love the festive season. Hashtag kids. Hashtag my handsome nephew. Hashtag thirty-six weeks and glowing. Hashtag never felt better.'

'Yes, yes.' We walked outside and found Angus. Matthew was a no-show, presumably in the bushes or perhaps up a tree.

'Gus, come,' Robyn yelled. He dutifully walked over. 'I love your costume. Let's do an Insta post!' She high-fived him. 'Hashtag Christmas.'

He grinned and a few mates joined in.

'Okay, let's do this quickly.' I stood Robyn, Angus and his friends in front of the school Christmas tree. The sun was still beating down, but I'd adjust the light later to simulate evening. All the boys were dressed similarly to Angus. A couple wore antlers. 'Ready?' I positioned my camera.

'Hey! What's going on? You can't take photos of kids.'

I looked around. Several other parents were taking pictures, presumably to post on Facebook.

A woman stepped forward, her face flushed angry and red. 'I know who you are.' She strode into Robyn's personal space. 'You're that disgusting woman hashtagging about your wonderfully perfect pregnant life and posting impossible images of flawlessness.'

Robyn faltered. 'I-I'm only doing my job.'

'You're setting a very bad example for teenage girls with all your airbrushing and pretence.'

'I'm sorry. I didn't mean—'

'Didn't mean, didn't mean. You're a babbling filthy whore.'

Onlookers gasped. I turned to Lexi. 'What the?'

'She's Susie's mum, Cissy,' Lexi explained.

I glared at her. 'Cissy? Really?'

'Mum, I don't choose the names. Go defend Robbie.'

'Excuse me.' I stepped between the women. 'My sister is heavily pregnant and doesn't need this stress.'

'What she needs is to be taken down,' Cissy barked.

'Cissy, is it?' I started.

'Cilla!'

'Sorry, Cilla, but bullying is a crime, and as a parent, you should know better.'

'I'm not bullying and who are you, anyway?'

'Kate, Lexi's mother.'

She stared at me blankly.

'I'm the mother of the teenager your daughter has been attacking online. Lexi, fell out of a tree yesterday while watching Susie and Hunter canoodling outside school grounds.'

Cilla laughed. 'I hardly think that's my problem. Your daughter should've been taught how to climb.'

'And perhaps your daughter should've been taught not to bully others online.' I looked more closely at Cilla, eyes squinting. 'Wait, are you Chill86?'

I retrieved my phone from my bag and started furiously scrolling.

She gasped. 'What?'

'Chill86?' I said, holding up my phone. 'I knew there was something familiar about your posts. When not trolling, you sometimes post happy snaps like this.' My screen filled with a sunny beach portrait of Cilla and Susie.

Robyn inhaled. 'Why?'

Matthew, torch in hand, joined the group. 'What's going on?'

'Cilla,' I replied, pointing to the woman, 'Or rather Chill86, has been trolling Robyn online, and her daughter, Susie, has been doing the same to Lexi.'

'This isn't the place for domestics,' Angus's principal, Mrs Jordan, butted in, trying to shush the growing cluster.

Meanwhile several dogs had broken free from their restraints and had gone rogue; stealing whatever sausages they could find, defecating in rose bushes, and generally making nuisances of themselves.

'Hang on.' Arnaud appeared out of the throng. 'Aren't you and Cilla sisters, Mrs Jordan? I've met you and her at numerous sporting events. That would make you Susie's aunt, wouldn't it?'

Matthew piped up. 'It just so happens, I found Susie and Hunter in a tree.' He stepped aside to reveal two ashen-faced teens, then nodded towards Lexi.

She shrieked, then covered her mouth with her good hand. 'Mum!' Lexi pulled me aside and whispered, 'I think they were having sex.'

'Pardon?'

'In trees. The grass in parks is too itchy.'

Way too much information. I'd never take Angus to the local park again for fear of being hit on the head by some naked teenager falling. Surely, this wasn't normal. Thirteen-year-olds weren't romping around in parks having sex, were they? I refused to believe it. But then again, why wouldn't they? I was at school with several girls who weren't virgins at thirteen. But now, it seemed so young. Far too young.

I hugged her tight.

Arnaud dipped his head. 'So, Principal Jordan, you condone online bullying?'

And rampant tree-climbing sex, I thought to myself.

'Of course not,' she replied. 'If everyone could please calm down and take your seats to watch the second half of the concert. The children have been practising all term. And through the generosity of one of our favourite parents, Mardi Downes, you'll all find a delicious Christmas treat in a decorative paper patty, on your chair. Be careful not to sit on it.' She held up a square of White Christmas. 'My favourite.'

'When you go at her for Mardi stealing Dana's baking glory,' Lexi whispered to me, 'you might want to mention that *Rudolph* forgives bullying.'

I nodded. 'The irony isn't lost on me.'

'You should also mention *Frosty the Snowman*. Unacceptable patriarchal behaviour.'

❄

After the concert, while Lexi, Gus and Matthew searched the grounds for vapers, Robyn, Cilla and I found a quiet bench, ate White Christmas, and Cilla told us her devastating story.

'I'm sorry you lost your bub at thirty-four weeks, Cilla. I couldn't imagine,' Robyn said, eyes misty.

'No,' I agreed. 'I'm sorry, Cilla. It would have been heartbreaking for you and your family believing they were weeks away from welcoming a newborn.'

She hung her head. 'Susie was only three. She was so excited about being big sister to a baby brother. We'd already named him.' She bit her lip. 'But then as I thought we were on the home stretch, my baby passed away. No reason. My husband and I never recovered. He left two years later. Said he couldn't deal with the sadness. What about my sadness and the fact that my body had failed me and couldn't nurture my baby to term?'

She started to cry.

I wrapped Cilla in my arms. 'I'm so sorry. I can't imagine the trauma you've endured.'

'It's been Susie and me ever since,' she sobbed. 'We have no other family.'

Robyn stiffened. 'I'd like to get to know you, Cilla. I have a great family, obviously excluding Kate, but I don't have a partner either.' She gulped. 'I'm really scared about being a single mum. Scared of fucking up.'

'Well, if you want to know about fucking up' – Cilla chortled – 'I'm your gal. It's been ten years, and I still haven't dealt with my grief.'

'Would it help to see someone?' I asked.

She nodded. 'Yeah. I'm so embarrassed and ashamed. Saying outrageous things online. Taking out my anger and sadness on strangers.' Cilla took a deep breath. 'Poor Susie. Mimicking my behaviour. I honestly had no idea she was trolling Lexi, Kate. I'm so sorry. I really dropped the parenting ball there.'

I rubbed Cilla's shoulder. 'You're not the only one guilty of that.' I was thinking about how our collective behaviours had led to rampant mental health issues, not only affecting adults, but our children too. Okay, Robyn was a social influencer, projecting unattainable perfect lifestyles, but I was the photographer airbrushing those lifestyles. I wasn't squeaky clean. Far from it.

'If we're taking honesty pills,' Robyn said, 'I'll accept that I'm part of the problem. Hell! I am the problem! My Instagram posts give me social anxiety. Of course I can't live up to the flawless image of myself.'

I laughed. 'Excuse me?'

Robyn nodded. 'I'm owning up.'

I took her hand. 'So could we stop the madness, at least for Christmas?'

'But I still haven't got the perfect family Christmas photo.'

I shook my head. 'That's what we've been saying, Robbie; there is no perfect photo.'

Just then, Matthew, Lexi and Angus appeared.

Standing, Cilla said, 'I could try and take a half decent one of you all.'

Robyn and I stood, and I handed Cilla my phone. 'Thank you.'

'No airbrushing?' Cilla asked.

'None,' Robyn agreed, then paused. 'And you'll get your troll army to lay off?'

Cheeks flushed, Cilla nodded. 'I'll do my best.'

Minutes later, given our combined exhaustion and Cilla's limited photographic skills, Robyn settled on a snap taken in front of the school Christmas tree. Angus appeared cross-eyed, Lexi poked out her tongue and held up her broken arm, I looked beyond worn out, Robyn screamed fat. As for Matthew wielding his torch? Plain demented.

All of us looked awful. I was very happy.

Before letting Robyn post it to social media, I showed Lexi the photo.

'Ha... good choice,' she said, examining it. 'Robyn reminds me of times when I'm cramping so much I want to kill myself, but then the Panadol kicks in and I pull myself back from the brink.' She sighed. 'Like I don't ever want to be a woman but then, do I want to be a child and cuddle my dog every day for the rest of my life?'

'I absolutely know how you feel. But I'm your mum. I can take the weight off your shoulders if you'll let me.'

'Not when I'm in a tree, Mum.'

CHAPTER 53

Monday morning, walking with Diane, I filled her in about the washup from the concert night.

She laughed. 'I picked a bad day to have oral surgery. I realised something was up when an email from the school appeared in my inbox on Saturday.'

'Almost unprecedented,' I agreed.

The email, coordinated with all the primary and high schools in the district, and co-signed by their principals, stated that the schools were "*committed to stamping out online abuse and trolling. Please contact your school principal directly to ensure matters are swiftly dealt with so they don't fester and infect the community.*

"The uncivilised behaviour demonstrated at (redacted) primary school on Friday night was unacceptable and will not be tolerated a second time. This behaviour is un-Christian especially at Christmas when civility, inclusivity, and goodwill to ALL is paramount.

"Finally, we wish all our community a joyful and relaxing holiday season and look forward to welcoming you and your families back next February."

'As for Mardi? Why would she pretend those treats were from her?'

Diane thought for a moment. 'Because there are people in this world who'll grab any opportunity to steal glory—'

'I was never after glory.'

'Doesn't matter. She saw a chance and snatched it because she knew you wouldn't brag about the delights because they were Dana's creations to boast about, not yours.'

'Dana would never boast. It's her job.'

Diane waved me away. 'It's a pity Mardi took them. Happily for her, she knew you wouldn't confront her when she stole the credit for baking them.'

'I didn't bake them.'

Diane clicked her tongue. 'Again, yes, I know. You're not listening. It's a micro version of the Sarah Stanthorpe situation. You don't confront – whether small or large. You're easy prey.'

Tears welled.

'Sorry, Kate,' Diane said. 'Truth bombs sting.'

❄

'Mum, Bugs is under my bed,' Angus said, running into the kitchen, tears streaming down his cheeks. 'He's dying.'

'What?' I flew upstairs and into Angus's room, Lexi and Angus keeping pace behind me.

'Bugs, Bugsy boy.' I got down on my hands and knees and looked under the bed. It was a wonder Angus could see anything beneath a mass of clothes, books and toys.

'Bugsy?' I could see him curled up on some clothes on the far side against the wall. I tried coaxing, but he wouldn't come. I crawled further under the bed. He appeared to be in great pain and—

'Oh God!' I hit my head as I crawled back out from underneath the bed.

Lexi and Angus were standing close by.

'Mum, what is it?' Lexi said, voice shaky.

'Get me – I don't know, towels, lots of towels.' I tried to remain outwardly calm. 'Hurry. Not the good ones. Angus, go downstairs and get me the dog box, the one we take Rupert to the vet in. Hurry.'

'Why not Bugsy's box? Is he okay?'

'Gus, get Rupert's box now.' I lowered my voice. 'Please.'

He ran away and Lexi rushed back in with towels.

'What, Mummy? Tell me. Is Bugsy dying?' She was crying. 'Tell me.'

'Sweetie' – I caught my breath and took the towels from her – 'Bugsy's having babies.'

There were five of them – five tiny, blind little bunnies, each not much bigger than my thumb. They couldn't have been more than an hour old. As quietly and slowly as I could, I laid Bugs and his – make that *her* – babies in the dog box together with a towel, water and lettuce.

'Do I have to go to school?' Angus asked.

'Yes, you do.'

'And me, Mummy?' Lexi whispered.

I raised my eyebrows. 'Yes, Lexi, you too. Besides, Bugs needs his rest as well. He, I mean she, has had an eventful night. She'll still be here when you get home this afternoon.'

Angus's face scrunched. 'So Bugs is a girl now?'

'It would appear so.'

'When did she change into a girl and start having babies?'

'We'll figure that out later, Gus. Please get ready for school. Scoot. We're going to be late.'

I put Bugs and her children in a quiet, warm corner of the lounge room, and shut the door, away from Rupert and Cleo's prying eyes.

❄

With luck on my side, I'd be a free woman within hours. I intended to see Fern, tell her what I thought of Graeme, and leave. She deserved to know the kind of person she had working for her. Genius or not, if he was intimidating me, he was probably harassing others as well. There was no way Fern would stand for that kind of behaviour.

I dropped Lexi at school and then Angus as the final bell rang, which was remarkable given I'd been a rabbit's midwife less than an hour ago.

In the car park at Image Ink, I called Mum. 'No, not good timing, but there'd never be a good time. Yes, five of them. Are you sure you don't mind popping in this afternoon? I'll be home just after lunch. Thanks.'

I clicked off my mobile and closed my eyes. Opened them. Then closed them again. Barely three metres ahead of me stood Fern and Graeme. She moved towards him, cupping her hands around his face. He didn't pull away. He turned to the side and kissed her hands. I couldn't believe my eyes when they kissed then, passionately.

Graeme wiped his lips and smiled smugly at me. He whacked Fern on her backside and sauntered into the building.

'Do you hate me?' Fern asked, walking up, when she saw they'd been caught.

'I'm... I don't know what to say.'

'Gray and I—'

'No. Please don't tell me.' I swallowed hard. 'Did I mention my rabbit's given birth to five babies? We thought he was a boy. How wrong can you be? Five! We have six rabbits now.'

We sat on the steps in the morning sun.

'Great, but about Gray – it's okay, really. We've... we've been together a while now. It's not ideal, of course, but we make it work.'

'Please don't tell me more, I mean it. You're too good for him. Would the children like a bunny?' I was gabbling to stop myself from thinking about what I'd just witnessed.

'But the sex! The sex is awesome.'

I didn't want to hear about Fern's adulterous sexual encounters, but it was too late. Visions of Fern clinging onto a filing cabinet in the office supplies room while Graeme penetrated her with quick thrusts from behind raced through my mind.

'Graeme excites me like no man I've ever had. He makes me tingle. I feel alive when he's inside me.'

Bile rose in my throat. Graeme was an evil, immoral pig. An ape who seduced others in quiet corners of pubs, who chatted them up in office hallways while they tried to work and attempted to have sex with them while on location shoots. I wanted to tell her he was a sloppy bad kisser! And he wore ill-fitting trousers. But I couldn't. (The last two weren't true, anyway.)

'Say something.'

'I-I don't know what to say.'

'Terry and I aren't like you and Matthew. We don't have the camaraderie you two have. With us, it's always been a competition. Who earns the most money? Who drives the flashiest car? Who's winning the most awards? The competition never ends. And as far as sex is concerned, well... let's just say there are no surprises.'

It never occurred to me Fern and Terry were unhappy. They looked perfect together, not like a couple in crisis.

'I had no idea.'

'Why would you? We put on a convincing show.'

'But the children...'

'What about them? They don't know. Graeme and I aren't about to run off together and live happily ever after. He's available. We both have needs, desires. I find the time to accommodate him and he, let me tell you, certainly accommodates me. End of story. Besides, Terry hasn't looked at me that way in years. To him, I'm plain old Fern. I'm the mother of his children, not a high-powered magazine exec overseeing ninety staff. He doesn't appreciate me. When Graeme looks at me there's pure lust in his eyes. He wants me. Graeme thinks I'm clever, loves my body—'

'Oh God.' I put my head between my knees. 'I'm going to throw up.'

'It's not that bad. I can handle it. Terry's not interested in me.'

'How can you say that? You have four kids.' I looked up at her briefly before the queasiness seized me again.

'Exactly. Four kids. They're my reality. The rest is illusion, keeping up appearances. Do you know how hard I work to keep it together? My perfect life, my perfect children... It's all a lie. I'm living a lie.'

I was staring at her open-mouthed. Never in a million years would I have guessed Fern and Graeme – Graeme! Of all people!

'Don't look so shocked, Kate. We all have our secrets. I didn't set out to cheat. At first Graeme and I flirted, it was fun. After Lily was born, I made a special effort to get back into shape. Went back to swimming laps three mornings a week. I walked and worked out at the gym to lose the baby weight. Do you think Terry commented or even noticed? Do you think he noticed I was on the lemon detox diet for months on end? I was starving myself to look attractive for him. I got my legs and eyebrows waxed, all for him, so he'd want me. Desire me again. But did he? No. No. No. He didn't say one bloody word about it. There was never any *Fern, you're looking great.* I got nothing. Not one word of encouragement. And pelvic floor exercises! I have bladder control like you wouldn't believe.'

'I'm so sorry. I didn't know.'

She waved my sympathy away. 'When I came back from maternity leave seven months ago, Graeme was still here, still keen on me and still flirting. He was pure charm, so good for my post-baby ego. Every day he was here, regular as clockwork, praising me. I know he was probably trying to get me into bed...'

'You think?'

'What? You don't think I ached to fuck him as well? Without strings? I was desperate for it. Desperate to have mad, passionate sex that didn't come at a price. *I love you, Terry. You're the greatest, Terry.* None of that. Zero mother guilt.'

I'd rarely heard Fern swear before, let alone say *fuck*. I felt uneasy. Squeamish.

'You know what, Kate?'

'Please don't tell me.'

'Ha! Terry says he can't go down on me because I'm a mother now. What a load of rubbish. For ten years, I've missed out. I'm shocking you, aren't I?'

Seriously, I was going to throw up. 'Maybe you shouldn't be telling me this.'

'With Graeme, I can think about myself and my own needs. Graeme and I are both selfish. But we also connect professionally. Graeme is a talented artist, brave. Inspirational.' Fern smiled. 'So now you know.'

'It's not just sex?'

'No. It's not just sex. Truly.'

'Why don't I believe you?'

'Look, Graeme can be a rat. I know he cheats. And he has every right to. I come with baggage – a husband and children. He was entertaining a woman at his home late the other night when I arrived unexpectedly.' She giggled. 'He quickly got rid of her. Made her climb out the window, but I knew he'd been with someone. Then we did our—'

'What?'

'Oh yes, he does that. He's a bastard. But he gives great—'

'I really need to use the bathroom.'

CHAPTER 54

After I threw up, I sat slumped over the toilet seat for a very long time. A video was running behind my eyelids, and I couldn't do anything to stop it. I closed my eyes. Opened them. Blinked. Nothing worked. The tape playing inside my head kept on and on, becoming more horrific and humiliating with each passing second until the finale, when, fully exposed, I finally saw what had happened with Graeme that night.

We drank champagne at the bar... moved to a dark corner... Graeme told me there was *no way you're forty* and kissed me, his hand strayed under my shirt and massaged my nipples. We left together... fell into the back seat of a car... my car!

Graeme climbed on top of me and told me he had *a special birthday surprise* for me. I pulled his shirt off... barely noticed people walking by and peeking in. The police knocked on the door and told us to stop what we were doing and get out of the car... we caught a cab to Graeme's apartment.

At Graeme's... I tripped as I stumbled up the path and through his open front door... I drank even more to celebrate my birthday. Gin, maybe vodka. He chased me into his bedroom.

The images flashed faster and faster. My drunkenness. Graeme's face. The bedroom. Graeme's bed. He ripped at my clothes. The two of us rolled around the bed.

Then... minutes later... the front door opened... a woman's voice called out. Graeme pushed me out the open bedroom window, practically naked. Clothes and shoes tumbled out soon after and hit me on the head.

I scrambled to my feet and hid in the bushes, dazed and confused. Finally, I dressed and walked to the deserted street in search of a taxi.

Mum's words rang in my ears. *The trick is to learn from our mistakes and move on. We all have to... Forgive yourself. Vow to become a better, stronger and wiser person... That's what life is about. None of us is perfect.*

Everything was quiet when I got home that night. I flipped on the kitchen light and picked up a picture Angus had drawn. It showed the two of us in our garden. He was kissing me and giving me flowers. He'd drawn a speech bubble bursting out of his head. Inside it were the words *Happy Birthday, Mummy. Hope you had a good night. I love you. Love Angus. Xxx*

Mum got out of bed and tried to tell me about Lexi drinking vodka and orange juice. *Kate, do you understand what I'm saying? I almost had to take Lexi to hospital. I was scared out of my wits. Why didn't you answer your phone?* But I was too far gone to understand.

I remembered walking into the bathroom. I turned on the shower, undressed and stood under tepid water for a very long time, crying.

Then Mum called from outside my bedroom the next morning. 'Katie, it's after seven.'

❄

'Everything all right?' Fern asked from outside the toilet stall. 'You've been in there forever.'

'Fine,' I mumbled. That word again.

'Okay. We'll talk more later. I'll take you to lunch.'

I didn't reply. Food was the last thing I needed. After she'd gone, I walked out of the cubicle and splashed my face with cold water. I'd been an idiot many times before in my life. Example – when the pet shop owner told me the rabbit he was selling was male! The time a new boyfriend told me he loved me, and I believed him, so I had sex with him on the second date. The time I drank a tumbler of vodka – neat – because Robyn told me it would cure my headache.

Very wrong.

Or the time, about half an hour after drinking said tumbler of vodka, I mistakenly thought the police walking towards me were male strippers. Wrong again. But it all paled in comparison. This was a catastrophe, a cataclysmic disaster. I couldn't see myself getting over this nightmare in the six-week period I'd allotted to overcome each new crisis.

Fern was nowhere to be seen. I had to focus. Focus on getting out of the building and never coming back. I brushed my hair and applied my lipstick as best I could with my shaking hand.

But as soon as I stepped into the corridor, I came face to face with him – Graeme Grafton.

'Hey, hey, Fern told you our news? Don't look so downhearted, babe. We can still get it together. But Fern tends to get twitchy about my other lady friends.'

'Excuse me?'

'Come on, you love it. All women do. I'm the exciting, ego-boosting guy you've been looking for. Don't tell me you haven't had fantasies about me, fantasies you can't share with your precious husband. Fern and I know all about fantasies, we act them *all* out. They come to life in the shower, on the beach, in the office kitchen—'

'I get it. Thank you.'

'I can be your real-life fantasy too, just like I'm Fern's. She wants it badly. And after she comes, she goes. No rings, no strings. I'm cool with that.'

'You are *the* most disgusting man I've ever met.'

'That's not what you said the night you were in my bed.'

'I was out of my mind.'

'And now you're out of your mind with jealousy. Don't be. It makes you look old and even more ridiculous, if that's possible.'

'You need help, Graeme. Not the once a week, three hundred dollar a session kind of help, I'm talking about the Switzerland, three month intensive stay, six hundred thousand dollar help! You make me sick.'

Tick number three on my to-do list.

But the experience wasn't as uplifting as I'd hoped it would be. I was confused. Never would I have thought Fern would have an affair with Graeme. Risk her marriage to Terry for him? If she needed male attention, surely, she could do so much better.

Graeme smiled, turned, and walked away. I felt stupid, sad and, yes, ridiculous. I walked in the direction of the studio, determined not to lose it. As if I hadn't already.

CHAPTER 55

'How do you do it?' I asked Mara a few minutes later in the studio.

A woman with a bandaged ankle was standing on crutches beside her.

'This is Simone,' Mara said with a happy smile.

I nodded weakly to Simone, blinking away threatening tears.

'Tough few weeks, hey?' Simone asked.

'Understatement. I don't know how you can work with Graeme without itching to stab him in the back every minute of the day.'

'We have each other.' Mara slipped her arm through Simone's. 'If I didn't have Simone, I'd go mental, which is almost what happened when she was sidelined with a broken ankle.'

I sighed. 'I'm sorry I couldn't be of more help.'

'You did great, Kate, but Simone and I know how to handle Graeme.'

'Most of the time.' Simone looked down at her foot. 'Anyway, I'm back now, and even with these crutches, I feel stronger than ever. Together, Mara and I can take on the bastard and win.'

'But what with Fern and everything,' I began.

'So... you know?' Mara asked.

'Yeah – you too? I still can't believe it. I keep asking myself, *why*?'

Mara sucked in her cheeks. 'Who knows? You do what you can to get by, and I guess those two fulfil each other's needs. Simone and I have had endless discussions. Graeme's a bully – brilliant and eccentric when he wants to be, but a bully all the same. If he can intimidate you, he will, if only for the purpose of being intimidating.'

'His weakness,' Simone added, 'is he likes to be dominated, which is the basis of his relationship with Fern. She dominates him because of her position here.'

'Still...' I didn't want the image of Fern's perfect life shattered. I looked up to her, admired her. Wanted to be like her. I'd thought Fern had it all. She had four children. She had Terry. She was the boss. Why did she need more? Why did she need Graeme? But who was I to judge? I'd almost had sex with the guy myself. Not to mention my Arnaud fantasies.

I couldn't face Fern right now. I'd come in tomorrow and see her. I left the building, got into my car and drove away.

What if Matthew found out? It was all I could think about. What if I'd destroyed my marriage over someone as pointless and worthless as Graeme Grafton?

I had to see Mum. Talk to her. Hear the truth about what I said to her that night after I'd come home after being with Graeme. Maybe my memories were distorted. Perhaps I'd only dreamed about being at Graeme's apartment. Part of me clung to the hope none of it had really happened. Perhaps only a vile hallucination.

CHAPTER 56

Two hours later, after driving to the beach and sufficiently numbing myself by playing *all* the *Waffle* and *Octordle* archives, I drove home.

'How's the wedding planning coming along?' I asked Mum, having checked on Bugsy, then sat at my kitchen bench, sipping tea. 'String quartet booked?'

'All done.'

'Good,' I replied distractedly. 'Maybe I should look in on Bugs again.'

'Stop.' She reached for my arm. 'Why don't you tell me what this is all about. Is it the magazine? Fern's called twice on the landline. I assume that's not normal.'

I blinked. 'What did I tell you that night of my birthday? After the drinks?'

'Oh... You were in a dreadful state. Worse for wear. I didn't want to bring it up until you were ready.'

'When did you ever think I'd be ready? Please, tell me what I said.'

'Only that you'd made a terrible mistake. You mentioned

Graeme and that his girlfriend had walked in on you both and you were thrown out of the bedroom window…'

'God, no.'

'God, yes, I'm afraid. After your shower, you insisted on taking a Berocca. Then I gave you a couple of headache tablets and put you to bed.'

'I made a mistake, a really bad mistake.'

'I'm so sorry, love.'

'It's not your fault, it's mine. I'm the disgusting one. How could I do that to Matthew, to the kids, to you? Why? I didn't have sex with him, but I might have, had we not been interrupted. Why did I do it?'

'It was a cry for help. A plea for someone to notice you, love you.'

'Not Graeme Grafton!'

'No, but maybe Matthew? We all make mistakes, wish we could turn back the hands of time in the hope we can undo something that happened. What's important is we learn and try not to repeat them. Life is about forgiveness and acceptance.'

'No, you haven't, Mum. I'm a terrible person. No wonder Lexi—'

'Stop it. Just stop. It's over. A lapse in judgement that will never happen again, will it?'

'No… definitely not,' I whispered. 'I couldn't live like that. I know women who do, but not me. I… I don't even know if I can live with myself as I am.'

'You can and you will. It's over and done with. Time to get on with your life. Forgive yourself and move on.'

'Should I tell Matthew?'

'Katie, only you can answer that.'

'It was a mistake. A stupid drunken lousy mistake.'

'Then forgive yourself. It's the only way you'll be able to move forward.' She poured me more tea.

I sniffed. 'It's a week until your wedding. What do you need me to do?'

'Write my vows?'

'Ha. You're on your own with that.'

'I didn't say much at our first wedding, only what the priest handed me, including saying that I would "love, honour and obey" Bob.'

'Times have changed. Very few women would say that now. Imagine what Lexi would say if she heard that?'

'Lexi would say what, Mother?'

I stood and hugged my daughter as she barrelled into the kitchen and dropped her school bag. 'We're drinking tea and Nanna's brought over her famous chocolate cake.'

Lexi's eyes widened. 'Yum.'

'Sit, and I'll cut you a piece,' Mum said. 'Ice cream too?'

Lexi nodded. 'Thanks, Nanna.'

'How's your arm, darling?' I asked. 'Keeping up with your pain meds?'

'Yes, but the plaster's so itchy.'

'That means it's healing.'

She poked out her tongue and accepted cake from her nanna. 'So why did I hear my name as I walked in?'

'I was telling your mum that I'm going to write my own wedding vows this time, not like the first time when I married Pop, and basically said, "I do", and that I would "love, honour and obey" him.'

'Nanna. No!'

'Nanna, yes. It's what was done back then. This time, I'll write my own words; something that reflects the genuine love Bob and I share.'

'I should think so.' Lexi licked her spoon of chocolate icing. 'As your bridesmaid, I insist. Death to the patriarchy and all that.'

'Touché,' I agreed. 'All good for your final day of school tomorrow?'

Lexi shone with happiness. 'Yes, my assignments have been graded.'

'And?' My top lip twitched.

'I'll never be Einstein, but Mrs Westley told me I've passed.'

I jumped out of my chair. 'Congratulations, I'm so happy for you.'

'Final year percentages will be emailed next week but Mrs Westley said I'll definitely be moving up.'

Mum beamed. 'Clever girl.'

'Don't expect miracles, loved ones.' Lexi finished her cake. 'The school's probably just worried about getting sued.'

'Ooh, yes, darling,' Mum cooed. 'I want to know all about your arm, and the skirmish at the carol concert.' Giggling, Mum cut two more pieces of cake for her and Lexi. 'Don't leave out any sordid details.'

I picked up my bag. 'I'm off to pick up Gus. I'll leave you teenagers to it. I'll check on Bugs on my way out.'

'I love you,' Lexi cried as I disappeared through the door. Distant cackling ensued.

CHAPTER 57

'You scared me,' I said sometime later when I turned with the hose and accidentally sprayed Rupert with water meant for the hydrangeas.

'I didn't mean to.' Matthew was standing at the back door. 'The grass is alive.'

'Probably because it's finally seeing sunlight.' I nodded in the direction of the trimmed conifers.

I turned off the hose and walked toward him. He smiled. 'I spoke with Lexi about Bugs. Five new rabbits, hey? And she's passed the year?'

I nodded. 'Amazing what can be achieved under pressure.'

He wrapped his arms around me. 'I spoke with Mum. She and Dad are looking forward to the wedding.'

I raised my brows.

'Yes, sure she was shocked.'

'We all were.' I exhaled. 'You know I still haven't forgiven her for giving me that book.'

'Let it go. At least Mum remembered your birthday. So, how'd it go with Fern?'

'I wanted to finish today, but there are still a few loose ends. I'll stay until Friday. Any remaining nativity spreads, I can file remotely. Now Simone's back, the main reason for me being in the office is for access to their library of files. Plus...' I gestured for Matthew to follow me inside. 'Dana and I get on so well. I'll miss her.'

I pulled out a roast lamb from the fridge courtesy of Dana.

'Nice.'

'Nice? It's a succulent roast lamb with nutty pesto stuffing! To buy this, we'd have to take out a second mortgage.'

Matthew's eyes widened. 'And it hasn't been artificially tampered with?'

I laughed. 'Not that I'm aware.'

'Even though I haven't met her, I'll miss Dana too!' Without warning, Matthew kissed me. 'You won't miss Fern?'

I bit my inner cheek. 'Yes, of course, but I'm sure we'll still see each other.'

'And the one Fern called a genius. Graeme...'

'Grafton.' Close to tears, I slid the lamb back into the fridge and stepped away from him.

'Not so fast.' Matthew caught hold of my arm. The touch of his fingers felt warm and strong. The way they had all those years ago. 'Another five mouths to feed...'

'We're keeping them all,' Angus shouted, galloping into the kitchen with Rupert. 'Mum said so.'

Matthew grinned. 'Did you?'

'Don't be ridiculous, though I guess we have to keep them for a few weeks.'

Angus shrieked with joy and fell on the floor with Rupert.

Matthew brushed hair from my face, and I felt an intimacy between us I hadn't experienced for a long time. 'Katie, I know how much your photography means to you.'

He pulled me close, enveloped his arms around me and hugged me. All at once I felt a longing for him. And love...

'Hold whatever thought you're having.' Matthew pulled away and reached for a bag on the kitchen bench. 'Your extraordinarily late birthday present,' he said, passing it to me.

'What?' I peered inside, pulled out a small box and opened it. Chanel Allure. 'My favourite. Thank you, sweetheart.'

'You have no idea the effort I put into buying this. Women spraying me all over the place. I walked around for days smelling like a gardenia. I'm surprised you didn't say anything.'

'I've been a bit preoccupied.' If only I had spoken up, I could have saved myself a lot of heartache.

'Do tell.'

'Actually,' I said, spraying myself with the gorgeous scent, 'there's something I want to show you. We'll need to drive though.'

'I'm intrigued.' His lips brushed mine.

Angus looked up; interest sparked. 'Where are we going?'

'Mum's taking us on an adventure.'

'Well, I'm not staying here on my own,' Lexi chimed in from the living room.

I swear there's no privacy in this house.

'All right, everyone in the car,' Matthew ordered. 'Yes, you too, Rupert.'

❄

'Why don't we come here more often?' Matthew asked as we strolled down a narrow winding street looking at simple workers' cottages housing potters, painters and sculptors. A suburb not far from our own but so different – a well-known artists' enclave with galleries, cafés and clothing designers, some successful but most of them just starting out.

'Great minds think alike,' he continued. 'I was here—'

'Let me show you something,' I blurted.

We walked around the corner to one of the cottages, which had a *For Lease* sign plastered across its window. I peered through one of the windows. It was still a wreck as it had been several weeks ago when I first saw it, but in my mind, I could see a gallery of my portraits in the front room, an office to one side.

'Imagine the possibilities, Matthew.'

'You don't have to imagine. Why don't you lease it and build your dream studio here? I met with the real estate agent and—'

Ah. The woman outside the café.

'I almost rented it as a birthday surprise, but knew this was something you needed to do on your own.'

'Really? I'd been thinking about it for months, then when Fern's offer popped up…'

'You decided to give corporate life another go. But now I reckon all you need is a nudge along, right, kids?'

'But—'

'Who knows what's going to happen down the track? What do you say? Your own photography business? Being your own boss and taking control of the photos you want to create?'

'Awesome, Mum,' Lexi piped up.

Matthew chuckled. 'See? Even Lexi thinks it's a great idea.'

'So do I,' Angus chipped in.

'It's unanimous. What's holding you back?'

'Fear,' I replied honestly.

'Come on, life's an adventure. Where did agonising over Sarah's book get you? Nowhere. And it turns out she's not so special. She had to stoop to stealing your work to get published. What does that tell you? If you want something badly enough, you have to go for it. Make it happen. Don't worry about the process so much, or the mere thought of action will cripple you with anxiety. You can do this.'

'I could enrol in a Photoshop course, get up to speed with digital...'

'That's our girl!' Matthew's smile was wide. 'Have faith in yourself. We do.'

CHAPTER 58

'Fern,' I said when I walked into her office the next morning. 'We need to talk.'

'Thanks for coming back.' She closed her door and we sat together.

Inside, I was shaking. 'Not for long.'

'Before you say anything more, I've been looking at the circulation numbers for your nativity posts and they're through the roof. The combination of your photos and Dana's quirky recipes is a huge winner.'

'Thank you, but—'

'Hear me out. I know you don't want to stay, and I understand, but if I could formulate a workable plan where you and Dana could team up for special events throughout the year, like Anzac Day, Easter—'

'I can't work with Graeme.'

'You wouldn't. And apart from meeting with Dana, you could work from home.'

I sucked in my cheeks. 'Actually, I've decided to rent a studio—'

'Brilliant. So you'll think about it?'

'There's something I need to tell you.' My eyes filled with tears. 'I was the woman in Graeme's bed the night you went over.'

'I know. He told me.'

I gasped.

'It's okay. He likes to hurt me. Thinks it gives him the upper hand.'

'Fern, I'm so sorry. I'd never normally—'

She held out her hand to stop me. 'You and me both. But I'm in too deep now. Trapped. You, however, are not. You have a great family and an amazing talent.' She hugged me. 'I know you're going to be a huge success no matter what you decide to do.'

I pulled away and wiped my eyes. 'That's very generous of you.'

She sniffed. 'You've got me tearing up now.' She paused. 'Okay, so where are we at with your amazing nativity montage?'

'I've still got Boxing Day through to New Year's Eve to put together.' I glanced at my watch. 'Dana and I are meeting in fifteen minutes to run through ideas.'

'Excellent, and you'll think about coming on board for special occasions next year?'

'If you keep Graeme under lock and key.' I stood. 'One more thing—'

She grimaced. 'Do I want to hear?'

'I think so. I've contacted a solicitor about Sarah's book. We'll see what happens.'

'Fantastic. I'll support you any way I can. I was there when you took those photographs and you deserve recognition, not to mention compensation. Please count on my support.'

I walked to my meeting with Dana, thinking about Fern, and how she must struggle every day. What did she call it? *Keeping up appearances.* Like me, Mum and countless women, we resisted admitting our dreams and desires, and banished our failures to the deep recesses of our minds, not wanting to let them consume us. And like Fern, was I guilty of disguising reality with a façade of perfection? No, that's one thing I didn't need to feel guilty about. Try as I might to be perfect, I'd never achieved it. My reality was a distant cousin to perfection.

CHAPTER 59

'I'm never going to fit into my dress if I keep eating this,' I said to Mum, devouring yet more chocolate cake at her kitchen bench.

'Are you really fine about your Dad and me marrying?'

Nodding, I said, 'I think so. I've learnt some things about myself recently.'

'Sweetheart,' Mum started.

'Is that why you're giving Dad another chance? Why you're forgiving him after all these years? Is it because he made a similar' – I searched for the right word – 'slip up?'

'Sometimes things just happen,' Mum said quietly. 'I can't remember how it even started. Your dad was so busy at work. He never had time for me, for the two of us. At least that's the way I saw it. He lost interest in me. And what with you and Robyn being social butterflies, spending weekends with your friends... I was lonely.'

'Not when we were planning our holiday?'

'By then it was too late. It had already started.'

'Dad's affair?'

'Kate, Dad didn't have an affair. He thought we were living a perfectly comfortable life. I was the one who was lonely when he went to work every day. I made his salami and pickle sandwiches and kissed him goodbye at the front door, but I wasn't happy. I was depressed and isolated. It was so easy to...'

'To what, Mum?'

'To crave something more... something exciting.'

'And?'

'I was the one who found someone else. I was the one who had the affair. It started before that summer.'

'That's not true! It was Dad! He was with another woman. You were distraught, heartbroken, a complete wreck. You worshipped Dad. You're not remembering correctly.'

'I am.'

'I don't believe you. You're covering for him. You'd never do that. Never have—'

Mum put her hand under my chin and lifted my head. 'What, Katie? An affair?'

I nodded.

'Yes, I could, darling. And I did. It wasn't your father who strayed. It was me.'

'Oh my God! Who with?'

'A friend. It doesn't matter. It was over within months. He was married too. I guess we were both bored. I had no idea it would turn out the way it did. It wasn't until after that I realised how much I'd hurt your father and how much I'd hurt myself and you girls in the process.'

'But why?'

'Why do any of us do the things we do? For excitement... because we're bored... but sooner or later, we have to take responsibility for our actions. I'm not proud of what I did.'

'Why didn't you tell me?'

'I tried, but honestly, I was a coward. It was easier for me to let you believe that your dad strayed. Life moved on. You married Matthew. Lexi was born. We got on with our lives.'

'Yes, but without Dad.'

'I tried to reconcile with him, to apologise. When I flew to Melbourne and found him in bed with *that* woman, I was shattered.'

'But you were still married.'

'Legally married, but memories play tricks, Katie. I've been trying to tell you. Dad left three months prior. It was easier to say Bob was working away from home – which he was – in Melbourne. But soon after, I realised I missed him, that I'd made a huge mistake. When I found him at the Windsor, I was heartbroken. Until then, I'd expected we could put the affair behind us. But when I saw him with her, part of me died.'

Mum took a moment. 'They got married as soon as our divorce came through. Bob's the kind of man... well, he didn't want to live alone, and I guess he made his decision not to.'

'I can't believe you're only telling me this now. It's been twenty-five years.'

'I never stopped loving your father. But the occasional bunch of roses and a night on the town would've made me happier. I didn't want to take another lover or divorce him. I wanted your father to notice me, to shake things up.'

'You certainly did. What happened with the other man?'

'Oh, I'd ended it with him before I went down to Melbourne. His wife was none the wiser. I was the one who ended up losing. After a couple of years of feeling sorry for myself, I got on with it. I had to. Bob had a new life, with a new wife. You and Robyn had your lives. I was thirty-six. I had to sort myself out or wither and die.'

'All this time I thought you were the victim.'

'Katie, I was never the victim. Well, I was a victim of my own stupidity.'

'But our family?'

'I was wrong, very wrong. I never stopped loving Bob or feeling responsible for what happened. But your dad and I have talked about it all. The past is the past. There's nothing we can do to change it. The present and the future, that's what's important now. Bob and I are together again and will be for another twenty or thirty years. I know it doesn't compensate for what happened all those years ago, but it's a start.'

'I don't believe you. You can't be serious. That's almost twenty-five years of my life you're talking about! All that time, I've hated Dad, twenty-five years he's missed out on being a father and a grandfather.'

'I'm so sorry, Katie.'

'Sorry's not good enough. Dad's the reason I keep expecting Matthew will one day leave me for another woman – because my father did.'

'But your father didn't.'

'I know that now, but all this time I've thought I wasn't good enough. I thought Dad left the family because of something I did... because I wasn't enough... and somehow, I was to blame.'

'Why would you think that? You were a teenager.'

'Why wouldn't I? I was a teenager. We were planning a holiday... my mid-term report arrived. You and Dad asked me why I'd done so badly at maths, and I told you I didn't need it... I was going to be a photographer. Soon after, Dad left. We didn't go on the holiday and Dad never came back to live with us – but it was you all along. You're the one who destroyed our family.'

Dad cleared his throat. 'Kate, I need to say something.'

Mum quickly reached out to him. 'How much have you heard?'

'Enough.' He kissed her and then walked up beside me.

'Is it true?' My voice wobbled. 'Is Mum covering for you or is she telling the truth?'

He grasped my hand. 'I'm sorry, Katie, Mum's telling the truth.'

Mum burst into tears, and I quickly followed. 'But why? Why did you let us believe—' I couldn't finish my sentence.

Dad took a breath. 'Pip and I met when we were young. Very young. Fourteen. We married at eighteen and we were parents at twenty. Twenty, Kate. Can you imagine?'

I shook my head.

'We were in love. Of course we were, but that responsibility at such a young age. Robbie coming along two years later. We lost track of ourselves.'

'Because we were on a treadmill,' Mum chimed in.

'I was consumed with providing for our growing family,' Dad explained.

Mum crumpled in his arms. 'I'm so sorry, Bob.'

'Hey,' he said, wiping her tears. 'We're okay, love. Nothing to be sorry for. We both made mistakes, and hey, look at us, we've made our way back to each other.'

'Dad,' I said, cutting in. 'Do you love Mum, in a death till we part way.'

Tears streamed down his cheeks. 'I do.'

'And, Mum, do you love Dad and promise never to lie to your daughters again?'

'Yes,' she replied shakily.

'Okay! Good. I love you both. Let's do this.'

Mum made me another cup of tea – my fourth, I think – and I sat at the kitchen bench in a Lipton-induced daze and cried with Mum and Dad. Thinking about the lost years, the years I spent blaming Dad and hating him for a family break-up that wasn't his fault. Okay, he had something to do with it – he'd neglected Mum – but he didn't deserve all the vitriol I'd hurled at him over the years.

CHAPTER 60

Freud once said only unsatisfied people had fantasies, but fantasies were what kept me going during those wakeful hours between two and four o'clock in the morning when struggling with thoughts of inadequacy and despair.

I rang Diane.

'None of us need to apologise for our fantasies,' Diane said, voice steady and reasonable. 'As long as they remain just that. There's a huge difference between fantasy and reality. Are you talking about Arnaud?'

'I guess, but I don't want him in the real world. I don't think I ever did... well, maybe a little. He was a diversion. Who I really want is Matthew.' But it's so easy to get distracted – and then, bang! One little indiscretion. Well, it can destroy a marriage like it had destroyed Mum's and no doubt would also destroy Fern's. I didn't want it to happen to me.

'So how are things?' I asked.

'Not so good. We're not splitting up, at least I don't think so, but now he's talking about going to his parents' home for Christmas Day.'

'Just David and the boys?'

'No, all of us.'

'Perfect! Barbecue, beach cricket, sun, sand and surf.'

'Not quite. They're traditional. So even though it will be thirty-five degrees in the shade, they always have a turkey roast for lunch—'

'I'm not really a fan of turkey. Dry, somewhat tasteless.'

'Exactly. And indoors! Stuffy and cramped.'

'Could David convince them for a more relaxed lunch this year? You could volunteer to bring the prawns and beer?'

'Doubtful. Now spill.'

'Working those few weeks at *Delicious Bites* made me realise I need to continue with my photography professionally. I'm not giving it up again. There's so much more I plan to do with my life. So, wearing my new push-up bra, I'm going to embrace the new era, brush up on my photography and computer skills and rent myself a studio.'

'Good,' Diane said. 'I'm thinking of embracing the new world as well and going back to uni to study child psychology.'

'Really?'

'Well, if you can't beat 'em... I can start in February. Tomorrow morning, you know the drill.'

'You do know it's summer and stifling hot by seven am?'

'Ah, so you want to start walking at four in the morning?'

'Forget I said anything. We'll stick to the plan.'

Diane was right. February was just around the corner. We just had to make it through another few weeks. By then, Mum and Dad would have settled into domestic bliss, Robyn's baby would be almost a month old and Lexi's arm and bruises will have healed. And I hoped I'd be ensconced in my new studio.

❄

I don't know how long I was standing staring into space before Lexi tapped me on the shoulder. 'Earth to Mum. What are you doing?'

'Thinking. How are you feeling?'

She shrugged. 'Feeling better now that school's finished for the year. And I'm excited for Nanna and Pop's wedding.'

'Speaking of which, I need your help.'

We walked inside, and Lexi followed me to the linen closet where I pulled out several ancient albums. Photos of Robyn and me when we were kids – in the snow, the beach, celebrating birthdays. All with Mum and Dad smiling in the background, adoring us. There must have been times, lots of them, when we fought, but looking at these snaps you'd never guess.

I sat down on the sofa, Lexi beside me.

'Will you help me put together a slideshow to play at Nanna and Pop's wedding?'

She grinned. 'Too easy.'

'I never imagined I'd be sitting here as a forty-year-old woman and my beautiful daughter would be a bridesmaid at my own parents' wedding.'

'Guess not.'

'Funny how things turn out. I always thought Nanna and Pop would be together forever. That nothing could break them up.'

'Yeah, I thought I'd be with Hunter forever.'

'I had a boyfriend when I was a little older than you' – sixteen, actually – 'and I thought we'd be together forever as well.'

'Really? You had another boyfriend? Besides Dad? What happened?'

'He dumped me.'

'No wonder!' Lexi pointed to a photo of me in my school uniform. Hair parted in the middle with two long mousy-brown plaits covering my ears. White socks pulled up past my knees. 'Tragic, Mum. Look at your hair!'

'His name was Brett. I wish I could see him again. Show him my beautiful kids and the life he missed out on.'

'You don't mean that, do you? What about Dad?'

'Well, if I'd stayed with Brett, he'd be your father. You'd be none the wiser.'

'But you were still at school.'

'Yes, but I was in love. At least I thought I was.'

Looking and laughing, we flipped through pages of photos.

'Mum, I don't think I can be thirteen anymore. I'm over it. I want to move straight to being an adult.'

'Why? All that responsibility... having to find a career.'

'It's gotta be easier.' Lexi took a deep breath. 'Friends, school, exams, boyfriends, it's so hard.'

'I know, Lex. And I don't think it'll get easier – but you're going to have wonderful times as well. Really great times with friends and boyfriends. Even school can be a lot of fun.'

'Then why do I feel so sad and lonely, and angry with you?'

'Because, as much as I don't like to admit it, you're growing up. You're trying to find your place in the world and where you fit in.'

'Mum, please don't get mushy.'

I sighed. 'How's your arm?'

'Sore... If I tell you something, will you promise not to freak out?'

I had to answer quickly or lose the moment. 'I promise I won't freak out.' Inside, I was freaking out, and she hadn't even said anything.

'You're not gonna like it.'

'Try me.'

'Hunter broke up with me because...'

I was going to faint.

'I wouldn't blow him.'

Oh God. I was freaking out big time. I couldn't breathe. When I was younger, oral sex was part of my fantasy agenda, not something you did after knowing a guy for ten minutes.

'Did you hear me? I said—'

I put my hand up to silence her and took a deep breath. I knew that boy was up to no good when I first met him and saw the pornographic T-shirt he was wearing. I was right. I *am* a perceptive mother. 'I heard you, sweetheart.' Wait till I get my hands on him. Imagine what Matthew would say. He'd die. He'd fall down dead in front of me.

'I wouldn't join in party games like rainbow kissing... you know what rainbow kissing is, don't you?'

'Yes.' Diane had filled me in. 'How do you feel now?'

'Kind of relieved. He doesn't love me like he said he did, or he wouldn't have hooked up with Susie so quickly. The boob pics. Probable sex in trees.'

I hugged her. 'I thought you were joking about sex in trees.'

She glared at me. 'You're so old. Anyway, I am going to do all those things.'

'What? We all do boob pics, but sex in trees?'

'I don't mean all that stuff. I just mean, I'm curious. And what do you mean boob pics?'

'Well—'

She held up her hand. 'Ugh. Please don't.'

I didn't know whether to cuddle or smack her.

I hugged her. 'When you're twenty-five, I'm sure you'll be ready for a proper boyfriend.'

Lexi rolled her eyes.

'Seriously, thanks for telling me, Lex.'

'You're not angry?'

'Why would I be angry? You're smart and you'll do what feels right for you. Although you are only thirteen—'

'And a half.'

'And a half. You know, you can talk to me about anything. Maybe I won't always agree with you, but I trust you and I'll always love you and try to listen to your side.'

'Even when you're furious, like when I cut off my hair?'

'Don't push it.'

'You know on your birthday, when I had friends over?'

'The vodka, orange and chilli night?'

'It was really stupid. I couldn't even taste the vodka.'

'Yes, it was stupid and incredibly dangerous – you could have ended up in hospital having your stomach pumped, or worse.'

'I'm sorry. It was the first time. So many girls drink cruisers, I thought it would be fun.'

Good grief! There was a vast difference between drinking a full glass of vodka with a dash of orange and drinking a Bacardi Breezer, but I kept quiet. I didn't want to encourage her experimentation. It would happen soon enough without my prompting.

Even so, I made a mental note to check her phone photos from time to time, and I wondered when, if ever, I'd be able to tell Matthew about this conversation. I was having enough trouble digesting it myself. I'd run it by Diane first.

'We all do silly things, Lex, even parents and grandparents. But the key is to learn from them, move forward and try not to repeat the same mistakes.' (Yes, Oracle. It would be nice if I could take some of my own mother's advice now and then.)

❄

Robyn turned up with her own stack of albums a couple of hours later.

'I'm really scared, Kate. I'm going to be a shitty mother.'

'We all think we're going to be shitty mothers. I still think I'm a shitty parent, but you learn as you go along. You'll see. The first thirteen and a half years are the hardest.'

'I guess I won't be going trekking in Nepal.'

'Not for some time, no.'

'Or painting in Umbria.'

'No.'

'Galapagos Islands?'

'Doubtful.'

'I'm going to have this baby, aren't I?'

'Yep, very soon I'd say.'

'And then I'll be a mother.'

'You sure will.'

'Promise you'll be there for me?'

'Always.'

'I hate my bloody hair... and this stupid nose ring is just... stupid.'

'Your hair will grow back. And the nose ring is... fine.'

'You think?'

'Yeah.' I wrapped my arms around her. 'Now, enough about you, Lexi's waiting for your round of photos to add to the slideshow.'

Twenty minutes later, Lexi tore into the room. 'What are you two doing? Nanna's hysterical.'

'What?'

'Mum, get a grip. You never have your phone when it's really important.'

Robyn smirked.

'I'm not happy with you either, Robyn.'

'Lexi—

She waved her phone in front of me. 'Nanna!'

I grabbed it. 'Mum?'

She could hardly speak. 'I didn't book the caterers.'

'What?'

'You heard. I didn't book—'

'Shit.'

Robyn winced. 'My baby.'

'Shush.' I glared at Robyn. 'Not you, Mum. I'll deal with it.'

A minute later, I was on the phone to Dana. 'It's not going to be pretty,' she said. 'Glazed ham; prawns and sausages on the barbecue; mango, avocado and lobster salad.'

I laughed. 'Champagne and beer.'

'Ha-ha. If only all our Christmases and weddings could be this idyllic.'

CHAPTER 61

On Christmas Eve Eve, after the kids were in bed, Matthew and I made love. It was sweet and romantic. I drifted to sleep. My dreams weren't about Arnaud or any other fantasy. Tonight, Matthew was the man in my dreams.

In the early morning hours, I felt Matthew's hand resting lightly on my thigh. The barest pressure, but the heat... Then his fingers found their way, teasing me. He slid his fingers inward and leaned over to kiss my neck, then lips, raking my throat with his tongue, biting, nipping. I could taste the earthy honey on his breath. Instinctively I pressed against him, moaning. This wasn't a dream. It was so much better. The real deal. My life.

At daylight, Matthew loved me, cuddled me, kissed me and bounded out of bed. He showered, left his wet towel on the floor, dressed, made me a cup of tea and brought it up to bed. I breathed a sigh of contentment.

Determination and faith. I've got the determination. Matthew's got faith. He really does have faith in me.

I'm not sure if I've resented Matthew all these years because I gave up photography after Angus was born – I mean, we both wanted children and I was the one with the womb and the breasts – but he's right. I can't spend the rest of my life blaming him and the kids for not pursuing my dream. I must at least give it a try. It's time for me to step out and do something for myself.

Until now, it's always been others who have defined who I was as a person – Matthew, Lexi, Angus, Mum, Dad, Robyn. And it's not like I don't want to continue being a wife, a mother, a daughter and a sister, but the time has come to look after myself as well. And I was more determined than ever to succeed.

An alert came up on my phone, an advertisement for February's issue of *Delicious Bites*. Ha! Fern had stood her ground. My photo was on the cover. *My photo!* I allowed myself a tiny smile. I wonder if Fern had walked over Graeme's dead body.

'Mum, are you getting up?' Angus was standing in the doorway, Cleo wrapped tightly in his arms. 'She's trying to eat the babies.'

I rolled over and glanced at the bedside clock: five minutes past seven. 'I guess I should.' I dragged myself out of bed and wandered into Lexi's room. 'Wedding day, darling.'

'Later,' she mumbled from under her blanket.

I opened her curtains to reveal the brilliant sunshine outside and Lexi poked her head out from underneath the covers.

Four hours later, even with her broken arm and bruised face, Lexi looked lovely, angelic. I almost didn't recognise her. So tall and grown up in her pale-pink, silk halter-neck dress.

'Don't start thinking I'm going to look like this all the time.' Her cheeks glowed from the soft, barely-there blush the make-up artist had applied.

I took her good arm and slipped it through mine. 'Wouldn't dream of it.'

'I'm not your little girl anymore, Mum.'

'I know.'

'But I'll still be your little boy.' Angus rushed towards me for a hug, a mini-Matthew, wrapped in a tux.

'Will you, Gussy?' I scooped him up with my free arm.

Matthew was smiling. 'Ready, gorgeous people?'

'As ready as we'll ever be.' It was time. This was no dress rehearsal.

❄

'Bob, I've had twenty-five years to stop loving you,' Mum said, eyes misty, voice strong. 'I could have traded you in, but you were such a comfortable ride.'

I glanced at Robyn. 'Did our mother really say that?' I mouthed.

Robyn nodded.

'I couldn't. I didn't. When I saw you at the gallery, my heart skipped and it's still skipping. You are the man of my dreams. You always were and always will be. Forever. I'm so thankful you've given me a second chance... us, and our family. Bob, I love you. Will you twirl with me again?'

There were no dry eyes when Mum and Dad danced to their wedding song, Frank Sinatra's 'Fly Me to the Moon', a second time. After a full thirty seconds, all the party stood to dance. Matthew with Lexi, me with Angus, Carol and Bernard. Dana jigged amongst us.

No arguments, not even a tense moment. We didn't need *Family Conversation Starters* cards. We were doing well all by ourselves.

There are three sides to every story, just as there are three sides to every person. There's how you see yourself, how others see you and how you really are – the truth.

But the truth is... well, the truth is too hard to live with sometimes. That's why we tell stories, and purposely forget significant facts. It's why we daydream and create reckless and exciting fantasy worlds. It's to save us from hurt and protect us from the pain and drama of everyday life.

As the clock ticked over to Christmas Day and Matthew snuggled in and cupped my breast, Robyn cried from the guest bedroom. 'The baby's coming.'

This time I knew it was for real.

ALSO BY LISA DARCY

My Big Greek Holiday

❄

Lily's Little Flower Shop

❄

Should You Keep A Secret?

ACKNOWLEDGEMENTS

Thanks to everyone at Bloodhound Books UK for seeing Kate's potential, especially co-founders and publishers, Betsy Reavley and Fred Freeman. I enjoyed the challenge of weaving in the Christmas theme, and I absolutely adore the cover!

To my editor, Ian Skewis, and senior editorial and production manager, Tara Lyons, thank you both for your dedication to detail and for making *Christmas Actually* a more engaging and believable read.

Thank you, Andrea Barton, my amazing first reader, editor and friend. I love our long chats and laughs. It must get tiresome talking me down off the ledge. Huge props for giving me the confidence to keep writing. Thanks, Michael Cybulski, my agent and NAC Literary Agency CEO. I am always grateful for your encouragement and enthusiasm for my writing.

To my always amusing, often irreverent children, Josh, Noah and Mia; previously, I have thanked you for allowing me the space to write and for (mostly) accepting mediocre dinners of chicken and salad, and spaghetti bolognaise, on frequent rotation throughout the years. Happily now, you're all independent adults living your fulfilling adult lives, with careers, partners, and cats (Mia!), and most importantly, culinary survival skills.

An occasional phone call would be nice.

For those who have read my previous novel, *The Pact*, I mention my partner and I bonding over musicals, pasta, wine, and cat wrangling. These days, it's more green salads, steps and word games. Cat wrangling continues, as does as our passion for musicals. Love you, Chris.

A NOTE FROM THE PUBLISHER

Thank you for reading this book. If you enjoyed it please do consider leaving a review on Amazon to help others find it too.

We hate typos. All of our books have been rigorously edited and proofread, but sometimes mistakes do slip through. If you have spotted a typo, please do let us know and we can get it amended within hours.

info@bloodhoundbooks.com